I0631798

DOC SAVAGE

The Wild Adventures of Doc Savage

Please visit www.adventuresinbronze.com for
more information on titles you may have missed.

PYTHON ISLE
WHITE EYES
THE FRIGHTENED FISH
THE JADE OGRE
FLIGHT INTO FEAR
THE WHISTLING WRAITH
THE FORGOTTEN REALM
THE DESERT DEMONS
HORROR IN GOLD
THE INFERNAL BUDDHA
DEATH'S DARK DOMAIN
SKULL ISLAND
PHANTOM LAGOON
THE MIRACLE MENACE
THE ICE GENIUS
THE WAR MAKERS
THE SINISTER SHADOW
THE SECRET OF SATAN'S SPINE
GLARE OF THE GORGON
SIX SCARLET SCORPIONS
EMPIRE OF DOOM

Also from Altus Press

The Wild Adventures of Tarzan

RETURN TO PAL-UL-DON
KING KONG VS. TARZAN

DOC SAVAGE

MR. CALAMITY

&

THE VALLEY OF ETERNITY

TWO DOC SAVAGE ADVENTURES

BY WILL MURRAY & LESTER DENT

WRITING AS KENNETH ROBESON

COVER BY JOE DeVITO

ALTUS PRESS • 2018

MR. CALAMITY & THE VALLEY OF ETERNITY copyright ©
2018 by Advance Magazine Publishers Inc.

© 2018 Condé Nast. The Doc Savage character is © Advance
Magazine Publishers Inc. d/b/a Condé Nast. "Doc Savage" is a
registered trademark of Advance Magazine Publishers Inc. This book is
published under license from Advance Magazine Publishers Inc.

Front and back cover images copyright © 2018 Joe DeVito. All rights reserved.

*No part of this book may be reproduced or utilized in any form or by any means,
electronic or mechanical, without permission in writing from the publisher.*

First Edition — February 2018

DESIGNED BY

Matthew Moring

SPECIAL THANKS TO

*James Bama, Jerry Birenz, Gary A. Buckingham, Condé Nast, Jeff Deischer,
Norma Dent, Dafydd Neal Dyar, Elizabeth Engel, Dave McDonnell, Matthew Moring,
Ray Riethmeier, Rick Scheckman, Christopher Wood, Howard Wright,
Gary Yarber, The State Historical Society of Missouri, and last but not least,
the Heirs of Norma Dent—James Valbracht, John Valbracht,
Wayne Valbracht, Shirley Dungan and Doris Leimkuehler.*

COVER ILLUSTRATION COMMISSIONED BY

Nicholas Cain

Like us on Facebook: "The Wild Adventures of Doc Savage"

To Our First Patron,

The One and Only Jack Juka.

Mr. Calamity

Chapter I

THE SWIMMER IN THE SKY

THE COPPER-HAIRED GIRL told everyone who inquired that she was heading up into the Bighorn Mountains to hunt jackalopes.

"I hear that they're as thick as jackrabbits up here," she was heard to say.

The young woman was too attractive for men to laugh at her directly. But behind her back, they averted their vision and repressed knowing grins.

For the jackalope was a mythical animal, a purported cross between an antelope and a hare, both of which were plentiful in the Bighorn Mountains.

Ever since some Wyoming card had mounted antelope antlers on a stuffed jackrabbit, the jackalope's fame had spread beyond the borders of the rugged Western state.

No such creature actually existed. The copper-haired girl knew that, but she had her reasons for telling that particular untruth.

Asked her name, she declared it to be Darla Dell. That was a fib, too. Her name was not Darla Dell. Any more than her natural hair was the metallic hue of a newly-minted penny.

The supposed Darla Dell rode out on horseback from the town of Bison one morning, a Winchester rifle in the saddle sheath, and an ancient single-action .44-caliber revolver snug in the holster of a cartridge-belt slung around her girlish hips.

She was slender and pretty and somewhere in her twenties. Her hair and tanned skin partook of a warm coppery hue. Her

1

brown riding boots were worn, but had a fresh polish. A cotton shirt and white whipcord breeches hugged her delectable form. There was a ragged tear in her gray suede blazer. A milk-white Stetson was suspended down her back with the chin strings knotted in front of her lithe tanned column of a throat. She looked every inch a girl of the modern West, which was not exactly the case either.

Alone, she rode into the foothills of the Bighorn Mountains. Behind her dark-lensed sun-glasses, which she never took off, entrancing eyes searched the terrain.

Saddlebags were filled with the necessities of Western life, as well as assorted prospector tools. For that was what the young woman calling herself Darla Dell was truly about. She was prospecting.

Among her possessions was a pan for sifting gold from sand, various picks, and other implements of the sourdough.

Darla Dell was not seeking gold exactly. Not that she had anything against gold. If she found it, she was going to take it. This section of Wyoming was not known for gold. There were other riches waiting to be gleaned. Jade for one. The Cheyenne had treasured it, and what they left behind was valuable still.

Darla Dell didn't much care whether she found gold or jade or silver or whatever. She just wanted to stake a claim, and pocket the profits. Darla Dell was a very determined young woman. Today, she was determined to turn her summer vacation into a profitable enterprise.

Water was scarce in these bone-dry mountains. Along about 11 o'clock, Darla Dell took advantage of her canteen, drinking about a quarter of its contents. Replacing the canteen sling on the saddle horn, she gazed about.

By this time, she had climbed high above the arid flatlands. If there had been sufficient trees to justify the term, it might be said she was above the tree line. Trees were as scarce as water in this part of Wyoming. Almost as scarce as the nonexistent jackalope.

There had been a recent rain. In fact, two days of it, but one couldn't tell from looking about the foothills. The blistering sun had dried up all but a few stubborn mud holes.

The morning's activities had thus far been a bust. This did not deter Darla Dell—or whatever her real name might be. Prospecting was an activity that required patience, among other virtues.

Dismounting, Darla Dell took the reins of her mount and led her along. Finding gold or jade was not something one did atop a horse, but by leading it.

From time to time, she stopped and applied a pocket magnifying glass to an interesting outcropping. Each time she made a little noise of disgust and continued on.

"I hope you're not in a hurry to go home, Lightning," she told the pony.

The animal made a little bit of a snorting sound that could be interpreted any way one wished.

Darla Dell gave Lightning a reassuring pat along the side of her magnificent neck. The horse was one of those equine specimens that one rarely sees outside of a Hollywood cowboy picture. She was a chestnut filly, with a flowing mane as black as dyed mink. Her switching tail was flaxen in hue.

Along the pony's cumber—hindquarters—was burned a brand. A circle containing what appeared to be a jagged scorch mark. The jagged line suggested a streak of lightning.

Now horses are normally branded with the name of the ranch to which they belonged. Notwithstanding the fact that this pony's name was Lightning, this was purely coincidental. In the parlance of this corner of Wyoming, the pony belonged to the string owned by the Circle Bolt Ranch. Bolt for thunderbolt. A jagged slash bisecting a circle constituted the brand.

As brands go, it was not typical. But very modern.

Leaving Lightning to wander about, Darla Dell walked into the noon part of the day, discovering nothing worthwhile, yet her demeanor suggested that she was having an interesting time.

It was about to get more interesting. Far more than Darla Dell imagined.

Noises in the brush alerted her that something was prowling.

Quicker than a rattlesnake reacting to a cowboy's hard boot, Darla Dell yanked her old-fashioned .44-caliber revolver out of its leather holster. The steel of the barrel and cylinder was not nickeled or blued or otherwise treated against rust, and it was of the finest quality conceivable. The grip was ivory. The worn holster, by contrast, exactly fitted the contour of the big weapon, indicating long usage.

Western movies like to portray the regulation cowboy as quick on the trigger and apt to shoot a man as say hello. In actuality, the working cowboy kept his revolver handy for rattlesnakes and the occasional coyote.

The brushy sounds coming from up ahead did not sound like any of these critters.

Lightning made a nervous whinny when her ears pricked up at the sound. Darla Dell reassured the chestnut pony with a murmuring voice and a steadying hand.

Presently, a man stepped out from behind a hillock and into view. He was not mounted, nor was he leading a horse of his own.

"How do?" he greeted, lifting one hand in a calming gesture of peace.

"Howdy," returned Darla Dell, lowering her six-shooter.

"I ain't no rattler, if that's what you're thinkin'," remarked the man.

Darla Dell laughed without a trace of nervousness. Her demeanor was wholly unafraid. Her smile was natural, if a trifle guarded.

"You spooked my pony," she explained.

"But not you, huh?" laughed the other. His grin was infectious, and it caused a galaxy of freckles to parade across his sunburnt nose and cheeks.

"I don't spook easy," returned the girl, and it was no boast. One could tell that by her confident tone of voice.

The cowboy held his sun-bleached hat crown-downward and peered intently at the damp sweatband. The color of his hair was close to the look of pine shavings.

"What's your name?"

"Darla Dell. Yours?"

"Hud. Just call me Hud."

"What are you doing up in the mountains without a horse, Hud?"

"Oh, shucks, I'm tryin' to get down *off* the gol-durned mountain. Looking for the swimmin' hole that happens every time it rains."

"I didn't see anything like that," returned Darla Dell.

"Well, it's a fair piece southwest of here. And that's where I'm bound." Hud looked the girl up-and-down appraisingly and asked, "You're not from around here, are you?"

"No. I hail from back east."

"Is that right? Well, where are you stayin'?"

Darla saw no harm in telling the truth. Besides, it would be downright unfriendly not to. Wyoming and its people were that way.

"I'm bunking at the Circle Bolt Ranch."

Hud whistled sharply. "The Circle Bolt! Mysterious place. People don't rightly know who owns it. The owner is hardly ever around."

"The owner is a friend of mine. He's kind of a hermit. Lives back east, too."

A big grin wreathed the face of Hud the cowboy. "Then that explains matters, don't it? Well, I'm not here to pry into anyone's affairs, so I'll just mosey along. Nice meetin' you, ma'am."

"Same here," said Darla Dell, holstering her impressive six-gun.

Clamping his hat back onto his head, the range bumpkin continued along his way, trooping down the mountain in search of his watering hole, and Darla Dell thought to herself that it was a mighty long walk merely to take a swim. But on the other hand, the cowpoke looked as if he were in dire need of a bath. Some folks in this neck of the woods still practiced the cowboy habit of bathing on Saturdays. And it did happen to be a Saturday.

DARLA DELL thought no more of the cowboy for the balance of the day in which she ranged the Bighorns, sometimes on horseback, but most often on foot in search of wealth for the taking.

It was a clear summer's day. Not a scrap of cloud cluttered the steely Western sky. The celestial dome was the metallic blue that open sky sometimes achieves when atmospheric conditions are just right. Meteorologists might explain the phenomenon, but it meant that the solar disk was unobstructed. Its rays beat down relentlessly. Darla Dell made frequent stops for water, and avoided taking her white Stetson off the wealth of coppery hair that smoldered like red gold in the harsh sunlight.

The hour approached four in the afternoon when Darla noticed that she was feeling light-headed.

Soon, she was swaying in her saddle, trying to keep upright. But the spell that was creeping over her brain was stronger than her determined will.

Reining in her pony, she slipped to the ground and lay down in the dirt. She concentrated on her breathing, for that was the recommended cure for altitude sickness—which is what she had acquired.

The sickness had crept up on her, unnoticed. As an outdoors girl, she knew about it, had been warned that, if she ventured too high up in the mountains, the lack of oxygen would stealthily do its work.

So Darla Dell lay there, waiting for the disorienting weakness to pass.

There was nothing much to do, lying on her back in the sun. So she searched the sky with eyes still protected by sun-glasses. If there had been any clouds, she might have counted them, but clouds were absent.

Shielded eyes shifting about the blue bowl above, something caught her attention. Something high in the sky.

At first, she thought it might be a hawk circling.

The thing in the sky was, in fact, circling. But it was no hawk. It lacked wings, for one thing. Also, it was too big to be a hawk.

From the distance, which was half of a mile, it was difficult to tell the exact size of the circling thing.

Darla Dell had a pair of binoculars stuffed in her saddle bag. With considerable effort, she got back on her feet and harvested them, training the lenses on the unusual oddity in the sky.

She almost dropped them.

A breathy gasp escaped her parted lips. For she could see that the thing in the sky was a man. And that he was swimming about in circles.

"Impossible," she burst out.

When that frank utterance failed to alter the situation, Darla Dell put the field glasses back in front of her eyes and gave the focusing screw some attention.

She had removed her sun-glasses for this, of course. And had there been an observer other than her pony, they would see that Darla Dell's eyes were an interesting color. They were warm yellow, a little like honey, but with a metallic glint.

Darla attempted to make out the features of the man who appeared to be swimming in circles.

That he was swimming was undeniable. His hands and arms were frantically churning and scooping while his feet were kicking in an equally agitated manner.

"A man swimming in thin air!" she exclaimed.

At this distance, which was respectable, it was impossible to discern the features of the swimming man. Only that he did not appear to be wearing much in the way of clothing.

As Darla Dell watched, the man's exertions became labored. Frantic kicking of his feet, along with the slowing sweep of his arms, showed definite signs of fatigue.

Evidently, the swimming man had reached the limits of his physical endurance, for he faltered, stopped and began to sink— sink hundreds of yards up in absolutely thin air!

Sensing what was coming, Darla Dell flung herself into the saddle, and lashed her chestnut filly in the direction of the stricken man as rapidly as safety permitted, her altitude sickness all but forgotten.

Safety did not permit her to keep her field glasses trained on the man in the strange predicament, but she could see his tiny form etched against the impossibly blue sky.

The man was not exactly falling. Rather, it appeared as if he were sinking—sinking as if he were immersed in water.

That, too, was impossible. There was no moisture in the sky to speak of. No cloud had troubled the unbroken expanse.

The man sank and sank. His arms flailed about, as if clawing for something to grab hold of. It was somehow sickening. Suddenly, as if something invisible had let him go, he plummeted to earth.

"Oh!" Darla Dell exclaimed.

Spurring Lightning, she charged for the spot where she knew the man would land. And land hard.

Darla Dell did not look like a young woman who was afraid of much, but as she approached the rocky place where the body had presumably landed, her eyes grew narrow and her face showed strain.

It was evident that she knew what to expect and was unafraid to confront it, regardless.

The man's body had landed in a flat section of greasewood scrubland. She could see him lying there, face up, arms and legs splayed like a starfish that had been deposited on a sandy beach by a tide.

Dismounting, she walked the rest of the way, leading the pony, whose skittishness was evidenced by a nervous whinnying and other equine utterances.

The man was not naked. He wore shorts. That was all.

The patch of earth upon which he had fallen should have been dry as an antelope's skull, but it was not. It was moist.

Moreover, precipitation was pattering down upon the body, lightly but steadily. Raindrops made tiny pits in the sandy soil.

Darla Dell looked up. No clouds. Not even scud. There was no place from which the rain could have come. And rain did not emanate from empty sky. She knew that for a certainty.

The rain finished falling as she entered the zone of moisture. Then it ceased.

The ground squirmed and writhed in spots. Blinking, she toed at the disturbances. Wiggle worms and pollywogs were flopping about in the mud.

"Strange," she muttered. They should not have been there. Not unless they, too, fell from the sky.

Once beside the body, Darla Dell got a good look at the man's face. It was twisted as if the last sight he had absorbed had filled him with an unutterable horror.

The man's face was familiar. Even without the shade of his cowboy hat, the freckled features were unmistakable.

It was Hud. The cowboy who had been in search of a natural bath in a watering hole that came and went with the seasons.

Evidently, he had found his watering hole, for he was soaked to the skin. He was also dead. The height from which he had fallen ensured that outcome. Nudging him at several spots, Darla Dell felt bones that had been broken if not shattered. The unfortunate man's entire skeleton had been disjointed and pulverized by the fall.

Again, the copper-haired girl looked up. Her honey-hued orbs searched the sky.

The man had shown every outward indication of swimming in circles like a goldfish trying to get out of an aquarium bowl. The bright sun made searching the upper atmosphere difficult, but of course there was no goldfish bowl, nor was there any body of water in which a man could swim suspended hundreds of yards in the sky.

And yet the evidence that a man had done exactly that lay shattered and broken before her.

As a final raindrop splashed one cheek like a tear, Darla Dell murmured to herself, "I reckon my vacation plans have gone to pieces."

She did not sound entirely unhappy about it.

Chapter II

VANISHED SWIMMING HOLE

THE COPPERY HORSEWOMAN rode back to the town of Bison as rapidly as common sense would permit.

She urged the animal along at a brisk canter, knowing that running her at a gallop would cost more time than otherwise. Only in Hollywood films are horses urged along at full gallop over long distances by actors who didn't know any better.

Eventually, she drifted into the small town situated east of the Bighorn Mountains and west of the Black Hills, found the general store and dismounted, tying the reins of her mount to a hitching post that had probably been there since the days of the infamous Hole-in-the-Wall Gang.

Striding into the establishment, she told the proprietor, "I must use your telephone."

Despite being the county seat, Bison boasted only one public telephone, and this was it. It was a crank affair, a long box of oak about twenty years out of date. It was bolted to the wall in a corner of the store next to the feed bin.

Lifting the Bakelite handset earpiece, the woman calling herself Darla Dell gave the crank a furious winding until central came on the line.

"Connect me with the Circle Bolt Ranch, please," she requested. "It is urgent."

"Hold your horses," returned the operator, who was not used to being rushed.

"Please hurry," repeated Darla Dell.

Presently, her party came on the line and a querulous voice asked, "Who is it?"

"It's you-know-who. I stumbled across some mighty interesting trouble."

The voice seemed to frown. "What happened to your plans to prospect for everything under the sun and strike it rich?"

"I can do that tomorrow. Can you pile into your jalopy and get over here?"

"If it's worth my time. I'm tinkering with a television contraption I'm trying to perfect."

"Whatever it is," countered the copper-haired girl, "it can wait, just like my prospecting."

"If you say so," sighed the querulous voice.

"I do say so," returned Darla Dell firmly before hanging up.

Turning from the instrument, she noticed the store proprietor staring fixedly. Men stared at her a lot. That was nothing unusual. Not that it was especially welcome. He seemed to be chewing something. The coppery girl assumed that it was tobacco.

"Have you anything cold to drink?" she asked.

His jaws stopped working. "Pop. What flavor?"

"Black cherry. Do you have that?"

"Fresh out of black cherry. How about orange?"

"Orange pop gives me the hiccups. I'll settle for grape."

The proprietor went to the icebox and removed a tall bottle of grape soda, which he placed on the counter, saying, "That'll be a nickel, please."

A nickel was laid down next to the bottle and claimed. The proprietor had already popped the cap with an opener.

Darla Dell walked out to the sidewalk, which was a raised platform of planks, and drank slowly, honey-hued eyes behind her dark glasses thoughtful.

Before long, the proprietor drifted out to join her. He struck up a conversation. His breath did not smell of chewing tobacco. It was odd, half familiar, that odor.

"What's the urgency?"

The coppery girl hesitated. "What urgency?" she retorted finally.

"I couldn't help but overhear you say something about trouble...."

"You misheard me. I didn't say *trouble*. I asked for my friend to get out here on the *double*."

"Sounds urgent," mused the proprietor, chewing methodically. His masticating produced a puzzling noise—a soft squeaking.

"Don't you have bare shelves in need of stocking?" Darla Dell suggested pointedly.

"Pardon me then," said the proprietor, drifting back into his store.

"He must not get a lot of company," sniffed Darla Dell, returning to her grape pop.

Finishing it, she remounted her pony and began riding in the direction of the Circle Bolt Ranch, with the expectation of encountering the person she had summoned.

The vehicle she encountered in due time was a battered station wagon, of a type common in this part of the country, and used to convey people and tools across the vast empty distances that comprised the state of Wyoming.

The station wagon braked to a halt, making dust move lazily. As Darla was dismounting, an undersized man with sail-like ears and two gold front teeth stepped out from behind the wheel and demanded, "Why didn't you wait for me in town?"

"Because we're not going to town," retorted the copper-haired woman. "The trouble I spoke of isn't in town."

The new arrival studied Darla Dell, who was a morsel of femininity outside of the common herd of women or girls. His scrutiny did not seem to reflect any noticeable appreciation of that undeniable fact, however.

"Lead the way, then," said the puny man, climbing back behind the wheel.

The horsewoman gave her mount a gentle tug by the reins, and led the way.

The station wagon struggled with the rough terrain, but it was the type designed for conditions in which roads were indifferent and sometimes nonexistent.

On the way to the spot where the dead man lay, they encountered the mud hole.

Darla stepped off, and began inspecting it.

She was shortly joined by the driver, who asked, "What is this?"

"It looks like a mud hole. Recognize it?"

The puny man looked as if he was ill-tempered in general, but now he displayed that quality in abundance.

"Did you drag me away from my tinkering to look at an ordinary mud hole?"

"No, of course not," flared the girl. "But this may be part of the trouble. Are you familiar with this spot?"

The undersized man dragged a battered hat off his head which was definitely not in the Western style. He walked around the spot, studied it with pale eyes and said, "It seems to me that this is a swimming hole when there's enough water to fill the pit."

"I thought so," said the other tightly. "This must be the swimming hole Hud said he was headed for."

"Who is Hud?"

"The dead man I called you about. Let me take you to him."

"Dead man?"

"I think he drowned, but that's only my opinion."

Without waiting for a response, the copper-haired woman swung onto her steed with the lithe grace of a cat springing onto a chair, and galloped away in a pulsing roll of hoofbeats.

The terrain was dusty, and between the horse's hooves and the tires of the station wagon, they kicked up a drifting cloud of the mouth-drying stuff.

"Rats!" complained the man behind the wheel of his wagon. "Looks like I'll get no work done today."

IT was another twenty minutes before they came up on the spot where a dead man had made his landing.

The patch of moisture was well on its way to drying, and for a moment Darla hesitated, thinking she might have the wrong spot. There was no body, nor any signs of blood. The body had not burst open upon striking the earth, she remembered.

Doffing her dark glasses, she gave the surrounding terrain careful scrutiny, recognized two boulders and a bit of prickly pear cactus and said aloud, "No, this is definitely the spot."

The puny one was out of the station wagon by this point and was looking around unhappily.

"Where is the dead man you told me about?"

Darla Dell did not immediately reply; she was walking the terrain in her boots, until she came upon a spot where the ground was concave. For the concavity was not regular, but it was enough to tell her that this was the place where the dead man had fallen from the sky.

"The body landed at this exact spot," she told the other. "I'm confident of that fact."

The frowning fellow did not know what to say at first. So he yanked at one ear in agitation.

"Suppose," he suggested, "you start at the beginning. If there is a beginning. Because I don't see any dead man."

The copper-haired woman put her brown fists on her hips, and looked as though she wanted to take out her six-gun and perforate something in sheer frustration.

"I met a man not far from here," she related. "Said his name was Hud. Hud told me he was on his way to bathe in the swimming hole."

"The mud hole back yonder a ways?"

"Probably," she concurred. "Perhaps an hour later, I happened to notice something in the sky. It was a man. He appeared to be swimming. Swimming in circles."

The puny fellow growled, "Probably a mirage."

"Mirage, my saddle sores," she sniffed. "I put my binoculars on him and I saw him more clearly. He was way up there, maybe a half a mile high in the clear blue sky. Just swimming in circles, like he was trying to find dry land, but couldn't locate any."

"A half-mile up, you say?"

"At least. Now this next part may be hard to swallow."

"I'm already gagging."

"Try to keep your dinner down," she advised tartly. "This man swimming in the sky started acting as if he had run out of steam. He slowed down and stopped swimming. Then he began to sink. At first, the sinking was slow, but then as if he dropped out of something that held him up, he plummeted to the earth. I rode for the spot as hard as I could, and I found him lying here. Dead."

"You sure about that?"

Darla nodded vigorously. "I checked him over. Practically every bone in his body was broken. He had fallen a great distance. That wasn't all that had fallen. The ground was wet, just as you see now. But it was moist from raindrops still falling. Falling from a cloudless sky."

The man looked up, scrutinized the sky and remarked, "I haven't seen a cloud all day. Matter of fact it looks like we're starting on another dry spell."

"This part of Wyoming," said Darla frankly, "is practically a desert."

"No argument there. What's your point?"

"I saw a man swimming in the sky, as if he was immersed in water. Then he fell out of whatever he was swimming in, and when he landed, raindrops were still falling. He was completely wet. It was Hud, who had gone to bathe in the swimming hole."

"Well, there's no water in the swimming hole now—unless you count the muddy mess."

"Two questions nag at me."

The runty man eyed the other dubiously. "Only two?"

Darla whipped off her sun-glasses, revealing scornful eyes of amber. "Don't be wise. The two questions are how did the man get up into the sky, and what happened to the water in the swimming hole?"

The other scratched at the nape of his neck as he muttered, "I can think of a third question. Namely, did you keep your hat on all day? The sun is pretty strong out here."

The copper-haired woman whirled on the runty man and the look on her attractive face was not pleasant.

"Are you insinuating that I'm heat-addled?"

"Well, I'm wondering which part of your story is mirage, and which part comes from being out under a baking sun all day. Either way, I'm inclined to see this as a problem of too much sun somewhere."

Darla Dell firmed her delectable lips, narrowed her eyes, and said stubbornly, "I saw what I saw. There's no taking that back."

"So where is the body of this Hud?"

The woman looked around in frowning frustration. "Darned if I know."

There was a thin silence as the pair shared an impasse.

Finally, the undersized fellow suggested, "We might wander back into town and ask after anyone named Hud. See if he's missing."

"It's a start," said the woman dispiritedly. Looking at the other challengingly, she demanded, "And what if there is a Hud and he's missing?"

"In that case, you have a swell mystery to unravel."

The concerned look on the woman's face suddenly altered. It brightened. A little bit of an intrigued smile worked her sun-bronzed features.

"If I do, Long Tom, promise me one thing: Don't call Doc into it. We'll solve it ourselves."

"No promises," said the puny individual addressed as "Long Tom."

"Stinker!"

"This is probably nothing," added Long Tom. "But if it turns out to be something, from what you describe, it might be something big. Doc will want to play a hand in it."

"Just hold off until I get the ball rolling in some way, so when Doc pulls up in his sky chariot, it will be my mystery he's pitching in to solve, and not one of his own."

"Suit yourself," Long Tom said, climbing back behind the wheel and starting the engine. "You found this impossibility. It's yours until I say otherwise."

"Who appointed you sheriff of all Wyoming?" the girl snapped back.

Long Tom didn't wait. He sent the station wagon hurtling back toward town at high speed, leaving the young woman to scramble onto her saddle and do her best to keep up.

Despite the seemingly shabby treatment she had been accorded, the bronze-and-copper girl was grinning happily.

Chapter III

HANG ROPE

RUNTY LONG TOM flung his station wagon along the rutted roads of northeastern Wyoming with suspension-punishing violence. He was an impatient sort of cuss. It showed in the lead-footed way he drove along, not pacing his vehicle so that the girl whose real name was Pat was not left behind, but instead accelerating sporadically.

Long Tom could not help himself. His temperament was not the most moderate.

Perhaps it was the long nights he had put into electrical work in his basement laboratory back in New York that had done it, although the windowless confines of the former wine cellar were usually blamed for his unhealthy mushroom complexion.

Soon, the girl and her horse were lost in the dust clouds created by his spinning tires.

Long Tom was not exactly a gentleman when it came to women. He was not unnecessarily rude to the fair sex, but he seemed immune to their charms for some reason.

A gentleman—especially a Western gentleman—would have loitered so that a girl following on horseback could catch up from time to time, but Long Tom had a powerful hankering to get back to the Circle Bolt Ranch where he had been conducting electrical experiments.

Pat had characterized him as a hermit, and this was allowably true. Long Tom liked solitude. He preferred to be left alone when he was in an experimenting frame of mind. For the puny fellow was no less than Major Thomas J. "Long Tom" Roberts, the world-renowned electrical engineer. Long Tom was considered one of the preeminent men in his field, and he was almost entirely self-made.

Experimenting with electrons and developing complicated electro-mechanical devices was how he made his way in the world. Finding the peaceful privacy to spend arduous hours doing so had vexed him for quite some time.

Recently, a distant relative had passed on to his reward and Long Tom found himself heir to a modest ranch in the shadow of Big Butte, here in the Powder River breaks.

Long Tom had flown out in his personal plane to inspect the place, fully intending to sell it for what he could get, when he decided that the solitude of the lonely little spot was conducive to electrical experimentation.

Renaming the place the Circle Bolt, he set up shop and got busy with transformers and dynamos. Before long he was contentedly making progress on any number of lines of inquiry. It was a kind of quiet paradise, but it was certain to be disturbed, life being what it was.

The first disturbance was Pat. Patricia Savage to give her full name. She might be styled a businesswoman or an adventuress, or both.

Long Tom was not entirely pleased when Pat dropped in, unexpected and unannounced, but neither was he entirely displeased. For Pat was the cousin of the famous Doc Savage, who is known far and wide as the greatest adventurer and scientist the Twentieth Century had yet seen.

In his more adventurous moments, Long Tom was part of the Doc Savage outfit, a compact group of experts who followed the bronze man in his unusual occupation of rectifying wrongs and punishing evil-doers, while traveling the globe in order to exact a measure of justice in this often-unjust world.

In her own adventurous moments, Pat Savage was continually horning in on her famous cousin's undertakings. Only rarely did she succeed in tagging along. For an occupation, she ran a high-class beauty salon and gymnasium catering to the wealthy on New York's Park Avenue. It kept her busy and usually out of Doc Savage's hair. It was also well on its way to making her very comfortable in the cash department. But Pat Savage was never one to settle for mere creature comfort. She had an eye for gold and a yen for wealth.

"What are you doing here in the middle of nowhere, Wyoming?" Long Tom had asked when Pat had presented herself at his doorstep, distressingly unannounced.

"I needed a vacation from the city," said Pat as she barged in and surveyed the litter of electrical equipment choking the parlor. "It's too hot back east."

"Isn't your place air-conditioned?"

"It sure is," Pat returned cheerfully, "but there's nothing like the wide-open spaces to give a gal a sense of being renewed."

Long Tom cocked a pale orb in her direction dubiously.

"You," he remarked, "have something up your sleeve. And it isn't your arms."

"I was reading in a magazine that you can find gold and jade and other precious items just lying around for the taking in the Bighorn Mountains."

"Possibly," said Long Tom guardedly. "So, you're a prospector now?"

"I was in the mood for a vacation and I don't want to waste my valuable time. I brought along everything you could want, from a prospector's sifting pan to a pick ax. I just need some place to plump down for the night."

Long Tom might normally have put up an argument, but this was Pat Savage. He knew better. Pat had a tongue as tart as a green apple. And she knew how to wield words to cutting effect.

"Just stay out of my hair," he snorted. "I'm busy working."

"Don't let me keep you up. I know you hold odd hours."

Pat almost immediately rode up into the mountains, leaving Long Tom to tinker to his heart's content. Two days had passed peacefully until Pat summoned him out into the airy open spaces with her wild tale of a frantic swimmer circling in the sky.

The whole crazy yarn had peeved Long Tom considerably, and he was in a rush to resume his tinkering. The puny electrical genius was destined not to do so for quite some time, as he soon discovered when, in steering around a draw, he almost ran into a knot of riders.

These riders were a strange clutch and collection of individuals. They were dressed for the range, in flannel shirts and denim. They sat on their horses like statues, blocking the way.

Seeing them, Long Tom immediately braked.

All of the men were masked. Coarse flour sacks were fitted over their heads, ragged holes crudely excavated so that their eyes could see out. They sat in their saddles with their rifles resting on their stocks, the barrels pointed upward. None of them wore hats of any kind. In a land where a man was known by the type of hat he wore as much as by his choice of steed, this alone constituted a bad omen.

The most disturbing thing was that the horses also wore flour-sack masks. Evidently this quintet thought it prudent to conceal not only their own faces but the equine countenances of the mounts they rode.

It was a comical sight in its way. But Long Tom was no humorist. He saw nothing funny about a group of masked riders and their equally caparisoned steeds.

And so the puny electrical wizard applied his brakes, causing the station wagon to jounce to a stop and become embroiled in the trail dust that hung in the air, there being no wind to blow it around.

Once the station wagon stopped rocking on its springs, the riders snapped down the muzzles of their rifles, pointing the destructive ends at Long Tom visible through the dusty windshield.

One man growled, "Climb out, gent. Careful like."

ALTHOUGH looking feeble and unhealthy of both frame and complexion, Long Tom Roberts was not yellow. Another man might have sat safely behind the wheel and assessed the situation. Not Long Tom. Hearing this challenge, he stepped out and thrust his jaw in the direction of the hooded riders.

Seemingly oblivious to the pointing rifle bores, Long Tom demanded, "Step to the way. You're blocking the road."

A high-pitched tittering laugh was emitted by one of the flour sacks, which puffed out around the area of the owner's mouth. "Road? I don't see any road."

A clump of greasewood disgorged a long, lathy individual, clutching a Winchester rifle. A gunnysack, perforated with eyeholes, encased the man's skull.

His Winchester whacked twice by way of foreword, causing a covey of sagehens to flush from cover and go winging off.

"Claw yourself a fistful of sky!" he commanded, his voice as metallic as the parting twang of overstretched barbed wire.

Long Tom became even more irate.

"What's this all about?" he demanded. "Better not be a holdup."

"What makes you say that, little fella?"

"I don't have my wallet with me. And I don't like bandits."

"We're not bandits," rasped the gunnysack-masked man. "We're vigilantes. You're the dude who owns the Circle Bolt spread, ain't you?"

"What's it to you?"

"Maybe you heard, but there are some outfits in this neck of the woods that raise mules. Not cows or horses."

"I haven't had time to meet any of my neighbors as yet," said Long Tom.

"You see," advised the one who appeared to be the leader, "mules have been disappearin' from the range, and it's been costin' folks money. It all started a couple of months ago. First a mule here, and then a donkey there. The next thing you know there's a shortage—a *suspicious* shortage."

Long Tom's hands were hardening into fists and his eyes took on the pointedness of flint arrowheads.

"What's that have to do with me?"

"Didn't you take over the Circle Bolt around two months ago?"

Face hardening, Long Tom asked, "What if I did?"

"Well, it's kinda like this. Folks around these parts have got to talkin' among themselves and they started noticin' the coincidence—if you know what I mean."

"I'm getting your drift, if that's where you were drifting," Long Tom said harshly. "And I don't care much for the insinuation."

"Some blackguard's been rustling mules. We think you're the cultus hombre behind it."

"Well, I'm not."

"Prove it."

"Prove I'm the rustler," snapped Long Tom impatiently.

A lanky man slid off his horse, and began approaching; others followed suit.

The gunnysacked leader kept his Winchester trained on Long Tom until all the others joined him. Soon every gun barrel was arrayed in his direction and Long Tom found himself surrounded.

"If you're thinking of arresting me," retorted Long Tom, "I'll have you know that I am a—"

Before the slender electrical wizard could properly identify himself, one man pulled a heavy rope out of his saddle bag and Long Tom's eyes popped open when he saw that it had already been woven into a stout noose.

There was a cottonwood tree nearby and two masked men walked the noose over to it. They began throwing the dressed end up into the branches in a way that made their intentions plain.

"What was that you were going to say?" grunted one of the road agents.

"I said my name is Long Tom Roberts. Maybe you heard about me."

"Long Tom, you say. That's a funny moniker. Kind of an owlhoot name, if you ask me."

Murmurings of agreement went around the masked group while the noose was being settled into place. When it was done, the loop hung twice as high as undersized Long Tom stood.

"I guess you're going to need to borrow one of our horses," said the spokesman of the group.

The other men laughed raucously.

"You'll have a sweet time getting me into the saddle," warned Long Tom. "And I don't lynch easy."

"I suppose we could just shoot him," a masked man suggested casually.

"That wouldn't be right. Rustlers ought to be hung, not shot."

"We could shoot him some, hoist him up on the horse, stick that scrawny neck into the hang rope, then let gravity finish the job," another ruminated.

The hooded men had been drifting closer. They discussed their intentions openly.

Long Tom didn't seem like much. He was too short, too thin, and too feeble-looking to worry them. Upon casual inspection, he suggested a pushover.

But when the leader got within reach, Long Tom socked him in the jaw in such a way that the gunnysack turned red at its lower portion, and the man's Winchester rifle flew out of his calfskin-gloved hands.

Long Tom moved like a streak of lightning. He seized the Winchester in both hands, swapped the barrel around, and the intimidating muzzle was suddenly pointed at his tormentors.

"*Whoooee!*" exclaimed one. "The bantam dude sure is a hellion, ain't he?"

Another taunted, "Be careful with that, little fella. That Winchester is almost as tall as you."

Some of the flour-sacked vigilantes laughed. Perhaps they did not take Long Tom seriously because they heard he hailed from back East, where men didn't necessarily know how to handle firearms.

That was their mistake. Because Long Tom did. He demonstrated this by jacking a round into the chamber and knocking a hole through the top of one flour sack with a single snarling slug. The rider felt his hood jump, and clawed at his covered skull, feeling for blood. But Long Tom had not even grazed the scalp.

Amid the whinnying and the snorting of rearing horses, there was a sudden scurrying for shelter. There was not much of that to be had, but the mood of the ambush swiftly changed.

Booted feet made a *crunch-crunch-crunch* in the sandy gully floor.

The ambushers got behind the shelter of their horses, demonstrating that the cowboy isn't always respectful of his mount, the way Hollywood portrays it.

Gloves came off of hands and were used to slap at the horse's flanks.

The spooked animals were suddenly running in all directions. Long Tom had to dodge wildly to avoid being trampled.

Two men jumped him. And a fistfight ensued. The two cowpokes outweighed and out-towered the puny electrical wizard considerably. It looked as if a massacre of fisticuffs impended.

One did. But not in the way appearances suggested.

The two masked men took wild swings, but neither one connected. Long Tom danced in between them and began jabbing at the triangular tents that showed where their noses jutted and blew out air with their fierce exertions.

Long Tom did not have to hit either man a second time. His bony fists connected, mashed noses to a crimson pulp. He stepped back as his first vanquished foes smacked down into the dust of the gully.

Whirling, Long Tom set his sights on his next victim and a six-gun lifted and flashed downward.

Steel made a wooden sound on bone. Long Tom gave a spasmodic leap into the air, collapsed without having seen who had hit him.

Bending, his conqueror lifted the insensate electrical wizard's skull by his hair and struck it again—but not too hard.

"That ought to keep him for about an hour," the victor proclaimed.

The others gathered round, surveyed their fallen friends. They studied Long Tom lying in the dirt.

"What did he say his name was?"

"Roberts. Long Tom Roberts," spat a man.

"That name sounds vaguely familiar to my ears."

"Well, his face doesn't look familiar to my eyes. So let's just fetch him up in the saddle and walk the two of them on over to the noose and be done with it."

"This is bad business, lynchin' a man."

The leader wearing a bloodied gunnysack mask felt of his jaw. "Rustling mules is a bad business. And if we're going to keep things calm around here, we need to send this pigeon winging on his way to his reward."

Grimly, the masked group picked up Long Tom, while another confederate walked the horse over. They got Long Tom up in the saddle, stuffed his booted feet into the stirrups. Two men held him there as they led the dun horse over to the cottonwood tree and its gently swinging noose.

Chapter IV

DEVIL IN GREEN

PAT SAVAGE WAS fuming once she lost sight of Long Tom Roberts' station wagon.

The dust of its rattling along hung in the air, and she was forced to tie a bandanna neckerchief over her lower face to protect her nose and mouth from inhaling too much of the stuff. The handkerchief was a muted gold, not quite matching the honey coloration of her eyes.

Knowing that she had no hope of ever overhauling the station wagon, Pat permitted her mount to move at her own pace, and prepared to arrive at the town of Bison when the pony got around to it.

"Drat that ornery woman-hater," she muttered.

That last was perhaps an overstatement. Long Tom Roberts wasn't exactly a woman-hater, but he had never shown much interest in the fairer sex and consequently lacked the customary masculine gallantry. Long Tom was also accustomed to doing things his way, and getting back to his electrical experiments was obviously uppermost in his mind. Thus, Pat was left behind.

As she rode along, Pat ruminated over the many peculiarities of the morning, beginning with the man swimming about in the sky.

A hallucination produced by altitude sickness, it was not. Of that, the copper-haired girl was convinced.

As she trotted along, Pat spied a new apparition.

This appeared to be a cowboy. But one unlike anything she had ever before beheld.

The puncher was up in the rocks, and he stood out like a lizard against the starkness of his surroundings.

He looked dressed for Sunday church, or perhaps a rodeo. The colors of his cowboy outfit were outrageous. He had a hat, but it was cocked half off his head, showing flaming red hair. His head was long and narrow, his outthrust jaw fashioned like a lantern. He appeared to be a small man, but his legs were long, suggesting that he wore boots with unusually high heels.

The combination of the iguana-green shirt and the flaming red hair reminded Pat Savage of a Christmas tree.

No self-respecting cowboy would go about duded up so, and Pat immediately marked him as an Easterner, or at least someone not familiar with cowboy ways.

"I wonder if there's a dude ranch hereabouts," she murmured to herself. "Something catering to cowpokes from Boston."

The spectacle on the rocks appeared to be preoccupied with something. The man was looking down. There was no sign of a horse. High up there amid the rocks, a horse could easily be concealed.

Pat Savage was an outgoing girl, one filled to the brim with curiosity. This cowboy looked like a character, so she became interested in him.

Cupping her hands before her mouth, she called up, "Hello there!"

Her voice carried, but evidently not far enough. She raised it significantly.

"I said: Hello up there! Can you hear me?"

The lizard-green fellow showed that he did. He started, swung around and displayed blazing eyes whose color nearly matched his outrageous shirt. Turning about showed a neckerchief tied about his neck that was as fiery as his hair.

The fierce green eyes narrowed. The man reached down and lifted what looked like an elderly blunderbuss of a shotgun and pointed it in Pat's direction. Methodically, he cocked two exceedingly ornate hammers, one at a time. The hammer style made Pat think of twin devil's horns.

The copper-haired girl gasped and then suddenly realized that her own neckerchief was tied over the lower part of her face, making her resemble a common owlhoot.

Swiftly, she yanked it off and simultaneously shook off her white hat, revealing her metallic tresses.

"I'm no bandit!" she called up.

Whether the man heard her or not, it was too late to alter consequences.

He pulled the triggers of the side-by-side shotgun. Both barrels gushed flame and Pat's horse gave a wild jump.

THE JUMP was something spectacular.

Pat had broken horses back in her youth, and was no stranger to a sunfishing stallion. Evidently stung by buckshot, the chestnut pony released a great whinnying scream and took to the air.

The bound—no one word fit—proved to be prodigious. Lightning vaulted into the sky like Pegasus unfolding powerful white wings. Seeing the ground disappear beneath her, Pat took hold of the horse's muscular neck with both arms, clinging for dear life.

Instinct caused her to shut her eyes while bracing for the hard impact she was certain to experience. Pat hoped neither one of them broke their necks. As she waited expectantly, the sensation of rising continued.

It seemed to go on for an unnervingly long time. Normally, Pat Savage was not a girl easily seized by fear. The sensations of lifting and rising persisted so that every time she was about to open her eyes, she squeezed them more tightly shut.

"I'm not afraid to look," she muttered to herself.

When she did, however, she discovered to her horror that the ground was very, very far beneath her horse's flailing hooves.

Pat shut her eyes tight, her pretty face bunching up in expectation of imminent catastrophe.

"This time I know it's altitude sickness," she gasped. "It must be. This just isn't possible!"

When she landed finally, tangled up in her mount, the wind and all consciousness was knocked out of her.

Pat Savage and Lightning lay insensate while the searing Wyoming sun baked them patiently. From time to time, both twitched. But neither one stirred.

Chapter V

CRACK-SHOT REDHEAD

LONG TOM ROBERTS stood stiffly erect, booted feet straining for balance on the cantle of the Cheyenne tree saddle on which he had discovered himself to be standing.

Over and over, he croaked: "Whoa, girl! Whoa! That's a girl—whoa!"

His words were strange, low. His lungs barely managed to pump them past the rope which was taut from his neck to the cottonwood limb directly above.

The mealy-nosed dun mare swished her tail and kicked a rear leg forward at a fly biting near the saddle cinch. With the bronc's movement, the rope from the scrawny electrician's neck to the limb went taut as a bowstring.

"Whoa, girl!" he rasped.

His arms writhed, straining to get free of the lass rope which bound them. Moving up and down, his crossed wrists rubbed the rope knots against his back. It was no dice. They wouldn't loosen.

The dun was getting tired of standing. Bridle reins were knotted to the saddle horn. The animal would walk off before long.

Long Tom thought about what would happen when the animal started off. His thin face contorted. His mouth opened wide and his breath came and went out with a sound like wind in a rocky canyon. He stretched on tiptoes and tried to take the rope in his teeth. The knot was back of his left ear, out of reach.

The mare kicked at another fly.

"Whoa, girl!" The two words were a bare whisper. Long Tom rolled his eyes about, turning his head as much as he could. He tried to shout "Help!" but the sound could not have been heard forty feet away. His eyes were beginning to stand out; his face was getting muddy looking.

Long Tom's gaze sought the departing hoofprints of a knot of horses and followed them until the trail lost itself in the greasewood that whiskered the canyon bed. Nowhere in the canyon was there a sign of the animals or riders. The masked vigilantes had ridden off only minutes ago, leaving him strung up to suffer exquisite tortures until the dun mare walked out from under him. Then he would hang....

Prophetic omens, five turkey buzzards floated, foul black flecks in the morning sky.

The slender electrical wizard had come to only to find himself being strung up. The stringing up was peculiar. Normally, the condemned man is seated in his saddle, and at the appropriate moment, a hat smacks the animal's flanks, sending it racing off, leaving the unfortunate rider to swing by the neck.

For some reason, Long Tom's tormentors had arranged matters so that he hung so high by the neck that his feet touched the saddle. He had been bound, of course. He discovered that almost immediately.

Somehow the vigilantes had managed to steal away, leaving the horse behind to finish the grisly job without their participation. The horse wore a flour sack over its head. It had been rearranged to blind the animal, and thereby prevent her from following the others. But Long Tom did not know that.

Perhaps they were squeamish about hanging a man. Possibly they had other concerns. All Long Tom knew for certain is that he was standing precariously balanced on the saddle and the horse beneath him was growing inpatient. It was a wonder that he had not already expired. The pressure of the noose around his neck had evidently awakened in him some deep instinct for survival, enabling him to throw off unconsciousness.

Long Tom's lungs swelled and collapsed with the effort of trying to shout for help. None of his words were more than tearing hisses.

The end was nearing. His tongue ran out to dampen his lips and he did not draw the organ back between his teeth. The mare swished at the fly. She shook her head, throwing it up and down violently. Then she snorted and walked off.

Long Tom suddenly hung by the rope about his neck. He kicked a little, feebly. His lids did not close over his protruding eyes. His orbs became glassy by slow degrees. Swirling red and black nothingness came in a rushing flood.

There was a roaring in his ears, and consequently he did not hear the gunshot that changed everything.

THE GIRL was a redhead, her hair curly. The green in her eyes was deep; the red in her rather large mouth was healthy. She was slender and hardly more than twenty years old. Her cheeks were pale under her sunny tan and her breathing came in uneasy spurts as she worked over the prostrate form of Long Tom Roberts.

Long Tom lay loosely on his back. Astride him, the red-haired girl alternately compressed his ribs and released them. The pallid electrical wizard was just commencing to breathe again.

He coughed, choked. Over on his side, he rolled. He lay there a bit, his coughing spasms blowing little clouds of dust upward.

After a bit, he put both hands on the ground and lifted himself to a sitting position. Vacantly, as if he had doubts about what he was seeing, Long Tom peered at the fluffy-haired girl.

She was no beauty, but she looked nice. Her nose was snub, chin small and firm. Her mouth was drawn tightly. Her slender form was swathed in blue denim overalls and a jumper a size too large for her. Scuffed riding boots encased tiny feet.

He coughed, mumbling in a weak and vaguely awed voice: "Where's your harp?"

The girl looked faintly puzzled. She asked, "How—how do you feel?"

Long Tom squinted about. Nearby lay the noose which had been about his neck, along with some two feet of heavy rope. The rest of the rope was still tied to the cottonwood limb. The girl's horse, a white and tan paint, muzzled inquiringly at the deceptively luscious green of a Spanish bayonet clump a few yards distant.

Long Tom ventured in a more stable voice, "I guess I'm not a goner and you're not any angel." Coughing, he rubbed his throat and added, "You cut me down?"

The girl shook her head violently. "There wasn't time. I took aim and parted the rope with a Winchester bullet...."

Long Tom would have whistled had he the strength. "Lucky shot!"

"Crack shot." The woman stepped back, her green eyes snapping. "Nothing lucky about it."

Then she swung about and picked up a short .30-30-caliber saddle gun. She pointed the rifle muzzle at him, but did not say anything.

Long Tom eyed her, managing a wry twist to his mouth that might have been a grin or a grimace. "Folks sure have funny customs in this neck of the woods."

The girl asked three questions rapidly, "Who are you? Why were you strung up, and who did the dirty deed?"

Long Tom looked at the brown spots on the girl's pinto horse. When he answered her, there was nothing in his voice to show how much of what he said was the truth and how much was not.

"Brown is the name. Joe Brown. I don't know why I was strung up. I'm new in these parts. I was headed for town when a clutch of masked men threw down on me with guns and left me hanging by a rope necktie. I don't know who they were. They wore flour sacks over their heads."

"Vigilantes," hissed the girl. Holding the .30-30 muzzle so

he could stare into it, the redhead backed up until she could grasp the reins of her pinto with one hand.

"You're lying," she said in a certain voice. "You're the one who has been stealing mules and shipping them across the Big Horns. You were caught red-handed and hung."

"Hanged you mean," grunted Long Tom.

The girl ignored that. "You were—alive—when I found you," she stated haltingly. Her voice was filled with horror. "I couldn't— I couldn't just stand by and watch you strangle. That's why I cut you down with a bullet." Her tone hardened. "You had better get out of this county if you know what's good for you!"

She remounted her pinto with a furious flounce. Her oval face was hard.

"You're far from the trail," Long Tom protested. "I'm no horse thief, never mind a mule rustler."

The girl swung the destructive end of her rifle in the direction of the horse Long Tom had lately stood upon. It was wilding about blindly, endeavoring to shake off its flour-sack blinders.

The girl snapped, "Your masked confederate tells a different story."

"Not my horse," Long Tom said weakly, knowing how lame his declaration sounded.

The Winchester regarded him again with its single black eye. It was no more or less ominous than the girl's emerald regard. "You get out of Campbell County, Mr. Mule Rustler! Or your name is mud. Muddy mud!"

Snorting under the bite of her spurs, the pinto galloped down the dirt highway.

Regret was in Long Tom's face as he watched her depart.

The paint was soon out of sight down the canyon, and the roll of hoofbeats eventually died.

"She might not be any angel," Long Tom muttered, "but she was good enough in a pinch." He rubbed his tortured throat. "This Big Powder country is a tough country."

He looked around, wondering where Pat Savage was. She should have caught up with him by now.

The mare on which he had been suspended was standing off a ways. And he noticed the flour sack stretched over her elongated head, ragged holes corresponding to equine eyes still askew—although through violent shaking that animal had succeeded in getting one dark orb lined up with a hole, which help quiet it down.

Something like a rough laugh leaped out of Long Tom's sore throat.

"That handy girl jumped to a pile of conclusions. Guess I can't blame her too much."

There was no sign of his station wagon, Long Tom suddenly realized. It certainly made sense that the vigilantes had left behind a horse. One had taken the wagon. Probably they will come back for the horse, unless it, too, had been rustled and that crime would have been laid on Long Tom's doorstep as well.

Grumbling to himself, he strolled over to the waiting mare, ripped off the flour-sack mask, and climbed aboard. A thought struck him. He twisted about in the saddle and looked at the horse's hindquarters. There, he saw a brand. He did not recognize it, but the undersized electrical expert had put no special effort into learning the brands of the numerous outfits scattered about this far-flung portion of Campbell County.

The brand was a puzzling one. Most were easy to read. A numeral 4 entwined with the letter "J" signified the Four-J Ranch, for example. The Y-Cross outfit was another that was self-evident.

This brand was not. It consisted of two oddly-shaped ovals side by side and connected by a burn line. Each oval contained what looked like a scorched hyphen. They made Long Tom think of ghostly, sinister orbs. He could not imagine what that outfit would be called.

It was a long ride back to the Circle Bolt, but Long Tom had no interest in returning home just now. Pat Savage was sure to be along shortly, and he intended to meet up with her.

After that, there would be plenty of time to track the vigilantes whom Long Tom fully intended to punish with all the power contained in his compact fists.

Chapter VI

SKY HAWK SURPRISE

THE DUN MARE rolled along easily, her gait something between a canter and a trot. It was nearing noon by the scorching sun when the peace of the late morning was shattered abruptly.

Long Tom had been riding along like any other self-respecting Wyoming rancher when the plane had shot down out of the sun-bathed heavens and began spewing hot lead about him.

There was little warning. The brilliant midday sun cast a moving shadow, a shadow that flitted swiftly, ever-changing in shape. A roar, a thunderous rumble like the clamor of some mad monster, literally filled the air, setting even the rolling rangeland atremble.

A great winged yellow-and-black monster hurtled close to the earth, breathing fire and smoke that exhaled the foul stink of exhausted oil and gas. Tiny bursts of sand puffed like the fall of raindrops across the sandy bottom of the blowhole, a pit hewn in the natural stone of the hilltop by centuries of wind and torrential rains.

Long Tom wrenched a Winchester rifle from its saddle scabbard and beat the deadly stream of smoking metal to the overhang by inches. His horse galloped frantically away in the opposite direction, screaming in mindless fright.

"Damn this difficult day!" he gritted.

The expression was pregnant with feeling. Long Tom hugged his knees closer and flexed boot heels further under the painfully scant shelter of the overhanging lip of the crater-like depression. Not more than an arm's length away the procession passed, a nerve-tingling *whang, whang* of squashed lead on the solid stone of the pit's side.

Above the thunder of the plane's motor and the whistle of wind through its struts came the staccato, spiteful snarl of the machine gun that was stirring the loose grains and rounded marbles of sandstone into volcanic action.

The craft shot across the pit with less than thirty feet between its undercarriage and the electrical wizard hugging the inadequate shelter of the overhang.

The instant the shadow ceased to darken the crater, Long Tom hastily untangled his lanky form. He launched into frenzied activity. The ship would return quickly, flame playing about the muzzle of the weapon projecting from the fuselage belly.

The .30-30 rifle barked once, then again and again. As fast as he could work the lever, Long Tom shot, with the edge of the pit slightly over waist high, forming an armrest. Already the plane was turning, banking until it hung edgewise over the sage and cactus strewn range.

A burst of lead hissed about his oversized ears, and Long Tom dropped again into his narrow retreat. During the seconds before the pilot again brought the rapid firer into play, his mind became a maelstrom of baffled fury.

The motor's mutter again became a mad roar, and once again hissing lead gouged and spattered across the blowhole's bottom. This time the pilot's aim was not good. It was his third attempt at exterminating the pale electrical expert. The stream of biting bullets missed by twenty feet.

The buzzard-like shape had scarcely passed overhead when Long Tom systematically began emptying his rifle into the black body of the speeding biplane.

Three shots did the work. The craft banked about viciously, and was again coming head on when the whirling propeller dissolved into a flying mass of splinters.

Flying against a slight breeze, it almost instantly lost headway. A hundred feet above the earth, there was no time for the attacker to maneuver his aerial steed.

The range was far from an ideal landing field. Sagebrush, the sandy soil washed from its roots by melting snow and flurries of rain, stood in knotty patches everywhere. Cactus and scattered clumps of greasewood added their bit to the irregularity of the terrain.

The ship touched the earth, bounced, struck again, and then stood on its nose, plowing along for fifty feet before it ended in a cloud of dust, rending metal and torn linen. The crash broke roughly into the comparative silence that had followed the howling of the motor.

LONG TOM, .30-30 firmly in hand, left the shelter of the blowhole and ran toward the wreck. Discovering his wiry dun snorting and milling one hundred feet away, reins tangled over a clump of sage, he altered his leap-frog race down the hill. He flung himself into the saddle. Once again astride the mare, a few seconds sufficed to cover the quarter of a mile to where the wreck was rapidly becoming a smoking mass.

Fire, starting at the ruined engine, was licking with greedy tongues of red along the black fuselage and out on the yellow wings. Pungent orange-colored smoke billowed upward in choking masses.

Long Tom hurled himself off his horse and into the blazing, smoke-shrouded inferno. By sense of touch alone, he located the still form of the pilot, crumpled limply under the smashed framework of the ship. The fellow was not pinned and he dragged the still form free without trouble.

Eyes watering and temporarily blinded, Long Tom staggered several yards with his unconscious burden. A muffled boom, followed by a louder roar of greedy flames as the gas tank exploded, lent zest to his steps.

He dropped the pilot and squinted painfully at the burning

wreck. Flame swathed it from nose to tail. Even the tips of the yellow wings were a blazing bundle. Useless to make another attempt to enter the burning machine in search of a possible second passenger. But Long Tom was morally certain there had been only the one person in the ship.

The electrical genius inspected the unconscious flyer out of watery eyes. The grease-stained flying suit on the slender form was burned black and smoking in spots. Long Tom hastily extinguished the smoldering places with his fingers. Then, struck by a astounding suspicion, he jerked the leather helmet from the pilot's head.

It was a girl!

Tumbling masses of pine-colored hair, a long bob that fell well down her smooth neck cascaded from under the removed helmet. Even, delicate features—although smoke-blackened— had given him his first stab of realization.

Gingerly, Long Tom took the girl's slender wrist in his thin fingers, feeling for her pulse. He was unable to find any, but she suddenly opened her eyes and sat up, groaning slightly.

"What was the idea of strafing me?" he demanded peevishly.

It was probably not the most gentlemanly question to ask, but under the circumstances the pale electrical wizard's disposition was on the irate side. He was not having a particularly successful day, and it was getting under his pallid skin.

Apparently, the girl saw him for the first time. Her head jerked back, and her hand wrenched back from his grasp, dropping to her side.

Staring into her widening eyes, Long Tom saw strong emotions pass in rapid review. Surprise, fear, hate, then grim resolution seemed to grip the attractive brown orbs in quick succession.

Suddenly there came a movement followed by a blinding flash almost in Long Tom's eyes. Then another. He was only dimly conscious of a sickening double shock—that the girl had produced a short-barreled pistol from the pocket of her flying suit and was discharging it at point-blank range. Diamond points of fire played in a purple mist before his eyes. Then everything became a whirling vortex of red-shot blackness.

Through the confusion and shock, Long Tom heard her voice, shrill and accusing.

"That's my dun mare you were riding, you—you horse napper!"

Chapter VII

BLISTERING TREK

LONG TOM ROBERTS' recovery was accompanied mostly by many disagreeable sensations. Chief among these was a stabbing pain in his head and a dull ache somewhere about his shoulder. Too, there was still the pungent odor that had associated itself with the burning of the wrecked airplane.

Gingerly, the scrawny electrical wizard shifted about, but subsided when a stabbing pang shot over his body after he moved his left arm. His sleeve, he saw when the whirling mist had cleared before his eyes, was clammy with crimson that oozed from a hole halfway between his elbow and shoulder.

Long Tom felt the side of his head. It was moist and sticky. When he examined his fingers, the tips were scarlet. Then he sat up. His head throbbed with the effort, racking his body.

The girl was nowhere in sight. Nor was the dun mare standing where she should have been.

With infinite effort, Long Tom turned his head until he had searched the entire horizon. Not a living thing in sight. The gaunt skeleton of tubing, bent and twisted, that had been the framework of the plane lay a few yards away. Streamers of black fabric, a few still smoking, dangled and whipped in the breeze. Smoke blew in wispy plumes from the still-smoldering padding of the cockpit.

Long Tom cocked a speculative eye at the sun.

"Two o'clock," he grunted from the wisdom of much practice telling time from the solar orb.

"Been out about two hours," he solemnly assured himself. "That gal gunslinger took that mare and made tracks."

After a pause, he added, "If she was telling the truth about the ownership of that nag, she's no more horse thief than I am."

The breeze shifted. Smoke, the pungent odor predominant and sickening, began to blow over him. Long Tom coughed a time or two, then weakly stumbled further away, where he commenced a personal inventory.

He had been shot twice. Once through the fleshy part of the arm, and another bullet had grazed his right temple. The first was a clean drill. No bones or arteries were broken. It was the latter that had brought unconsciousness.

The sickly-looking electrical engineer bound his arm tightly with a plain bandana from the hip pocket of his work-worn corduroys, his mind full of mystified wonder. Blood no longer welled from the wound, but there was a dull ache that became a pronounced stab when he moved. Several minutes passed before he could stand erect without feeling ill.

Long Tom rarely looked healthy of complexion, but that was appearances only. He had seldom been ill a day in his life. Furthermore, he was a wildcat in a brawl. Consequently, he was unaccustomed to infirmity.

Practically nothing but the metal framework of the airplane was left. The spruce wing beams had burned almost completely away, the gaunt aluminum ribs dangling from the wire braces.

Creeping over to the wreck, Long Tom prodded among the ashes with one of the loose ribs, but found nothing. A feeling of relief washed over him when he ascertained that nothing resembling a charred body lay among the wreckage.

Having no other option except the time-honored custom called "Shank's mare," Long Tom began the weary trek back to the Circle Bolt Ranch. Walking cleared his head and as his brain became less muddled, his comments grew fierce.

"Fifteen lousy miles," he growled. "And all because of that trigger-happy gal pilot!"

Having vented his displeasure, Long Tom settled down to the prolonged and disagreeable hike through the desolate Powder River Basin.

High-heeled cowboy boots are not conducive to a pleasant stroll. Especially when the owner has a bullet hole through the arm and has been painfully rapped on the skull with another.

Long Tom discovered this unhappy fact in the first hundred yards. After a mile was put behind him—seemingly by inches—it became a monotonous, stumbling, headachy grind. Cowpaths and ancient buffalo trails all led toward Greasewood Creek, a mile away, which made them useless to the hiker.

Through long habit Long Tom wore an undervest of chain-mail construction, which would turn most pistol bullets. He wore this now, and it had deflected the slug fired into his upper chest, the shock of which had produced unconsciousness after glancing off his skull. The other bullet—the painful one that had struck his arm—had done the only significant damage. This led Long Tom to wish that the woman's point-blank aim had been better.

"Just my luck she wasn't a dead shot," he muttered to himself.

Ten miles or so behind him loomed the frowning mass of green timber, red sandstone and steely granite of Big Butte. Strung out, flanking Big Butte on either side were three lesser buttes. They were known locally as the Pumpkin Buttes, due to their striking color and rounded shape, or owing to the wild pumpkins that grew in the area. Accounts varied.

Toward this impressive group—North Butte, Middle Butte, Big Butte and South Butte—Long Tom Roberts had been loping purposely when the mysterious lady flier had popped up, determined on exterminating him.

Long Tom had a homestead, little more than a rough-hewn log cabin and a rickety stable, under the frowning shadow of Big Butte. The cabin, on the edge of eighty or ninety acres of luscious meadow, level as a floor, was the retreat which Long Tom expected to shelter him while he worked on his electrical experiments.

A cow ranch it had been. Not much more than a backcountry spread. A great uncle had owned it, but he'd never had the money to do much about the place. The bulking, majestic mass of Big Butte, the chaotic primeval canyons and timbered peaks of the "badlands" that flank the buttes, formed an ideal setting for solitude. The babbling waters of Greasewood Creek, a spring-fed hurried torrent the year around, held trout fit for a king.

Sixty miles it was to Gillette, the rambling, sunbaked and blizzard-swept conglomeration of board-fronted stores and weather-beaten, whitewashed stockyards that was the little Wyoming cattle-shipping town. Thence, shimmering bands of steel led into the east where Long Tom's Uncle Hicks expected guests for his proposed dude ranch establishment to arrive. But it never quite panned out.

"That female person," he growled ruefully, sidestepping a spiny bed of cactus, "sure got my dander up."

Thoughts of the fluffy-haired blonde caused Long Tom to associate her with another female ball of fire, namely Patricia Savage.

Swiveling his head around on his sunburned neck, Long Tom looked over his shoulder and remarked, "Pat should've happened along hours before this." This realization caused him to frown so deeply that his high bulbous forehead became a corrugation of wrinkles.

So much had happened to him between the drygulching, the near lynching and the aerial ambush that he had all but forgotten about Pat. Now worry rode his face and he got to wondering.

Long Tom became possessed of a profound and gnawing thirst. He reached the white-walled sink of an alkali hole, but the water was bitter and nauseating. He sat down for a few minutes, feet dangling over the edge of a tiny gully, resting and hoping that Pat Savage might turn up.

Pat failed to happen along. Thus, Long Tom reluctantly picked himself up and resumed his difficult trek.

AN hour passed and the sun commenced to hang low in the Western sky.

"Five miles more and I'll be to the horse pasture," he told himself firmly. "Maybe I can catch one of those bony nags my uncle left me."

The fiery disk of the September sun was sinking into the purpling masses of a brilliant painted sunset when Long Tom finally snared a mount from the horse pasture. The victim of his cautious stalking, an aged sorrel cowpony, wise with the mellow wisdom of sixteen years under the saddle, was a sway-backed blessing.

Thumping the friendly old roan over the ears with his good hand to guide him, Long Tom made better progress. Coyotes began to howl mournfully from distant hilltops with the first murky shadows of darkness. The staccato, shrill medley of their tongues gave an eerie touch—a sound once heard, not soon lost to memory.

Before long, Long Tom encountered another rider.

The fellow was short, thick-bodied and tremendously long of arm and leg. His skin was as shriveled and hard-looking as cowhide which has dried carelessly in the sun. A tobacco-yellowed mustache concealed his mouth and humorous wrinkles banked his grayish eyes. In age, he might have been any-where between forty and sixty. His clothes looked as though they had been worn continuously over a long period, and the slicker roll behind the saddle was bulging as if it contained food and possibly a soogan for a bed.

His star-faced grulla bronc was rather bony.

"*Daw-w-w gone!*" It was Laramie, the Circle Bolt's tobacco-chewing foreman who vented the astonished exclamation when Long Tom Roberts tottered weakly into view.

The grizzled old cow nurse forked his mount, and grunted, "I can see you're a-bleedin'. So just foller me."

Reaching the ranch house, Laramie dismounted, helped Long Tom from his saddle and assisted him through the front door.

"What ails you?" he wondered.

"Ant kicked me," Long Tom growled back, the corners of his thin mouth twitching from pain. The light of the oil lamp had blinded him temporarily. He braced his lean form against the rough door jamb.

"It must've been some helluva ant," Laramie grunted. "It looks to me more like you got a bullet to the arm an' another through that hat you took away from me with them educated cards."

The foreman studied him out of narrowed eyes.

"Well, what happened to the station wagon? You run it off a cliff or something?"

"I managed to get myself bushwhacked," grunted the under-sized electrical wizard. "The station wagon got away with the bushwhackers."

"That's kinda a jugheaded thing for a smart feller like you to let happen to him," snorted Laramie as he helped Long Tom into a chair. "Better fill me in."

Long Tom did, leaving out no detail, even to the piney color of the stunning young lady's hair and eyes. He finished while the bowlegged puncher, who boasted some little skill as a doctor of man and beast, sterilized and bound his wounds.

"You weren't bushwhacked," he grumbled. "You were drygulched."

"I was nearly lynched," snapped Long Tom.

"That, too," admitted Laramie while Long Tom suffered under the ministrations of the foreman who was more experienced doctoring horses and cattle than humans.

The slender electrical genius winced and made screwed-tight faces often.

"The way I figure it," Laramie ruminated, "those vigilantes who tried to string you up as a mule thief were themselves horse thieves. That would explain why they had flour sacks over their horses' heads. They rustled them in order to do the dirty work and not leave honest tracks."

Long Tom moaned. "I had that part pretty well figured out during my hike. That girl in the old plane spied me riding along on the stolen horse and decided to separate me from my mount with bullets."

Laramie nodded somberly. "She must of had a powerful mad on to do it the way she did."

"Who owns a private plane like that in these parts?" asked Long Tom fiercely.

Laramie considered as he cut himself a plug of tobacco for chewing. "I've seen a plane like that from time to time, but I don't rightly know who owns it. All the spreads around here are so far apart it's hard to get to know your neighbors unless you make a project out of it."

"You'd think a plane would be conspicuous."

"These are modern times," said Laramie thoughtfully. "Some folks have discovered that an aircraft, especially one of those old crates, is pretty durn near perfect for runnin' down stray cows or footloose cayuses."

"I take it you've seen no sign of Pat Savage?"

"None. Should it worry me?"

"It scares the daylights out of me, given what I ran into today. Pat can usually take care of herself, but she should've turned up long before now."

Chewing methodically, Laramie remarked, "Well, we've lost the light, but if you're willin', we can saddle up and mosey around."

Long Tom looked thoughtful. "If we still had the station wagon, that would make a lot more sense. But we don't."

"Yep. And them two crates out in the north meadow, your bus and Miss Patricia's, are practically useless at night. Even if you could spot a body by some miracle, landin' at night is tantamount to plain suicide." Laramie made a face. "Might be smarter to hold vigil and see if she turns up. And then there's that other thing."

Adjusting the temporary sling Laramie had fashioned for his wounded arm out of an empty flour sack, Long Tom looked up sourly. "What other thing?"

"The fact that you've been branded as both a mule filcher and a horse thief by two entirely different parties. Might not be such a smart idea to be goin' about showin' your face around, even if it is after dark. You're lucky to be alive after the trouble you barged into."

"I didn't barge into any trouble," snorted Long Tom derisively. "Trouble landed on me with both feet."

Laramie's laugh was on the wild side. "Both feet, and a pair of devil horns and spiky tail to hear you tell about it! Haw!"

The slender electrical genius declined to join in the merriment. He felt of the fresh bandage wound around his aching scalp. It felt dry. A good sign.

After he settled down, Laramie suggested, "Why don't you get some shuteye and I'll hold vigil for Miss Patricia. If she don't turn up, you'll need your strength for the search tomorrow mornin'."

Long Tom appeared reluctant, but finally he said, "Wake me if anything important happens."

Chapter VIII

GREASEWOOD MAGIC

LONG TOM ROBERTS spent the balance of the night in a somewhat turbulent state of mind. Sleep came only at scattered infinite intervals. His mind staggered back to the events of the evening of the day before, and he jolted awake every time he drifted off to sleep and his imagination put him back standing on the saddle of the stolen horse, his neck suspended in a coarse noose of hempen rope.

Uppermost in his mind were worried thoughts of Patricia Savage. He considered calling Doc Savage in New York, but the bronze man could not possibly reach Wyoming before dawn and by then the upset electrical wizard would be back in the saddle, searching. Aside from that factor, he had promised the bronze-haired girl that he would not call Doc into the matter prematurely. Long Tom now regretted that promise.

The next morning, Laramie woke him with the sound and smell of frying eggs and bacon. The old puncher served as cook, foreman and whatever else was necessary. Long Tom, in addition to being somewhat of a hermit, was on the miserly side and did not care to run a full ranch operation. It was hardly necessary, anyway. The Circle Bolt boasted a handful of cowponies and a single milk cow, but no herd of cattle.

Long Tom was no cowman. He just liked his solitude. And since he intended to spend only a few weeks out of the year at the ranch, Laramie served as the solitary caretaker whenever the owner was away, which was almost all the time.

After a hasty breakfast, they drove a rocking spring-wagon back along the road where Long Tom had last seen the golden-eyed girl.

Laramie's thinking was simple. "In case she's injured somewhere, we'll need to bring her back in the wagon."

"Don't talk like that," snapped Long Tom. But he did not disagree with his foreman's thinking. It was sound.

So off they rattled, with an extra horse trailing behind. The wagon pitched and rolled behind two big-footed draft horses.

They combed the trails traveled the previous day, but found no trace of Pat Savage or her horse, Lightning.

"Got me an idea," said Laramie suddenly.

"What is it?" Long Tom wondered.

"Let's mosey over to that crashed plane. I have a notion to look it over kinda careful-like."

"No time for that," snapped Long Tom.

Laramie puckered a sun-withered mouth. "I'm also thinking that if Miss Pat noticed it, she couldn't help but look it over, too. Maybe thinkin' it was a search plane in trouble. If so, she'd leave us a trail to follow."

"You might have an idea, after all," admitted Long Tom.

Chewing methodically, the old cowboy turned the wagon around and drove the snorting team toward the spot.

Eventually, the big, rubber-tired vehicle came upon the scorched metal tubing and twisted mass of wreckage. It was ten o'clock by the sun when they rode up on the scene of the plane crash.

Laramie bawled a sonorous "Gee!" and "Whoa thar!" and dragged on the manila jerk line, bringing the horses to a stop.

A couple of burned clumps of sage, wind-blown bits of charred linen and a few blackened wires marked the place. A brownish stain still colored the alkali-whitened patch where the girl shot him. A dozen empty, powder-marked cartridges littered the sandy bottom of the blowhole. Long Tom picked up several bits of soft metal, mushroomed into fantastic shapes. They were the machine-gun bullets that had flattened about him and very concrete evidence they were.

These items were the only traces remaining of the short, explosive thriller of the previous afternoon.

"Well, I'll be a Texas maverick if this ain't funny business," Laramie grumbled, stepping off and poking about in the wreckage.

"Nothing funny about it," Long Tom groused shortly.

"Why would a gal pilot rear up and pepper you like she done?"

"Feeling salty, maybe," corrected Long Tom. He made two wide circles around the spot before he gave up hopes of finding a trail. Disgusted and puzzled and no little interested, he walked back to the plane wreck.

Stamping about the wreckage which still smelled of burned fuel, he told Laramie, "Here is where the lady lead-slinger almost got me."

Laramie inspected the charred weapon with interest.

"Them's the kind we had in Uncle Sam's army," he explained after a curious examination. "They're bad medicine, all right."

Long Tom nodded. He also had been in the big scrap, so his knowledge was of a first-hand nature. That the big machine gun was bad medicine was something he did not have to be told.

Together, they removed the machine gun, discovered its mechanism was hopelessly ruined, and narrowly escaped getting shot again when a shell in the weapon's mechanism exploded.

The two men flung themselves in opposite directions until the machine gun settled down.

Laramie whistled as he sat up in the dirt. "Daw gone! She's still got some kick in her, don't she?"

Long Tom climbed to his feet and dusted himself off with his one good arm.

"We should give the horses a rest," he decided. "I'm going to saddle up the cowpony and Indian around and see what I can find. You stick here for a while."

"You betcha." Laramie chuckled. "Don't get perforated any more than you can help it."

"Stop riding me," Long Tom snapped back.

"Then quit bein' such an Eastern jughead in your ways."

The scene of the plane crash was on the outskirts; in fact, it lay on the very edge of the badlands' abrupt beginning. The rocky canyons and warped peaks, virtually impenetrable except by a few rough trails, formed a buffer that had effectively discouraged the inroads of dry farmer and cattleman alike.

Long Tom pinned his mount toward this wasteland. The ancient sorrel rolled along easily, his gait something between a canter and a trot.

TOWERING almost a mile above the surrounding districts, Big Butte was unique unto itself. On top, it was level as a table and as barren, nothing so much as a gigantic mesa, which it was not, technically.

Its flat summit was accessible, if one was willing to tackle a stiff wind, and it had the reputation of being a former Indian stronghold. Indeed, rifle pits, broken arrows and, once in a while, bits of rusty weapons were found to substantiate this legend.

North Butte had been the scene of a spirited and bloody conflict between cavalrymen and marauding Sioux back in the early 1880s, over fifty years back.

Long Tom headed his cowpony toward Greasewood Creek, crossing on the way the rotted furrows of the old north trail to California, the Oregon Trail, aged and long since unused, but still well preserved by the dry climate. Along the stream wound the trail that led to his little spread in the scenic paradise under Big Butte.

Greasewood Creek narrowed, became a leaping, babbling torrent of foaming water. The stream twisted and rose, while the frowning mass of the badlands pressed closer and closer as if to throttle its noisy sound.

The trail was a threadlike path that wound precariously under overhanging cliffs and across narrow ledges where the merest misstep would mean at least a plunge into icy waters, or possibly a smashing fall to the jagged rocks below.

Long Tom was thinking, if Pat had become lost or her horse crippled, the golden-eyed girl would surely have made her way to the river, drawn by its thirst-quenching attractions.

Rounding one of these narrow ledges, the sorrel stopped so suddenly that Long Tom jarred against the well-forked cantle. Greasewood Creek poured in a roaring medley of sound over a little waterfall, filling the cleft-like canyon with a booming roar that drowned all sound.

Long Tom looked up, for confronting him was a rider.

The undersized electrical wizard blinked. He blinked several times. For the unexpected apparition appeared to be a byproduct of the morning heat, a mirage in human form.

The fellow's attire was green, violently so. He wore a tan hat at least a size too big for him, for it squatted down on his head and swallowed his eyebrows whole. The heavy brim made his ears conspicuously lopped.

The man had an ancient shotgun, matched barrels dull with age.

His vivid green eyes flared when he saw Long Tom. He lifted the ungainly blunderbuss.

"Stand steel, hombre!" he shouted in an exaggerated South-of-the-border accent.

Despite the handicap of his flour-sack arm sling, Long Tom launched himself from his saddle and collided with the man just as the shotgun discharged.

"*Oof!*"

The pair landed in the dirt as their horses shied and snorted nervously.

Long Tom was quite a scrapper, and he possessed a temper

that was fierce when aroused. It had been aroused for the better part of a day now, and he was happy to take the cork off.

Using one fist, he began pummeling the other, but the green rider had the advantage of two good fists, and he used them.

As a result, Long Tom found himself being battered and unable to defend himself properly. He was still rather weak from his ordeal of the previous day. Having his wounded right arm in a sling was no advantage, either.

The green man grabbed up his formidable shotgun and clubbed Long Tom with the stock.

The force of the blow would have knocked out a less stubborn individual, but Long Tom Roberts was made of sterner stuff. Nevertheless, he was dazed, and momentarily lost control of his senses. Violently-colored sparks and stars swam before his wavering vision.

His ears told him that the man had remounted and was taking off in a clatter of hoofbeats.

Groaning, Long Tom got control of himself and tried to stand up. But he could not. All his wiry strength had been knocked out of him.

The slender electrical wizard possessed sufficient presence of mind to examine his limbs for damage. He was pleased to discover no shotgun pellets had entered his body at any point.

That accomplished, Long Tom looked about and lost interest in his own well-being. His pale eyes clicked over to Greasewood Creek where he spied something that made him blink rapidly.

In the middle of the rushing creek, there was a stretch that was muddy. The creek bottom stood exposed to the blinding sun for only a few seconds. Then the tumbling river rushed in, covering it. The restored river continued to course along as if the patch of exposed mud had never existed.

Eyes popping, Long Tom stared at the spot, wondering if he had been hallucinating.

And something else happened that was equally strange.

There was a sudden cloudburst. Or so it seemed. It was brief and the water soaked Long Tom thoroughly.

But when the slack-jawed electrical genius looked up, there was not a cloud in the sky and no source from which the precipitation could have fallen.

After a bit, something struck him on the head. He grabbed at it. A live trout. It flopped about, squirming between his thin fingers. Long Tom threw it into the creek.

"That blow must've done something to my brain," he mumbled. And despite the danger, he lay back down and stared up at the clear blue sky, waiting for the spell to pass.

Chapter IX

GUN TALK

A S HE LAY supine, Long Tom Roberts reflected upon his unusual situation.

His thoughts drifted back to Pat Savage's urgent summons and her wild tale of a man swimming about in circles in the sky until he plummeted to earth, as if overcome by a crippling fatigue.

At the time, Long Tom had credited it to a touch of altitude sickness, but now he was not so certain.

These last few minutes of events were taking place at a reasonable altitude, that is to say, no particular height. The badlands hereabouts featured many high elevations, but Long Tom had not climbed any of those fantastic precipices.

Altitude sickness could not account for the vision of an interrupted creek and its swift refilling. And the trout that had fallen out of a clear azure sky had been solid enough to fillet and fry.

He struggled with his memory of the muddy waterhole in which the missing cowpoke, Hud, had supposedly sought.

Could that swimming hole's contents somehow have been transported skyward, taking the man with him?

It seemed preposterous. But the more the baffled electrical wizard contemplated it, the more his brain tugged at the corners of the mystery.

If the swimming hole had been catapulted skyward somehow, it was reasonable to assume gravity would bring it back down, along with any contents, such as a trapped swimmer.

The theory was reasonable. No question about it. Extremely reasonable. An agency that might elevate a swimming hole was a bit of a puzzle, true. But many inexplicable things had in the heart of them ordinary explanations.

The truly baffling part centered around the possibility of the swimming hole having remained suspended high in the sky, containing the captured cowpoke. What had kept it up there for so long? And what had caused it to fall back to earth, along with the unfortunate Hud?

Those were the questions that made the electrical genius' brain hurt in a way that had nothing to do with a concussion.

Finally, Long Tom rearranged his flour-sack arm sling, and sat up. He clucked at his horse, which obligingly trotted up. With difficulty, Long Tom managed to clamber back into the saddle, one-handed.

The feel of its worn leather hull brought his thoughts careening back to the near hanging he had endured. He was developing a distaste for Wyoming, or at least this desolate section of it. The appeal of solitude was giving way to the inconvenience of constant trouble.

As he forked his mount back in the direction of the isolated spot where the smashed plane had come to rest, something in the sky caught his canny eye.

It was white and it scooted high up in the blue.

At first, the slender electrical expert mistook the thing for a bird, but careful attention showed that it was no avian specimen.

Shielding his eyes from the sun, Long Tom followed it. Suddenly he exploded, "That looks like Pat's Stetson!"

That comment was likely a product of hope and not recognition, for at the great distance, one white Stetson could be mistaken for another. But since the golden-eyed girl had last been seen wearing such headgear, Long Tom flew into a conclusion.

As he rode along, Long Tom paid attention to the rugged

ground beneath his pony's feet. He was keeping an eye out for any signs left by the green-togged rider.

The ground was too stony to take hoofprints, so he paid more attention to the hat flying about high above it.

It was not particularly windy by Greasewood Creek, where the Pumpkin Buttes acted as a windbreak, and it was clear from the behavior of the whirling Stetson that there was plenty of wind at the higher elevations.

"That chapeau," muttered Long Tom, "doesn't look like it wants to land."

Abruptly, there came a crack of gunsound and the Stetson gave a flip and changed direction like a wounded bird.

It tumbled a bit, then righted itself somehow, and continued gliding about, pushed by playful winds.

Another crack and the Stetson jumped almost straight up. When it came down, it fell like a rock.

Echoes made it impossible to track the source of the gunshot, for that must be what it was. It was the bark of a six-gun. Whoever triggered it was a pretty fair shot. For twice the shooter had nailed the fast-moving target.

"Might be Laramie having a little fun," Long Tom told himself reassuringly.

Another thought struck him. He voiced it aloud.

"Maybe it's Pat herself, trying to fetch her Stetson out of the sky with a bullet."

Again, nothing more substantial than hope lay behind that declaration.

This was proven when Long Tom rounded a rocky outcropping and spied the wielder of the revolver.

It was a female. But not Pat Savage. This girl possessed fluffy pine-colored hair and sat on the same dun mare that she had so preemptively requisitioned after the previous shooting.

Long Tom sat in his saddle staring, mouth falling open when he found himself looking for the second time into the muzzle of the six-gun in the young lady's hand. For she had spied him and brought both her mount and her aim around in his direction.

The young woman's face hardened. Reading purpose in her brown eyes, Long Tom hurled himself suddenly sideways, just as the weapon barked thunderously. Then he leaped to safety behind a jutting tusk of the stony point.

A female voice rang out. "Thought I'd perforated you permanent-like yesterday! Clear out of this county lest I hole your thievin' skull!"

No more shots were fired. Long Tom cautiously poked his hat around the corner, then followed it with his head when it did not attract a bullet. The trail was empty!

It was a little uncanny. Without a gesture beyond the single shot, the girl had fled. Long Tom mounted his horse, whose temper not even the end of the universe could shake, and spurred madly in pursuit.

Search as he might, the total result of his hunt was an absolute zero.

The dun mare she had taken from him was vastly superior to the ancient sorrel in speed, if not in experience and staying qualities. With only two or three minutes start, she had disappeared completely, which was not remarkable. Any one of the craggy canyons could have easily swallowed horse and rider. The polished boulders, packed earth and scattered loose stones offered no discernible trail.

Finally, Long Tom gave it up as a bad job and headed back toward the plane wreck.

His course took him past the white Stetson, which had by this time fluttered to the ground. Bending awkwardly in the saddle, he scooped up the bullet-riddled thing and examined it carefully.

"Pat's, right enough," he decided.

He gave the inside of the crown a sniff and frowned. He had

hoped to smell fresh perspiration, but no such luck. Evidently Pat had not worn the hat for several hours, if not longer.

His pale eyes searched the elevations comprising the chain of frowning buttes, and he came to a firm conclusion.

Long Tom kept his conclusion to himself.

The wound in his arm ached. It had been jarred when he slid so abruptly off the horse. He readjusted the sling to give a little more comfort and urged his mount on.

VERY soon the narrow canyon through which Greasewood Creek ran widened. It spread out fanwise on either side. Lying between the surrounding walls of massive sandstone and red rock was a natural meadow decorated with scarlet spikes of Indian paintbrush.

Amidst these wild flowers, a solitary cabin stood decaying in the sun. It possessed a deserted air. Swallows popped in and out of the corrugated iron eaves, where they had apparently nested.

Long Tom rode absent-mindedly out of a fringe of scrub pines. No sooner had he done so than things began to happen.

Spa-a-n-g-g! A bullet struck a tree a dozen feet away and ricocheted, humming like an angry hornet.

This time Long Tom kept in the saddle. Instantly, he was back in the belt of trees, spurring for shelter. Other bullets cut needles and cones from about him, one hissing so close that it stood his hair on end. Or so his prickling scalp felt.

Safely concealed, with the granite bulk of a score of boulders the size of small dwellings between himself and the sharp-shooter, Long Tom pulled to a halt.

"This searching business," he told the panting roan, "is getting more mixed up every minute."

A fringe of underbrush, dwarf pines mostly, ran completely around the meadow. Long Tom tied his mount to a scrawny briar that grew out of a crack in the solid rock. The spot was well hidden; only one passing a few yards distant would discover the horse.

Drawing close to the cabin, he used added caution, moving from thicket to thicket searching the ground ahead carefully. The brush extended almost to the cabin wall.

A single window, two small sashes in size, pierced the rear of the structure. Long Tom reached the opening unmolested and raised his eyes cautiously.

A man was crouched at the window, facing the middle distance. Reclined rather, for he half lay, half sat on a rude stool. One arm was bound tightly to his side with ragged white bandages. Additional wrappings, apparently improvised out of torn flour sacks, swathed his torso.

Resting on the windowsill was a businesslike carbine. The man held the weapon with his one good hand and was watching the line of trees across the meadow closely. His face had a worried look.

Long Tom scrutinized him for a full minute.

The fellow looked as if he had been through a scrape, for his clothes were dusty and torn here and there. But Long Tom recognized the man's duds.

"Laramie!" he hissed.

The fellow whirled, and averted a catastrophe only by common horse sense. Lead would surely have flown wildly. But this man kept his finger out of the trigger guard and that precaution conceivably saved Long Tom's life.

Lowering his weapon, Laramie exploded, "I almost shot your big ears off, you know that?"

"What are you doing holed up here?" demanded Long Tom.

"I might return the favor by asking what are you doing skulkin' around this cabin?" countered Laramie.

"I ran into that girl again. She's been shooting at me some more."

Laramie grunted. "Gettin' to be a bad habit with her."

"Shooting back didn't make a lot of sense, so I retreated after leaving my horse tied up."

Opening the door, Long Tom stepped in and the two men huddled, eyes watching the windows.

"I have a story to tell," Laramie said at length.

"That makes two of us," declared Long Tom.

"My story is a mite unbelievable," cautioned Laramie, his eyes looking slightly guilty. "You're gonna think that either I've swapped my chewing tobacco for locoweed or I'm the tallest liar this side of Cheyenne."

"We'll swap yarns. You go first."

Laramie was scratching at the back of his wrinkled neck where the sun had reddened it most.

"I was waiting by that plane wreck when I happened to notice a white Stetson flyin' around the sky. Naturally, I thought of Miss Pat. So I began walkin' in that direction."

"I saw it, too," commented Long Tom. "That blonde gal began shooting at it until it dropped out of the sky."

"That's when I ducked back, since I don't cotton to wild lead-slingin' here in the badlands," admitted Laramie. He went on. "In my caution, I happened to mosey into the rocks where I encountered the most doggone fellow you ever did meet. Except you never met him."

"Was he dressed in green, like a leprechaun?" asked Long Tom suddenly.

"Had the Irish red hair, too," clucked Laramie. "So I guess you did meet up with him."

"Unexpectedly," allowed Long Tom. "He opened up on me with a double-barreled scattergun, but he missed."

"Did me the same favor," said Laramie. "Only he didn't miss me by much. I got me a skin full of rock salt and I'm grateful that's all it was."

"What happened to him after that?"

"It's what happened to me that I hesitate to offer." Laramie did more scratching, then squinted his wrinkled eyes as if trying to assemble the most sensible words he could.

"After the scattergun blasted me, I was blown back a ways, but I kept going. Next thing I knew I didn't know anything. When I woke up, I was a long ways away from that old rock. In fact, I landed in this meadow. All my bones ached and I can't figure out how I got here so fast."

"Whoa," said Long Tom impatiently. "Back up a bit. You say the shotgun blast threw you all this way? That's got to be two to three miles, as the buzzard flies."

"That's not the impossible part," the old codger admitted. "The blast flung me in the opposite direction from where I landed. I plumb blacked out. When I came to my senses, I was tangled up in an old cottonwood. I don't know how I got here. But no horse-drawn wagon dragged me this far. My pocket watch told me that much. So, when I got myself back on the solid soil and reassembled, I hunkered down in the cabin, fearin' God knows what devilment might transpire next." He cleared his throat nosily. "That's my story and she's a fact."

Tugging absently at an oversized ear, Long Tom closed one pale eye in thought.

"You got the better of me," he admitted at last.

"How so?"

"My story isn't anywhere near as preposterous. But it's in the general neighborhood. I ducked the green bird's blast, but somehow Greasewood Creek went dry in the middle for a short spell of time. I couldn't see how. But the water rushed in to make it whole again. After that there came a short downpour, followed by a live river trout landing. I've been thinking that it might be the river water coming back down to earth."

"It would take a powerful shotgun to blast a section of creek clear up into the sky," Laramie mused.

Long Tom frowned. "I didn't think it was the shotgun until you spun your yarn. Now I don't know."

"That makes two of us," allowed Laramie. "What happened to the gal?"

"She's still out there, but it's Pat I'm more worried about. Her hat was flying around like it blew off one of the buttes. She might have climbed one if she lost her horse."

"Makes sense that she might've done that. But where is Lightning? And shouldn't Miss Pat be up on a butte, waving her arms for us to see?"

"Don't make me think mournful thoughts," said Long Tom. "I think it's time to bring Doc Savage into this confusion."

"We're pretty far from any telephone, and that ornery gal is out there with her loaded-for-bear smoke-wagon and an over-eager trigger finger. She's warpathin' something ferocious. If she sees me coyoting around with the likes of you, she's liable to brand me as a maverick, too. With hot lead. How do you propose to navigate this conundrum?"

"By tracking down that girl, for starters," said Long Tom tightly.

Laramie squinted. "You sound plenty sore with her."

"That's not the point. No sense in hunting for a telephone if she's going to take potshots at us from the rocks. I need to settle with her first."

The old cowboy gave his pants a hitch. His tongue, pulling away from the roof of his mouth, made a little click of sudden disapproval. "That kinda talk usually leads to the parties involved unravelin' cartridges at one another."

Long Tom's mouth hardened. "If it comes to a fight, I'm game."

"You'd do that?"

"She shot at me twice. I'm starting to think it might be a pleasure."

"In that case," said Laramie reluctantly, "you're the boss, so you lead the way. And if you're still wearin' that bulletproof vest of yours, don't think poorly of me if I stand behind you most of the time."

"Let's get cracking," said Long Tom with firm conviction.

Chapter X

MULE MYSTERY

PAT SAVAGE WOKE up to the blaze of the Wyoming sun stabbing hot needles into her golden eyes.

The glare was something awful. Groaning, she reached up for her Stetson and encountered only her hair, which had been dyed copper to disguise its bronze sheen.

The difference between copper and bronze was not very great, but to Pat Savage it had been a reasonable precaution, as were the dark sun-glasses that concealed her striking golden eyes.

Pat sat up with difficulty. Her back ached, and her face was so dry and hot that she realized that she must have been lying in the sun for a good many hours.

Shielding her eyes from the blazing sun, she looked up and attempted to ascertain the time.

The position of the sun caused her to exclaim, "It can't be!"

Suddenly remembering that she was wearing it, Pat checked her wristwatch. It was broken, the crystal face shattered. She lifted it to her ear. It no longer ticked. The hands read 11:32.

The position of the sun suggested that it was approximately 9 o'clock in the morning.

"No wonder my noggin aches so much," she complained.

At the sound of her voice, Lightning emitted a dismal whinny.

Twisting around, every muscle and joint protesting the effort, the copper-haired girl discovered Lightning lying on her side. She did not look good. Her eyes were watery and her chestnut flanks heaved with the struggle to keep breathing.

Climbing to her feet, Pat made a circuit of the mare and saw the sad truth. Lightning's left foreleg had a disquieting bulge in it that could only mean one thing.

"Broken," she murmured. Kneeling down, she patted the horse's trembling cheek. "I'm sorry, old gal," she said soothingly.

The horse gave a pitiful bleat of a sound and a solitary tear ran down from one moist eye.

Pat gave the horse reassurance for a while, then stood up and took stock of her situation. She had not done this before, concern for the animal being uppermost in her mind.

Pat saw that she was high up, and for a moment she began to wonder about her mental health. It started to come back to her that she had been blasted by a shotgun wielded by a weird little man in green and she and her mount had leapt prodigiously into the sky.

Going to the rocky rim of her perch, Pat saw how high they had landed and whispered one word wonderingly. "Impossible."

No horse could leap so high, she knew. And from the looks of her surroundings, there was no trail up. Therefore, the horse could not have fled into the rocks and clambered up to this rocky perch. The golden-eyed girl made a circuit of the butte's lip just to be certain.

Returning to the stricken horse, she said, "Lightning, that was a leap that would have outshone Pegasus."

The stricken horse offered no rejoinder.

Getting down on her knees, she checked the animal again and discovered a leakage of blood seeping from the flank pressed to the rocky summit.

"Looks like you collected some buckshot," she said sympathetically.

Pat reached under the horse, felt around the coarse hairs and found something lodged in a small wound. She brought it out and examined the bloody pellet.

It was not buckshot at all. It wasn't any kind of lead. It was nearly transparent, although yellowish.

Wiping it off on her sleeve, she examined it in the harsh sunlight. "Rock salt!"

Frowning, Pat said, "This stuff must sting. I've heard of varmints who stuffed rock salt into their scatterguns to teach people a lesson without seriously harming them, but I don't understand why it would make you jump like you were wearing seven-league horse shoes."

Of course, the animal could not have executed such a mythological feat, Pat quickly realized. Yet she could not account for how she and Lightning arrived at this lofty perch where only the buzzards normally roosted.

Pangs of hunger stirred in her stomach and reminded Pat that she had not eaten since breakfast the previous morning. If she had any hope of reaching the safety of the valley floor, she needed to get about her business.

This included some unpleasantries. Beginning with the disposition of Lightning.

Fighting back tears, her chin trembling a little, Pat took the Winchester out of its saddle scabbard, cocked it once and slipped up behind the horse, placing the muzzle against the back of its long skull without touching horseflesh.

"I'm sorry, Lightning," she whispered.

Closing her eyes, Pat Savage pulled the trigger and the horse's head rocked as a convulsive shudder coursed along its spine, causing the tail to flutter and whip about. The last animation ceased within less than a minute.

Pat did not look back as she jacked another round into the receiver and began picking her way down off the high elevation. She had never had to put down a horse before, although it was not an unusual thing in the wilderness of British Columbia where she had been raised by her father, now deceased. But she was horsewoman enough to know what to do when the time came. Still, the appropriateness of the action, and the mercy she had shown the loyal animal that would have eventually died of starvation, roiled her emotions as few things ever had.

Unsteadily, Pat picked her way down, climbing, sliding the Winchester ahead of her where necessary, moving as fast as her weakened condition would permit. For Pat knew that if she allowed herself to be stranded high among these rocks, she might be forced to resort to consuming horse meat in order to survive long enough for rescue to arrive.

Since rescue was not guaranteed, taking her chances climbing down was her only sensible option.

It stood to reason that Long Tom Roberts and Laramie would have been searching for her long before this hour. The fact that they had not yet located her suggested they were looking in the wrong places.

The golden-eyed girl showed that she had some traits in common with a mountain goat as she worked her way around obstacles, shifting horizontally whenever tumbled rocks obstructed her descent, and so eventually reached the ground.

Pat had a rough idea of where she was, but very rough. She knew that Long Tom's little ranch lay to the east and her best bet was to head in that direction. The town of Bison tempted her, but it was too far a hike.

Tucking her Winchester under one arm, Pat began her trek. Her Frontier six-shooter hung heavy in its contoured holster, the ivory butt protruding. Inasmuch as it rivaled an anvil in weight, the heavy revolver had stayed put through all of Lightning's acrobatics.

LUCK was with her. Or rather, Lady Luck returned to smile on her after a particularly trying absence.

Pat was walking along when a dusty blue roadster came hoicking along the graveled road, throwing alkali dust into the air. Had this been a better traveled area and a true highway, Pat might have considered cocking her thumb like a hitchhiker, but she was the only person around for miles and this was the Wild West, after all.

The motorist pulled over and asked, "Where is your horse?"

Pat choked back a sob and croaked, "Had to shoot her."

"Tough break. Busted leg?"

"Not as busted as my heart," Pat admitted.

"Where are you bound?"

"The Circle Bolt Ranch. It's at least ten miles up ahead."

"Never visited the place, but I've heard of it. I'm headed for the town of Bison. Would that suit you?"

Pat did not have to consider that for long. "It would suit me just fine. They have a public telephone."

The driver reached over and pushed open the passenger side door. Pat hopped in, slamming it behind her.

Getting the car back in gear, the motorist sent it jouncing along. He appeared to be a tall, athletic individual, solidly muscled without being too sturdy with a head so square it might have been planed into shape by a carpenter. His boots were rich and had a little bit too much silk embroidery; his pants looked as though they had been cut to fit his well-shaped legs; while his shirt was rather gaudily purple, and his hat was too flamboyantly big and white.

HE was not young, but did not appear old. Yet out from the cuffs of his shirt poked quantities of thick white hair. He appeared to be a simple, outdoorsy fellow, possessing sharp lead-colored eyes. Some women might have considered him handsome in a rangy way, but Pat wasn't one of them.

His smile was friendly enough. "What's your name, girly?"

Cautiously, Pat said, "Quitt. Juanna Quitt."

"Nice name. Shame about your horse."

Pat said nothing; she did not want to dwell on the subject.

"My name's Oakley Wood. I'm with the Lynx Eyes outfit."

"Funny name for a ranch."

"It's kind of a funny ranch. We don't run cattle, or even horses. We raise mules. These breaks are mostly all mule range."

Pat nodded distractedly.

"I'm off to Bison to talk to the sheriff. Overnight, we lost a few more. It's getting to be like a contagion, these vanishing jacks."

Clutching the open window as she bounced in her seat, Pat frowned. "What kind of rustler would steal mules?"

The other laughed roughly. "A mule rustler, naturally. I fear it's been going on for a while now. Not just our mule outfit, but a bunch of others are losing stock. It's a big mystery. In fact, there are rumors floating around that the rustlers operate out of the Circle Bolt Ranch." Turning his head, he eyed her speculatively. "Would you know anything about that?"

"A good friend of mine inherited that ranch. He's no mule rustler. In fact, there's just him and his foreman at the place now."

"Well, it was just a rumor I was repeating," said Wood. "No offense intended. Five or six men are doing the deed. They change the brands with an acid that makes the new brand look like the old one, even to gray hairs in the scars on the inside of the hide. They take the mules across the Bighorns and ship them from Worland on the Burlington branch line that runs up the Bighorn basin."

Wood speared a cigarette out of the pocket of his purple shirt and managed to light it from a jeweled lighter while holding the steering wheel straight with a knee.

"Five or six men are doing it, like I say. I suspect who one of them is. Every time that I followed them, the other hombre shows up in the breaks to help with the brand blotting. He's always masked. I ain't seen his face, nor have I been able to trail him. I don't know who he is."

"Who's the one you know?" Pat asked curiously.

"I don't rightly want to say. No point in casting aspersions based on suspicions. But that's why I'm headed into town. I want to share those suspicions with the sheriff. The days of taking justice into your own hands in these parts are over and done with."

"It pays to abide by the law," commented Pat.

"That ain't all," Wood went on. "The brand they put on those rustled mules is Miss Crater's Lynx Eyes. The Lynx Eyes is one of them changed Window Sash brands—it'll blot out everything on this range. All of them that's losing mules, at any rate. J.C. Mott's brand is the Half Circle. He's the biggest loser and that's the one who's making the biggest fuss about lynching the culprits, once we catch up to them. I'm trying to head that off."

"You sound sure of your facts," commented Pat.

"Sure am," Wood said flatly, exhaling tobacco smoke with his comment. "The Lynx Eyes is a small outfit. Like most of the brands in this section of the Big Powder country, it had origi- nally been a horse outfit but with the slump in the demand for horses following the World War, had turned to raising mules. You see, the wiry, tough little range jugheads, bred to big-boned jacks shipped in from the East, produce a hearty variety of mule greatly in demand among the small cotton farmers of the southern states. The Lynx Eyes is two egg-shaped loops with the little ends together and a short dash in each loop. The Half Circle happens to fit in that dash and the Leaning Dash is just the size of the dash in the Lynx Eyes. They even ship the pilfered jugheads from Worland under Alta Crater's name."

"Are mules difficult to rustle?" wondered Pat, not because she was truly interested but because she wanted to keep her mind off her troubles.

"Nope. We ship them to Alabama and Georgia and the cotton country. Whoever's rustling them could do that, too, once they get them past the brand inspectors. Acid could be used to blot a brand so it'll look like it's been there for years," he added.

"How interesting," said Pat thinly, her voice drifting off.

Soon they pulled into the town of Bison, said their goodbyes, and Pat made a beeline for the general store.

Noticing Pat coming in and seeing her sun- and wind-burned complexion, the proprietor clucked, "Black cherry pop, ma'am?"

"Open up two," said Pat. "I will need to make a telephone call first."

Striding over to the long oak box of a telephone, Pat set her Winchester rifle down, leaning it against the wall.

Giving the mechanism a crank, she got the operator and said, "I would like to place a collect call to New York City."

"What number?" asked the operator crisply.

"The party I wish to speak to has several numbers. No need to bother about them. Just tell the New York operator to connect to Doc Savage in Manhattan."

"Did you say Doc Savage?" the operator gasped.

"Yes, and I do not care to repeat it. Please, hurry. This matter is urgent. Tell him Juanna Quitt is calling."

The general store proprietor was finishing stripping the metal caps off a pair of cold black cherry soda pop bottles and his eyes went wide. He had been chewing furiously in the background, his busy teeth made squeakings like fingers stroking freshly soaped saddle leather.

Turning, he stared at Pat, looked her up and down from the crown of her coppery head to the toes of her well-worn riding boots. His eyes became narrow and suspicious.

Setting the cold bottles on the counter, he listened intently. That he heard only half the conversation that followed seemed to intrigue him all the more, given the portion he did overhear.

A striking voice finally answered, saying, "Is that you, Pat?"

"Well, of course it is," said Pat breathlessly. "I told you if I ever ran smack into trouble and didn't want to identify myself I would use the name Juanna Quitt."

"A peculiar name," said the distinctive voice.

"You can take it to mean that I'm quitting my excitement seeking and handing over my share to you, starting immediately."

"You have run into a little difficulty in Wyoming?"

"I wish it was only a little," confessed Pat. "It all started when I rolled up into the Bighorns to do a little prospecting. That was when I saw the man swimming in circles in the sky."

"Such a thing is impossible, as you certainly know."

"Impossible, but I saw him. As I watched, he started to flounder, then sink slowly. Finally, he plummeted to the earth. I called Long Tom and we found the place where he landed. But the body was gone. But that wasn't the weirdest part. The spot where the body should have been was wet from a recent rain. But there wasn't a cloud in the sky, Doc."

A strange sound came over the wire. Mellow and melodious, it might have been the eerie keening of a western wind flowing through the sandstone spires which dot the Wyoming badlands like limbless specters. It emerged from the telephone diaphragm like a fugitive creature composed of pure sound that had wandered in from another dimension. Eerie and unearthly was this tuneless trilling.

Pat ignored the musical interlude and asked, "I take it you are intrigued?"

"How high up in the mountains did you get?" questioned Doc Savage.

"Pretty high. But I know what you're thinking. It wasn't altitude sickness. That is, I did have a spell of it. But that's beside the point. A body did land from a great height. It's just up and disappeared."

"It sounds like hallucination produced by altitude sickness," stated Doc Savage.

Pat stamped a booted foot in annoyance. "But it wasn't! And that's not the worst of it."

"Continue your report," Doc said calmly.

Pat resumed her recitation, telling how Long Tom had left her in the dust to ride along until she encountered the weird little fellow in vivid green clothes and a John B. Stetson hat too big for him.

"He uncorked an old scattergun in my direction and stung my horse. The horse naturally bolted, then kept on going. I closed my eyes and we must have landed pretty hard, because I woke up almost a day later high up in the rocks." A catch came into her voice. "I had to put the horse down, Doc. It was awful. But there was no way that horse could have gotten up that mountain. There was no path. I don't know how we landed there. Honestly, I don't. But I managed to climb down and hitch a ride into town."

"What about Long Tom?"

"I don't know what became of him. I imagine he is out searching for me somewhere in those badlands. Doc, I believe you should come out. I think you should fly here now. There's a powerful mystery out here. I don't understand it, but very strange things are happening, and I've just about had my fill of trouble."

The line hummed for fully a minute and longer.

Then the distinctive voice of Doc Savage said, "Endeavor to locate Long Tom. Let him know that you are safe. Then stay put until my arrival."

"So you don't think it's altitude sickness, do you?"

"Not all of it. Perhaps some aspects of it. But as mysteries go, you seem to have uncovered a particularly intriguing one. Await my arrival."

"Thanks, cousin," said Pat in genuine relief. "You won't regret this. Just remember, however, this is my mystery before it's yours. I expect to participate in its unraveling."

"We will see about that," said Doc Savage noncommittally.

PAT was grinning when she hung up and turned to claim her refreshments. Then she noticed the expression on the proprietor's stunned face. A man suddenly struck by lightning might wear such a face.

That expression took her aback.

Pat said firmly, "That was a private conversation, I will have you know."

The proprietor appeared tongue-tied. Pat took that for assent, scooped up one of the cold bottles and began drinking thirstily.

She downed the pop in one continuous pull. When she set the empty bottle down on the counter, Pat noticed the proprietor's face. It had a crafty look.

"I thought I overheard you talking to a fellow named Doc Savage."

"Mind your business," said Pat tartly.

"I've heard tell of a Doc Savage who liked to go around, busting trouble and putting his nose in other people's business," mused the man.

Grasping the other bottle, Pat ignored him.

"Do you have trouble you want Doc Savage to bust?" the man asked tightly.

"Do I need to repeat myself?" asked Pat, lifting the bottle to her lips.

"I think I would like to hear more about this trouble, Miss."

Pat took two swallows, then paused.

"You overheard all you're going to learn." With that, she fished out a dime, dropping it on the counter where it rang jarringly before settling down.

"Keep the change," said Pat, stalking out into the dusty street.

The proprietor made no move to interfere. But once the door banged shut, he ran to the long telephone box and gave the crank a vigorous revolution.

"Connect me with the Lynx Eyes Ranch," he bit out nervously. "And don't you dare listen to this conversation, you hear me?"

A furtive voice soon came on the line and said, "Who's this?"

"Get Buck on the line. Pronto."

"Buck ain't here. Went off somewheres without sayin' exactly where. What's doing?"

"Trouble," the proprietor said hurriedly. "Tall trouble. I got some hot news. That damn Doc Savage is coming to town. He's looking to mix up into something strange."

"What would be happenin' out here that would interest *that* guy?"

"I don't know. But if Doc Savage shows up, this entire section is liable to be turned upside down. Savage has a way of doing things like that. All he has to do is show up and matters will commence earth-quaking."

"You don't think he's comin' out Wyoming way alookin' for the missin' mules, do you?"

The proprietor chewed slowly as he considered the question. "It doesn't sound like a big enough deal for Doc Savage to mix into. But he has a reputation of helping people who need help. And so many mules have gone missing that the whole county is riled up. It could be a bunch of owners have pooled their money together to hire him."

"Doubt it. I heard this Doc Savage doesn't work for pay. He's some kind of altruist. He steps into a fracas for the sheer and abiding pleasure of it."

"Whether he's looking for mules or has bigger fish to fry, he's going to blow this territory wide open just by stepping into things. We have to head him off at the pass."

The other grunted shortly. "Laying low sounds smarter to me. Let Doc Savage blow through the Bighorns and right out again when he's concluded his damn business."

The masticating proprietor shifted the cargo in his mouth to the opposite cheek. As he did so, his eyes shifted in the opposite direction. "We can't take that chance, and you know it. Listen, I overheard this from a strange mohairrie that's been staying at the Circle Bolt dump. You know the place. That's the one around which all the rumors have been circulating."

"Suppose we turn this to our advantage," said the telephone voice. "Maybe we can tie this girl into the mule-rustling business. Just like we hung that little fella the other day."

"That's another thing. Nobody's brought in that body yet.

And the dun we strung him up on hasn't showed up either. That I heard of."

"Nobody could've wormed out of that noose alive. So that's one rustler dead. If we take care of the girl, that will make it two. And that no-cow ranch will likely get closed down as the center of the whole mule rustling operation."

"O.K., I'll go take care of the girl. Tell everybody to lay low for a while. That Doc Savage is bad medicine."

"Pure poison," agreed the other.

The proprietor hung up, and extracted a serviceable six-shooter from a wooden box. The weapon's muzzle was bulldogged to less than half of its manufacture length. Stuffing this into his belt and covering the worn handle with his flannel shirt, he barged out of the general store and went in search of the girl known as Juanna Quitt, his masticating teeth squeaking as they punished whatever was in his mouth.

He had not gone very far when he spied a familiar face.

"Buck!"

Scowling, the other crossed the street, his face a thundercloud of wrath.

"Anybody ever tell you that your mouth is too big for Wyoming, Kip?"

"What's the matter, Buck? You look snake-bit."

"Don't call me Buck in town," gritted the other, pulling the general store proprietor into the shade of an alley. "You know that's not my real name."

"I slipped up. Sorry. But you need to hear what I got to say. Brace yourself. Doc Savage is coming our way."

"Doc Savage!"

"Yeah. And there's no telling what kind of a mess of forked lightning he's fixin' to tie into."

"He's earned himself a big rep the world over," agreed the other.

"That bronze devil ain't human, I'm telling you! He can do

anything! Listen: I'm hunting a girl who just left my store. She's connected to him somehow."

"Describe her."

The other man did. When he was finished, he patted his midriff where the bulky six-gun was concealed.

"Funny," said the one who didn't wish to be called Buck. "A fine-looking filly fitting that description stomped into the sheriff's office a few minutes back. I think it was her."

The starch went out of the proprietor's fierce expression. "If she's in with the sheriff, I can't do much about the situation."

"Not with your face hanging out for all the world to see, Kip."

The store owner said suddenly, "What say we loiter a bit? Lie in wait for when she comes out."

"*If* she comes out. But you have the right idea. Only you're going about it the wrong way. I have some ideas along that trend. Let's hie back to your store and I'll spread them out for you...."

Chapter XI

PREDICAMENT

TOGETHER, LONG TOM ROBERTS and Laramie crept out of the ramshackle old cabin and picked their way in the direction in which they believed the girl lay, probably in ambush.

The way brought Long Tom toward his roan, which he reclaimed.

The placid sorrel was still standing among concealing briers, stamping listlessly at flies and breathing wheezily. The ancient animal started snorting, but Long Tom placed a smothering hand over her nostrils and mouth, quieting the creature. "Pipe down, Sparkplug," he hissed.

Taking the reins, he led the horse along while Laramie followed. Their eyes got busy searching the rocks and declivities through which they crept.

Laramie particularly studied the ground, seeking signs. But only well-spaced patches of dirt took tracks, and so they put off that particular activity.

After a bit, he took the reins in order to free up the puny electrical engineer's good arm, climbing heavily into the saddle.

Long Tom carried a peculiar pistol before him. Larger than a conventional automatic, it was mechanically complicated in a fashion suggesting enormous firepower contained in a compact housing. That it was capable of spewing large quantities of bullets was evident in the ammunition drum mounted ahead of the trigger guard. This was a supermachine pistol, a remarkable weapon perfected by the inventive genius of Doc Savage himself. Each of the bronze man's aides carried one. Long Tom swept the muzzle around to match the direction of his gaze.

The way took them back up into the mountains. They moved with appropriate caution.

The old horse shied at a jackrabbit which had waited until it was almost under the horse's hooves before it shot away from its dugout bed under a sagebrush. Laramie pulled the nervous animal back to the trail.

"Quit spookin' that way!" he grunted at the sorrel. "You ain't got nothing on your mind but prairie grass and oats." The outburst seemed to remind him that he had a plug of tobacco in a pocket. He extracted it, plopped it into his mustached mouth, and began masticating methodically.

The horse shied again, snorted. Laramie leaned in and stroked the animal's neck quietingly. "Girl, you're getting worse than a new-branded calf. You bein' a she-horse, you won't savvy, but an old terrapin like myself—"

The sound which stopped his words—a bullet made it—was like the hiss and pop of a bullwhip. The slug came out of the rocks ahead. It tore into his shirt front, opened a hot groove below his left arm pit and went off into the distance with a shrill squawl.

The impact knocked him back in the saddle. While still jerking back, he decided what to do. His burly frame loosened and he fell as if fatally hit. Tense muscles broke his collision with the hard range sod.

The sorrel snorted and ran away with a great hammering of hooves.

Alerted by the commotion, Long Tom switched his super-machine pistol from single shot to full automatic. Squeezing the trigger, he sent a moaning blast into the rocks. The mechanism spurted a tumbling shower of smoking brass cartridges. The rivet-gun bawling of the elaborate weapon was reminiscent of a bull fiddle whose bass string had been plucked to vibrate in a prolonged manner.

Another rifle bullet came through the sage with a terrific ripping.

Laramie grunted, "I didn't fool that cuss none," and hastily rolled into a gully that was no wider or deeper than his body. "Don't worry about me none, Long Tom!" he added. "I'm scored, not scragged."

He fired one of his sixes in the general vicinity of the bush-whacker's gun flash, then went down the gully a ways with the scuttling movements of a scared crawfish. No lead came snapping back at him.

For his part, Long Tom ducked into the brush. He sneaked along fifty yards, the gully getting deeper, then veered off to the right through the sage. His listening ears detected a faint scratch that sounded like a cactus thorn on a boot. Convinced that whoever had tried to dry-gulch them was retreating, he quick-ened his pace, trying to get the drop on the bushwhacker. The sagebrush, as high as his belt, made for excellent concealment but hard to get through silently.

Long Tom's feet ground through a cactus bed, the thorns on his boots making sounds like the squeaking of cold snow. In stumbling over an anthill, he kicked up a shower of fine gravel. Breathing a low oath, he slackened his pace a bit.

Whang! It was a gun. But no lead came in his direction.

From concealment, Laramie grunted, "Daw gone! Who could she be shootin' at now?" He lifted his body and crawled through the sage and around rocks with no great effort at silence.

Whang! Whang! Whang!

Laramie's howl came shrill and rather canine, like a dog that had gotten its hind leg caught in a bear trap.

"D-a-a-w-w gone!"

The shooting stopped. Silence clamped down.

A sound ahead—the creak of strained saddle leather. Long Tom jutted up, supermachine pistol in hand.

The muzzle lifted to the level of his elbow. Through a break in the rocks, he could make out a paint bronc, and the woman climbing onto the saddle. The pine-haired girl!

She rode away, the paint in a dead run, never suspecting Long Tom's presence.

The undersized electrical genius sighted carefully and switched the weapon back to single-shot operation. He had a perfect bead on the woman's departing back, but hesitated.

Shooting a woman was not something he relished. Shooting one in the back caused a disgusted sound to arise from deep within him.

Frowning sourly, he lowered the weapon. The retreating figure was no longer a threat, anyway.

Staggering slightly, Long Tom wheeled about and raced to where the shots had exploded.

A man was sprawled in a clearing in the sheltering sagebrush. Laramie! Long Tom sagged down beside him.

Laramie said grimly, "The dodgasted hussy's lead ventilated one of my legs!"

Long Tom Roberts explored swiftly, then yanked off one shirt sleeve, tore it into strips, and did some emergency one-handed bandaging. Laramie pitched in to help tie knots. Using his good arm, the wiry electrical wizard dragged old Laramie into the shelter of roadside boulders. It was several minutes before anyone said anything.

"You didn't shoot her, did you?" Laramie asked Long Tom.

"Didn't have the heart."

"Nor the brains, I reckon."

"I resent that!" snapped Long Tom. "If I had shot her out of the saddle, she might've broken her neck in falling."

"Horseflies! You could've shot the cayuse in the rump. Those tricky bullets you use probably would have put the animal to sleep eventually. Not likely to have caused rider or horse any injury."

"Now that you mention it…" muttered Long Tom.

"Goldang! Be careful with that leg," ground out Laramie. "Her first shot didn't do much damage, so I skinned up until I could see her waitin' in some rocks beside the trail. I lost sight of her after she started shiftin' around. I knew she was fixin' to make mischief. So when the fireworks started, I turned loose in the air, thinking it would scare her off. But she shot one of my pins out from underneath me before I knowed what had happened. She sure knows how to get a bead on a gun flash."

"You positive it was her that leaded you?"

"What do you mean—? Of course it was her! Who else would it be?"

"Only I thought that last burst was rifle shots. She didn't look like she had a Winchester. Only a six-shooter."

Laramie craned his sunburned neck around and searched the rocks with his wrinkled gaze.

"If you're right, that means somebody else skulkin' hereabouts."

"Trouble doesn't ever seem to run out of steam around here, does it?" complained Long Tom.

"No, it don't. But I recognized that gal. That's Alta Crater. She runs the Lynx Eyes outfit, her and her brother, Hud."

Long Tom blinked. "Did you say Hud?"

"It sounded to me like I did. Did it sound that way to you?"

"Don't be so cranky," said Long Tom. "Hud was the name of that cowpoke that Pat Savage met before he ended up swimming in circles in the sky."

"You say you found him dead?" asked Laramie.

"Pat said she did. But when I showed up, the body wasn't where it was supposed to have landed."

"If Hud Crater up and died, Miss Alta might not likely know about it yet. In fact, she could be ridin' the range in search of him. No wonder she's so loose with her lead. She's got to be worried sick about her brother by now."

Long Tom scratched his chin thoughtfully. "That could explain why she was flying around in that plane. She wasn't looking for missing stock, but for her lost brother."

"I wouldn't want to be the one to break the news to her," muttered Laramie. "Folks say she has quite the temper."

"I can testify to that," said Long Tom sourly.

"So how do we get out of this hellacious predicament we are in?" Laramie wondered. "If we show our hats outside these rocks, we're liable to collect hot lead where our brains normally roost."

The offhand remark gave the pale electrical wizard an idea.

SHIFTING around, he found a long branch that had come off a cottonwood tree. He balanced his hat atop this, then lifted the arrangement as high as he could, while keeping to the shelter of the boulders.

The hat had no sooner popped up than it went flying. The branch was rudely torn from Long Tom's grip.

The crack of a rifle shot followed an instant after that.

"We're pinned behind these rocks, and I don't mean maybe," Long Tom informed Laramie.

"Here," grumbled Laramie, "stick my hat on that branch. You bait him into takin' another shot."

"What good will that do?"

"You do it and I'll let you know."

Taking the battered old hat, Long Tom repeated the operation, and got practically the same results. The hat acquired a bullet hole, jumped up several feet, but Long Tom managed to latch onto the whirling headgear this time.

Laramie scooted back from whatever he had been doing, and said, "I got a quick look at the bushwhacker."

"Was it that girl?"

"If it was, she's got a funny way of goin' about things."

Long Tom looked at the old foreman questioningly.

"The bushwhacker with the rifle is high up in the hills," explained Laramie. "I didn't get much of a look at him, but it didn't matter. He had a flour sack over his head."

"Flour sack! That's what those would-be lynchers were wearing."

"Looks like one of them would like to conclude the unfinished job of stringin' you up for a lowdown mule thief."

Long Tom felt of the bruise-blue welt banding his throat and swallowed hard once.

"Don't look now," he muttered, "but our predicament just went from bad to worse."

"Don't you worry none, Long Tom. They'll hang you over my dead body."

Long Tom Roberts said nothing. He took cold comfort in those rough words of reassurance. For he was thinking that where there was one lurking man wearing a flour sack, there was likely to be more of the same. And the badlands of Wyoming was not a place where the law ventured much. Gunshots might not summon help.

Looking at his supermachine pistol, he frowned. The weapon was a wonder, but it was no rifle. For all of its fearsome power, it lacked the range to reach up into the high hills. On the other hand, the rifleman wearing the flour-sack hood was in a perfect spot to pick them off if they dared venture from the tight confines of their stony shelter.

"We'll just have to lay low until the sun sets," he told Laramie.

"That's a good idea. Or it would be if my leg would just stop leakin'."

Long Tom examined the man's thigh, tightening the tourniquet he had tied there.

"It doesn't look like an artery was nicked," he advised. "But we've got to get you to a doctor before you lose too much blood."

"I take back what I said earlier. If they do hang you, it *will* be over my dead body. I'm powerful sorry about that. But I didn't mean to collect a bullet in my leg bone."

Before Long Tom could reassure the old foreman, there came creeping sounds from another direction.

Turning, they saw the unexpected.

It was the woman with the fluffy blonde hair. Alta Crater. She was on foot.

Sighting Long Tom, her face went hard. She trained the muzzle of her big six-gun on him.

Half under his breath, old Laramie growled, "Now's your chance to shoot that filly—if you got the stomach, that is."

Long Tom did not hesitate. It was either her or him.

Squeezing the trigger, he got off the first shot. The answering shot came from the six-shooter, and a splatter of hot lead *spanged* off the rocks behind him, stinging like flying wasps.

The girl gave out an ugly *ugh!* of a sound. She collapsed.

Scrambling down, Long Tom seized the smoking six-shooter and handed it to Laramie, saying, "That mercy bullet will keep her out of action for an hour or so. When she wakes up, we'll have to explain ourselves."

"That part'll be easy," grumbled Laramie. "But the part I'm not lookin' forward to is tellin' her about her brother, Hud. She won't cotton to that. No, sirree. Alta Crater will be a powerful handful of trouble once she wakes up. Mark my words. She's a regular wildcat, that one is."

Long Tom grated fiercely, "So I noticed. This superfirer packs plenty of mercy bullets. If I have to shoot her every hour, I will."

Chapter XII

JUGGED

PAT SAVAGE MARCHED into the sheriff's office. It was a tiny place, the sheriff's quarters in the local calaboose occupying the same modest building that looked as though it had been built before Wyoming had achieved statehood.

The sheriff looked up, saw the sorry state of Pat Savage's hair, complexion and clothing and asked, "What befell you?"

"Exactly what I've been wondering," quipped Pat. "But never mind that right now. I thought I would look in on you since I'm the gal that everybody's searching for."

"You don't say?" said the sheriff, standing up. "And what might be your name?"

"I've been going by the name of Darla Dell, but that's because I've been on vacation and wished to remain incognito."

The sheriff of Bison looked slightly blank. Evidently 'incognito' was a word not found in his personal vocabulary.

"I just had a talk with a local feller. He tells me he brought into town a girl who looked a lot like you. He said she gave her name as Juanna Quitt."

"I called myself that, too," confessed Pat. "But that's not my real name, either."

At this point, the sheriff became extremely interested. His face bunched up into a frown and his dark blue eyes got little sparks in them.

"You say you're the gal everybody's looking for. What exactly do you mean by that?"

"I'm the one who got lost overnight on my way back here. I had to shoot my horse, because it—er—pulled up lame. No doubt my friend Long Tom has stirred up a fuss about my absence."

"I don't know anyone by that name," advised the sheriff slowly.

"Long Tom Roberts owns the Circle Bolt," said Pat. "I've been his guest for the last few days."

"Is that right? But no one's come calling about any missing gal."

Pat's pretty face acquired a quirk in the corners of her mouth, narrowing her eyes. Her eyebrows crowded together, almost touching.

"I would have thought that he would have organized several search parties for me by now," admitted Pat.

"Not that I know of," said the sheriff. "The only thing I hear out of the Circle Bolt is rumors. Rumors of mule rustling."

Pat batted her golden eyes.

"Mules? Long Tom doesn't own any."

"Mules," advised the sheriff, "have been going missing these last few weeks. Just about the time that the Circle Bolt passed into new ownership. Folks hereabouts have been putting two and two together and auguring out loud."

Pat flared righteously, "Long Tom Roberts would no more rustle a mule than he would kick a puppy."

The sheriff looked thoughtful. "You say your friend goes by the name of Long Tom. That's kind of a piratey-sounding name."

Now Pat was becoming frustrated. "Do you mean to tell me you've never heard of Long Tom Roberts, the electrical engineer?"

"Can't say that I have. Tell me more."

"Long Tom is one of the men who works with Doc Savage. Surely, you've heard of Doc Savage."

"Doc Savage I've heard of," admitted the sheriff. "He's a real hellbender from back East. They say he rearranges the affairs of entire continents, smashes gangs that the G-Men can't touch, and is probably only five or six years away from conquering the moon for science."

"You," said Pat, "have definitely heard of Doc Savage. Then you would know that anybody who associates with Doc would never stoop to rustling, whether it's horses or mules."

"I'll accept that theory," said the sheriff. "Now let's get down to who you are. How many aliases do you have, anyway?"

"As I've already told you," said Pat impatiently. "I'm here incognito. I don't want to attract attention, so I go by different names. You see, Doc Savage is my cousin."

"Now that's an impressive tallish tale you tell, but is it true? That's what I'm wondering."

"If you don't believe me, just stick around. I called Doc Savage from the general store. He'll be here as fast as he can fly. He'll vouch for me."

And the sheriff fell silent. He was appraising Pat Savage with wise, speculative eyes.

"Funny you would go missing overnight and no one would raise an alarm," he mused.

"Nothing funny about it. I ended up on top of a butte with my horse."

"Which butte?"

"What are the big ones called? I don't know all their names."

"How did you and your horse end up way up there? None of those buttes could be climbed by a horse. Unless it had wings."

"That, I cannot explain," admitted Pat. "Someone in a foul temper uncorked a shotgun at us. And the next thing I knew, we were flying through the air."

A dark frown overtook the lawman's sunburnt features. "Did you happen to subsist on any wild weeds when you were out there overnight?"

"I haven't had a bite to eat since yesterday's breakfast. Why do you ask?"

"Oh, some who get lost out in the badlands get to chewing on a plant called the locoweed. It causes them to imagine things."

Pat looked as if she were getting angry, but then she remembered something.

"If I was imagining flying up into the buttes, I wasn't the only one. Before I fell victim of the little man in green, I happened upon a cowpoke named Hud. He was going for a dip in the swimming hole. An hour or so later I saw him swimming in the sky. Swimming in circles, then he looked for all the world like a drowning man. He fell. He was dead when I got to him. I called my friend Long Tom right away, but by the time we got back to the spot where the body fell, there was no sign of any body."

"Hud! Do you mean Hud Crater?"

"I don't know which Hud I mean," admitted Pat. "The Hud I met didn't introduce himself formally. He was just a passing acquaintance."

"This is mighty interesting. There's a Hud Crater who went missing from the Lynx Eyes spread a day ago. His sister Alta has been combing the badlands, looking for him. Now you say he's dead."

"I'm sorry to say he's dead. Fall must have killed him. But I can't for the life of me imagine how he got up in the sky the way he did. Even after it happened to me, it's a puzzle."

"No one found any body, but that doesn't mean there isn't one." The sheriff lapsed back into a period of contemplation. When he came out of it, he marched over to Pat Savage and said, "I am placing you under arrest, whatever your honest name might be."

Pat's eyes lit up like candles. "Arrest! Whatever for?"

"Suspicion."

"Suspicion of what, may I ask?"

"Just plain vanilla suspicion," advised the sheriff. "I'll work out the details later. Right now, you're going into the jug, while I go look for Alta Crater and let her know that her brother may or may not be dead. And while I'm at it, I'm going to nose around the Circle Bolt Ranch and see what I can see."

Pat warned, "Doc Savage will not be pleased to learn that his only cousin has been jailed for no good reason."

The lawman was unmoved. "From what I hear about Doc Savage, he has a sympathetic understanding of the law and its ways. If you're who you say you are, he'll appreciate my placing you under protective custody while the ball of knotty twine you just laid on my desk gets untangled. Well, come on. We ain't got all the livelong day."

PAT SAVAGE was too weak from her ordeal to resist—not that she thought that would be a good idea.

The sheriff confiscated her six-gun, remarked, "Some flame-thrower!" in an admiring tone, locked it in his desk, and walked the copper-haired girl into the single cell the town of Bison boasted. She was locked in like a common criminal and sat down on the wooden bench that might have been occupied by the Sundance Kid in a more colorful era.

"This just isn't my day," she moaned.

"From what you say," observed the official, "it hasn't been your day so far this week."

"You are very perceptive," said Pat, folding her sinewy brown arms defiantly.

Without any further ado, the lawman went out, got his automobile, and took off into the Badlands.

As she settled down onto the rough wooden pallet, Pat Savage wondered, "Whatever could've happened to Long Tom?"

Pat did not have long to stew in the calaboose, for only a few minutes later, a man entered the sheriff's office, whose door had not been locked.

The man wore a gunnysack over his head. He wore a pair of tooled leather cuffs on his wrists. From under his shirt, he extracted a gun—a revolver with its barrel bulldogged short.

He waved the weapon about aimlessly until he came to the iron bars of the cell door.

Seeing the masked man, Pat stood up abruptly.

"If you're looking for the sheriff, he just left," she told him.

A strangely muffled voice said, "So I saw. But it's you I'm looking for."

"Me? Whatever for?"

"I need to break you out."

"But I don't want to be broken out," protested Pat. "The sheriff locked me up fair and square, even if I don't agree with him. If I go with you, serious charges could be lodged against me."

The tall man in the gunnysack hood rattled around the sheriff's office, found an old-fashioned brass key on a ring, and brought it over to the iron door. This he inserted into the big lock, and the grating and squealing of the mechanism made Pat feel as if going with him would be tantamount to stepping onto the gallows.

"I'm staying right here," she said firmly.

"You're coming with me. Like it or not."

The barred door was swung open, and the gunnysack jailbreaker strode in.

"You don't look like you have much fight in you at the moment," he said confidently.

Pat demonstrated the error of his ways when she stepped up and smacked the nickeled revolver out of his fist before he could react.

The gun made a *pop!* A foul genie of smoke bloomed forth. Evidently, the bullet that discharged had a faulty supply of powder. The noise was hardly anything. The bullet jumped into the ceiling and cracked it.

As the weapon clattered to the floor, Pat leapt for it. But so did the other.

They wrestled about on the floor for a time, grunting with

effort until their hands wrapped around the short-barreled six-gun and they were strenuously tugging in opposite directions.

Pat's strength was not up to its usual level. Nevertheless, desperation lent her a certain determination of thew and tendon. Much to her surprise, she began making headway.

Abruptly, the would-be kidnapper released the revolver and Pat fumbled it around in both hands, trying to get her fingers wrapped around it in proper order. One tapering forefinger found the trigger. Too late.

The jail-breaker reached out, snagged her coppery hair and used it to slam her head into the floor three times in quick succession.

With a groan, Pat collapsed on the floor, limp. The revolver was stripped from her loose fingers.

"If you can't skin a rabbit one way, you flay it another," grated the gunnysack-headed one.

Picking himself up off the floor, he dragged Pat out of the cell by her heels and to the rear door.

He yanked off the gunnysack, poked his head out the back door, looked both ways until he saw no witnesses. Then he dragged Pat to a waiting brown sedan.

As he did so, it could be seen that his anxious face was that of the proprietor of the Bison general store, the fellow called Kip. But there were no witnesses and Pat Savage had entirely lost consciousness.

So when she was dumped into the trunk of the machine, the bronze-skinned girl was oblivious to that unsettling fact.

Climbing behind the wheel, the kidnapper sent the automobile scooting out of town, attracting almost no attention as he did so.

Chapter XIII

LEAD MEDICINE

THE SUN STARTED sinking. With a sullen heaviness, it disappeared behind the string of sandstone tabletop formations locally known as the Pumpkin Buttes.

Men began arriving, some on horseback. But at least one automobile engine could be heard in the vicinity. Most ominously, it ran without its headlamps on, preserving the slow-creeping murk.

Laramie grunted to Long Tom, "You reckon that's the U.S. Cavalry?"

The pale electrical genius shook his head violently. "Reinforcements."

It was sufficiently rocky that the slender electrical wizard could peer around boulders and perceive some of the arrivals. They wore flour sacks over their heads. It made them look ridiculous, like overgrown boys playing at being Halloween spooks.

Crawling back to Laramie's side, Long Tom advised, "That flour-sack headed gang is here. Somehow the sniper mustered them."

"How could they—way out in these badlands?"

Long Tom considered this as the sun continued going down.

"They must've been called by heliograph signal, or something," he decided.

Laramie's tobacco-stained mustache drooped forlornly. "What?"

"By flashing a pocket mirror so that the sun's reflection makes Morse code dots and dashes," Long Tom explained. "They couldn't manage it any other way."

"Are we surrounded, or what?"

The undersized electrical expert jerked his body about, peering toward every compass point, looking for signs of skulkers while listening for the sounds of approach.

Perceiving nothing, he undertoned, "There's no telling where some of them are. But it's a sure bet they're going to wait until it gets dark."

"Moonrise ain't far off," Laramie offered hopefully. "Maybe an hour."

"They can't snipe at us without moonlight," reminded Long Tom. "So it's a standoff until somebody makes a move."

Laramie spanked his gore-soaked bandage and grunted, "Well, I ain't doin' any movin' myself. Not with this bum leg." The grizzled old man eyed Long Tom in the fading red light. "If you have a notion to take off, I wouldn't think poorly of you for doin' exactly that."

Long Tom's eyes flashed with a hint of anger. "I don't desert wounded men."

Laramie laughed shortly. "I was just thinkin' you might fetch reinforcements to come at the reinforcements that's just been fetched up. Try to even things up a bit."

Long Tom said nothing. He thought so little of the idea he refused to give it breath.

His eyes went to the girl, still lying in the dirt and the rocks, sleeping completely unawares. Cooling breezes played at her fluffy hair, but otherwise she did not move.

Up to this point, the sniper with the rifle had not spoken. Perhaps emboldened by reinforcements, he lifted his voice.

"You down there!"

Laramie exploded, "Don't answer that! He'll aim for the sound of your voice."

"I know that," growled Long Tom. "I was in the war."

"Plumb forgot. Pardon my fidgetiness."

The sniper's voice carried again. "You're surrounded and outnumbered," he hollered. "Come crawling out of your burrow with your hands held high, like you hope to snag a cloud. We won't shoot you."

"Sure he will," snorted Laramie.

Another voice suddenly spoke up. "And we won't hang yuh, neither. Even though yore a no-account range bum and deserve to have yore neck stretched by a rope."

That was no special comfort either.

Laramie ventured, "Sounds to me like they aim to finish the necktie party that got out of hand yesterday."

Long Tom remained mum. He was beginning to get the drift of things. Although he couldn't see very much, his imagination placed a gunnysack hood over the head of the loud-voiced sniper.

Opined a voice from another direction, not loud, but strong, which carried on the wind.

"He ain't takin' the bait, Quest."

"Didn't think he would," mumbled the man. The mumbling was strange. It sounded like the fellow had something in his mouth and was trying to talk around the obstruction. Perhaps it was the muffling effect of a hood.

The one addressed as Quest went on. "We'll just have to beat the sagebrush for them. Try to take 'em by surprise."

Long Tom was listening with his oversized, sail-like ears. The sound seemed to be coming from the east, and it was not high. Quest was not up in the tall rocks.

Narrowing his eyes, the runt-sized electrical genius put all his efforts into gauging the distance of the two conspirators.

The muffle-voiced Quest said, "Work around to their position. Move low so you're not seen."

The other complained, "How can I be seen when I can't even see where I'm goin'?"

"Just feel your way. You can do it. You know this territory."

"If you say so," the other allowed. Sounds made by creaking boots came.

Twisting suddenly, Long Tom cut loose with the supermachine pistol. A long saffron tongue leaped out of the spike-snouted muzzle. The weapon moaned like an alarmed ghost.

The muzzle flashes helped, for as Long Tom corrected his aim, he spied a skulking figure. It went down. The man fell on his back, and his boot heels struck the ground hard a moment later.

"You got him!" exulted Laramie. "Pretty fair shootin'."

Lead ripped and sang. The blasting roar of guns sent echoes thumping like the laughter of some evil monster. Bullets began spanking off the rocks all around him, indicating that Long Tom's muzzle flash had been seen.

There was more than one rifleman. That forced Long Tom and Laramie to stay under cover while the one called Quest lit out for shelter of his own.

AFTER a bit, the shooting died down and the weirdly-mangled voice came distinctly now.

"You there! We got a bead on you now. You can't hold out all night."

Long Tom said nothing.

"What say we talk medicine?" Quest called out.

"I think he means bad medicine," grunted Laramie. "Probably poison."

Laramie cautiously peered around the side of the sheltering boulder. No part of a human was in sight, but a Winchester barrel rested across a flat rock, dimly visible by starlight. Nearby floated the shadowy silhouette of a high-crowned hat.

Laramie didn't think there was a head in the hat. There wasn't. The sharpshooter was trying to pull a fast one.

Slight movements of the gleaming barrel showed that the rifle was being aimed. The old cowboy leveled his six-shooter carefully and let fly. The muzzle released a clap of powder noise. The slug hit the Winchester barrel squarely.

A man squawked as the rifle stock knocked against his jaw. The Winchester bounced, then fell, discharging upon landing.

Pin-n-g! Pe-e-e! The bullet ricocheted off the boulder directly behind them.

Laramie made sudden spitting sounds. "Daggum it! That last slug came so close to my face it felt like a bumblebee a-tryin' to get into my mouth!"

After a bit, there came the mechanical mutter of an automobile. Consternation broke out among the reinforcements. It was sudden movement—shifting about and whispering voices that could not be distinguished.

The motorcar crept along, its headlights throwing shifting shadows among the hulking boulders. Long Tom and Laramie both took a chance and scanned the high rocks for sniping skulkers.

Both men were particularly surprised to see a handful of hunkered-down heads made shapeless by pale flour sacks.

"I count six," said Laramie.

Then the motorcar rounded the bend and someone recognized the car.

"It's the damn sheriff!" a voice howled.

The voice carried. No order was given. Evidently, panic over took the men in the flour-sack hoods. Rifles and six-guns began hammering metallic hail. Lead popped and sang and the echoes thundered out once more.

The windshield of the sheriff's automobile shivered into a glassy shower.

Fortunately, the vehicle had been moving at a cautious pace out of respect for the difficult terrain. The sheriff immediately lost control of his vehicle and the front tires jerked to the left, then the entire machine went blundering into a gully.

Long Tom and Laramie watched in horror as the machine careened out of control and dashed itself against the rocks. Its trunk lid flew up like a startled bird's wing when it crashed to a stop.

The silence that followed was awful. They had expected screams, possibly groans or other indications of life, no matter how damaged. But there was nothing. Just silence.

Laramie breathed, "I reckon if that was the sheriff, he's a goner."

Long Tom did not contradict that assessment. He came to the identical conclusion.

A voice twisted with a species of awestruck horror sprang up.

"I think we done murdered the sheriff! We are shore up to our necks in quicksand now."

No one spoke for a long time. It was clear that the shooting of the sheriff's automobile had not been planned. The hooded gang had been spooked by the lawman's arrival, and had reacted out of panicky fear.

After an uncomfortable silence, the mumbling voice of Quest lifted. "It's tough luck. Tough for the sheriff. But he barged into our gunning bee. We'll just put it on these mule rustlers—after we string them up."

"You hear that?" Laramie hissed.

"Exactly what I figured on," said Long Tom, squeezing the grip of his supermachine pistol. "But they'll have a swell time taking us when they try."

"We just gotta hold out 'til the moon rises," Laramie encouraged. "Won't be long now."

But they did not have that much time. For not far along, another automobile put in an appearance, and the sounds of hammers being cocked on assorted pistols and rifles came all around them like a brief stirring of crickets. It was a brown sedan.

This machine slowed to a halt and a man poked his head out. The head was smothered by a ragged gunnysack hood, although neither Long Tom nor Laramie could see that fact in the darkness.

Headlights made a harsh blaze beyond their sheltering rocks, but they dared not poke their heads out lest they be sniped at.

The man who had stepped out of the machine demanded, "Quest! Where are you?"

"Here, but I can't show myself on account of we got that scrawny fella treed."

The man's voice lifted. "Better listen up then. All of you. I broke that nosy girl out of jail. She's in my trunk."

High amid the rocks, someone called down, "What gal?"

"That copper-haired mohairrie who says she is the cousin of Doc Savage, that's who. I busted her out of the jug. The sheriff had taken off."

"That's his car down in the gully with him dead behind the wheel," mumbled Quest.

The new arrival did not respond immediately. But after a bit, he ventured an opinion. "Between Doc Savage and the dead sheriff, our troubles sure are overflowing."

"We'll string the girl up with the other one, and leave it to Doc Savage to sort out."

"Is that smart, Quest? Doc Savage is no ordinary lawman. He won't clear out of Wyoming until he's gotten to the bottom of matters."

Quest grunted, "Savage is not here yet. So we got to move fast. Doc Savage is going to put the kibosh on our little racket, but all that will blow over in time. Mark my words."

The remark was almost humorous, since the man's words were jumbled and sometimes half recognizable.

Then Quest barked, "Yank that girl out of the trunk and set her in the headlights."

This was done and Pat Savage was laid in the gravel and dirt where the headlights bathed her supine form.

Quest called down, "Take a look. If you two don't surrender, my sharpshooters will start using that girlie for target practice."

Long Tom and Laramie swapped looks, and their expressions were not healthy.

Laramie scowled. "Them jaspers are plumb skunky—the polecats!"

"Be smart," Quest warned. "You're sitting ducks."

Old Laramie emitted a gritty chuckle. He raised his voice. "Try and make us quack, you gizzard-slitting mule thief. We're hombres who aim to shoot back."

"Somebody take the first shot," directed Quest.

SURPRISINGLY, the sound of a bullet being jacked into the receiver of a Winchester came audibly. This was followed by the crack of a bullet.

A little geyser of dust exploded not six inches from Pat Savage's head. Neither Long Tom nor Laramie saw that, but they heard it distinctly. Their imaginations filled in the rest.

Laramie said, "Why don't I crawfish myself out? They may not know about you."

"Stay low," growled Long Tom. "Keep an eye on the other girl."

He stepped out, pale hands empty and slowly lifting into the sky.

Moonlight painted him and made him look spectral, doing nothing good for his normally sallow complexion.

"You got me," he said sullenly.

"Yeah," grated Quest. "Dead to rights."

The man who stood with Pat Savage in the headlights strode forward, six-gun held before him. This was the proprietor of the Bison general store, but Long Tom did not know that, owing to the man's gunnysack disguise.

Long Tom held his hands out at his sides as if he were unsure whether to lift them fully skyward or be prepared to employ his fists.

"Reach higher," prompted the gunman.

Long Tom made a move in that direction, but only with one hand, his left. The right hand wriggled out of its arm sling, swept behind him, and yanked out the supermachine pistol which he had tucked into the small of his back, where his belt held it firmly in place.

The weapon came around so fast the man with the six-shooter did not have time to squeeze off a shot. Long Tom cut him down with a furious burst of mercy bullets. The fellow collapsed. Then all around him, bullets began spanking off hard rock and pounded into the ground with ugly *chucking* noises.

Long Tom was moving fast. He plunged into the headlight glare, fired two short bursts in different directions, stuffed his hot gun into a pocket, and threw Pat Savage over his good shoulder.

The driver-side door had been left open and Long Tom deposited her into the front seat, rather roughly. Shoving her over, he got behind the wheel. Without bothering to clap the door shut, he got the sedan in motion.

Assorted slugs started drumming the roof. Long Tom doused the lights. The absence of illumination produced the expected effect of causing everyone to be more blind than they would otherwise have been.

Consequently, no one could get off a clear shot.

In that interval of consternation and confusion, the undersized electrical wizard wrenched the car wheel and sent the machine as close to the shelter of rocks as he could.

"Laramie!" he called out.

But the wily old cowboy had already divined Long Tom's intent. He had crawled up and was lurching in the direction of the machine.

He got the passenger-side door yanked open, crammed his thick body in, squeezing Pat Savage between himself and Long Tom Roberts.

Laramie chuckled raggedly. "I see you collected Miss Patricia. What about Miss Crater?"

"We'll come back for her," said Long Tom, sending the brown sedan lurching ahead.

As getaways went, this one was hastily improvised. The absence of illumination appeared to be in their favor. But it was not helpful in terms of navigation.

Long Tom was forced to creep the car forward, straining with his eyes, trying to hold to the dirt trail that passed for a road through the badlands.

The crunching of dirt and gravel under the crawling tires seemed as loud as popcorn popping. That was imagination, of course, seasoned with fear. The machine inched forward, but no shots snapped in their direction.

The gunmen sprinkled around them were no doubt struggling with their optic nerves. Probably other nerves as well.

Somebody had a flashlight. And it popped a rod of light that was quite intense after the unrelieved darkness.

The luminous rod flickered and flashed about, finally locating the slow-moving machine.

Craning his head about, Laramie spotted the other end of the thread of light, and without respecting the glass at the sedan's back window, he squeezed off a single shot, breaking the glass and causing the flashlight wielder considerable pain and distress.

"Winged him!" Laramie exulted.

His joy proved short-lived. For a rifle bullet found the left rear tire and the inner tube let go with an explosive *pop!*

Skinning his lips back off of his teeth, Long Tom gave the gas pedal more pressure, but the machine only dragged itself along for a few yards before he realized that the effort was futile.

Applying the brakes, he unlimbered his supermachine pistol and scrutinized it. "The indicator on this thing says I have twenty shots left. Maybe that will be enough." He gave the weapon an adjustment that set it to fire single shots.

"I got five shells in my six, and another dozen in my pockets,"

Laramie said firmly. "We might not have 'em outnumbered, but we can take a bunch with us."

Long Tom said, "No sense sitting here waiting for them to sneak up on us."

With that, the grim-faced electrical wizard opened his door and stepped out, pistol at the ready. On the other side of the front seat, Laramie did the same.

No longer propped up by the two men, Pat Savage slumped down, showing no signs of being aware of her peril.

Chapter XIV

GREEN DEVIL AGAIN

THE DARKNESS WAS so absolute that nothing much transpired for several minutes. Quiet reigned. Somewhere, a prairie owl uttered a questioning, disconsolate hoot.

No one could see to shoot. It was a discouraging situation. Not that Long Tom Roberts feared a gun fray. Circumstances had backed him into a tight corner and the only sensible way out was to blaze away.

On the other side of the brown automobile, Laramie complained, "Long Tom, I'm feelin' poorly. Loss of blood, I'm thinkin'."

"Well, get yourself behind the machine and be ready to shoot your best."

"Damnblast it! It's darker than a bat's worst nightmare. What are we gonna use for light?"

Long Tom answered that question by removing a small flashlight from his pocket. Cranking the spring-generator that provided power, he placed it on the trunk of the automobile and stepped away.

The pocket torch's ghostly beam naturally attracted attention.

Several bullets arrived in short order and made the light jump around.

Long Tom had kept his eyes peeled for the gun flashes he knew would come.

There was no point in shooting up into the rocks. The distance was too great for the superfirer's limited range. But closer by,

108

he sent tiny hollow bullets snapping. They whizzed like wasps, dashing themselves apart with small splashing sounds.

Return fire was both sporadic and spiteful. A bullet sang off a nearby boulder, causing both hunkered men to flinch, knowing how wild slugs could ricochet with lethal consequences.

Crouched behind the sedan, Laramie uncorked a careful shot, followed by another. A man yelled out in the darkness, followed by a stream of blistering cuss words. The air almost turned blue from his vehement cursing.

"That'll teach you gunsters!" barked Laramie with gleeful satisfaction.

A rifle bullet zinged down, dislodging his hat. Profanity erupted from his lips.

"Sure hope Miss Patricia didn't hear that," he mumbled, catching himself.

To his immense surprise, a sleepy voice murmured, "Hear what?"

Long Tom yelled, "Pat! Are you awake?"

Pat groaned. "Barely.... Where am I?"

Laramie answered that pained query. "In the middle of a shootin' affray, Miss Patricia."

Pat took this in silence. The silence was brief. When she spoke again, her voice was both clear and determined.

"Somebody," she requested, "hand me a proper shootin' iron."

"Fresh out, I'm afraid," said Laramie.

"Darn!" fumed Pat. "How many are we up against?"

"No tellin' for sure," returned Laramie. "But there seem to be plenty of 'em. A regular cavvy of coyotes."

Laramie squeezed off another shot, but he missed his target. Nothing much resulted.

Pat had crawled out to join him. She kept low.

The moon was coming up now, shedding silvery luminance. Coyotes greeted it with low yipping wails. The solitary owl contributed a mournful mouthful.

The creeping lunar illumination gave the ambushers a glimpse of something to shoot at. The sniping began in earnest.

A nearby six crashed, and Laramie's right leg acquired a surplus joint between knee and ankle. The shock made his face dumbly blank. His fingers let the still-smoking revolver fall into the dirt. The collapse of the leg toppled him over to the right.

Pat pitched against the stricken man and undid his belt, twisting it about his calf to stem the flow of blood.

Another revolver blazed. Something fanned Pat's cheek. The bullet tore a ragged, gory trench across the back of Laramie's flannel shirt, the furrow burning like a string of bee stings.

"Daw gone!" he howled. "Pot them critters for me, Miss Pat."

Pat got the .45 pistol he had dropped. The weapon was hardly in her fist when it exploded twice. Gunsmoke squirted from the jerking cylinder.

Laramie took a long chance—he let his body slump loosely. He opened and shut his stiffly outstretched hands. He shouted as if he were dying.

Fooled, a skulking man swung his gun on Pat.

Pat's six-shooter barked first. The man screamed, put his arms across his middle, one atop the other, as if to cover up something suddenly very dear to him. His weakening legs let him down rapidly. He collapsed half across the roadway.

On the other side of the automobile, Long Tom Roberts sent mercy slugs whining into the lunar-lit landscape. Most of these dashed themselves against buff-colored sandstone, splashing their anesthetic contents harmlessly.

Someone higher in the rocks showed that he was an expert with the Winchester. He sent one bullet down that clipped off a lock of Long Tom's pale hair. Long Tom felt the breeze and snap of its passing, but had no idea that the lock had been shorn. He was too busy searching for fresh victims.

The sniper's second bullet did something almost impossible. Silently, the man aimed for Long Tom's wrist, just in back of the weapon. Instead, he struck the barrel, and the force of the slug yanked the compact weapon out of Long Tom's tight fist.

The supermachine pistol was snatched away as if by an angry ghost. Long Tom's fingers stung and he grabbed his wrist, staring at the empty fist with disbelief coming into his eyes.

The weapon went skittering across the hood of the car and careened past Laramie. The old cowboy crawled toward the spot where the weapon landed. The grinding agony in his leg and back made him yelp shrilly. Bullets beating the dirt around him, he took hold of the weapon with both hands. But he saw that the supermachine pistol's short barrel had been knocked off true by the force of the bullet. His sun-seamed face fell.

"Useless!" he said disgustedly.

To cover for the old man, Pat Savage was triggering the six-shooter methodically. It blew out its last bullet, along with spitting sparks.

"Empty," Pat moaned.

Laramie coughed, "Got some spare shells in my pocket. Hold on."

The mossy old cowboy jerked about, and tried to dig into his pockets, but the effort combined with the biting pain and loss of blood proved too much. With a leaky sigh, he simply fainted.

Pat saw this, and jumped toward Laramie.

That was when the hooded men marched out of the rocks and surrounded the automobile like a tribunal of white-headed spooks.

Long Tom groaned, "We're sunk!"

"Sunk, my foot," snapped Pat.

Then a shotgun was directed toward her face, and the mumbling voice said, "Unless you want to be buried with a pound of buckshot in you, kindly subside nice and gentle-like."

Pat subsided.

She was quickly disarmed and helped to her feet. Two men surrounded Long Tom and his fists balled up so tightly they turned white as bone. He looked as if he was about to take a wild swing at somebody, but Pat Savage hissed, "Don't! It's sure death."

The frail-looking electrical expert let out a slow breath and seemed to deflate. He made no move to defend himself. His fists were concrete.

"Hoist 'em high!" a faceless voice commanded.

Reluctantly, their hands crawled above their hat brims.

The surrounding group wore flour sacks over their heads and their assorted sizes were as varied as one might expect to find in cow country. Few stood out noticeably.

One was a little taller than the others. He stepped forward. A gunnysack enveloped his head. He was the only one wearing a gunnysack hood. His shirt was a flannel so faded that its original color was impossible to discern by moonlight. His dark trousers were corduroy.

He spoke in an ugly, scraping snarl like the sound of a rasp shaping a shod bronc hoof. "My name is Quest. Just Quest. No first name. Get me?"

"We get you," growled Long Tom. "What's this all about?"

"Seems to me that we have some unfinished business," mused Quest. "Something about mule rustling."

"You have the wrong party," said Pat vehemently.

She was ignored.

"March," ordered Quest.

So they marched.

They were driven a short distance at the point of rifles. When they saw the cottonwood trees and the waiting horses, they were not surprised by the hempen ropes being fixed in place. Regulation nooses swung in the shadows like twin dooms.

Long Tom squared his jaw, but said nothing.

Pat flared, "You boys wouldn't hang a woman—would you?"

No one commented. The hooded men were very silent. Disquietingly so.

At this point, cords were produced and their hands were tied behind their backs. There followed an attempt to lift them in the saddles.

This resulted in a brief mêlée in which skinned knuckles and cruel kicks predominated. One attacker swung his revolver barrel club-wise. A gun barrel came into contact with hard skullbone. In mid-swing, Long Tom saw stars and his fist failed to connect with a hooded jaw. Rifle butts slammed down on Long Tom's back and Pat's shoulder. They were driven to the ground and, after that, manhandled into the saddles.

Nooses were set around their necks. In the distance, the coyotes seemed to grow quiet.

Pat said bravely, "Doc Savage will make you pay for this."

In his abnormal voice, Quest retorted, "Doc Savage will bring a lot of trouble, no matter *what* we do here tonight. So we might as well be about our business."

Long Tom began uttering some choice words, which caused Pat Savage to remark, "I never suspected you possessed such a colorful vocabulary."

Quest chuckled. "He's just upset because this is his second hanging. Usually a rustler only gets his neck stretched once."

"You know he's not a rustler!"

Quest said flatly, "There's been so much mule rustling in these parts, someone's going to have to hang for it. Better you two than any of us."

Pat blazed, "So you're the rustlers!"

"Don't tell anyone after you get to the pearly gates," said Quest ghoulishly. "I don't want Saint Peter eyeing me funny when I get around to showing up."

"You monsters! Hanging innocent parties for your own crimes."

One of the hooded vigilantes said, "Let's be done with this, Quest. No point in draggin' our feet."

"No, no point in dragging our feet." Quest agreed. With a mumbled chuckle, he added, "But these two will be kicking their heels up in another minute or two. So let's get these horses moving."

Before the horses could be spanked into action, a new arrival put in an appearance.

In the full blaze of moonlight, he was a remarkable sight.

THE APPARITION might have stepped out of a particularly shoddy Hollywood movie production.

He stood tall, spindly, and slightly knock-kneed. His high-heeled boots gave him added height, as did the oversized hat. But it was his outfit that arrested their attention. It was not quite a rodeo outfit. But it bordered on the ridiculous. An Eastern dude having taken in too many cowboy pictures might attire himself in such outlandish duds.

Green was the predominant color, although his bandana was red. The neckerchief did not quite match his carroty hair, which was a little long and sprayed out from under the brim of his hat.

In the moonlight, his eyes gleamed a lizard green. His skin was so pale that it was clear that he was no outdoorsman, certainly no native son of Wyoming.

Despite the grim solemnity of the occasion, the masked vigilantes emitted furious chuckles and other sounds indicating mirth.

"Get a load of that greenhorn!" exclaimed one.

"What would you call him?"

"A walking calamity of colors!"

"He's kind of a Christmas-colored dude, ain't he?"

"Let's call him Christmas!"

"Why don't yuh call me Mr. Calamity?" the other said levelly.

Then he lifted an ornate percussion scattergun and showed the double maw to everyone.

"A dying Crow medicine man gave me this. He said it was full o' powerful medicine. Reckon he was right because I never have had to reload it. Every time I pull the trigger, calamitous happenings commence."

His accent was atrocious. It was not Wyoming. It was not even Western. It was Hollywood. And it was ridiculous.

But the ominous maw of the double-barreled shotgun smothered all atmosphere of the ridiculousness.

They saw that two turkey buzzard feathers were tied to the fore-end of the ugly weapon. One black and one white. The scattergun looked to be about fifty years old. The cocked hammers resembled devilish horns. Worn scrollwork patinated with age decorated the receiver. The side-by-side barrels measured thirty inches in length.

Quest spoke up. "What are you fixing to do, stranger?"

"The old medicine man handed me this ripsnorter and said that I should keep strangers off o' these rocks. It was kind of a special charge."

Quest drawled, "In case you haven't noticed, we have business here. *Hangtree* business."

The double maw shifted to the west and the Christmas-colored apparition said, "Take yore business elsewhere. This is Crow territory."

"I never heard that," snapped one of the vigilantes.

"I'm telling yuh to mosey along. Do your hanging somewhere else. Else I'll let loose with this devil gun."

Quest said tightly, "In case you haven't noticed, Christmas, you're outnumbered considerably."

The ridiculous apparition showed nerve. His shotgun did not waver an inch.

"Yuh won't like what this hammer gun puts out. Not one little bit."

Pat Savage spoke up, "You better listen to him. That shotgun doesn't spit buckshot, birdshot or anything remotely like it."

Quest turned. "What would you know about it?"

"Too much. He turned it on me yesterday."

"You don't look much the worse for wear."

Pat said thinly, "I gave you fair warning."

Shrugging negligently, Quest turned his glittering colorless eyes back on the absurd jasper in green.

"The way I see it," he told the other, "you got two charges to uncork, provided you pull both triggers at once. Then we're going to drill you like a rattlesnake."

The other held his ground. "I can take yuh. I can take yuh all."

Mr. Calamity said it with such low vehemence that Quest hesitated. The ridiculous figure did not seem to have any particular fear in him.

While hesitant cloth-rimmed eyes gleamed in the moonlight and the situation poised on the brink of disaster, something passed over the moon, intercepting the light.

Everyone looked up.

It was a plane. It had come up so quietly no one had noticed. In truth, they heard no motor drone even as the plane passed overhead, winging west and slightly to the north. Floodlights sent out funnels of illumination, as if it search of something.

A steady hissing filtered down, echoing off the clustering bluffs.

Pat and Long Tom exchanged surprised glances.

"Doc!" Pat declared.

"That's his plane all right," whispered Long Tom. "I recognize the whisper of those silencers. Nobody but Doc has them."

But the aircraft passed by, continuing on into the darkness of the western horizon.

Pat moaned. "He didn't see us, did he?"

Before Long Tom could reply, Quest made his move.

The hissing plane had drawn all eyes. In that interval, the vigilante leader saw his opportunity.

Swiveling his six-gun about, he aimed in the direction of Mr. Calamity, so-called. His trigger finger tightened.

His target, however, was swifter. Calamity pulled back on one trigger and then the other.

That was when everyone took his newfound nickname seriously.

Two violent blasts seared the night, and several vigilantes were struck by whatever the scattergun had vomited forth. They were knocked off their feet, momentarily turned about, and otherwise disadvantaged.

None fell to the dust. Instead, they began rising into the night, flailing and floundering as they moved skyward.

Abruptly, Quest hurled himself to one side, slamming into the dirt and rolling into the shelter of a rock.

Slipping around, he tried to get the long steel barrel of his six-shooter set atop his stony shelter while he sought a bead on the green-clad cowpoke.

Before he could squeeze off a shot, something that felt exactly like a metallic vise took hold of his wrist and shucked the heavy weapon from his unresisting fingers.

Chapter XV

THUNDERBOLT OF BRONZE

A METALLIC HERCULES had appeared, seemingly from nowhere.

None of the assembled necktie party had discerned his approach. This was explained by the fact that the giant had dropped down out of the sky like a silent thunderbolt.

The modern Hercules had descended by parachute. The silken bell was blacker than the night sky, and therefore not noticed. None of the lynchers had been looking upward, anyway. Thus, they failed to take notice of the nemesis that the night had apparently deposited in their midst.

Huge fingers with a grip like steel had disarmed the vigilante calling himself Quest. Those same fingers took hold of the man as if he were but a young boy. They manhandled him briefly, slapping his clothes, tearing off his cartridge belt as if it were mere cheesecloth. This act alone suggested prodigious strength.

The steely hands transferred to Quest's pulsing neck. Fingers were about his throat, squeezing. Quest's tongue popped loose of his mouth. His eyes protruded as well. Such was the obdurate strength in those metallic digits.

Quest had the momentary impression that he was being strangled. But this was a product of panic and imagination combined. The squeezing fingers found a spot near the back of his neck and began kneading it. Quest's hold on consciousness began to ebb.

Still possessed by the panicky sensation of imminent death by strangulation, the outlaw began floundering and kicking. It was to no avail. Nor could he speak and give outcry.

The bandit found himself more helpless than he could ever recall. The imminence of death produces in a man strange reactions. When he realized he could not defeat the thing that had utter mastery over him, Quest craned his head around to see what it was. He wanted to take the last sight of his conqueror with him to the grave. That was how helpless he felt.

Quest had time only for a glimpse. But what he saw stuck with him for the rest of his days, which were destined to be short.

His first impression consisted of eyes. They were golden, like those of an eagle. But no eagle possessed such metallic talons. A bobcat might possess golden eyes, but the face surrounding the orbs of gold was neither feline nor avian. The eyes were human, but not ordinary.

The twin irises staring down at him were intense in their focus. The cast of the surrounding face was metallic. In the moonlight, it appeared to be molded from hardened bronze. The features were handsome and regular, but somehow terrible in their cold expressionlessness.

Everything about that countenance was fixed and immobile. No anger dwelled there. Not even annoyance. Yet the eyes were terrible. Deep within their depths golden flakes whirled in an eerie agitation. There seemed to be anger there. Anger and wrath. But nowhere else on the bronze Hercules' metallic features.

The giant wore an unusual outfit of brown leather, a one-piece affair, the upper portion of which resembled a modern aviator's flying jacket. Beating his fist futilely against this leather-clad Titan, against his immediate surroundings, and even against his own pounding heart, Quest prepared to surrender his mortal parts to the terrible giant that had appeared from nowhere.

Then out of the corner of his eye, Quest spied the garishlycaparisoned creature who had dubbed himself Mr. Calamity. The fantastic figure stepped around behind the bronze giant, closed up his shotgun and detonated a double blast against his assailant's broad back.

The boom of the vintage hammer gun was an echoing knell. Both barrels had been unleashed. There was no doubting that.

The bronze Hercules was thrown forward by the blast. He lost his grip on Quest's neck. In landing, he cracked two of Quest's ribs. It felt as if a steer had been dropped upon him. The crushing weight of the bronze giant exerted itself only momentarily, however.

Abruptly, the metallic apparition began levitating upward. This time the expressionless bronze mask of a face showed a flicker of concern, but only that. The whirling eyes continued their ceaseless and uncanny animation. This feature picked up speed.

Kicking his legs and clawing at the empty air about him, the bronze Titan floated upward with increasing velocity. It was not long before he was lost from sight high in the diamond-bright field of starlight.

From nearby, Long Tom shouted, "Doc!"

Groaning and wincing, Quest stumbled to his feet and demanded, "Was that Doc Savage?"

Instead of answering, Long Tom looked about, saw that only three of the vigilantes were yet on their feet—the others having vanished—and made a sudden lunge from the back of his horse in the direction of Pat Savage, whose pretty neck had been inserted into a noose.

As a maneuver, it appeared to be unwise, if not reckless. Perhaps the puny electrical wizard realized that, with his bronze chief having vanished into the night sky, there was nothing to prevent Quest and his crooks from finishing the job of hanging.

Long Tom had one boot out of his saddle stirrups and swung it in a wild arc so that the rowels struck Pat's horse in the withers.

The horse backed up abruptly, crying out in pain as it did so.

It was a predictable reaction. That might have explained Long Tom's risk taking. For the horse backed Pat's head out of the noose, which had not been properly tightened.

The deadly loop swung free.

The bronze-skinned girl had showed no signs of struggling against her fate. Her arms hung limp, and her head had rested in the noose as if tired. A bruise visible on the side of her head explained why. A squeamish gunman had knocked Pat unconscious so that she would not suffer.

There was an unfortunate consequence to this action. Namely, that Pat's horse became spooked and began prancing about in agitation. She tipped over in the saddle. One foot tangled in the stirrup. Caught.

The nervous animal walked off, dragging the helpless girl in the dirt.

Long Tom's heart dropped into his boots. But he could do nothing about this. He found his head being jerked about wildly. Suddenly, his fear of strangulation by hanging was replaced by a near panic. His neck was likely to be broken and he knew it. He shook his head madly, like a canine attempting to shake off a constricting dog collar, but it was no good.

As it turned out, the pale electrical genius Long Tom did not have long to be concerned.

Three unusual things happened in close order.

FIRST, a body fell out of the sky with a heavy thud. The ground actually shook. The body must have fallen from a great height. This was followed by a second body. It made a less disturbing sound crashing into a clump of greasewood, but the finality of the second, along with the first, suggested that two men had died.

Long Tom remembered seeing two of Quest's gunmen being flung up into the sky by a pair of shotgun blasts. Squeezing his eyes shut, he steeled himself for the third thud, the one that would signify the return to earth of Doc Savage.

Instead, there was a distant crack and the rope above his head jumped violently. Another crack came. This time the hang rope parted and Long Tom felt the heavy braided strand slap his back hard. It was a welcome feeling. It meant that he could throw himself safely out of the saddle, the noose about his neck notwithstanding. Which he promptly did.

His landing was hard, and he rolled with it. He could feel his elbows scraping rock and grit. He could not protect himself because his hands were tied behind his back.

When Long Tom stopped rolling, he flung his head about wildly, eyes attempting to pierce the darkness.

Only two figures could be discerned, and those but dimly.

Quest was one. The strange little man in green was the other. Quest was struggling to his feet with great difficulty, one arm holding onto his side while the other hand attempted to lever himself up using a large boulder as a brace.

His gunnysack hood sat atop his head, but it was greatly askew. One eye was covered, while the other orb peered about wildly.

Contrary to his previous boast, the apparition in green was reloading his scattergun, and his intentions were plain. He was about to send Quest hurtling to his doom—hurtling straight up. Hurtling into the night sky.

Before he could close the shotgun properly, a stuttering sound came from one of the nearby buttes. It was a roar. Long and deep. It stuttered like a rivet gun.

Long Tom skinned his teeth into a grin. "That's a supermachine pistol!" he exulted.

Hollow metal capsules commenced busting themselves open against objects on the ground, releasing their chemical contents. There were a lot of them.

Neither standing man understood that properly. They only knew that they were being fired upon by what sounded like a powerful machine gun.

Plenty of shelter existed amid the rocks and boulders. But

that only worked for those who knew whence the withering gunfire emanated. Neither man did.

Both got the identical idea at the same time. They ran for one of the waiting automobiles.

Spurning the one with the flat tire and bullet-riddled body, they went for the other, a blue roadster.

Quest reached the machine first, flung himself behind the wheel, and pulled the door shut.

The goblin in green caught up to the rolling machine and yanked open the passenger door. He threw his shotgun in first, and the rest of him followed. That door clapped shut.

The dome light was on and Long Tom could spy the long-barreled scattergun lifting and being pointed at the side of Quest's hooded head.

"Vamoose us out of here!" howled Mr. Calamity in a shrill voice.

"What do you think I'm trying to do!" yelled back Quest.

That was the extent of their conversation, at least insofar as Long Tom's hearing went. The automobile accelerated, and the roar of its motor drowned out everything else except the stuttering of the supermachine pistol high in the air.

The ruby-red tail-light dwindled, then was obscured by stirred-up dust.

Soon enough, the sound of the motorcar became lost in the Wyoming vastness.

Long Tom contorted himself into a seated position and stared up in the sky, his pallid features aghast.

He had seen Doc Savage floundering in his upward ascension and knew what was to come. Stealing himself by gritting his teeth, he waited. He stared and stared into the moonlit sky, but saw nothing resembling a body tumbling about the inky heavens.

If his wristwatch had not been tied behind his back, the slender electrical genius would have consulted it. It seemed as if the bronze man should have arrived back on earth by now.

Fear and apprehension can distort a man's sense of time, so Long Tom continued to wait for the inevitable.

The inevitable never came.

Instead, before long a weird whirring sound smote his years.

Searching the horizon, Long Tom saw something lift up from Big Butte, display itself against the rising moon momentarily, and then drift downward.

It was a gyroplane. A true gyro—a nimble experimental aircraft capable of rising straight up and landing without need of a runway. It could also hover in place, which meant it was several years ahead of present-day aeronautical engineering.

Evidently, the dragonfly craft had alighted stealthily and silently upon the butte. Now it was seeking lower ground.

The whirligig craft was settling into the center of the roadway. As it approached, it kicked up whirlwinds of alkali dust. At first, Long Tom sealed his lips tight and closed his eyes. He would have liked to pinch his nose shut, but his fingers remained pinioned behind his back. He did his best not to inhale any sooner than practicable.

Finally, the windmill plane landed on rubber wheels.

The door opened and a man stepped out—a man so tall he had to duck to avoid being decapitated by the whirling rotor blades.

Long Tom opened a single eye. In the darkness, details could not be made out, but scrutinizing the shadowy man, Long Tom's heart gave a quick leap of hope. It was dashed almost immediately.

When the man straightened out, it could be seen that he was nearly as tall as Doc Savage. But his outlines were rougher, not as symmetrical as the famed Man of Bronze. Moreover, his fists were gigantic. Freakishly so.

The hulking man peered around and gave vent to an exclamation that caused booming echoes to resound off the nearby buttes.

"Holy cow!" he thundered. "Where is everybody?"

"Over here," Long Tom called out. "I'm tied up. Pat's somewhere around here. She's trussed up, too."

The huge-handed giant pounded forward, and moonlight found his features. They were long, mournful and vaguely equine. His dour lineaments made one think of cartoons of Old Man Prohibition back in bootleg days. He looked as if he rarely smiled.

The big fellow lumbered up, seized Long Tom by his scrawny shoulders and stood him on his feet without any apparent effort other than a grunting release of breath.

Spinning the slender electrical wizard about, he found his bound wrists. By exerting massive strength, he caused the bonds to snap apart.

Long Tom spun, feeling of his chafed wrists. "You practically tore the hide off me!" he complained sullenly.

During this outburst, the huge man rumbled out a question. "Where is Pat?"

"Last I saw, she was tangled up in her saddle stirrup, out cold, and her horse was making tracks, dragging her along with it."

THEY found the horse first, but no Pat. The bronze-haired girl they discovered lying in the waist-high fringe of sagebrush, insensate as before. One boot was missing. It had come off during the horse-dragging.

"Is she breathing, Renny?" demanded Long Tom.

Renny used his monster paws to pluck Pat out of the sagebrush, which had fortunately broken her fall. Ropes held her wrists together. The hulking man took careful pains to release her from bondage by bringing out a pocket knife and going to work carefully on the hemp.

Then he lifted Pat up in his arms and demanded, "Where did Doc get to?"

Long Tom hesitated, swallowed hard, then croaked out, "He landed O.K., but then he went shooting back up in the sky. He didn't come back down—that I heard, at any rate."

Renny closed one eye, and regarded Long Tom like a skeptical Cyclops. "Back up into the sky?"

"Let me show you," invited Long Tom as he led the way to first one and then another of the bodies of the two would-be hangmen who wore flour sacks for masks. One of them was not wearing his flour-sack headgear. He was clutching it in his hand. Evidently, during his upward flight, he had yanked it off in order to make sure he was not hallucinating. The flour sack remained clutched in the stiff fingers.

"Looks like they hit mighty hard," Renny rumbled.

"It took a couple of minutes for them to come back to earth, by my reckoning," Long Tom allowed.

Renny looked up. "I don't see anything up there, do you?"

"Not me," admitted the puny electrical genius. "But Doc should've landed by now."

"Knowing Doc," mused Renny in his rumbling tone, "he might have pulled a gimmick out of his trick vest and managed to save himself."

Long Tom regarded the smashed bodies at his feet. "These two looked like they fell more than a mile. What could accomplish that?"

"Search me," admitted Renny. He looked around, his disconsolate expression lengthening.

Renny was Colonel John Renwick, the civil engineer of Doc Savage's outfit. Setting Pat Savage down carefully, he blocked and unblocked his monster fists. His general attitude strongly suggested that he wanted to tackle the mystery with his bare hands, which were prodigious.

Those monster paws looked as if each one could barely be slipped into a quart milk pail. When Renny bunched them into matching mauls of bone and tendon, they took on the appearance of gallon-capacity jugs. The skin was red from outdoor work and the knuckles were scarred. Renny had unbounded confidence in those gargantuan hands, and not without reason. It was his boast that no wooden door had a panel so stout that it he could not wreck it with one blow of either fist.

Often in the past, when he was frustrated, Renny had simply hauled off and demolished the nearest door with a single blow. But there were no doors handy, so he worked his fists reflexively the way some men tugged on their earlobes or chewed the inside of their cheeks. It was a nervous habit. And an unnerving one if you got on Renny's bad side.

Finally, both men stopped staring expectantly into the star-spattered sky.

Renny had a question. Long Tom did, too. Long Tom got his out first.

"How did you find us? We heard Doc's plane whiz by without showing any sign of seeing us."

"Johnny was piloting that bus," boomed Renny. "That was to draw everybody's attention while we slipped up in the gyroplane, Doc and me. Doc parachuted out after we spotted you."

"That's what I was asking," snapped Long Tom impatiently. "How did you find us? We're in the middle of nowhere, Wyoming."

"You're a funny goof to be asking that question," returned Renny.

"Who are you calling funny?"

"You. You're hilarious—a regular panic. Have you forgotten the radioactive coin you carry in your pocket?"

"No," returned Long Tom peevishly. "And I don't carry it in my pocket anymore. It's in the heel of my shoe. That way I don't forget and leave it in the wrong pants pocket. But we use that token to activate the electroscope that opens the door to Doc Savage's headquarters. What does it have to do with this situation?"

"Doc took one of your experimental television receivers and rigged it up so it will display on a cathode ray tube anything that gives off radioactive emanations. We've been flying over this part of Wyoming, noses pressed to the screen. When Doc detected something in the air from the gyroplane, he directed Johnny to fly over and make it seem as if he saw nothing."

Long Tom nodded vigorously. "I get it now. Then you and Doc sneaked up in the gyroplane."

"Right. Johnny saw what was happening through the infra-red scanner on the big plane. He radioed us, and Doc decided there was no time to waste. He bailed out. With motors silenced, I landed on the butte after Doc parachuted down."

"Doc did a good job of busting up the hanging party, but he barely got started before one of the bad ones opened up with both barrels of a shotgun into his back."

Renny winced, then remembered something. "Wait a minute! Doc was wearing his bulletproof vest. Do you mean to say he got hit in the head?"

Long Tom shook his head again. "Not that I saw. But the guy with the scattergun wasn't putting out ordinary buckshot. It fired something that when it takes hold catapults you into the sky at a violent pace. Doc went skyward. He still hasn't come down."

They walked around and Renny produced a flashlight that could be manipulated so that it projected a fan or beam of light, even an intensely white rod. He used all three configurations to examine the surroundings.

The blinding beam disclosed a handful of bodies draped limp and broken amid the lower rocks. These unfortunates appeared to be gang members who had been perched high up and who had been struck by potent mercy bullets, which had promptly rendered them unconscious, causing them to fall to their doom. Renny had wielded the supermachine pistol that had unleashed this inadvertent mayhem from the descending gyro. The big-fisted engineer seemed unconcerned by what he had wrought.

"How many bad ones?" he thumped.

"I counted six, not counting the goofy-looking gink in green. They don't work together. Although he and the head guy took off in the same car when you opened up with your supermachine pistol."

Renny's frowning face grew more rugged of line.

"This is starting to sound complicated," he muttered.

"It's worse than complicated," ground out Long Tom. "It's a tangle of barbed wire and I don't know where the strands go, never mind what they connect to." Suddenly, he was peering around. "Where did Laramie get to?"

"Who's Laramie?"

"My foreman. I left him wounded behind a rock, where they couldn't string him up."

"Anybody else hiding?"

"Down in the gully back there," Long Tom said, jerking a thumb in the darkness, "there's a busted-up car. Behind the wheel there's the sheriff of Bison."

Renny scratched his curly hair. "Is he wanted, too?"

"No, he's dead."

"A dead sheriff really complicates matters," grunted Renny. "Who killed him?"

"The dirty gang of mule rustlers that just got busted up."

Now puzzlement roosted on the towering engineer's countenance.

"I've heard of horse thieves, beef rustlers, but not mule thieves," he remarked.

"These dead boys scattered about are the local mule thieves. I don't know who they are, but they decided to hang me and Pat for their own misdeeds."

Renny frowned. "Thinking to cover their tracks?"

"That's about the size of it," allowed Long Tom.

After failing to locate any surviving rustlers, they discovered Laramie lying in the rocks and Renny looked him over carefully.

"Got your leg busted up, old-timer?" the big-fisted engineer asked sympathetically.

Laramie didn't look as though he had much fire left in him, but suddenly he flared up. "Who are you calling an old-timer, you gallopin' galoot!"

Renny looked unperturbed and continued examining the man's wounds. He tightened the belt tourniquet about the oldster's calf, bringing forth a wincing "Daw gone!"

"There's a first-aid kit back in the gyroplane," he told Long Tom. "Maybe you should fetch it."

"Do I look like a dog-faced retriever?" snapped Long Tom.

Renny eyed him speculatively. "What's eating you?"

"Not much. It's just that I've been nearly hanged twice in the past twenty-four hours, and the last I saw of Doc Savage he was heading toward the moon. Now I can't figure out whether I want him to land or not."

Renny rumbled, "Neither outcome sounds welcome to me, either. O.K., you watch this old sourdough. I'll get the first-aid kit."

Laramie flared up anew. "Who're you calling a sourdough? I'm a ranch foreman, not some packrat scratchin' about in the creek bed for enough gold dust to buy beans and bacon."

Renny had no sooner started off than there came a distinct sound from nearby. Everyone jumped, including Laramie, who winced with the effort.

It was difficult to see where the noise came from. Renny's powerful flashlight splashed illumination around. A rising cloud of dust drew their attention. It had something of the shape of a toadstool in the spectral moonlight.

The big-fisted engineer and the diminutive electrician pounded toward the dust, their mouths hanging open, and their eyes a little sick.

"I hope that's not Doc," Long Tom moaned.

"Well, who else could it be?" Renny flung back.

Laramie called after them, "Are you gents fixin' to leave me here to die?"

But his plaintive cry was lost as their feet slapped the sandy soil in desperation.

Chapter XVI

FUTILITY

THE THING THAT plummeted from the sky was a body. No question about that. It landed with a hideous sound that suggested pulverized bones and smashed internal organs. The sound of its landing signified that it was very heavy. Heavier than a normal man.

Long Tom swallowed hard as he pounded toward the commotion while Renny's closed fists grew moist in the palms. Conversely, his mouth dried. Fear did that. It was not often that either man experienced the darker emotions. But Doc Savage was their leader, the man around whom they had gathered in the aftermath of the World War, now many years in the past.

Together with the other members of the Doc Savage organization, they had combed the distant corners of the globe, seeking peril and excitement. They found both in plenty. This only made them want more.

So it was that, when they skidded to a stop, Long Tom and Renny drew great sobbing breaths in through their lungs before their eyes could focus.

The crushed body was indeed large. And its overall color was a dark brown, the color of the flying outfit that the bronze man had worn during his daring parachute plunge.

But the inert body was not that of a human being. It took a little scrutiny to discern that happy fact in the dark.

Rather, it was a horse that had fallen from the sky. It was an ordinary looking horse, except for one peculiarity: the horse wore a gunnysack hood over its elongated head.

"Thank goodness," breathed Long Tom. "One of the horses must have been hit by wild buckshot."

"Why would buckshot whirl a horse a mile up?" wondered Renny.

"That's one of the mysteries," snorted Long Tom. "But that's Quest's horse. Quest was the leader of the group. He sported a gunnysack hood, while all the others had flour sacks covering their heads. It was the same with their mounts."

Renny grunted, "Must be local boys afraid of being recognized."

"That's my thinking, too," said Long Tom. He suddenly remembered something. Snapping his thin fingers, he said, "We should look for the girl."

"Pat? I left her back yonder."

"No, the *other* girl. Miss Crater, the sister of the man Pat saw tumble out of the sky."

Renny said, "I heard about that from Doc. Can't say I credited it much until I got here. Strange things seem to be falling out of the sky, and none of them are rain or meteors."

Long Tom said nothing. Foraging around, he found, to his increasing agitation, no sign of Alta Crater.

"What does she look like?" rumbled Renny.

Long Tom's disposition was approximately that of week-old cream. Sour. He whirled on the big-fisted engineer and snapped impatiently. "Other than Pat, she'll be the only woman in the vicinity. If you want to know the color of her hair, it was like pinewood, but fluffy. Otherwise, you're on your own."

With that, the pallid electrical wizard stalked off to do his own searching.

Renny made no move to follow. Although he stood six feet, four inches in his stocking feet, he knew that Long Tom had many of the propensities of a wildcat. Although perhaps the least impressive looking number of Doc Savage's group, Long Tom Roberts was probably one of the worst to pick a fight with.

Also, Renny understood Long Tom's peevishness. The fate of Doc Savage was looming over their heads like a threatening thundercloud. From time to time, Renny looked upward, as if hopeful of spying some sign of the missing bronze man.

Of course, that was ridiculous. But the whole matter was ridiculous. Men being hurled into the sky as if from a catapult. It was fantastic, unbelievably so. It got on the nerves.

Both Long Tom and Renny ranged the immediate vicinity, kicking through greasewood and cactus clumps, but finding no sign of the missing woman. Nor was there any indication that Doc Savage had landed anywhere.

Long Tom turned his attention to Laramie lying in the sagebrush.

"Are you much of a doctor?" the oldster croaked.

"No," returned the electrical genius. "But I can patch you up until we can get you to a medico."

Long Tom's bedside manner left a lot to be desired, but he got Laramie patched up well enough. Applying his own knowledge of horse doctoring, the old man offered his own suggestions, particularly in regard to splinting the bullet-broken leg.

"Ain't you going to take out one of the slugs?" he groused after Long Tom finished up.

"I don't want you dying of blood loss on me."

"Well, thanks for nothin'."

"If you live, I'm docking you a day's pay."

"For what?" roared Laramie. "I got all these perforations in your employ."

"For complaining so hard you make my eardrums hurt," snapped Long Tom.

Meanwhile, Renny's ranging search eventually ran its course. He got around to the crashed automobile and examined the man behind the wheel. The latter wore a five-pointed nickeled star denoting that he was a local sheriff or marshal.

"Dead," grunted Renny. He was not surprised. The car was a wreck. His flashlight disclosed all the grisly details. Renny wound the charging crank constantly to keep it going.

FINALLY, the two men gave up and rendezvoused by the spindly wingless gyroplane whose rotor blades creaked in the soft summer breeze.

Renny had scooped up Pat Savage in his immense massive arms and lay her in a back seat. The gyro was a cabin craft, a four-seater. There was not a lot of room for all that.

Long Tom asked, "Got any smelling salts?"

Renny rummaged around, found a small glass bottle, uncorked it and waved it under Pat's nostrils.

The pair expected an immediate reaction, but did not receive one.

"Maybe she has a concussion," rumbled Renny.

Long Tom looked worried. "That's bad if she does. I'll keep trying to rouse her."

Nodding, Renny lumbered off to collect Laramie and loaded him in back. The old foreman complained every step of the way.

"I had my share of aches and pains before this fracas of a night commenced, now I'm so perforated I can hardly stand to be manhandled."

"Pipe down," blared Renny.

"Where did you get those fists?" snorted Laramie. "Off a caveman ancestor?"

Renny grunted, "You should meet Monk sometime."

"Are his fists bigger?"

"No, but he's more caveman than any Neanderthal you might meet—provided there are any still around."

"I'll settle for being left alone to bleed in peace, thank you just the same," grumbled Laramie.

Renny deposited the cranky oldster in the gyro and asked, "Pat wake up yet?"

"No," answered Long Tom. "No choice but to let her sleep, and hope she's O.K."

Having exhausted all ground search possibilities, Renny and Long Tom decided to take to the air.

Long Tom made a move for the control bucket, but Renny's big paw intercepted his chest bone and held him in place while the loud-voiced engineer ducked into the gyroplane, seized the controls and slammed the door shut, leaving Long Tom to scoot around and take the seat on the other side.

The door was pulling shut when the ingenious synchronized motor caused the overhead rotor wing and the nose propeller to spin in unison. Alkali dust began whirling, billowing pale clouds charged with cold moonlight.

With amazing speed and mechanical agility, the machine warmed up, then jumped straight into the air like a nimble grasshopper.

There was a searchlight attached to the hull. It could be controlled by a dial that made it rotate. Long Tom switched it on and redirected the beam toward the flat tops of the Pumpkin Buttes.

"Any sign of him?" grunted Renny.

"No," admitted Long Tom. "Doc Savage did not end up on any of them."

Dejectedly, the slender electrical genius switched off the searchlight.

Renny sent the windmill plane scrambling up into the sky, canted it northeast, and said, "First order of business is to find where Johnny put down his plane."

"I forgot about him," snapped Long Tom, reaching for the radio microphone. The cockpit transceiver was already dialed to the private frequency used by Doc Savage and his aides.

"Calling Johnny. Calling Johnny, this is Long Tom Roberts."

A thin, reedy voice answered. It had an interesting quality of

scholarly precision. Each word and every syllable was annunci-
ated with great care and exactitude.

"Salutations. Commence your catechism of eventualities."

Long Tom and Renny exchanged glances. In the back, Laramie
piped up. "What language is he speakin'? Latin?"

"It's his own brand of English," said Long Tom sourly. "Most
folks can hardly understand it."

"Well, I hope his mother does. Be a terrible shame to go
through life not bein' understood."

"You leave my mother out of this, whoever you are!" Johnny
snapped, reverting to everyday English.

Renny's voice carried to the microphone. "I found Pat and
Long Tom. But we lost Doc Savage."

There was a momentary hesitation from the radio loudspeaker. Then:

"I trust that you mean misplaced."

"The last anyone saw of Doc Savage," the long-faced engineer
said mournfully, "he was climbing into the sky like a meteor
returning to its home planet. We waited for him to come back
down, but it never happened."

"Was he riding a rocket?" Johnny asked anxiously.

"He wasn't riding anything at all, he was just shooting skyward
like a rocket."

Long Tom interjected. "It's a long story, but others met the
same fate. Eventually, they came down to earth. They landed
hard. Dashed the life out of them. But we don't know about
Doc. He never returned to earth."

"No." Johnny's voice was clogged with apprehensiveness. *"Are
you saying that Doc Savage is dead?"*

Renny let out a great gusty breath that was like the sad sigh
of a tired old lion.

"You know Doc. He climbs out of the durndest fixes."

"In this instance," Johnny wondered aloud, *"where would Doc
climb to—the moon?"*

Long Tom interjected, "Where did you land, Johnny?"

"Open prairie to the northwest. It was the only safe place to set down. I've been waiting half the night, worried sick."

"Well, get into the air. We'll conduct a search for Doc."

Then Johnny Littlejohn asked a question that froze their blood.

"Are we combing the ground, or searching the sky?"

"Both!" snapped Long Tom. "What do you think?"

The blood-freezing effect congealed with his next words.

"I am thinking," said Johnny deliberately, *"that if Doc Savage is floating around in the sky somewhere, we are liable to bump into him with our propeller blades in the dark."*

From the rear, Laramie let out a startling grunt of laughter.

"If this don't beat all! I have heard some tall tales about Doc Savage, but the yarns you two were spinnin' put Paul Bunyan to shame."

"Butt out of this!" snapped Long Tom.

"I will not! Somebody has to talk sense. Doc Savage went climbin' into the sky, so it makes sound horse sense that he's back on the ground by now. No point in lookin' for a man in the night wind. He can't fly, can he?"

Neither man answered. Instead, Long Tom spoke into the microphone.

"Stay put, Johnny. We will join you. If Doc did fall back to earth, there's nothing we can do for him. But if he's somewhere in the atmosphere, we will resume our searching at first light."

"A consummately unsatisfactory plan, but I see no other recourse," said Johnny, and his radio transmission went dead.

The gyroplane beat smoothly through the night, encountering few air bumps. Following the radio signal from the plane, Long Tom worked the direction finder with one eye on the surrounding night, his beating heart high in his throat. Never before had he experienced such sickening fear over the fate of his seemingly invincible bronze leader.

Chapter XVII

ATMOSPHERIC ORDEAL

DOC SAVAGE HAD not been unceremoniously hurled into eternity, as was supposed.

The double shotgun blast that had torn up the back of his flying suit had done considerable damage to the tough outer leather, but the charge had been arrested by Doc's underclothing, which was of a chain-mesh construction able to turn all but military rifle slugs. It extended to include his elbows and knees, rather like a pair of winter long johns.

Both barrels had discharged at short range, throwing Doc forward onto the man he had seized, the hooded crook calling himself Quest. Unavoidably, Doc had been momentarily stunned. The contents of two shotgun charges arriving simultaneously will do that to a man, even one as powerful and well-armored as Doc Savage, who was seen in some quarters as a modern Sir Galahad.

How long Doc Savage might have lain across the man he had been intent upon subduing was not something that would ever be known. For almost as soon as the bronze giant had shaken off the first stunning blow, he found himself rising in the air.

This rising was remarkable. It was as if titanic fingers had plucked him up for inspection.

Except that there was no Wyoming equivalent to Paul Bunyan, and Doc Savage continued to rise. It quickly became alarming.

As the bronze man's stunned senses cleared, he became aware

that he was floating skyward at an accelerating pace. His head hung slightly downward, so he could see through the darkness toothy rocks below rapidly receding. Doc kicked experimentally, but encountered nothing solid. Nor did he expect to.

It was no secret that Doc Savage had been trained for the life's work that he had undertaken. This altruistic enterprise was the brainstorm of his father, who had blazed a similar path in life before him. When astonishingly young, Clark Savage, Jr.—not yet known as Doc—had been entrusted to a seemingly endless parade of scientists, experts, and other competent specialists, each of whom was charged with the duty of imparting all of their knowledge and training to young Clark.

By the time Doc achieved manhood, this had produced a virtual superman, a mere mortal somehow filled to the brim with all earthly scientific knowledge, as well as other skills necessary for the pursuit of adventure and danger.

A period spent in the army during the World War had rounded out young Doc's fighting skills, finishing the preparation for this tremendous undertaking.

In the course of his upbringing, Doc had been thrown into deep water, forced to penetrate unexplored caves, and learned to survive in conditions ranging from the Arctic to the Tropical, until he was sufficiently experienced that he could encounter any kind of danger and come out on top.

None of these experts had unexpectedly hurled Doc Savage skyward as if he were a cannonball. This was a new experience, an unexpected and unforeseeable peril.

Therefore, it was understandable that the bronze man, when initially confronted with the impossibility that he was being ejected into the upper atmosphere of the earth, would do some foolish things at first. After kicking about pointlessly, he clawed at the sky—which, of course, accomplished nothing useful.

Craning his head around, he could see four high buttes flash beneath his boots, their flat tops washed by spectral moonlight.

The bronze man had a good idea of how tall those buttes

stood and that was the last inkling he had of his height relative to mother earth.

As he accelerated upward, Doc became aware that his position grew increasingly hopeless. To fall from his present altitude would have been fatal. Unquestionably so.

And he was still rising. Rising fast. He did not yet understand why, only that his back hurt him.

Doc attempted to twist about in midair. It was more difficult than it should have been. The sensation of monstrous fingers plucking him skyward continued. From his parted lips came his uncanny and ethereal trilling. It was a long time in coming relative to the stark surprise that had overcome him. But the situation was beyond unusual.

It was impossible!

Quickly, Doc left off attempting to reposition himself. It would do him no good, he realized.

The night had been warm, but now the air was becoming cool. It was not the passage of wind that was creating the coolness. It was the height to which he was climbing.

Only a few years before, the United States Navy had sent up a manned balloon-and-pressurized-gondola into the stratosphere. Doc himself owned a dirigible that could also make stratospheric trips. Up in those upper reaches below the troposphere, the air was thin and there was no warmth. Ice could form on anything that managed to gain such a supernal height.

Doc Savage's presence of mind was a result of his scientific training and vast experiences. He was fully in control of himself. He could feel no sense of deceleration, only a steady acceleration. That told him he was in no danger of falling. At least not falling down. He was falling *up!*

Rapidly, he became aware that his immediate peril lay above him, not below. Should he continue up into the thinner reaches of the atmosphere, he would suffocate and be overcome by cold. Already a numbness was creeping into his fingers. He flexed them experimentally to keep them limber.

His breathing, which he fought to keep regular, became unsteady. Doc began to gasp as if winded. But he was not winded from exertion, for he was doing nothing strenuous of his own volition.

One bronze hand reached into the zippered opening of his flight suit and into an ingenious vest of many pockets. He always wore it into battle. From one receptacle, Doc pulled out a compact oxygen mask good for several minutes. Pulling this on, he set the mouthpiece in place and flicked a tiny switch that fed oxygen from the miniature pressurized tank.

When his breathing became regular, Doc made some lightning mental calculations.

Although he had yet to understand the phenomenon that had seized him, the fact that he seemed to be pulled up from his shredded back suggested that the power that had seized him was a direct result of the double shotgun blast. How this could be was immaterial at the moment. Doc deduced the possibility that imbedded shotgun pellets were somehow producing this counter-gravitational effect.

He still wore his parachute pack, although he had discarded his main chute by pulling on a quick-release ring upon landing. This had enabled him to disentangle himself from the chute without going through the cumbersome process of taking off the entire pack.

The difficult situation on the ground had made that necessary. Doc had landed close to the man with the gunnysack hood and knew he would have to overpower him first before he could remove his parachute pack.

Now he was glad that he had not. For there was still the reserve chute, which was bundled in the front of the harness.

In a normal air emergency, it would have been the simplest thing to deploy the spare parachute and drop back to earth.

If only this was an ordinary air accident. Doc dared not crack the chute while he still traveling upward. It might retard his ascent, but it was more than likely to have no other impact on his predicament. And if he began to fall—which he imagined was inevitable—the trailing chute could easily become entangled once he reversed direction.

Removing the parachute harness in order to shake himself out of the flight suit whose lining was filled with shotgun pellets, seemed to be the only course of action suggesting salvation.

First, Doc would have to get off the harness, yet hold on to it.

The cold of the upper atmosphere increased; it gripped him like icy tongs. His breath condensation created frost inside the mask. That told the bronze man that the functioning of the oxygen mask might cease at any moment due to icy conditions.

There was no time to waste.

With both hands, he went about removing the harness. This involved unbuckling buckles and straps, which took some time to do properly. Gripping cold slowed him considerably. His fingers felt like the inner bones were no better than brittle icicles.

But he got the thing done. A stab of disappointment entered his golden eyes when he saw that one of the straps was hanging by a shred of webbing. It had been punctured by the shotgun blast. Brief inspection showed the bronze man that it would not hold up against the shock of the parachute opening up.

Since that was not of immediate concern, Doc stuffed the harness under one arm, clamping it securely there. That the spare parachute was now all but useless was chilling. But no fear touched the metallic mask that was his countenance. Doc Savage was not one to surrender hope prematurely.

Employing his free hand, Doc ran the zipper down. Opening up the front of the flight suit, he tried to shuck himself out of the topmost portion. This proved to be more difficult than he imagined. Again, there was the clear sensation of a closed fist grasping the back of the shredded suit, impeding his efforts.

Doc removed from his equipment vest a simple clasp knife.

He got the blade out, and started cutting away, beginning at his waist.

It was now excruciatingly cold and the work was difficult. Doc made progress thanks to the keen blade. He was hampered from having to work entirely one-handed so that he did not lose the spare parachute tucked tight under one arm.

When the bronze giant had cut around as much as he could, he split one leather sleeve from shoulder to cuff.

That part proved easy. But the next was difficult—exceedingly so.

Doc shifted the parachute back onto the other arm, after pocketing the blade, which he would have preferred to hold between his teeth if not for the oxygen mask clamped there.

All the while he was accomplishing these tricky maneuvers, his metallic countenance remained impassive in a way that was unnerving, or would have been unnerving had there been any witness present at twenty thousand feet or more.

Reclaiming the blade, he slit the other sleeve, this time all the way to his fleecy collar. The blade slashed again, and suddenly Doc was free of the leather tunic.

That did it. The upper portion of the flight suit tore away, as if the upward force being exerted was entirely concentrated in the garment.

Doc was tossed about, buffeted by forces that stood in opposition to one another. One obviously was gravity. Another was high winds. But the third was the strange power that had been driving him, throwing him skyward, and seemingly into the stars.

Almost immediately, the bronze giant began to fall and tumble.

THE ACCEPTED method for righting oneself when falling out of an airplane prior to a parachute deployment was one Doc Savage had practiced many times. That time-tested procedure was designed to aid a man who is wearing his parachute harness and was not otherwise encumbered by a knife.

Attempting to pocket the knife Doc Savage lost it, and it fell. But the blade no longer mattered.

With movements that had a slight hint of the frantic about them, Doc attempted to wriggle himself into the parachute harness. This proved to be all but impossible. He was tumbling too wildly.

Giving up on a bad job, he inserted one arm into the appropriate loop in the harness. Then Doc did his best to become spread-eagled in midair and attempt to gain control over his fall.

Had he not been so high above the earth that the fall was considerable, Doc Savage was unlikely to have survived the next few minutes. Gaining control of his body proved tricky.

At one point, he found himself on his back. At another he was dropping head downward.

With a determination only a man facing his final moments of life could summon, the mighty bronze giant got himself oriented in the sky and, after three difficult tries, got his other arm into the harness loop. Unfortunately, that was the loop that was damaged.

But for the moment it held.

Getting the lower loops around his upper legs buckled in place took some doing, but finally the bronze man got first one and then the other firmly attached. He next tightened everything. The reserve parachute pack was suspended over his stomach.

Frozen fingers found the ripcord sheath, and took firm hold of the D-ring.

The bronze man appeared to hesitate. The whirling golden flakes in his eyes appeared to speed up as if doing calculations with lightning speed.

Doc wore a wristwatch that was a gadget unto itself. There was a tiny compass, a thermometer, a stopwatch, and even an altimeter built into it. This last was because Doc sometimes had need of such information when scaling mountains or high places.

The altimeter told him he was approaching the fifteen-thousand foot mark. This enabled him to calculate the time before he struck the earth. So skilled was Doc's trained brain that his calculation was accurate almost to the second.

There was time to try something fancy. It might work, it might not. But it was a chance.

Doc threw his limbs about, changing his orientation in the sky and shifting his body until he was falling in such a way and at such an angle that once he deployed his parachute, the minimum strain would be exerted on the left shoulder strap—the one that was weakest.

As an added measure, Doc raised his free hand and clamped bronze fingers around the torn portion of the canvas strap, to further support it. He possessed no illusions that even his prodigious strength could hold the webbing together if it gave way. But every precaution possible increased his odds for survival, no matter how dubious a chance it stood.

When he was set, Doc pulled the ripcord ring without hesitation.

The reserve chute billowed out. It was a good silk one, and it resembled oil smoke as it spilled out of the burst canvas casing.

As Doc continued to fall, the silken mushroom and its shroud lines swelled upward and outward. The bronze giant braced himself for the crack of its opening and the jarring shock of its arresting action.

They came as expected. Doc's limbs and torso were jolted and squeezed by the harness as the bell performed as expected. His gripping hand never let go of the weak strap, but it proved not to be sufficient.

With a stinging snapping that jarred his clutching fingers, the webbing surrendered to the sudden strain.

Doc was thrown crazily about as the harness became unseated. His opposite hand went to the other shoulder, knowing that this would be the place that let go next.

Doc pulled on the strap, endeavoring to keep it in place. Here he was not fighting tearing canvas cloth. Yet it was still an effort. Perspiration broke out on his metallic forehead. His eyes narrowed with exertion. Behind slightly parted lips, strong white teeth clamped more tightly.

Abruptly, Doc felt himself being thrown out of the harness. There was no preventing it. Centrifugal forces were at work, forces more powerful than human—even superhuman—muscles and tendons could contend with.

Doc's next maneuver appeared to be suicidal. But it was not. Giving up on the shoulder harness, he reached down and simultaneously unbuckled the webbing strapped snug to his upper thighs. They came away easily.

Using both metallic fists, Doc Savage clutched the straps. They snapped upward, pulling his arms with him. Had the bronze giant attempted anything like this reckless maneuver before this, there was no doubt that his arms would have been torn out of their sockets when the parachute first deployed.

Because the great black silken bell was already deployed, Doc needed only to hold tightly to the harness, which he managed to do.

Flake-gold eyes a little strange, the bronze man quickly found himself with both arms flying high over his head, clutching the bundled harness in his viselike grip.

That grip held. He continued his descent. But now survival depended entirely upon the strength of his digits and tendons.

Doc Savage's hands were formidable, although nothing on the order of Renny Renwick's monster fists. They were not misshapen, but rather exceedingly well developed. They were the hands of a surgeon, for this was Doc's primary profession. Considerable sensitivity had been trained into them. Yet they were also strong enough to accomplish physical miracles.

When young, Doc had trained his fingers to do amazing things. One of those amazing things was to crush raw potatoes simultaneously in each hand, pulverizing them with digital pressure alone. It took many months to accomplish this feat of strength and coordination. But all those months of preparation were now paying off.

Doc Savage's double grip was more than sufficient to uphold his more than two hundred pounds of bone and muscle.

Swaying under the parachute bell, the bronze giant would have liked nothing more than to get a glimpse of his wristwatch altimeter, but he dared not move any part of his body, lest it throw him out of balance, and endanger his precarious position.

It was possible to look down, but not to perceive the ground below clearly.

Not that there wasn't sufficient lunar light, but the terrain beneath him was so uneven that even by spectral moonglow, it was difficult to tell where he was—never mind where he might land.

Doc set himself, knowing that he still had a few minutes before his boot heels touched solid ground.

So it was with a distinct shock when the hard earth seemed to slam up beneath him.

Caught off guard, the bronze giant's powerful leg muscles absorbed the shock of landing. Due to the regrettable fact that his hands were clutched tightly over his head, he toppled over.

The combination of his crushing grip and frozen digits made releasing the parachute harness difficult. Doc stumbled and rolled until finally he came to a stop.

The Man of Bronze lay on his back a very long time, staring skyward into the night. His eyes held a shocked look. Never before had he come so close to death. The ceaseless whirling of the golden lights in the aureate depths of his eyes were strangely still. After a time, he blinked once, twice, and then rapidly.

Animation returned to his golden optics and his face radiated a rediscovered energy.

The parachute pack had been torn out of his hands, of course. Doc sat up, stared at his hands. They were like metallic claws now. The death grip he had had on the harness, combined with the bone-deep cold, froze the bronze fingers into talons.

Doc wiggled his fingers experimentally. Eventually, they responded, although with reluctance. Crimson flowed, indicating lacerations.

Climbing to his feet, he discovered himself to be standing very high above the Wyoming terrain. A glance downward showed that he had rolled close to the edge of the lip of a sheer drop-off. Had he kept going, there was little doubt that he would have tumbled to his doom.

A winding river shimmered to the west. Doc studied it by moonlight. He had made a practice of studying maps of all kinds, as well as aerial photographs, committing all details to memory. This so that whenever he found himself stranded in the outdoors, he could make good use of natural landmarks.

Doc recognized the river's contours. It was the Belle Fourche. This particular stretch suggested that he had landed on one of the highest elevations in all of Wyoming.

Doc now knew where he was. The knowledge caused him to trill in a combination of disappointment and disgust.

For the bronze man realized that, despite achieving the safety and solidity of solid ground, he was stranded!

Chapter XVIII

THE CALAMITY

DOC SAVAGE PASSED what was under the circumstances a most unpleasant night.

It was not cold at the elevation upon which he had found himself. It was windy, true, but not distressingly so. The movement of air was neither too cold, nor was it particularly warm. Doc would have preferred more heat, having spent an unnervingly prolonged period in the lower stratosphere.

His hands ached as much from cold as the stress of clutching canvas webbing for dear life.

He had no great amount of water. In his gadget vest was a flat case that contained concentrated fruit tablets. These provided nourishment and could be taken without water, provided they were carefully chewed and mixed with mouth moisture before swallowing.

Doc Savage found that his reservoir of saliva had been significantly depleted. So he chewed the tablets slowly, and forced the crushed tablets down his dry throat. The taste was nothing to boast about. All his efforts had been bent in concentrating the necessary nutrients. A few of the pills had a slightly citrus tang. Most were bland.

After consuming them, the bronze man decided that he would reformulate the pills to make them more palatable.

Once he had swallowed the last pill, and his hands began to feel better, he removed from another vest pocket a glassine packet. This he rubbed briskly between his palms—or as briskly as he could manage in their tender condition. This produced a pleasant chemical heat. Doc used this to warm up his finger bones. More than the concentrated tablets, this operation produced significant relief.

Wayward breezes pushed about the collapsed canopy of the parachute. Doc wondered if a sufficiently strong wind sprang up, he might maneuver the bell in such a way that it would fill and he could leap off the edge of his precarious perch.

He knew from memory that he stood over one thousand feet above the immediate ground and over five thousand feet above sea level. Probably not enough to safely descend via a parachute that had already taken a beating. Yet Doc was tempted. Or would have been, had there been an encouraging wind.

Among the items in his vest was one of the spring-generator flashlights, but Doc used this mainly to avoid venturing too close to the edge of the prominence. He knew where he was. He was not happy about it, but the bronze giant had been in worse predicaments.

Had he possessed reliable strength, he could have climbed down. In another pocket was a collapsible grappling hook small enough to fit into the palm of his hand. Yet another pocket contained a thin silken cord that could be knotted and used for a descent. Additionally, his normal finger strength was such that he could emulate a human fly and scale the side of a brick building by inserting his steel-strong fingertips between the mortar cracks.

The bronze giant was up to no such effort.

When morning came, the sun slowly illuminated the surroundings. He could see the red sandstone and siltstone cliffs above the Belle Fourche River. Ponderosa pines added touches of majestic greenery.

The area sprawled out, rugged and primitive. Geology was something Doc Savage had studied intensively, along with other natural sciences, such as petrology. He knew that back in the Triassic Period, approximately two hundred million years ago, the surrounding terrain had been a shallow sea. In fact, petrified oysters and other prehistoric shellfish were sometimes dug up at the base of the natural formation that had captured him.

Doc was more interested in the flat surface upon which he sat. It was hard gray rock. Litter told that vultures sometimes carried carrion up here to feast. There was other litter, including signs that modern humans had climbed to the summit in recent years.

Doc recalled that the summit had rarely been scaled due to its sheer rock walls. It could be done, but it was a discouraging undertaking.

For this was the plug of igneous rock the Cheyenne had long ago dubbed the "Bear Lodge Butte" and present-day Americans had renamed "Devils Tower." It was a fantastic natural formation that might have been a massive laccolith—a volcanic plug.

Doc inclined toward that theory, but he had never studied the formation in detail. He did recall that it was over forty million years old. Wyoming Indians of many tribes considered the place a sacred spot. It was visible a considerable distance. But its elevation prevented him from being seen, except from the air.

Walking to the edge, Doc lay down on his stomach and looked downward. This was the west face, which was the most climbable. The sides of the plug suggested deep gouges. Sioux legend claimed that a giant bear known as Mato had scored the butte on all sides while attempting to capture two young boys for supper.

Climbing down was not something the bronze man felt up to doing as yet. But if he did not make the attempt before sundown, Doc knew that his life would be once again in peril. He could go four days without water, although rain might increase his chances by another few days if it fell. But this was late summer. Rain was unlikely.

After reconnoitering the great tablelike surface, chasing away curious mice and chipmunks, the bronze man went to the center and gathered up the parachute fabric and made for himself a comfortable nest. It was the only creature comfort of which he could avail himself. It might become necessary to use it for shade against the blistering sun. If night found him still stranded, it would serve as a warm bed.

As the morning wore on, Doc monitored the surrounding area, looking for stray riders or passing motor vehicles. He saw nothing of either kind.

Then something strange caught his attention. He noticed it out of the corner of one eye.

It was an aircraft.

From one of the innumerable pockets of his vest, Doc removed a slim black tube which he quickly telescoped into a small but powerful spyglass.

The sound of the moaning motor told him it was not one of his own buses, but it represented an opportunity to capture the pilot's attention.

It proved to be an Air Mail plane. One of Uncle Sam's speedy ships, winging its way westward. Probably bound for Salt Lake City, or points farther west.

Had it been night, Doc Savage could have lit a flare which he carried, but it was early morning so he removed a smoke generator from his vest. This steel tube produced black smoke through chemical action. Doc armed it, tossing the thing a few feet away. Immediately, one end began belching a dark pall that swiftly intensified.

Glancing toward the passing plane, he discerned no alteration in its course. No doubt the pilot mistook the evil-looking smudge for a brushfire, rather than a distress signal.

Doc had no way to attract the pilot's gaze other than stand up and wave both arms vigorously. He did this for a few minutes without result, then realized that the black parachute might better be employed as a signaling device.

Gathering up the shroud lines, Doc dragged the collapsed canopy around in circles. Since the silk was as black as coal, it would stand out against the smooth gray rock of the tabletop mesa.

It appeared to work. The mail plane banked sharply, sliding in his direction.

Doc Savage gave the silk another dragging turn around the table top, then dropped it and took to waving his arms as best he could. They were stiff and sore.

It became clear when the aircraft dipped that the pilot had noticed him.

Something exceedingly strange transpired.

AT FIRST, Doc noticed what appeared to be a disturbance in the stunningly blue sky. There was a lack of clouds, so he had a clear view of what happened next.

It was difficult to describe. It was as if the azure of the sky had taken on the qualities of a slightly darker blue sea. It was difficult to make out, even with someone possessing the visual acuity of the Man of Bronze.

Undeniably, the clear blue sky turned dense and discolored. For the phenomenon originated behind the Black Hills to the east, climbing into the sky like a cloudburst going in the wrong direction.

This was not rain. It was nothing like rain. It was something else. Something uncanny.

The pilot appeared not to notice the disturbance, for his attention seemed to be upon the solitary figure balanced atop Devils Tower.

And so, oblivious to the changing atmospherics, the Air Mail plane blundered into the disturbance, whatever it was.

The results were catastrophic. Unbelievably so.

The propeller came apart. The nose of the mail plane was pushed inward, the motor slamming into the control cockpit. The droning aircraft jarred to a shaky stop. And then the rest of the plane began disintegrating.

The exact manner by which this happened made it look as if

the high-winged monoplane had blundered into an obstruction that could not be seen. Something palpable, but invisible—or nearly so.

The plane shuddered, its component parts popping at every rivet and spar. Wing bracing wires sprang loose. Those disturbing details Doc witnessed through his spyglass.

Destruction of the Air Mail ship was rapid, and complete. Doc watched to see if the pilot threw himself clear, but knew that he must have been crushed by the bizarre aerial impact.

But that was not the most astonishing thing. The fragments of the aircraft, which included the shattered wings, did not fall to earth as they would normally.

Instead, they simply floated about as if suspended in some invisible solution. The suspension utterly defied gravity. But the pieces of the plane which had been violently disbursed soon settled down to drift about in some unknown medium that was almost indistinguishable from the blue sky.

Doc studied this through his telescope. His flake-gold eyes whirled strangely. Then he made, without being aware of doing so, a tuneless vocalization that was an unconscious habit invariably prompted by stress or surprise. The melodious emanation sprang forth, startled and a bit aghast, before ebbing into nothingness. It made an eerie accompaniment to the phenomenon in the sky.

Plane fragments whirled about aimlessly in a confined space that seemed as large as a football field, perhaps larger.

There was no explaining the destruction of the aircraft. The weird suspension of its remains was utterly inexplicable.

Then the motor began falling, as if gravity had discovered it. Doc had his eye on it because this was the heaviest surviving piece of the aircraft. Not that it was intact. It was obviously not. But most of it was. The engine began to fall first with a slowness that was agonizing, and then with increasing speed.

Watching this phenomenon, the bronze man thought back

to his experience on the previous night when the reverse had happened to him. It was not pleasant to relive.

Slowly, inevitably, the other portions of the aircraft also showed signs of sinking. They did not fall. Not yet. But they sank as if in water. Gathering momentum, the disintegrated ship picked up velocity. As the bronze man watched, fascinated, the dismembered aircraft plummeted back to earth. Doc thought he could see the pilot mixed in with the debris. The pilot did not flail about, nor did his form appear to be whole. There was no question that he did not survive the strange impact.

Doc observed the whirling conglomeration of parts disappear behind the Black Hills. Dimly, he could hear the impact of the engine echoing. Sounds of the other pieces landing did not carry to his ears.

There was nothing to be done. Doc Savage made painful fists on either side of his erect body. Knuckles showed white against the bronze of his skin.

Before very long, a sprinkle of rain struck him in the face and he could see all around him other droplets. Yet there was no cloud in the sky.

Doc Savage thought back to the strange story Pat Savage had told him of the man seen swimming in the sky whose body had landed in a moist patch where no rain should have fallen.

That gave the bronze man a lot to consider. Inasmuch as his hope of immediate rescue had come to pieces before his eyes, he gathered up the silken parachute again, made a comfortable place to sit and commenced his mental chewing.

Doc spent an hour at this, then he removed from a large flat pocket something that looked like a cigarette case but was not. It consisted of a silver metal casing, a grilled loudspeaker, and a few buttons and dials.

It was a radio transceiver. Battery operated. Its range was very limited and Doc knew that he had drifted far from the spot called Pumpkin Buttes, impelled by stratospheric air currents.

The bronze man had not wished to employ the device prematurely because its short battery life made it risky to waste.

Now he pressed a button in the side, began speaking into the loudspeaker which also served as a microphone.

"Doc Savage calling Doc-1. Doc Savage calling Doc-1."

"Doc-1" was the designation for his big speed plane, the one Johnny Littlejohn had been piloting the night before. He knew that Renny in the gyroplane radio would also be tuned to this frequency.

What Doc did not expect was that they would be within range of the radio transceiver. Nor was he surprised when he failed to raise either aircraft.

It stood to reason that his men would be conducting an aerial search throughout the day. It was Doc's plan to signal them at intervals in the hope of becoming lucky.

For the bronze man was not greatly disturbed when no one replied. In another hour or so, he intended to try again.

In the meantime, Doc considered all that he had seen and heard, and bent his master brain to the task of solving this new mystery Pat Savage had stumbled upon.

Chapter XIX

GRIM SEARCH

THEY TOOK OFF at first light.

Long Tom piloted the streamlined bumblebee of a gyroplane, since he was somewhat familiar with this portion of Wyoming.

He and Johnny Littlejohn had carried Pat Savage to the big bronze-painted plane, where she had passed the night quietly. The unconscious girl had acquired numerous scrapes and bruises, but was not seriously injured.

Eventually, the copper-haired girl awoke, sat up, felt of her neck and stared about wildly, her golden eyes stark.

Wrinkling her forehead at her surroundings, she gulped, "Wh-where am I?"

"In Doc's big bus," Renny told her.

Struggling to get to her feet, for she had been lying in the rear, Pat said, "Let me speak with Doc. I have a lot to tell him."

"You'll have to wait."

"Nothing doing! Kindly step out of my way."

Pat stumbled then. She noticed one boot was missing. She caught herself, grabbed hold of the back of a seat and flung herself into it, where she fumed like wood burning.

"I feel like I just climbed out of a nightmare," she declared. "Would it be too much to ask my cousin to come back and see to my health?"

Seeing the cut of her mood, Renny thumped, "We're searching for Doc. We don't know what happened to him."

This did not improve Pat's disposition appreciably.

"Let's hear your tale."

Renny told it as best he could, and as he rumbled along gloomily, Pat's expression grew slack and worried. The gold in her eyes got a little dull.

She brought her brown fingers to her mouth and her lips trembled. The fingertips shook, too.

"He can't be dead...."

Renny sighed like a leaky steam boiler.

"He went up like a rocket and never did come back down. We checked the immediate area. Now we're going to conduct a wider search."

Anger wrinkled Pat's nose. "Why didn't you search all night?"

"I know it sounds loco, but Johnny pointed out that, if Doc were somehow floating through the night sky, our propeller blades might damage him, living or not."

Now shock made Pat's eyes round and the tawny color of her features grew cold and drained.

"Doc," she gasped. "Oh, Doc!"

"We won't know anything until we find him," Renny assured her. "And one way or another, we'll find Doc," he added firmly.

The expression on the long-faced engineer's countenance was peculiar. Renny typically looked as if he had just returned from a funeral. Now the corners of his prim mouth quirked up and his eyes crinkled in a way that looked like a craggy smile was trying to break through the frowning granite of his countenances.

It was another peculiarity of Renny Renwick that the more morose he appeared, the happier he was. Conversely, the opposite was true. When he seemed close to smiling, that meant he was miserable. A grin denoted deep unhappiness.

On the floor of the plane near the rear was affixed a red quartz lens. A porthole of sorts. This was designed to work in conjunction with an infra-red lamp mounted on one wing. Other floor portholes were filled with clear Plexiglass.

Together, these permitted the ground to be observed as it rolled beneath the plane's bronze wings. The cabin was soundproofed and so its mighty motors reverberated dully.

Stalking over to the infra-red floor port, Renny stared downward, his big fists bunching.

"If you turn on the heat scanner," he called ahead to Johnny at the controls, "we might be able to pick up the warmth of his body."

It was a testament to how rattled the long-worded archaeologist was that he snapped back in unadorned English, "A body would be cold by now."

Hearing that, Pat Savage flung herself out of her seat, pushed herself forward and dropped into the co-pilot's bucket.

She stabbed the man in the pilot's seat with golden eyes gone brittle with scorn.

William Harper Littlejohn had been the name on his certificate of birth, but he was called, for some reason, "Johnny." There was near to seven feet of him, all of it hung on a frame a skeleton would have thought emaciated. He was about as bony as a living man could be. His studious face was narrow, and his hair worn full and long. His hair looked better fed than he.

"Listen to me, you long bag of bones," Pat scolded. "You turn on that infra-red scanner. And you turn on every gadget and gimcrack you have at your disposal. We're going to find Doc Savage, one way or another."

"Indubitably," said Johnny, regaining his self-mastery. He began flipping switches and myriad devices became illuminated.

Pat reached down into a seat pocket and pulled out a pair of binoculars. She began scanning out the side windows.

The terrain was rugged. Spindly sandstone spires, as well as the rocky totem-pole like formations known locally has hoodoos, divided the landscape. It was a forbidding spot. Wild cliffs, mesas and buttes broke stretches of prairie flats. Little water.

The colors were sometimes fantastic, and other times distressingly dull.

Locating one man, living or otherwise, in this vastness was not promising to contemplate. It might as well have been the Sahara Desert.

Over the cockpit radio, Long Tom's voice came acidly from the patrolling gyroplane.

"Anything?"

"Nothing," said Johnny. "You?"

"If I found anything, I wouldn't be asking you if you found anything, now would I?" retorted Long Tom in his most peevish tone of voice.

"Dry up, you sawed-off vacuum tube," returned Johnny hotly.

It was evident that nerves were rubbed raw. Ordinarily, neither man was particularly argumentative with one another.

And so it went. They criss-crossed northeast Wyoming, the airplane flying high enough to take in large vistas while the plodding gyroplane hugged the ground, looking to spot any movement visible there.

It was lonely territory, forbidding and desolate. The lack of habitations was disconcerting. Even the skies appeared empty. Evidently, few planes crossed this corner of the state.

One, however, did happen along. Pat spotted it from a distance. Training her binoculars upon it, she remarked, "I spy an Air Mail plane."

From the radio cubicle, Renny's foghorn voice boomed out, "I'll try to raise him on the government wavelength. Just in case he saw something."

Turning the dial to the proper setting, he began chanting into the microphone.

"This is Doc Savage-1 calling U.S. Mail plane over northeastern Wyoming. Come in, Air Mail plane."

Renny repeated himself several times, but there was no response. The loudspeaker merely hissed in a listless manner.

ABRUPTLY, the plane banked, and its maneuver seemed to suggest something unusual, for Air Mail planes normally fly as straight as an arrow between their point of departure and their destination city.

Pat exclaimed hopefully, "He may have spotted something on the ground!"

Whether the pilot had indeed seen something was never learned.

The government plane was far away. Only Pat could see it through her binoculars clearly.

The high-winged plane banked, changed its heading and ran smack into something. It came apart as if it had exploded from internal pressure.

"Oh, my goodness!" Pat yelled out. "It broke up!"

Aghast, Renny demanded, "The dang plane?"

"Yes, the plane! It seemed to explode but..." Pat's excited voice trailed off.

She had taken her eyes off the accident, so horrific was the sight. But now she brought the lenses back to her eyes and what she beheld filled her with uncharacteristic fear.

For the pieces of the plane were floating about as if in suspension—floating in the clear blue sky.

"It's not falling," she said in dull disbelief. "The pieces, I mean." Realization dawned upon her amazed brain. "It's just like that poor cowpoke, Hud. He floated around, too, until he started falling."

Renny had poked his unruly head into the cockpit, took the field glasses from Pat's hands and made good use of them.

"Holy cow! The plane pieces are just hanging in the sky. Not just hanging, swimming around. It's like gravity has stopped operating."

"Now do you gentlemen believe me?" Pat asked sharply.

"I never said I didn't," Renny thumped back. Then his pet expression came again. "Holy cow, it's starting to fall now!"

"Give me that," said Pat. Reclaiming the field glasses, she trained them on the phenomenon. As she watched in horror, the disorderly pieces of the aircraft commenced tumbling, slowly at first. Then with increasing speed.

At the controls, Johnny looked frustrated. He couldn't see a thing. The aircraft was too far away. He shifted the control wheel and directed the plane toward the bright patch of sky where the aircraft had come apart.

Noticing this, Pat Savage pleaded, "What are you doing? Do you want to fly smack into the same thing that wrecked that ship?"

"Is there anything there?"

"Not that I can see, but that doesn't mean there isn't something unseeable high in the sky. Something held that broken plane together until gravity got around to exerting its pull. Don't go near it, whatever you do."

Pat's normally warm voice was so charged with emotion that Johnny sheared the aircraft in the opposite direction, his thin features worried.

The skeletal archaeologist circled for a time, unsure what to do. It was as if the sky contained an invisible mine field and they had no idea what it looked like.

Renny had the binoculars again and was studying the ground where the pieces of the airplane were striking. They sent up spurts and then growing clouds of dust that were brown and red and very noticeable.

His "Holy cow!" was muted this time, freighted with wonder and puzzlement.

"What is it?" demanded Johnny.

Clouds of dust were being kicked up by the plane, but now they evaporated. And the ground became dark in a uniform way.

Renny studied this and decided, "Plumb looks to me like a cloudburst followed that plane down—kind of a localized cloudburst."

Johnny scanned the skies with his penetrating eyes. "No clouds of any type. Nothing to produce a cloudburst. Couldn't be. It has to be something else."

Renny rumbled, "I think I know rain when I see it, and I think I recognize water when it darkens dry soil."

"Rain doesn't fall from an empty sky. You know that."

Pat cut into the growing disagreement. "We should land and look for survivors."

Renny shook his head. "Long Tom will have to do that. There's no place for a big bird like this to safely touch down. And I wouldn't count on any survivors. There would only be the pilot, anyway. It's certain he's a goner."

Returning to the radio cubicle, Renny raised Long Tom and told his story.

Long Tom said nothing in return. Renny described the terrain in the general direction of the air accident, after which Long Tom responded, *"I'll be there shortly."*

"No sign of Doc Savage," added Renny. "But I guess you know that."

"I know that," replied Long Tom sullenly.

It was while they were circling the terrain that Pat Savage noticed the monstrous sheer mesa jutting up from the ground like a stupendous tree stump. Its color was a very pale gray mixed with hints of tan. Vertical black grooves ran from its rugged based to the flat top. They were impressive in an other-worldly way.

Studying the deeply scored sides, Renny wondered, "Isn't that the thing they call Devils Tower?"

This question was directed to Johnny Littlejohn who, in addition to being an archaeologist of great fame, was one of the world's foremost geologists. If anybody would know the landmark by sight, it would be him.

"Yes, that is Devils Tower. It is composed of porphyry."

Pat blinked. "Did you say 'pottery?'"

"No, *porphyry*. Phonolite porphyry, to be precise. And the formation is not, technically, a mesa. It is a laccolithic butte, a volcanic extrusion. It sits upon a broad mesa, which forms its base. During the Paleocene Epoch, roughly sixty million years ago, the surrounding Black Hills were uplifted, with the result that...."

Johnny's recitation of the geological history of the impressive volcanic remnant seemed to wind on and on. Pat Savage soon stopped listening. She was more interested in the look of the impressive formation than its geologic origins.

As the plane approached, she spotted something black moving upon the table top. It was quite large. It seemed to flutter like a dark flower in the wind.

"I wonder what that thing is...." she mused.

"What does it look like?" asked Johnny, squinting.

"A big black flower blowing in the breeze."

"How big can a flower grow?"

"If that's a flower, it's the size of the crown of a oak tree."

"Therefore," said Johnny in his scholastic tone, "it could not be a flower."

"You said that it was black?" demanded Renny, poking his head back into the cockpit.

Pat offered the binoculars. "See for yourself. Why?"

"Because Doc Savage's parachute was black."

Johnny, Renny and Pat Savage all exchanged violent glances.

Leveling a gigantic forefinger, Renny blared, "Fly over that mesa, pronto!"

Renny ducked back into the radio cubicle, dialed back to the Doc Savage frequency and began calling to the bronze man by name.

He received no answer. But that did not dissuade him. He kept calling, his thundering bear-in-a-cave voice punishing their eardrums with every syllable. It was as if Renny was determined to summon up the Man of Bronze by sheer force of volume alone.

Chapter XX

MYSTERY IN THE MUD

DOC SAVAGE HEARD the distinctive drone belonging to the motors of his big speed plane.

Extracting his transceiver radio, he turned it on and began calling.

"Doc Savage calling Doc-1."

The bronze man had to speak only once before the loudspeaker crackled with Renny's thunderous tones.

"Doc, is that you stuck up on Devils Tower?"

"It is. I've been up here all night. Where is the gyroplane?"

"Long Tom's got it. Let me raise him for you."

"Right."

Doc was able to hear the conversation that followed.

Long Tom said, *"I can be there in twenty minutes or so."*

"Did you hear that?" demanded Renny of Doc.

"Yes," replied Doc. "The gyroplane is my only way down. I am relatively undamaged, but my hands have suffered lacerations. They will need first-aid."

Renny asked, *"How did you manage to get up there?"*

"By falling down from a great height," stated Doc without humor or irony. "I was able to deploy my reserve parachute after my unfortunate encounter."

Pat Savage flung herself out of the chair and into the radio cubicle.

"Do you believe me now?"

"My education is complete," admitted the bronze man. "We will discuss this later. Renny, a United States Air Mail plane encountered trouble north of here. It has crashed."

"We all saw it go down. It was stupefying."

"That," said Doc Savage, "is probably the correct word to use."

With that, Doc signed off to conserve his strength. It had been a long night. And not exactly an enjoyable morning. He had started to wonder what chipmunk tasted like.

Long Tom set down the gyroplane on the south side of Devils Tower, where it was most level.

Doc retreated to the north, covering his face with a clump of parachute silk to protect his eyes from dust and the inevitable grit the whirling rotor blades kicked up.

The puny electrical wizard managed a perfect three-point landing, and the cabin door popped open. He came out on the run, carrying a canteen of water and a first-aid kit.

"Water first," requested Doc.

Long Tom unscrewed the cap and Doc drank steadily. To Long Tom's amazement, he drained the canteen, which was not small.

Then Doc dropped the canteen and held out his hands.

Long Tom examined them carefully, saw lacerations but nothing so deep that the tendons had been nicked. Under Doc's expert guidance, he began his ministrations.

Long Tom commented, "Probably should've saved some canteen water to wash out these wounds."

"Use the iodine instead," directed Doc.

Long Tom rummaged through the first-aid kit. "There's Mercurochrome in here."

"Save that for later."

Long Tom did his best, then Doc took over, doing his own bandaging.

That accomplished, they walked back to the gyroplane.

To Long Tom's surprise, Doc Savage claimed the pilot seat.

Evidently, he felt his hands were up to the task of piloting the dragonfly ship.

Once they were beating through the air, Doc Savage stated, "The first order of business is to investigate the mail plane wreckage." He repeated this into the radio microphone.

From the speed ship, Renny radioed back, *"We'll find someplace to land while you do that. We have a lot to talk about."*

"Correct," stated Doc, sending the gyroplane scooting northward.

THE AREA where the plane had crash landed was a muddy stew of disturbed ground and aircraft pieces. They had to land some distance away because the crash site was a vast mud hole.

"Where did all this water come from?" Long Tom grumbled as they picked their way forward, their boots becoming encrusted with foul muck.

Doc stated, "There is a lake not far from here. Or there was."

"Do you think the lake got thrown into the air?"

"Pat claimed that a swimming hole suffered the same fate, carrying with it an unfortunate man who happened to be swimming there at the time. If a lake had somehow been hurled skyward, its waters would not have been visible to the naked eye, except possibly as a discoloration against the clear blue sky."

Carefully, they slogged their way along, and soon encountered airplane parts, some quite small, but others were sizable. One wing was standing upright like a rigid shard of duralumin sail.

The deeper they ventured, the more trouble they had walking. The ground was impossibly muddy. Their boots made sucking sounds and they walked with great deliberateness. Once Long Tom's right foot got caught in the mud and Doc had to help him get extricated. They noticed pollywogs and wiggle worms struggling in the mire.

They found the pilot's battered head first. Further along, his lower body. The disintegration of the aircraft had torn the body to pieces. The unfortunate man's eyes were wide and staring in death. Doc closed them.

They did not expect to discover anything else of significance until Doc Savage spied a shape covered in mud. He directed his attention on it, studied the form briefly and decided it was worth investigating.

Reaching the shape, he discovered it was another corpse. Doc had watched the pilot's body fall and knew there had been no passenger aboard the government mail plane. This person therefore had not fallen from the demolished aircraft.

The body was lying face downward. Kneeling, Doc overturned it. His trilling piped up briefly. It was a woman, her hair and face covered in mud. The woman's bones seemed to have been pulverized, suggesting that she had fallen from a great height and not simply been caught in the deluge of water and aircraft debris. She wore Western garb, which included a split skirt favored by active horsewomen.

Despite that, her features were not badly damaged and Doc studied them, rather intently.

The bronze man called over to Long Tom. "Come here."

The slender electrical wizard grumbled as he made his difficult way over. When he halted, he released a low, feeling oath.

"Damn! That's Alta Crater...."

"Who is Alta Crater?" demanded Doc, standing up.

"She was the woman who kept trying to run me out of Wyoming, thinking I was a mule thief and general owlhoot to boot. She's the brother of Hud Crater, the bird that Pat saw swimming in the sky. She's from the Lynx Eyes Ranch from where a bunch of the mules have been rustled."

"This sounds complicated," remarked Doc.

Long Tom rubbed his jaw. "More than I figured. She was with us last night when Quest tried to hang me and Pat. After everything had settled down, we couldn't find hide nor hair of her. So, what's she doing way out here, miles from Pumpkin Buttes?"

"From the looks of it," remarked Doc, "she had been in the lake when it was levitated."

"That hardly makes any sense." Suddenly, Long Tom snapped his fingers. "You don't suppose that she had slipped into the car before Quest and the other one drove off with it?"

"Tell me more about that," invited Doc.

Long Tom went into a careful recitation of the events of the evening. When he had concluded it, Doc Savage was very quiet.

"It is conceivable that Miss Crater was somehow involved with the vigilante gang, or possibly with the other individual, the one in green who dubbed himself Mr. Calamity. But it's more likely that she became a victim of either of those individuals after she was discovered hiding in the automobile."

Doc Savage continued his examination of the body. He noticed that the woman's fingernails were broken. Examining this damage, the bronze man discovered coarse fibers caught in the nails. Removing one of these, he cleaned it off, put a magnifying glass to it.

"Gunnysack threads," he pronounced.

Long Tom exploded, "The rustler known as Quest wore a makeshift gunnysack hood! She must have tussled with him."

"This would seem to prove your theory, Long Tom. This woman was discovered in the fleeing auto and done away with for some reason."

"But why?"

Doc considered. "If she fought back, as seems likely, the gunnysack hood might have come off, revealing Quest's features. If Miss Crater recognized him, that might be a motive for murder."

Long Tom looked down at the late Alta Crater. "I wish we had something to cover her with."

Doc imparted, "We will alert the government authorities. Destruction of a United States Air Mail plane is a federal matter. Not to mention the emptying of a local lake. Let us return to the gyroplane and be on our way."

As they trudged back, Long Tom wondered. "Where are we bound?"

"It is first necessary to put our heads together and assemble our narratives. Your ranch is the most private place for that. We will radio government officials en route. They can conduct their own examination without us."

"We'll have to inform the town of Bison that their sheriff is dead. That's going to complicate matters, as well."

Doc nodded grimly. "Evidently, it has been a very violent last twenty-four hours in this section of Wyoming."

Long Tom grunted, "I'm starting to regret taking over my great-uncle's spread."

Chapter XXI

THE OPPOSITE OF GRAVITY

THE REUNION AT the modest Circle Bolt Ranch was unusually emotional.

Johnny landed last, owing to the necessity of picking out an appropriate spot on the prairie, where Long Tom's and Pat Savage's aircraft were parked.

The big speed plane was an amphibian, so it was necessary to drag the meadow several times for obstructions in the buffalo grass lest the float hull be damaged during the unavoidably bumpy landing.

Once the aircraft's motors ceased blooping, the gyroplane alighted nearby.

By the time it did, everyone had piled out of the big bronze amphibian and pounded in the direction of the agile dragonfly craft.

Doc Savage emerged, ducking under the slowing rotor blades. Only when he finally stood erect did his great size become apparent. It was an optical illusion of his symmetrical frame that, when standing beside some object which provided visual reference, his true stature was emphasized.

Although the bronze giant had passed the most difficult night of his remarkable existence thus far, he showed few signs of this. Rather, as he stepped forward, he resembled a being formed of indestructible metal. His hair, only a shade darker than his metallic skin, lay flat and smooth like a skullcap of hammered bronze.

Seeing him, Pat Savage gave a glad cry, rushed forward and threw herself into his arms.

Doc offered a somewhat awkward hug. Normally, the cousins were not prone to such outward displays, especially the bronze man, who had been schooled from childhood to keep his emotions under firm restraint.

Too, Doc Savage had not met his younger cousin until he was fully grown and she was a teenager. This was several years ago. So, although they had formed a close bond in the intervening years, they were not usually this familiar with one another.

"Oh," cried Pat, her voice choking. "We really believed you were dead this time. Dead beyond all hope."

Releasing her, the bronze giant said simply, "It was a very near thing."

"You'll have to tell us all about it. I imagined you'd been catapulted to the moon, never to return." Noticing his bandaged fingers, Pat asked anxiously, "What happened to your hands?"

"Circumstances forced me to hold my reserve parachute with my bare hands. The damage is not permanent, but it will be a few days before my fingers will function without pain or stiffness."

Renny was saying, "We tried every way possible to locate you. But we were afraid you were floating up in the air. We didn't want to mangle you with our propellers by blundering around blindly."

"As preposterous as that sounds," asserted the bronze man, "it was a reasonable precaution. I was catapulted into the lower stratosphere for a time. It is not impossible you might have plowed into me as I parachuted back to earth."

Johnny remarked, "I endeavored to locate you through the radioactive token you carried, but there appear to be significant deposits of radium and pitchblende in some of these hills. I could not tell one hot spot from the other."

"No matter," stated Doc. "Let's put our heads together and see where this mystery has its center."

Together, they entered the modest ranch house and they sat around on Western-style furniture while Pat made coffee, ham and scrambled eggs.

Doc Savage examined Long Tom's gunshot wounds, replaced his flour-sack arm sling with a better one and pronounced the graze wound to his temple well on its way to healing.

"Whoever tended these wounds," noted the bronze giant, "did a serviceable job under the circumstances."

"That was Laramie, my foreman," said Long Tom. "He's more of a horse doctor, but I guess he did all right."

Laramie had been returned to the ranch house overnight, and was sleeping. They let him be.

The aromas of breakfast soon roused the old Westerner, however, and he came limping out of a bedroom. When he saw Doc Savage, he blinked owlishly.

"Even sittin' down," he remarked, "you're a tall hombre."

"Take a seat, you old reprobate," snapped Long Tom. "Or you'll miss your fair share."

"Don't mind if I do," Laramie said, dragging himself into an empty chair. Turning to Doc Savage, he asked, "I hear you're a medico. I got me a busted-up leg. Maybe you got some pills for the pain."

"I will examine you after we eat," promised Doc.

Laramie grinned. "Grub before doctorin'. We'll get along just fine, you and me."

Doc Savage did not normally take stimulants, but to everyone's surprise, the bronze man drank two cups of coffee. Black with sugar. This uncharacteristic act told the others that his body was starved for energy.

Despite his injured arm, Long Tom helped with the cooking and caused jaws to sag when he reported, "Doc and I found Alta Crater in the mud around that Air Mail plane wreckage. Doc thinks she fell from a great height."

Pat's mouth went round and her eyes sharpened. "How terrible! She died just like her brother!"

Renny rumbled, "That can't be a coincidence."

Long Tom said, "We lost track of her last night, but it looks like she was hiding in that car when Quest and the other one took off. One of them may have thrown her in the lake, possibly to drown."

"You mean that lake up by Devils Tower?" Laramie demanded.

Doc Savage offered, "It appears that the lake was levitated in the same amazing manner as Pat's swimming hole. Suspended in the air, it became a huge body of organized water into which the Air Mail plane blundered, with catastrophic results."

Hearing this, Johnny mused, "Perhaps we should start our recitations from their point of origin, so that our accounts unfold chronologically."

Everyone understood him because it was a peculiarity of Johnny that he never used his jawbreaker words in front of Doc Savage.

Pat Savage interjected, "Let me suggest that we begin with breakfast, which we all heartily require. Then we can share our stories."

BREAKFAST was consumed with deliberation and no idle talk. At the end of it, Pat announced brightly, "I should go first, since it was my mystery to begin with." Her golden eyes lanced in Doc Savage's direction. The bronze man looked slightly uncomfortable.

Pat started with her encounter with the late Hud Crater while she had been out prospecting. She summarized all pertinent events up to the point where she had raced toward the spot where the cowpoke had slammed back to earth and summoned Long Tom Roberts.

During this recitation, Long Tom added, "There was nobody there when we got to the swimming hole. But Pat said Hud's corpse had landed hard a few hours before."

Doc Savage suggested, "Evidently, someone made off with the body for some reason."

"Probably Mr. Calamity, whoever he is," suggested Pat.

Doc nodded in agreement, but said nothing. He was on his third helping of eggs.

"Aren't we getting ahead of ourselves?" asked Renny. "I thought we were reciting this according to the calendar."

Pat resumed her story, detailing her strange encounter with the garishly-garbed shotgun wielder, and the bizarre circumstances that had deposited her atop a high butte, her escape and the circumstances that led to being unceremoniously jugged in Bison.

Doc paused in his eating long enough to comment. "Events so far indicate that Mr. Calamity wields a shotgun whose charge can produce inexplicable results."

Doc asked Pat to describe Oakley Wood and the masked man who abducted her from the Bison jail.

"Could they have been the same man?" asked Doc.

Pat considered. "Wood had an awful lot of white hair on his wrists and the other man—if it was another man—wore tooled leather wrist cuffs."

"Did you notice either man's boots?" pressed Doc.

Pat frowned unhappily. "I confess that I did not. Guess I'm a bum sleuth."

Laramie scowled without venom. "First things a body gets to noticin' out here is the cut and color of a man's boots."

"Please continue with your story," said the bronze man.

Pat obliged, reciting everything until the point she had been knocked unconscious during the attempted hanging, after which Long Tom Roberts told his side of the story.

Hearing how Long Tom had kicked her horse, forcing her neck out of the noose, Pat Savage flared indignantly, "If the horse had bolted in another direction, my neck might have been broken!"

"And if I hadn't done what I did," retorted Long Tom, "you were sure to die by slow strangulation. We were in a tough spot. I did the best I could."

Pat looked only slightly mollified. She felt of her neck and the rope burns there. Noticing this, Long Tom did the same. They shared an uncomfortable silence.

Doc Savage was particularly interested in Pat's account of the shotgun blast that had sent her and the unfortunate horse Lightning to the top of one of the high buttes.

"Were you struck by any of the charge?" he asked.

The golden-eyed girl shook her head. "No, thank goodness. Lightning took the brunt of it."

Doc Savage then went into his experience after having parachuted down into the midst of the frustrated lynching, with the intention of breaking it up.

He spoke simply and without emotion, but as the bronze giant related in stark terms the details of his stratospheric ordeal, all eyes got a little round and mouths started hanging open.

Laramie grunted, "You got more lives than a cat. In fact, it sounds like you might've used up all nine last night. I don't think all the Greek gods put together, from Apollo to Zeus, could have wrought the miracle you did."

Doc Savage said nothing. He looked a little uncomfortable; the bronze giant was by nature modest.

After all accounts had been absorbed, they began to pick the tangled ball of yarn apart.

Johnny mused, "It does not appear that Quest and Mr. Calamity are connected. Even though they fled together."

Long Tom grunted, "The last I saw of them, that Calamity character had a shotgun pressed against Quest's skull."

Johnny murmured, "One of them probably didn't survive the night."

Renny rumbled, "My money would be on Quest coming out the loser."

"What makes you say that?" demanded Long Tom skeptically.

"Because that shotgun seems to have stirred up an entire lake and Calamity is the one who knows how to use it. Therefore, it was him that caused that mail plane wreck."

"Makes sense," allowed Pat.

Doc Savage suddenly asked, "Pat, do you have specimens of those shotgun pellets?"

Pat shook her coppery-bronze hair. "I came across a piece, but didn't keep it. Reminded me of rock salt, but it was yellowish."

Johnny snorted, "Rock salt possesses no properties that defy gravity."

"Does *anything* known to science?" challenged Pat.

A long silence fell. Doc Savage and his men became queer of expression. They shifted in their seats.

Noticing this unusual behavior, Pat remarked, "You boys are holding out on me. What do you know that you don't want to talk about?"

Johnny cleared his throat. "A few years back we were all in the South Seas when a volcano coughed up a substance never before known. This substance had the properties of a powerful force that acted against all other objects." *

Long Tom nodded. "Yeah. Kinda like a reverse lodestone."

"You're not making an ounce of sense," Pat observed.

Doc Savage took up the tale. "The substance was dubbed 'Repel.' It acted upon physical objects in a way similar to the shotgun charge that inflicts such calamitous consequences."

Renny asked gloomily, "But this can't be pieces of Repel, can it? You can't hardly manage the blamed stuff. It pushes everything away. It's like the opposite of gravity."

Doc said carefully, "We appear to be seeing the effects of Repel. We don't understand the exact cause, but we cannot

---

* *Repel,* also titled *The Deadly Dwarf*

discount any possibilities. When the volcano coughed up that chunk of Repel, the stuff was catapulted across the Pacific Ocean and over half the continental United States of America. Reports were it first impacted somewhere in Wyoming before bouncing upward again and landing in the Lake of the Ozarks, Missouri."

Johnny breathed. "It might be conceivable that a fragment of Repel was driven deep into the earth, or shards scattered thereabouts during that first impact."

Long Tom said, "Well, why didn't they just fly up again? Repel pushes against everything, unless something strong is holding it down. For a long time, it was stuck in that volcano plug."

Doc Savage offered, "It might be wise to consider that there might be a deposit of Repel here in Wyoming and the individual who calls himself Mr. Calamity stumbled upon it, and somehow achieved control over the unstable element."

"Well, he won't be hard to find," Long Tom snapped. "He looks like a walking Christmas tree. He'll stick out like cactus in a snowbank."

Doc said, "We will not leave Quest out of our investigations."

Long Tom snorted, "His rustler gang is broken up and most are probably dead. He won't be much of a menace going forward."

"Any man willing to hang innocent parties to cover up for his own crimes will always be a menace," stated Doc. "We will run down Quest, as well as Mr. Calamity."

Renny rumbled, "Assuming either of them are still alive."

THE QUESTION was destined to hang in the air for not very long after.

The noon hour had come and gone; the day was heating up.

Doc had employed the telephone to speak with local, state and federal authorities. He held a special agent's commission with the Department of Justice and was given great deference. He relayed as much of his accumulated discoveries as seemed reasonable without inviting unhelpful skepticism, and promised to remain in close communication with all appropriate parties.

After he had hung up, Pat said, "You didn't tell them about the kidnapper's missing automobile."

"It might be too dangerous for ordinary authorities to attempt to run it down. That shotgun is formidable. We will find it."

But before they could get underway, a shadow passed over the sun. This brought several of them to windows, looking out to see what had blotted out the solar rays.

Pat spied the problem first. "Parachute!" she called out. "Someone is dropping in on us. And I mean literally."

There was a general rush for the door. Doc Savage was the first out.

The parachute was white, and the figure swinging from it was definitely green.

Long Tom burst out, "It's that Calamity character! Everybody get ready. He means trouble."

Supermachine pistols were produced, and safety latches thrown.

Doc Savage had his pocket telescope out and was studying the descending figure. His trilling filtered out, low and a little weird.

"He signifies trouble all right, but not the kind you mean, Long Tom," imparted Doc.

"What do *you* mean?" demanded Pat, shading her eyes against the sun.

Doc turned to her and said gently, "Go indoors, Pat."

Pat stood her ground. Her hands went to her lean hips. "Just because I don't have my six-gun doesn't mean I can't handle myself."

"The man dropping from the sky is not bringing a fight."

"How do you know that?"

"Because he is hanging in the shroud lines, completely limp. And he appears to have no head."

Pat put one hand to her mouth and looked a little sick. "Maybe I need a glass of water, after all. Excuse me, please."

Chapter XXII

THE HEADLESS DEVIL

THE BODY LANDED like a sack of unshucked corn. The color of the dead man's garb suggested that idea.

When his long boot heels hit the ground, he fell over to one side with a smack. Collapsing shroud lines and parachute material enveloped him, ironically enough, like a settling shroud.

Doc Savage rushed up, fell to pulling away at the parachute fabric, and swiftly uncovered the body.

It was an ugly sight. The man's head had been removed cleanly—probably with a corn knife, or some similar blade.

Going through the corpse's pockets, Doc Savage discovered no wallet or other items of identification. There was nothing to show who the man really was. A flicker of disappointment showed in the bronze man's eyes. The cognomen "Mr. Calamity" was hardly helpful.

The others stood around, watching. Doc Savage asked Long Tom, "Does this look like the individual you encountered?"

"Those are his togs, all right. But I can't tell for certain."

Renny was searching the sky with hard eyes. "Wonder where he came from?"

Doc Savage ventured, "He might have been catapulted skyward by a Repel blast, whereupon his parachute opened fully, the wind carrying the body in our direction by design."

Dropping his gaze, Renny grunted, "That means the culprit's around here somewhere. But where?"

The bronze giant seemed unconcerned by that possibility. He inspected the man's hands. They were soft and well-manicured.

"These are not the fingers of a working cowboy," decided Doc.

"I didn't get the impression that anybody duded up like that ever did much in the way of cowboying," Long Tom muttered.

The bronze man gave the nails careful study. Clinging to one was a fragment of what appeared to be yarn. He plucked it free, holding it up to the light.

Long Tom gave it his attention.

"Gunnysack fiber?"

Doc nodded. "We will take fingerprint impressions and see what they tell us," he stated.

"I'll get the fingerprint kit," offered Renny, bounding back to the big plane, which was crammed with scientific equipment.

Doc studied the man's fingertips. He possessed a nearly photographic memory and had studied the fingerprint impressions of known criminals in the F.B.I. files and elsewhere. It was entirely possible for him to identify individual fingerprints by sight, provided he had seen them before.

"I do not recognize these prints," admitted the bronze man.

"That doesn't mean he's not a crook," said Renny. "Just a crook whose prints you haven't seen."

Doc Savage continued his examination. The man did not appear to be wounded, except for the raw stump of his neck. This suggested that he had been decapitated while living, or, at the very least, while asleep.

Renny rumbled, "Bet that Quest bird done that."

Long Tom countered, "Until we're sure, no one can say that this isn't someone else's body dressed up like Calamity. It would be a smart way to make us think Calamity was dead."

"Until we run down Mr. Calamity's actual identity, either proposition is equally possible," allowed Doc Savage.

The bronze man had accepted the fingerprint kit from the big-fisted engineer and was pressing the dead man's fingertips onto index cards for future reference. He used a fine black powder to make the impressions, and not messy ink.

When he was done, Doc turned to Renny. "Carry the body into the barn. We will let the authorities know what landed here in good time."

Renny eyed the bronze giant. "Meaning you're not in a rush to notify anybody about this corpse?"

"The authorities are busy enough with what we've already given them," stated Doc.

They withdrew to the ranch. Pat and Laramie were filled in on the latest developments.

Doc Savage took that opportunity to examine the grumpy old Westerner, and redressed his wounds and did other things to decrease his discomfort.

"I feel like Alice," said Pat sullenly.

Johnny looked blank. "Alice whom, may I inquire?"

"Alice of the famous looking-glass. The one who fell down the rabbit hole."

"Oh," said Johnny, blinking like an emaciated owl.

Long Tom observed sourly, "No one in this mess is falling down anywhere. They keep falling upward. And I'm getting tired of it. It's getting on my nerves."

"Wait until it happens to you," warned Pat.

"No, thanks," retorted Long Tom. "I like keeping my feet firmly planted on the ground. That's where they're going to stay. I wish I'd never taken over this forsaken spread."

"A fine thing to say," snorted Laramie in the corner. "Leavin' an old man to die without honest work in this rugged paradise."

Pat Savage eyed Laramie dubiously.

"I thought you objected to being called old."

"I do. I mean I did. But I believe that I have aged considerably since last night."

Abruptly, Doc Savage signaled to Renny. The pair went outside. They went directly to the big speed plane, entered it and rummaged around in back. The rear of the craft was fitted with storage lockers and other compartments, all containing quantities of the types of scientific equipment that the bronze man habitually carried into battle.

Doc began making piles of parachutes. He handed one stack to Renny. The other he took himself.

"I get it," Renny said after a few moments of mental confusion. "These are going to be our aces in the hole."

"Important precautions," admitted Doc.

When they reentered the ranch house, Renny boomed out, "Come get your safety rations."

"Are we flyin' someplace?" grumbled Laramie.

"Not if we can help it," said Doc dryly. "Do not leave this building without donning your parachute."

Eyes widening with understanding, Johnny exclaimed, "A prudent precaution against peril!"

"Two of us have already experienced the potency of the strange shotgun Mr. Calamity wielded," reminded Doc.

The parachutes were naturally rigged for different-sized individuals, so Renny and Johnny had to swap. Pat exchanged with Long Tom, until they found rigs that would fit them properly.

Pat tried hers on experimentally and was surprised at how light it was. "I thought it would weigh a half ton."

Renny rumbled, "Cotton chutes are heavy, but these are silk jobs."

"Actually," corrected Doc Savage, "these are fabricoid. Lighter and more durable than silk. It will make it easier to move about wearing a main parachute and its reserve. But by no means will it be comfortable."

"Is that spelled 'cumbersome?'" laughed Pat.

Renny stepped outside in his parachute harness and wandered about, Long Tom following. The big-fisted engineer was curious about the Circle Bolt spread, about which he had heard little. His interest appeared to be confined to the livestock.

"Where do you keep your herd?" he boomed.

Long Tom pointed to the solitary milk cow standing chewing grass placidly.

"That's her."

"One cow?"

"There's only two of us. This isn't a working ranch. I don't have time for that. Gloomy gives reliable milk and we get along fine."

Frowning, Renny poked about in the barn and grunted, "I only see two horses."

"There were more yesterday. I lost a wagon, along with two good mares. You know what happened to Lightning."

"That I do," admitted Renny mournfully. "Shame about her. I guess if we're going to be riding about, it will be by air. And I don't aim to climb aboard that burro."

His attention on the horizon, Long Tom suddenly perked up at hearing the word.

"What burro?"

"The one standing in the far corner of the barn, of course."

"I don't own any damn burro!" Long Tom snarled. Raising his voice, he yelled, "Doc! Fresh trouble."

DOC SAVAGE and the others came running. They took a few minutes to don their parachutes and looked a trifle ridiculous pelting toward the open barn so encumbered.

"What is it, Long Tom?" Doc asked with controlled urgency.

The aggravated electrical genius pointed into the dim barn interior and clipped, "Unwelcome visitor."

Doc stepped inside, found the burro, examined its brand and remarked, "This is not your brand."

"It's not my mule," sniffed Long Tom. "That's what I'm trying to say. I don't know how it got in there, but it's fishy."

Long Tom examined the brand. Two loops connected by a dash, with a dash in each oval. "I don't know many of the local brands—ranches are spread out pretty far."

Using a cottonwood limb for a makeshift crutch, Laramie limped into the barn with difficulty, having decided to dispense with donning his parachute. He did not know how to assemble the thing, and his bandaged wounds made doing so painful.

Loping over to the animal, he grumbled, "That's no mule," he snorted. "That's a goldurned useless hinny."

Blank faces sprang up all around.

Doc Savage explained, "A hinny is the offspring of a female donkey and a stallion."

"You know your oats," Laramie said admiringly. "Mules are bred from jacks and mares and make for hardy work animals. This hinny is its weak sister." The oldster was studying the animal's hindquarters. "This is the Lynx Eyes brand. That's where some of the mules have been rustled from lately. Some sidewinder is tryin' to frame us, Long Tom."

"Everyone stand still," advised Doc Savage.

"Why?" asked Laramie.

"Just do as Doc says," snapped Long Tom.

Doc Savage's men had been trained to obey their big bronze chief. If he gave an order, it meant something. Something significant. Now they watched him work.

Doc Savage made a careful survey of the barn and immediate vicinity. He was looking for boot tracks. Of course, he found plenty. The bronze man followed the ones that had led out from the ranch house, memorizing their outlines and assigning them to the individuals he knew.

Curiously, he found no unfamiliar boot prints.

Doc did notice hoofprints, however. They meandered about, and so did the bronze giant, moving with an uncanny silence that belied his Herculean physique.

Some of these tracks he was able to match up to the solitary mule simply by lifting one of its hooves. Not that there is any doubt about the difference between a mule hoofprint and that of a horse or cow. There were scatterings of others. But no boot prints belonging to strangers.

It appeared as if the hinny had wandered into the barn of its own volition. Possibly accompanied by a steer or cow.

Doc checked the forefeet of Gloomy the milk cow and quickly decided that these odd hoofprints represented a different animal.

Once Doc Savage waved them out of the barn, Renny, Long Tom, Johnny and Pat Savage eventually joined in.

"Observe how the hinny's prints seem to come out of the rocks and go directly to the barn," he indicted.

Laramie grunted, "Anybody can see that. But who let her in? It weren't no cow."

"Yet there are cow prints present that do not belong to Long Tom's milk cow."

Everyone could see that, as well. Renny and Long Tom fell to scratching their heads in puzzlement. Johnny, perhaps to disguise his own bafflement, removed the thick-lensed monocle affixed to one lapel with a ribbon. This was a magnifying glass he used in his field work. Getting down on all fours, he studied the cow tracks through the lens.

"An enigmatic bovine conundrum," he pronounced.

Laramie nudged Long Tom and asked, "What did the tall skinny feller just say?"

"Why don't you ask him? I don't speak his lingo."

Standing up, Johnny announced, "These are not the tracks of a common cow."

"Not if it escorted a stolen hinny into somebody's barn," Laramie snorted.

Johnny assumed the stance and scholastic demeanor of a lecturer in natural science, which he was. "Either this cow has learned to walk upright like a man, or it is the only two-legged bovine that was ever calved."

Pat challenged, "Are you spouting nonsense now? Because you sound like you are."

Doc Savage interjected, "There are no two-legged cows, nor has a bovine ever learn to walk upright. But it is an old rustler trick to affix cow hooves to the bottoms of work boots to disguise the tracks of a human thief."

"Holy cow!" exploded Renny. "Do you mean to say that some rustler wearing trick boots walked the mule in and then took off, leaving no other trace?"

"Exactly," advised the bronze man. "Once again, Long Tom is being framed. Rather, the Circle Bolt Ranch is."

The slender electrical wizard took fistfuls of his pale hair in either hand and let out a kind of annoyed groan.

"This broken-down dump in the middle of nowhere is more trouble than it's worth!"

No one offered a word to the contrary. Indeed, Long Tom's lament was something they understood perfectly.

Renny did not help matters when he observed, "You realize this is going to point the finger at all of us when Alta Crater's body is recovered. Never mind that of her brother."

Pat Savage snapped her fingers sharply. Her face brightened. "I wonder...."

"You wonder what, Miss Pat?" asked Laramie with genuine curiosity.

"We have yet to find Hud Crater's body."

"Probably buried," snorted Long Tom.

Renny rumbled, "Unless that's him lying in the barn, minus his head."

Pat continued her musings. "I wonder if Mr. Calamity, whoever he might be, could have dressed that headless corpse in his ridiculous outfit and dropped it on us to close the noose of guilt?"

Long Tom felt of his neck and looked a little more pale than usual.

"I wish you hadn't used that word."

"Which?" demanded Renny.

Touching the raw purple-red welt encircling his throat, Long Tom winced. "Noose. I'm getting kinda sensitive to it."

Chapter XXIII

ASSIGNMENTS

DOC SAVAGE TOOK Pat aside.

"Other than the Bison sheriff, who knew that you had been arrested?"

"Just the sheriff. He was very discreet about it."

"What about the man who gave you a ride into town?"

"Mr. Wood? I don't know that he knew. I told him my name was Juanna Quitt, anyway."

"Events suggest that, when the sheriff spoke to Wood, the former may have indicated his intention to arrest you, Pat."

"You think Wood is Quest?"

Doc did not reply directly. Instead, he said, "Someone knew that you had been arrested almost as soon as it happened. What about the general store proprietor?"

"He was the nosy sort. Come to think of it, he was an old busybody the first time I barged into the store to use the telephone."

"We will have to look into both of them quietly."

Pat nodded in agreement. "No sense in stirring up the Bison authorities. They're bound to be touchy about their dead sheriff."

Doc's flake-gold eyes flickered. "At the moment, we can assume that no one knows of your arrest, at least officially. That means you are probably not a fugitive, except technically. But you should stay out of the town of Bison just to be safe."

Pat's chin became firm. "Doc, that sheriff confiscated my

grandfather's shooting iron. I'll need to fetch it back if I'm going to participate in future festivities."

"I will see what I can do about your six-shooter," advised the bronze man. "My advice to you is to stay indoors and keep your parachute about you at all times. Even when you are sleeping."

"That sounds mighty uncomfortable."

"Not as uncomfortable as a one-way ride into the stratosphere. Now if you'll excuse me, I'm going to use the radio in the big plane."

"Don't let me hold you up, cousin," Pat said with a trace of sharpness in her voice.

Doc Savage exited the ranch house so quietly his going was not noticed by the others for quite some time.

Old Laramie fell to studying Johnny Littlejohn.

The gangling archaeologist and geologist was freakishly thin, uncommonly bony and taller than a scarecrow nailed to a post.

Johnny wore his hair on the longer side, as if he played the violin. He was not known to play the violin. He was not that kind of longhair, but a scholar.

Laramie sized him up speculatively. Then he began unlimbering an assortment of Western insults.

"You," he clucked, "are built kinda like a rattlesnake on stilts."

"I resent that remark," said Johnny hotly. He clung to his dignity the way another man would hold onto his best suit of clothes. Johnny had once held the Natural Science chair in a famous university. He had opened up musty tombs in Peru and explored Egyptian pyramids no white man had ever penetrated. In his chosen fields, he was considered an eminent authority. One of the best in generations.

"If you close one eye," Laramie continued, "you look kinda like a walkin' needle. But with Eastern clothes on."

Johnny fidgeted with his tie; his neck began reddening. That meant he was becoming hot under the collar.

"Canards are the last resort of uncouth ruffians," he sneered haughtily.

Laramie went on unperturbed. "Furthermore," he observed, "you're so skinny you could probably take a bath in a shotgun barrel."

The big-worded archaeologist was not accustomed to such abuse. He did not seem to know what to do with his swelling anger.

At that juncture, Renny Renwick stepped in, demanding, "Why don't you pick on someone your own size?"

The old Westerner made a show of looking about the room. "I don't see anybody hereabouts who fits that description, especially you, big fists."

Renny lifted one of those stony-knuckled members, bunched it into a brick-red maul of bone, muscle and tendon, and warned, "If we weren't guests here, I would flatten your snoot."

Laramie appeared to be unaffected by the threat. "Your friend over there looks so mad he could bite himself. As for you, those fists fit you like a pair of feathers on a terrapin. Where did you get them? If you remember, take 'em back. They gave you the wrong size."

Now it was Renny's turn to fume. And despite his menacing fist, he knew better than to let fly.

In a low, rumbling voice, he growled, "If I pop off on you, there won't be enough left of you to snore. Get the picture?"

"Big fists, big talk. You got anything that's right-sized, you grim-faced galoot?"

This exchange started getting on Long Tom's nerves. "Knock it off, Laramie. These are my friends."

"Just entertainin' folks," said Laramie with a chuckle. "No need to be so touchy. I'm gettin' kind of ornery with all these hurts I've acquired. In fact, I'm feelin' mean enough to swallow a horned toad backward."

"I'll fetch you one," rumbled Renny. "And make you eat it raw."

Laramie grinned broadly—the grin magically turning his

homely face into a fountain of amiability. "Fetch two and we'll call it supper."

Pat Savage interjected, "I know all this mystery and confusion is getting everyone down. But if we're going to beat this menace, we're going to have to stick together."

Laramie snorted, "Mr. Calamity wore a ten-dollar Stetson perched on a two-bit head. Now he ain't got either. How are we gonna figure out who he is, or was. Or run him down if he's still livin'?"

"Doc Savage will do that," Pat said confidently.

"You folks talk about Doc Savage like he hung the moon in the evening sky," scoffed Laramie. "I ain't yet seen any sign that he's such-a-much. And I've been ramroddin' cow punchers and bronc busters all my days."

"Watch what you say about Doc Savage," exploded Long Tom. "And where do you get off calling yourself ramrod of this spread? You're little more than a glorified cook!"

Laramie glowered his indignation. "Better to be a cook than a crook. And you should eat more of my grub. It ain't fittin' that a respectable rancher should be so poorly-lookin'. It reflects on my cookin', which I take kinda personal."

"I'm tired of eating mutton four times a week," snapped Long Tom. "Especially mutton stew."

"Are you insinuatin' that I'm a lousy sheepherder?"

"Take it any way you like," snorted Long Tom.

Laramie glowered dramatically at his boss. "Somebody hand me a firearm!" he howled. "Gimme a lead-thrower! That's a towering insult. I'm gonna have me a personal massacre!"

IN THE middle of this verbal mêlée, Doc Savage reentered the ranch house.

"I have been in touch with the F.B.I. office in Cheyenne. At my request, they are going to canvass hotels and dude ranches throughout the state for reports of any red-haired and green-eyed visitor fitting the description of Mr. Calamity."

"What makes you think he ain't a common Wyoming no-good?" demanded Laramie.

"There was nothing common or, for that matter, authentically Western about his attire," stated Doc.

"What about my six-shooter?" demanded Pat.

"I neglected to raise the issue," admitted the bronze man. "For there was another matter that has arisen."

Everyone looked to Doc Savage expectantly.

"It appears that not only did the big lake vanish this morning, but other, smaller, bodies of water have been evaporating all day. An unidentified man has been calling local ranchers and threatening to make their waterholes go away."

Laramie interrupted, "That's powerful bad medicine. We ain't in a tough drought at present, but Wyoming is plenty droughty this time of year. Take away a rancher's source of water, he might as well shoot his cows and horses and pack up for Canada."

Doc Savage continued, "Some of these ranchers are finding notes in their mailboxes. The threats are the same. The notes are signed 'Mr. Calamity.'"

Long Tom grunted, "The bird's sure been busy today. I guess we know now why he's been doing what he's been doing. He's been testing that crazy shotgun of his, and now he's looking to cash in."

Renny boomed, "I don't figure this at all. If Mr. Calamity is the guy tricked out in green, who is sending those notes?"

Doc Savage said, "That is one of the main mysteries, but by no means the central one. It is time that we get active, brothers. Johnny, I want you to take the gyroplane and go prospecting. Start in the Belle Fourche badlands due east of the Bighorn Mountains. That's approximately where the Repel projectile made impact, according to witnesses. See if you can find any trace of it."

"Indubitably," said Johnny.

"Take Renny with you. His engineering skills might come in handy."

"Holy cow, that's a lot of territory. And I'm no prospector!"

"We know that the Repel stone left Fan Coral Island in the Pacific," advised Doc. "And that it landed in Lake of the Ozarks. In between, a boat on the Great Salt Lake in Utah was buffeted by waves raised by no discernible wind. Use those points to plot a trajectory. It should enable you to pinpoint where in Wyoming it bounced."

Renny nodded. His engineering skills included survey work.

Doc turned. "Long Tom, why don't you return that mule to the Lynx Eyes Ranch. Find out what they know. And inquire about Oakley Wood."

Long Tom nodded. "My hunch is that some of their hands make up that vigilante gang."

Doc nodded firmly. "The mule rustlings have all the earmarks of an inside job. No doubt some of the vigilantes are from other spreads, or are loafers hanging out in the towns. If almost all of them are dead now, we are simply concerned with getting information that will lead us to Quest and Mr. Calamity."

"What about me, Doc?" asked Pat plaintively.

"Remain here and look after Laramie. We may have use of your skills before long."

As she took in those words, Pat's frown turned into a half-hearted smile.

"You're not just stringing me along about that last part, are you, cousin?"

Doc said sincerely, "Mr. Calamity seems to be taking on a good section of Wyoming. We will have a lot of territory to cover. As developments take shape, your help may prove to be invaluable."

That seemed to satisfy the feisty Pat, if not exactly placate her.

"Fine. But I'm holding you to those words. Don't let me down."

Everyone except Pat and Laramie exited the ranch house and went about their assignments.

Johnny and Renny got the gyroplane off the ground first, while Long Tom saddled up one of the spare ponies and tied the mule to his saddle. The long-eared animal proved cooperative in starting off, but before long it started digging its heels stubbornly, braying noisily.

The scrawny electrical genius was equally stubborn, but it was a while before Long Tom prevailed and the two animals, along with their single rider, disappeared into the foothills.

Before he took off in the big plane, Doc Savage went to the headless body that had come down out of the sky via parachute.

In the privacy of the horse barn, he performed a superficial autopsy using a scalpel and other medical implements. His purpose was to locate any trace of a shotgun charge that might have been embedded in the man's body.

The bronze man did remove a few kernels of something. He studied these under a magnifying glass for a time. His face was very intense. His uncanny trilling came, ethereal and uncertain. When he finally allowed it to trail off to nothingness, Doc placed the fragmentary matter into a glass tube, which he promptly stoppered and pocketed. Then he went out to the waiting aircraft.

He left the headless corpse wrapped in a horse blanket on the barn's hay-strewn floor.

Claiming the amphibian, he closed up the huge bronze bird, took his seat in the control compartment and methodically clicked cockpit switches.

One engine warmed up, coughed some oily smoke, then the other followed suit. The plane was quickly jittering with motorized life.

Stainless steel props snarling, the speed plane turned into the wind, and Doc commenced his takeoff run.

Despite some bumpiness due to the uneven terrain, the takeoff was brisk and uneventful. The amphibian was soon moaning into the distance, bound for the city of Cheyenne.

Chapter XXIV

BIZARRE BANK ROBBERY

IN THE OFFICES of the Federal Bureau of Investigation
in Cheyenne, Wyoming, Doc Savage was received with
restrained but sincere approval.

The bronze man was not required to display the identification
card that proclaimed him to be a Special Agent. There probably wasn't a man in the Bureau who did not know who Doc
Savage was in general, nor understand his official standing with
the Department of Justice in particular.

Firm handshakes were exchanged with the Special Agent in
Charge, as well as with his immediate subordinate. The Cheyenne office was modest, owing to the sparse population of the
state of Wyoming and its far-flung cities and towns.

"We don't see a lot of business here, other than bank robbers
and such desperadoes," explained the Special Agent in Charge,
whose name was Heflin. "What brings you here, Mr. Savage?"

Doc Savage got right to the point. "An associate reported
that a man was seen swimming in the sky, after which he fell
to his death. His body subsequently disappeared."

The bronze giant gave the flummoxed F.B.I. men a moment
to absorb that remarkable statement.

Doc went on. "The missing man has been identified as a
rancher, Hud Crater. The body of his sister, Alta Crater, was
discovered earlier today, apparently a victim of drowning. These
two matters are connected. It appears that someone has control
of a substance or force capable of levitating bodies of water to

considerable heights. Hud Crater was immersed in a swimming hole when the water was levitated, conveying him skyward. Earlier today, a lake was similarly levitated, with the unfortunate result that a government mail plane crashed into the suspended water. The plane wreckage can be found northeast of Devils Tower, along with the bodies of Miss Crater and the government pilot."

"We heard about the plane crash," stated Special Agent in Charge Heflin. "Are you saying it was brought down deliberately?"

Without responding directly, Doc Savage continued. "The person responsible has been sending demands to ranchers, citing this unfortunate event, and warning that, if they fail to pay ransom, other water sources will be removed. He signs these threat letters with a presumably false name, Mr. Calamity."

Now the bronze man had the agents' full attention, for the destruction of a U.S. Mail plane constituted a federal matter.

Doc Savage laid on the desk two white cards containing the fingerprint impressions of the headless body that had landed at the Circle Bolt Ranch.

"These are the fingerprints of a person believed to have been involved in this matter," he explained. "This person is deceased, but his identity is not known. It is imperative to learn who he was."

"I'll have our fingerprint boys run these," promised the Special Agent in Charge, handing the cards to his deputy. The latter quickly disappeared from the office.

Doc Savage changed the subject abruptly. "Has this office been investigating the mule rustling centering on the Pumpkin Buttes area?"

Agent Heflin hesitated. "Normally, we leave rustling to state authorities. Rumor has it the mules are being shipped out by rail, which takes the matter across state lines. Why are you interested in common mule rustlers, Mr. Savage?"

"A gang of these rustlers ran afoul of the individual whose

fingerprints I provided. Most of the gang were wiped out in the skirmish. But the leader, a man known only as Quest, appears to have escaped with his life. He was last seen in the company of a mysterious man who may or may not be dead, and who controls the force that can levitate water."

"You think these two have joined forces?"

"That is one possibility," admitted the bronze man. "The other is that one murdered the other, leaving his weapon in unknown hands."

Doc Savage gave a brief description of the man named Quest, but other than his height and weight, there was not much to it. As for the one known as Mr. Calamity, Doc had significantly more detail, but only insofar as the individual's outlandish Western garb went.

The F.B.I. agent frowned. "We had a report last week about a holdup involving a culprit dressed exactly like that."

"What sort of holdup?" asked Doc.

"A mighty peculiar one," said Agent Heflin, pulling a folder out of a filing cabinet. He handed it to Doc Savage, explaining, "It was real road agent stuff. The motorstage from Gillette to Ten Sleep came upon a boulder blocking the highway. The rock was so big the driver couldn't get around it. The holdup man stepped out of a clump of greasewood and showed the driver the hollows of his double-barreled shotgun, ordered everyone off the bus, and made them empty their wallets and handbags. Then he disappeared into the badlands. The motorstage had to turn around and return to Gillette. Road's still blocked, Mr. Savage. Funny part is that big boulder wasn't rolled into place. It was the size of a house and there wasn't any scarp or high place it could have been heaved from. State Police couldn't figure out where it came from, or how it got there."

Doc Savage finished perusing the F.B.I. report.

"There can be no doubt that Mr. Calamity is responsible for the perplexing relocation of the boulder," he stated. "There seems to be no clear description of the bandit's face here."

Agent Heflin commented, "His outlandish duds distracted the witnesses." He frowned thoughtfully. "The only time you ever see or hear tell of anyone duded up like that, they hailed from back East, full of crazy ideas they got from Western movies and thriller magazines."

"Sound reasoning," said Doc. "A check-up on the dude ranches might be in order."

Heflin reached for his desk telephone, saying, "That's a good place to start."

Before he could grasp the receiver, the instrument rang. Slightly startled, the F.B.I. man lifted the receiver. "Yes?"

Heflin listened for several moments, interrupted twice, then slammed down the receiver.

He addressed Doc Savage. "You are not going to believe this."

"I heard every word," said Doc. "It appears the troubles are escalating."

The other agent returned at that juncture. He looked startled when his superior rapped out imperative orders.

"We need to drive up to Casper, Agent Hale. We'll fill you in along the way."

"My plane will be faster," suggested Doc.

"Lead the way," said the F.B.I. chief, grinning. "It will be a pleasure to work with you."

EN ROUTE, the F.B.I. head recited the report he had received for the benefit of Agent Hale, who drove the official car. Doc Savage had already absorbed the details, thanks to his acute hearing.

"A masked gang knocked off the Casper City Bank. They blew in, wielding shotguns. A bank guard stood up to them. One of them blasted away. The guard was not killed. Instead, he was slammed up to the ceiling where he got stuck. They had to haul him down with ropes. That was later. They robbed the bank without resistance. On their way out, they blasted someone who happened to get in their way. That poor soul went screaming skyward—screaming all the way into the clouds, according to reports. They later found him on the roof of a department store, dead. Every bone in his body was broken."

Doc Savage advised, "The gang needs money to finance their future plans."

"What about those ransom notes?" asked Heflin.

"It is doubtful that local ranchers took them very seriously. This bank robbery may also be a way of demonstrating their power, and changing stubborn minds."

The F.B.I. man said, "Every one of the robbers was wearing a flour sack over his head. So we don't have much to go on."

Doc nodded. "Those are the types of hoods worn by the mule rustlers, but most of them are dead now."

"Those rustlers had quite an operation, from reports," stated Heflin. "They had confederates scattered throughout the state. No doubt some of the gang survived the other night."

At the airport, they boarded the aircraft. Inside, Doc Savage handed the two agents parachute rigs, saying, "Put these on."

Neither man thought the request unusual, but both needed help buckling their harnesses properly.

The flight was brief. They had hardly gained altitude when the bronze man pushed the aircraft into a sharp descent.

After they landed in a modest Casper airfield, Doc Savage told the F.B.I. men, "Do not remove your parachutes."

Special Agent Heflin blinked. "Why not?"

"If the gang is still around," advised Doc, "you could be blasted into the sky. A parachute would be the only thing that could preserve your life."

Faces falling, the two F.B.I. agents kept their harnesses on. It made for a distressingly awkward ride in a taxicab, yet there was no avoiding it.

The cab pulled up in front of the bank while the local police were still interviewing witnesses.

The bank guard who had been pried off the ceiling was sitting in the back seat of a police radio car, refusing to step out. He was clutching the passenger straps on either side, his facial expression terrified. He had a black eye, evidently the result of his ceiling encounter.

The nervous man was saying to anyone who would listen, "I don't want to go up into the sky like that other fella. I hear he's dead."

After introducing himself to the local police, Doc Savage drifted up to the frightened fellow.

"Describe the men who did that to you."

There was something calming about the bronze giant's steady regard, a hypnotic quality of the whirling flake-gold eyes that could not be denied.

"They wore Halloween hoods. Rough clothes. Not much else stood out. The shotgun blast stung like crazy, but I don't seem to have much damage. Except that I conked my skull on the ceiling."

"Do you see the shotgun clearly?"

"No. Except that it was old. An antique."

Agent Hale inserted, "Might have been an old Zulu gun—a rifle with the barrel bored out and shortened to fire shotgun pellets."

The victim shook his head vehemently. "That scattergun was no Zulu. It was a side-by-side. I never saw one like it. But she kicked like no mule that ever lived, let me tell you."

"Thank you," said Doc, rejoining the police, who were conferring with the two F.B.I. agents.

A police detective reported, "The getaway car has been found on the outskirts of town. They must have switched cars."

Doc Savage said, "Take us there."

Three automobiles made a caravan, police sirens clearing the way.

The auto was a stolen one, a cream-colored coupé. Detectives were already going over it for fingerprints and other clues, but the gang was reported to have worn gloves, so police optimism was thin.

The bronze giant ignored the vehicle and instead studied the ground all around. It was blacktop, which did not take much in the way of tire tread impressions.

The F.B.I. agents also examined the immediate vicinity. They went about this business methodically, but uncovered nothing of interest.

"Looks like a dead end," Hale decided.

Doc Savage was studying the near distance. He noticed tiny specks of light out on the prairie. These were not visible to the ordinary eye, but his powerful optics detected two gleams. Removing his small folding telescope, he brought this to bear. These minuscule specks became visible under study.

"Spot anything interesting?" asked Heflin.

Doc observed, "It is possible that the gang took off on horseback."

The F.B.I. chief frowned doubtfully. "More likely they transferred to another motorcar."

"That is also possible," allowed Doc, pocketing his telescope. "Let me suggest that both avenues be pursued. Where might a horse be rented?"

One of the helpful Casper police volunteered, "I'll take you there, Mr. Savage."

"We will be in touch, Savage," said F.B.I. head Heflin.

Before long, Doc Savage had acquired an appaloosa stallion suitable for his size, a sturdy swelltree saddle, and was pushing out into the prairie north of Casper, in the direction of Gillette.

Despite appearances, the bronze man was not embarking upon a wild goose chase. Not in the slightest. His study of the surrounding terrain had disclosed tiny specks of mica, which had been reflecting afternoon sunlight.

During his rearing, Doc had spent a great deal of time out West in the company of working cowboys, as well as Indian trackers. From them, he had learned all the tricks. Chief among them was the arcane art of reading sign.

Doc knew terrain that did not take horse prints might nevertheless reveal to a trained observer the passage of riders. Bits of mica embedded in surface soil often was dislodged by passing riders, exposing their clean undersides to the sunlight.

The action of wind and blowing dust would soon diminish that reflective property. But the fact that mica specks gleamed here and there suggested a recent disturbance of the soil—and a fresh trail.

Pinning a mount almost as imposing as he, the bronze giant was intent upon following the trail. A cream Stetson shaded his metallic features. He was a striking sight as he broke into the prairie, his parachute pack firmly strapped to his Herculean physique.

If Doc Savage was bothered by the extra weight, he did not show it.

Chapter XXV

LYNX EYES

LONG TOM ROBERTS was no fool.

Having suffered numerous ignominious outrages at the hands of Wyoming locals, he was not about to lead the missing hinny boldly onto the Lynx Eyes spread and be mistaken for a mule rustler once again.

"I've had a bellyful of jackasses," he mumbled to himself as he rode along the dismal flats surrounding the Lynx Eyes Ranch. Buffalo grass dominated the prairie. Here and there a scrawny jack pine struggled for existence. Water was not plentiful this time of year.

This was mule range. More than one spread ran the hearty little pack animals. It was desolate country. Gophers and jack-rabbits far outnumbered the human population. Antelope and elk were a common sight.

Long Tom led the hinny by a simple rope tied to the pommel of his saddle. It was a considerable distance they traversed. By this time, the animal had lost much of her stubbornness. She ambled along disconsolately, elongated ears flicking at flies.

Approaching the Lynx Eyes spread at long last, Long Tom pulled to a halt, dismounted, and untied the hinny.

"Now you stay put, you miserable little troublemaker," he growled.

The animal twitched her long upright ears. Now and then the doleful orbs blinked a few times, but she offered no comment, not even a braying complaint.

Pulling together the rope, Long Tom remounted and continued on his way.

As he approached the Lynx Eyes bunkhouse lying baking in the sun, Long Tom cocked a battered hat over his eyes to increase the shade across his face. A neckerchief was tied around his throat to conceal the purple bruise encircling his neck like an engorged artery.

He did not know for certain if any of the hooded vigilantes had been Lynx Eyes waddies, but the suspicion was fixed firmly in his mind. There was no avoiding being recognized, but if he could put off that possibility, there was a chance of jerking out his supermachine pistol before trouble started popping.

The Lynx Eyes Ranch encompassed a small stream which carried melted snow and spring water down out of the hills and emptied it into the Big Powder River. A sizable spread, its corrals sprawled a net across a greasewood flat, the log ranch house resting on a knoll near the stream.

Two busters were halter-breaking young mules when Long Tom rode up. Another sat on a feed box, watching them.

By the bunkhouse, two more punchers had stopped making rope hackamores to watch him steadily approach with squinting eyes.

"Howdy," one said without much warmth.

"Howdy-do back," said Long Tom, trying to sound Wyoming-bred.

"What motivates you to drop by, stranger?" asked another.

"I came across a mule that maybe belongs to this outfit. He's wandering the road back there, looking lost."

Long Tom did his best to sound like a local, but he did not quite pull it off.

"You're not from around here, are you?" one wrangler queried.

Long Tom shook his head. "From back East."

"Passin' through?"

"Kinda."

"Well, if you're lookin' for work, we're short as hell. Some of our top hands up and vanished on us last night. If you're seekin' a piece of honest work, we might take you on. Provided you're not tenderfootish."

Another waddy said, "You'll find old Blab Crater in the big house. He's the one you should hit for a job. I don't think we're takin' on anybody permanent-like, so don't get your hopes up."

"O.K., I won't," said Long Tom. "Is Blab Crater the owner?"

"Naw, that'd be Miss Alta Crater. She's out looking for her brother, who's gone missing. Blab is their grandpa. He's kinda like the foreman. But not actually."

The cowpokes appeared to be bored and were casually conversational. One produced a muslin sack of tobacco and a red-backed book of brown rice paper. His blunt fingers moved with deceptive ease as he fashioned a smoke while he talked.

Long Tom decided to prime the pump a little bit more.

"Who's foreman here?"

"Right this minute, that would be old Blab," drawled another hand. "The actual article is among the missing. Probably lookin' for poor Hud. Hud's the one who got lost a couple days back."

Long Tom ventured, "I heard talk of a gang of rustlers operating in this area."

The puncher jammed his spreading spike into the strands of the rope he was making hackamores out of. He did not look up. His reply was laconic.

"I don't know nothing about it, stranger."

Another shifted uncomfortably. Numerous eyes narrowed by the intense Wyoming sun appraised him silently.

"Well, I'll drift in and make medicine with Blab Crater," decided Long Tom.

"I'd walk up to the big house kind of loud-like," suggested a waddy, "so you'll be heard. The old rip can't see so well no more. He might take you for trouble and splatter your innards in all directions." The mule wrangler's tone was dry as sun-baked alkali.

Long Tom moved toward the big house. Sagebrush lined the path on both sides. Beside it, halfway between the bunkhouse and the ranch house, stood a sagebrush cutter. The big implement, closely resembling a road-grader, was a dull pile of metal in the hot sunlight.

As he walked past, Long Tom noticed something pale stuffed inside. He paused, reached in and pulled it out. It was a gunnysack. An ordinary gunnysack. Except that two ragged holes had been cut into it. Holes for human eyes to see out of. The lower portion was rust-colored. Dried blood, from the feel of it.

That was all the pallid electrical wizard needed to prove that at least one of the rustlers who claimed to be vigilantes belonged to the Lynx Eyes outfit, its leader. It was a valuable clue. Long Tom decided to inform Doc, rather than take action himself.

STEPPING up to the big house door, Long Tom rapped on it loudly. Presently, a gravelly voice called out, "Come in!"

Doffing his hat, Long Tom did.

He encountered an old man sitting in a rocking chair, looking fretful and staring up at the cracked plaster ceiling. The old man didn't look as if he had shaved in a couple of days, and he was scratching absently at his whitish stubble.

"Who might you be?" he asked.

Long Tom gave voice to a deep sigh.

"The bearer of bad news, I'm sorry to say."

The old man gathered up his wrinkled features and pointed the entirety of his face in Tom's direction. His eyes became as narrow as that of a Sioux brave.

"That don't tell me your name, stranger."

"Long Tom Roberts. I took over my Uncle Hicks' ranch near Pumpkin Buttes. Using it for a vacation spot."

"Hicks! That would be the old Split-C spread."

"It's the Circle Bolt now."

"You run cows or mules?"

"I have a milk cow. Some horses, but that's about it."

The oldster chuckled dryly. "Another dude ranch in the making!" Then his face assumed a sober demeanor. "What's this you say about bad news? Is this about Hud?"

Long Tom hesitated, groping mentally, uncertain how best to put the words together, but he knew that he would have to break the awful news somehow.

"I'm not sure about Hud," he admitted, "but there's a reason to think he's gone to his reward. A witness saw him fall from a terrific height the other day. But they're still looking for the body."

The old man's weathered hands squeezed the rocking chair arms, and his sunburned knuckles got white.

"Alta's gonna be heartbroke," he said harshly. He looked as if he had a good grip on his emotions, so Long Tom proceeded with his unwelcome report.

"I'm afraid that Alta Crater isn't coming home, either."

This time the old man fixed Long Tom with a puzzled eye. His mouth sagged, revealing teeth like old yellow pegs. A few were missing.

The old man must have been a fire-eater in his youth, because his shoulders squared and his voice got rigid. "Don't drag it out, stranger—spit it out!"

"Her body was found in a lake near Devils Tower."

The man's gnarled fingers gripped more tightly, and he stopped rocking in his chair. He seemed not to know that he was doing that.

"Drowned?"

"That will be for the medical examiner to say," said Long Tom. "I'm sorry. I really am. I know it's tough to hear. But it had to be done."

"Well, it's done and done properly. I appreciate the neighborliness of bringing me the bad news. Now if you'll excuse me, I got to pull myself together."

"I have a few questions," Long Tom interjected.

The old man studied him.

Long Tom had his hat in his hands and was holding it by the battered brim. He turned this around as if it were a steering wheel and he was trying to hold onto the road.

"I didn't mention this before, but I work with Doc Savage. Maybe you've heard of him."

"The confounded King of Siam has heard of Doc Savage!" exploded Blab Crater. "City papers call him 'the bronze man of mystery,' and they pile on the superlatives like they were stacking flapjacks. The way folks talk, ol' Doc is a human alloy of Daniel Boone, Davy Crockett, Kit Carson, Pecos Bill and a few other fire-eaters of yore."

Long Tom nodded. "Doc's in Wyoming looking into some trouble here. Somehow it ties into the mule rustling that's been going on in these breaks. What can you tell me about that?"

"Not much to tell. This is mostly mule range. There's plenty of stock running loose. Rustlers take advantage. Mostly by moonlight. I should say, by *lack* of moonlight."

"Have any of them ever been identified?"

"Not one. The rustling hasn't been going on but three months. How does this tie into trouble big enough for Doc Savage to tackle?"

Long Tom hesitated. He didn't wish to get into the more fantastic parts of recent events.

"We hear that the leader calls himself Quest. That name mean anything to you?"

The old man shook his head. "Can't say I ever heard of a local boy with that name. But if those rustlers can be run to earth, their punishment will be swift and certain as sunrise."

"Last night Doc Savage piled into a pack of them. They came out the worse for wear. They won't be rustling your mules, or anything else, anymore," Long Tom added grimly.

Something like a smile twisted the old man's features. "Hud and Alta would be pleased to hear that news. I guess it comes too late for them, though." A tear leaked from the corner of one eye. The old man seemed not to notice it.

"Some of your boys tell me that you're short-handed today. A few of your wranglers haven't come back."

"Out looking for Hud, I suppose. They been out practically every night."

"Doc Savage has a suspicion that some of your hands might belong to the rustler group. If that's true, they won't be coming back, either."

The old man's features quivered, like a spiderweb unexpectedly disturbed by a freshening breeze.

While Blab Crater was absorbing this morsel of information, Long Tom pressed him.

"Who were the ones who went out last night?"

The old rancher gathered his thoughts, composed his features, gripped the arms of his rocking chair and resumed his rocking. His jaw moved as if he were chewing tobacco, but there didn't seem to be anything in his mouth. Maybe he was chewing the inside of his cheeks with worry.

"Let's see, there's Slim Jim Bowen. Dizzy Allen. Off Swiggert. Clayton Shoulders. And our foreman, Buck."

"What's Buck's last name?"

"Quane. Buck Quane. Been with us near to a year. But I don't take Buck for no mule rustler."

"I heard a man named Oakley Wood works here, too."

"Well, you heard wrong, feller. Never heard that name before. Sounds kinda made-up, if you want my opinion."

"I must have misheard the name," allowed Long Tom. "If Quane or any of the others come back, don't tell them I was here. Or let on about Doc Savage. We'll check back with you."

Long Tom turned to go when the old man spoke up. "I almost plumb forgot. Who do I see about Alta's body?"

"Doc Savage will be looking into that for you."

"Kind of him. But what does my granddaughter drowning at a lake have to do with Doc Savage's business?"

Long Tom hesitated. He did not wish to add to the old man's unimaginable grief. On the other hand, he felt that Blab Crater deserved to hear the truth. And sooner was probably better than later.

Long Tom shifted his feet. "Doc Savage believes that Alta Crater might have been drowned on purpose."

"Who would do that?" the oldster roared.

"That's one of the reasons Doc Savage is on the warpath right now."

The old man lifted himself up, stood erect, and his face took on a weird energy that made him seem several decades younger. Hot tears streamed down his weathered cheeks.

"You tell Doc Savage for me that old Blab Crater is on the warpath, too. If our paths cross, I'll stand right by him. Shoulder to shoulder, and shot for shot."

"I'll tell him," promised Long Tom. And he stepped out to the harsh sunlight, walked past the sagebrush cutter, paused briefly. Making sure he was not seen, he pocketed the gunnysack hood.

He gave the bunkhouse a wide berth before claiming his pony and riding off.

His pale face was grim. He thought about what the old man had said about the missing foreman named Buck Quane. And how much Quane sounded like Quest.

As clues went, it was no shining jewel. But Long Tom Roberts was dead certain Doc Savage would be interested in hearing about it.

Chapter XXVI

PAT MAKES HER PLAY

PATRICIA SAVAGE WAS an impetuous young woman. British Columbia had birthed her. She had grown up in its untamed evergreen wilderness, and some of that wildness had imprinted itself upon her spirit. Perhaps she would have lived out her days there, but the death of her father, combined with a visit by her cousin Doc Savage, changed the direction of her destiny.*

After relocating to New York City, the young woman had established a beauty salon that swiftly grew into a combination spa and gymnasium on fashionable Park Avenue. The establishment had made her, if not exactly wealthy, extremely comfortable for a woman of her young years.

This did not satisfy Pat. Mere money never would. Pat lusted for excitement, adventure, travel and to see all the wide world could offer her.

Most of all, her ambition was to join Doc Savage's band of trouble-busters. The bronze man had steadfastly denied her membership. Not because Pat Savage was not capable. She was. Pat had horned into many adventures and done well for herself.

But modern as Doc Savage was in most ways, in one way he harbored an old-fashioned streak. Pat was his only known living relative. Also, she was undeniably female. Doc did not wish to see her in danger as a general rule, nor was he willing to risk losing her during the course of one of his peril-fraught exploits.

---

* *Brand of the Werewolf*

Often, Doc simply put his foot down. Sometimes this worked; most of the time it did not. Pat was persistent. In desperation, he would try to hoodwink Pat into tearing off on a wild goose chase. The bronze man was tireless in his ingenuity. He believed Pat should attend to her business and, when she got around to it, snare a husband and settle down.

Pat Savage had shown no special inclination toward marriage or bringing children into the world. She had the pioneer spirit—no doubt obtained from her late father—as well as a stubborn streak that might be blamed on the Savage blood in general.

In this instance, even though she had stumbled across the beginnings of the present mystery, Pat was willing to play along until her opportunity came. Although she hated every minute of it, the bronze-haired girl was prepared to stick out her vigil over Laramie until the others returned.

It was not easy. The old man had been wounded in several places. He ached. He moaned. He complained. He chewed tobacco constantly. Loss of blood had made his hide as pocked and wrinkled as though he had been soaked in green persimmon juice.

Pat had taken the time to wash the coppery dye from her wealth of hair, and to scrub the make-up that had given her bronze skin its copper tint. When she was done, Laramie appraised her and grunted, "Before, you shone kinda like a new-minted penny. Now, if you stood stock-still, folks would mistake you for a statue of Diana the huntress come to life."

Pat laughed musically. "I feel like myself again. Darla Dell was getting into too much of the wrong kind of trouble to suit me."

Laramie inveigled Pat into several games of checkers until Pat's boredom became too much.

"Is Laramie your real name?" she asked at one point.

"Nope, it's a nickname. I acquired it young. It's fit me ever since."

"What's your honest moniker?"

Laramie stopped chewing, seemed to hesitate.

"My last name is Scow."

"First name?"

The old cowboy tongued his wad to the other side of his mouth thoughtfully. "I don't usually talk about it. In fact, I kinda disremember it."

"Is it a secret?"

"No, it's just that I buried it long ago."

Pat smiled. "Surely, you can cudgel it out of your memory."

Laramie frowned. "Promise you won't tell the others?"

"Cross my heart and hope to barge in on some fresh excitement before the sun goes down."

Laramie was chewing ferociously by this point. When he spoke a single syllable, Pat had difficulty understanding him.

"Say that again?" she prompted.

"Elk! I said Elk. My first name is Elk!"

Pat blinked. "So, you're Elk Scow?"

"No, dadblast it! I'm Laramie. Just plain Laramie. Elk Scow I buried out in the prairie when I was a tender pup."

Pat cocked her head one way and her eyebrow the other. "Why did your parents name you Elk?"

"I never did get around to prying it out of them. I guess they liked the sound of it." Laramie seemed disagreeably tired of the subject. "At least, they didn't name me Moose, like my big brother."

THE OLD man was shifting around in his seat. Suddenly, he gave a wince of pain that grew into a grunt of agony.

"What is it?" demanded Pat, rising suddenly.

"I think I popped open one of those dodgasted stitches."

"Let me see," said Pat solicitously.

Carefully, she examined his wounds, saw fresh crimson leaking from a bandage, and exclaimed, "You're bleeding again!"

Laramie looked for himself. "Dadgum bullet hole opened up," he grunted. "Well, make it stop if you can, Miss Pat."

Pat did her best. But the wound was deep and she had difficulty staunching the blood.

Finally, she gave it up. "We have to get you to a doctor," she decided.

"Nearest sawbones is over in Bison. We don't have an automobile, since Long Tom managed to lose it somewheres."

"We'll take my personal plane. It's faster. I'll help you into it."

Laramie hesitated. "Doc Savage told us to stay put."

"He did. But he didn't tell us to sit around helplessly while you slowly bleed to death. We're going to see the doctor. And, while I'm at it, I'm going to collect my six-gun."

"You'll just be huntin' trouble," cautioned Laramie.

Pat gave a game little grin.

"Nothing wrong with looking for trouble," she retorted. "It's what kind of trouble you find or don't find that matters."

Laramie averred through his pain, "I have a hunch, Miss Patricia, that the trouble will have a way of finding you."

"Let's hope trouble doesn't happen along before I've got my six-shooter back," Pat declared with even determination.

She assisted the old Westerner to his feet and to the ranch house door. But not before helping him into a spare parachute harness. Then out they went.

"Why do I have to wear this dadblamed contraption?" he groaned as he leaned on Pat's shoulder.

"Lately, folks have been falling both up and down," Pat reminded him. "This will keep you safe."

"It ain't natural," groaned the old cowboy.

"You'll get no argument from me," said Pat. "But Doc insisted, so we're following his orders."

Laramie eyed the bronze-skinned girl. "You," he pointed out, "appear to pick and choose how much you obey Doc Savage, according to your own lights."

"I'm a full-blooded Savage," retorted Pat.

"Meanin'?"

"It's another word for maverick."

Chapter XXVII

THE DISINTERRED

RED AND RESPLENDENT, the afternoon sun hung over the crest of Big Butte as Long Tom Roberts rode grim-faced back to his ranch. He kept a close watch for any strange riders. He saw none.

From time to time, he cast a careful glance backward in the direction of the Lynx Eyes spread. He half expected to spy the dust of trailing horsemen. But he saw none. He did not trust the hands who worked there.

He was not twenty minutes along in his thumping journey when the buzzing of an aircraft motor smote his ears.

Shading his eyes, Long Tom looked up. A small plane was buzzing overhead. He studied it. It was a modern bus, possessing a fuselage of ivory, with shiny gold wings and trim. His face twitched with certain surprise.

"That's Pat's bus!" he exploded. "What's she doing tearing around loose?"

Since he possessed no means to find out, Long Tom studied the ivory-and-gold aircraft and realized it was winging in the direction of Bison. That meant one of many possibilities. Pat could have been summoned by telephone or short-wave radio, possibly by Doc Savage. Or that old Laramie had taken a turn for the worse and she was rushing him to the hospital.

Forking his horse, Long Tom changed direction and galloped toward Bison. He wished for his station wagon, but there was no telling where it was hidden. The pint-sized electrical genius had kept a canny eye peeled for it at the Lynx Eyes place, but he didn't want to appear nosy and attract suspicious attention.

As Pat's plane disappeared over the hills, Long Tom slowed down, realizing that he would have to pace himself or risk exhausting his mount. Wyoming settlements were distributed far apart on the theory that the best neighbors lived on the other side of the horizon.

Before long, a cluster of dry-farmer shacks came within sight, and his attention turned toward those. He was not familiar with this spot, or its tenants. Little better than hovels, the shacks were constructed from rough-sawn pine planks, sod, logs, and a few flattened tin cans for roofing. The peculiarities of the climate, the absolute lack of prolonged spells of rain, made the common sod about as effective as any other building material, although lacking in certain sanitary qualities.

Long Tom noticed a semi-dugout structure, the walls of sod with a roof of the same material laid over a framework of cottonwood poles. It was a mean-looking structure. Long Tom would not have given it a second glance except that he spotted something familiar.

From a distance, he could not be certain, but there stood a spring wagon, to which was attached a pair of draft horses. The wagon was nothing special, but the horses looked familiar.

"That's my rig!" he exploded.

Abruptly, Long Tom decided that Bison could wait. He turned his steed in the direction of the shanty.

A single dusty road led to the spot. It was scarcely worthy of the designation, a couple of deep ruts that wound over the sandy rolling range, here and there spreading into two more pairs of ruts where they had grown so deep that "high centers" developed.

As his horse thumped easily along, Long Tom made out the spring wagon and horse team clearly. It was definitely his rig.

In the bed of the buckboard was stretched out something shapeless and dirty, swathed in a sun-faded horse blanket.

Dismounting silently, Long Tom walked the horse toward

the buckboard. He kept one hand on the horse's chin to keep it quiet. The pony was obedient.

No one seemed to be around, but outward appearances could be deceptive. Often, they were.

Holding onto the reins, Long Tom crept up to the buckboard and made a murmur deep in his throat after he got a better look at the bundle wrapped in the horse blanket.

It possessed the correct shape to be a body. One end was rounded, while the other came to a kind of point. The latter made him think of feet encased in riding boots.

Reaching in, Long Tom undid the rounded end and uncovered the head of a man. The man's face was caked with dirt and his pinewood-hued hair was likewise clotted with sod.

The man appeared to be on the young side, and dead for only a day or more. Everything indicated that he had been recently disinterred. Dirt was clotted deep in his ears, in his still nostrils and around the corners of his eyes, as if soil had been packed down around them.

The door to the mean hovel was open and its smoke-blackened interior gaped empty and odorous.

Frowning, Long Tom went to the next shack.

Before he could approach the rude door, a young woman stepped out. She held a clumsy weapon in both hands. It was a single-shot buffalo rifle, Spanish War vintage. The barrel end looked big enough to jump into.

"If you know anything about buffalo guns," she grated, "this cannon will tear you apart."

Long Tom was so intent upon the deadly bore that he neglected to look at the wielder's face. Thus, he recognized her voice before his eyes got around to scrutinizing her features.

It was the green-eyed redhead who had saved him from the hangman's noose not two days before.

"Well, what are you waiting on?" she hissed. "Grab the lowest cloud you can manage."

Obligingly, the puny electrical wizard hoisted both hands.

The arm in the sling was only partially cooperative, but Long Tom managed to hoist it to shoulder level. He was in no mood to be shot again. Particularly was he of no mind to be blown apart. As long arms went, the buffalo rifle was more fearsome than any shotgun.

"If you so much as wiggle an ear," the redhead warned, "I'll bisect you where you loop your belt!"

Long Tom decided to get the upper hand the best way he could.

"That's my wagon standing over there," he said, jerking his head in that direction. "It went missing a day ago."

"Well, I found it running loose when I was looking for my sweetheart. I was driving it into town to turn over to the sheriff when I found… him."

Long Tom blinked. "Found who?"

The woman's voice was as hard and brittle as broken glass. "My boyfriend. That's him in the wagon over yonder."

LONG TOM didn't know what to make of the redhead. He attempted to match her hard-boiled tone of voice.

"He looks dead."

"He *is* dead," she said without much emotion.

"Looks like someone recently dug him up."

"That was me," admitted the woman. "For two days, I've been searching high and low for him. Searching hard. We were supposed to be married. It was a secret. Not even his family knew. Then he up and disappeared. After I found your wagon, I came across a fresh grave by the side of the trail. The person who dug the grave didn't do too good a job. Didn't dig deep enough, I reckon. Coyotes had scratched around and pulled loose one arm. When I saw the hand, which was half gnawed, I suspected the worst. So I dug him up. It was Hud, all right."

Her voice lost control near the end, and her chin was a-tremble. But she firmed both of them up with visible effort.

Long Tom all but exploded. "Hud Crater?"

"That was his name. What do you know about it, stranger?"

Long Tom told his story. "I inherited the Circle Bolt Ranch from my Uncle Hicks. A friend of mine named Pat Savage met Hud on his way to a swimming hole. A few hours later, she thought she saw him swimming around the sky like a fish out of water. Then he tumbled down. When we went to see where the body landed, it wasn't there anymore."

"That story doesn't exactly stack up straight."

Long Tom requested, "Do you mind putting down that blunderbuss? My arms are getting tired."

Her brittle eyes congealed into the semblance of greenish ice. "I *do* mind. If you have more story to tell, spit it all out."

Long Tom did his level best, picking up from where he experienced his first hanging, moving on to the arrival of Doc Savage, and up to the present point. He described Mr. Calamity in detail without producing any sign of recognition from the woman's emerald eyes.

The redhead listened with her pale mouth making dubious shapes. Finally, she put down the buffalo gun and said, "That yarn is too crazy not to be true. Not that I completely swallow it. But I believe in Doc Savage. I read about him in big national magazines. He's practically a one-man F.B.I. If you work with Doc Savage, you must be right as rain."

Long Tom dropped his hands, fumbling the wounded one back into its supporting sling. Prudently, he did not make a grab for the buffalo gun. He knew better. If the cannon went off, he would be dead before his eardrums registered the blast.

"Why don't you borrow my wagon and take him back to the Lynx Eyes?" he offered.

The redhead shook a lock of loose hair out of one sad eye. "I think I'll do exactly that. Bison is too far, anyway. By the way, my name is Lola Collins. I was planning on being Mrs. Hud Crater." Her tone sank to a subdued half-whisper. "But I guess I'm going to have to make other arrangements, once I get around to them."

Long Tom said nothing. He owed the grieving woman his life, and harbored no quarrel with her otherwise.

"Why do you think that varmint in green killed my Hud?"

Long Tom scratched his head in thought, his sour face all but puckering. "It might have been an accident. And when he discovered that he had slain a man, the killer decided to bury the evidence."

"So Hud wasn't murdered?"

Long Tom shrugged unimpressive shoulders. "Did Hud have any enemies?"

"No, but he was powerful mad at them mule thieves. Suspicion was falling on the Lynx Eyes brand. Could be someone wanted to do away with him."

Long Tom had very little to offer in that regard. "One thing is for certain: Doc Savage will get to the bottom of this. He always does."

"Well, when he does," said the woman, stalking off to claim the buckboard, "kindly pass on to him my top regards. Tell him Lola Collins will always be his friend."

The woman checked the body, climbed onto the wooden seat, and got the horses and the buckboard turned around.

"One last thing," she called back. "When I dug up poor Hud, there was something else in the grave with him. Something that didn't belong to him."

"What was that?" Long Tom wanted to know.

"It was a head. Human head. It wasn't Hud's, so I left it there. Couldn't think of anything better to do about it."

Long Tom's eyes narrowed. "Where did you find this grave?"

"A couple miles west of Pumpkin Buttes. Look for the hoodoo with the one eye. It's the only one standing out there. Although why anybody would want to lop off somebody's head like that is beyond me."

Without any other goodbye, she rolled off. Her expression

was fixed in silent grief, and the wind in her red hair looked as if it was on the point of igniting.

Long Tom Roberts got back on his horse and flung it in the opposite direction, thinking that the ridiculous-looking man in green, Mr. Calamity, was well named. He was stacking up to be the author of a lot of grief and misery in this corner of Wyoming.

Long Tom soon found that hoodoo. The lonely sandstone spires were often found in clumps or clusters. This one stood alone. Some bored cowboy had emptied his revolver into a spot high up, making it look like a narrow Cyclops without arms.

The slender electrical genius dismounted when he came to the section of disturbed earth. Having no shovel or any other tools, he used his bare hands to excavate the grave.

It took some digging around, but he found the head. Like that of the late Hud Crater, this head was encrusted with sandy soil. Long Tom hauled it out by the hair, held it up to the dying sun and turned it around. He was not outwardly bothered by the grisly artifact.

The head appeared to have been cut off cleanly. Long Tom showed no surprise there. He had already harbored suspicions.

Examining the hair closely, he noted its color. Using a thumb, he opened one eye. The lifeless eyeball retained enough of its original configuration that its color could be determined with certainty. Studying this, Long Tom let out an off-key whistle of interest.

"The stew," he murmured, "is thickening up. Doc Savage will want to see this."

Turning, he went back to his horse, stuffed the head into a saddlebag as best he could, closed up the strap, and climbed back into the saddle.

Somber of face, Long Tom continued on his way. It was now very late, and dusk was creeping in. The ride back to the Circle Bolt was likely to take most of the night....

Chapter XXVIII

BETRAYED

AFTER LANDING AT the dusty airstrip that passed for Bison's airport, Pat Savage went to the modest operations shack and requested an ambulance.

"What's the problem?" demanded the radio operator.

"I just flew in an injured man. He's bleeding from a gunshot wound."

"I'll get the ambulance, but I have to call in the sheriff as well."

"Just summon the ambulance first, if you please?" urged Pat, dashing out to return to the plane.

The ambulance arrived first, but the sheriff was not far behind him.

While Pat was enumerating for the internes all of Laramie Scow's injuries, the sheriff's noisy flivver pulled up and he got out. The man was squat and broad. The ends of his mouth curved down nearly to the end of his jaw, which, together with a pair of watery gray eyes, made him seem on the point of tears. A nickeled star was pinned to his chest.

"What seems to be the trouble here?" he wanted to know.

Of course, it was not the same sheriff. It could not be. That other man had perished.

Pat said forthrightly, "My name is Patricia Savage, cousin of the famous Doc Savage. This man is the foreman of the Circle Bolt Ranch, and he was injured in a shooting yesterday."

"How does Doc Savage figure into this?"

"It's a long story," confessed Pat. "I'll be happy to tell you the bare bones, once my friend is taken care of properly."

"We'll go to the hospital together then. You can ride with me. My name is Gates. They call me 'Easy.' Sheriff Easy Gates."

They watched Laramie being loaded into the back of the ambulance. The old Westerner gave Pat a wink and a thumb-and-forefinger circle signifying the O.K. sign.

"Don't worry about me none, Miss Pat," he called out. "I've been plugged a time or two before. I'm practically half-lizard. My limbs always grow back."

Sheriff Gates pulled open the passenger side of his flivver and started to wave Pat in. Then he stopped. "You might want to take off your parachute, Miss. You seem to have forgotten it in all the excitement."

Pat hesitated. "If you don't mind, I'll leave it on. You never know when it might come in handy."

Wrinkles of suspicion twitched the sheriff's windburned features, but he shrugged and said, "Suit yourself."

Pat got in. The sheriff slammed the door shut and she almost immediately bumped her head against the roof of the flivver. This was because she was sitting on her parachute pack.

The sheriff got the contrary machine into gear and said, "Let's have your story, miss."

The flivver shook jerkily with a loose, tinny rattle bred from the unpaved, ungraded roads, chugging and sputtering as it progressed.

As they followed the ambulance, Pat did her best to weave her tale while leaving out the inconvenient portions, particularly the interlude during which she had been previously arrested by the late sheriff of Bison. She carefully skipped over the part about seeing a man swimming in the sky.

The sheriff asked, "You say the F.B.I. is on the case now?"

"Due to the mail plane crashing. That's a government matter, you know."

"It's big, all right," allowed the sad-looking lawman.

They went directly to the Johnson County Hospital where the sheriff questioned Pat while they waited for the doctors to patch up old Laramie Scow.

"Does Doc Savage think that colony of mule rustlers is back of all this hooraw?" asked the lawman.

"If he does," admitted Pat, "he hasn't said. But he hardly ever talks ahead of the point where he busts loose and cleans up matters. He's peculiar that way."

Sheriff Gates nodded. "I heard that about him. Read it somewhere."

The lawman considered his next words for a time.

"We found some dead bodies out near Pumpkin Buttes," he drawled. "Rustlers. We know that because they were wearing sacks over their heads. Got 'em all down in the morgue."

Pat's eyes brightened. "Have any of them been identified?"

"We're keeping it quiet, but some of them have. They're Lynx Eyes brand hands. Others are too busted-up to be identified. It looked like a few fell off the high buttes, although I've never seen a dead body pulverized so. Some of their faces—" The lawman caught himself. "Well, I guess I don't need to go too carefully into the details. But from what you say befell them out there, they could've benefited from wearing parachutes," he added dryly.

"I was unconscious when most of that was happening," Pat affirmed. "In fact, I'm lucky that I wasn't lynched."

"I see. Well, I suspicion the gang had spread themselves out instead of bunching up. They can't all be Lynx Eyes boys."

"Doc Savage will be interested in that."

"I'd like to talk to Doc Savage. Do you know where he is at the moment?"

Pat shook her head firmly. "He took off for Cheyenne, but I haven't heard from or of him since."

"Reason I ask is that I am the new sheriff. We found the previous one dead in his car near where those rustlers were found. That's why we're keeping it quiet. If any of those rustlers survived, they're liable to be guilty of killing the lawman."

"I don't know anything about that," said Pat hastily. "As I said, I was unconscious practically the entire time."

The sheriff eyed Pat suspiciously. The bronze-skinned girl had been pacing, but now plunked down into a seat, sitting on her parachute pack.

The lawman made a face, narrowing his sun-squint eyes and altering his weather-seamed countenance remarkably.

"Wouldn't you be more comfortable taking off that rig?"

Pat sighed. "I neglected to mention that Doc requested that we always wear our parachute packs in case we encountered Mr. Calamity again."

"From what you say, that sounds sensible. But you have to admit it's mighty peculiar, you walking around wearing a parachute pack without being in an airplane."

"When you stumble into the kind of mysteries Doc Savage and I like to tackle," said Pat sincerely, "you get used to matters that are peculiar."

"That brings to mind another matter. An old airplane was reported crashed out Pumpkin Buttes way. No sign of the pilot, but it's gotta be Alta Crater's crate. It's the only one in these parts fitted with a machine gun."

Pat did her best to look surprised. "Whatever for?"

"Miss Crater is the headstrong type," the lawman supplied. "She had that Gatling gun bolted on the undercarriage so she could give demonstrations of aerial gunnery at the annual Frontier Days shindig down in Cheyenne. At least, that was her stated reason. Personally, I think she's plain hot-blooded."

Pat grimaced. "I've been accused of that very thing myself."

The sheriff fell silent.

Pat also lapsed into silence. She was thinking of her grandfather's frontier-era revolver, locked in the late sheriff's desk. She was scheming for a way to recover it without giving away the fact that she had previously been in custody. As much as she cudgeled her brain, she could come up with no possible way to accomplish her goal.

Eventually, the doctor came out and said, "We have staunched the hemorrhaging finally, and given the patient something to let him sleep. He should pull through just fine, if he is smart enough to stay in bed."

"Thank you," said Pat fervently, shaking the doctor's hand.

There was no point in looking in on old Laramie, since he was asleep, so Pat and the sheriff exited the hospital.

OUTSIDE, the sheriff asked, "Can I drop you anywhere?"

Pat smiled with relief. She had feared arrest. "The best hotel in town. There's no point in going back to the ranch just yet. Doc has exiled me for the moment, but I have a feeling my time is coming."

The sheriff obliged and let Pat off at a respectable looking brick pile, the Hotel Buffalo.

"Be good if you stuck around town," the lawman said in parting. "I might have more questions for you."

"Happy to oblige," said Pat. She smiled inoffensively. "Unless duty calls, of course."

She registered using her own name, and took a few moments to freshen up. But only a few.

Already, a scheme had hatched in her mind.

Pat had suspicions about the proprietor of the general store. The sheriff had not mentioned any such person as among the dead down at the morgue. She decided to drop in and get herself some black cherry pop.

At the top of her right boot, she carried a small automatic pistol in a hideout holster. It was something she kept on the plane for emergencies. It was not her favorite weapon by any means, but the pistol was small and easily concealable. She carried two magazines, one of which was mercy bullets. The other was in the gun.

After checking the weapon, she placed it in a pocket and

exited the hotel. She left her parachute pack behind. It was risky, of course, but the golden-eyed girl knew she would be too conspicuous wearing it. Especially if any surviving members of the gang were in town. A woman wearing a parachute pack in the middle of Bison would stand out like a sore thumb, not to mention the utter ridiculousness of it.

It was a short hop to the general store, and Pat peered in before entering.

The proprietor she had twice before encountered was not behind the counter. Instead, a young man held forth, looking fresh-faced and honest. Dimples dented his cheeks.

Pat went in boldly, greeted the man with a cheery smile and asked, "Do you have any black cherry pop, preferably ice cold?"

The young man returned the smile and his eyes seem to light up at sight of the bronze-haired girl's pleasing shape. He went out of his way to dig out a bottle of black cherry from the ice chest and opened it up for Pat, setting the sweating bottle on the counter.

"Five cents, please," he said. "You must be new in town."

"Just visiting," returned Pat, slapping down a nickel. "Do you mind if I drink it here? I'm thirsty as all get out."

The proprietor was only too happy to let Pat have her way. The golden-eyed girl was a vision.

"What's your name, gal?"

"Dell," said Pat. "Darla Dell."

Pat sipped the refreshing beverage, then asked, "Whatever happened to the man who was here the other day?"

"But you must mean my cousin. Kip Farr is his name. This is his place. I'm just minding it while he's away."

"Where did he get to, if you don't mind my asking?"

The young man blinked, wondering if Pat's interest meant that he was out of the running for her attention. He hesitated briefly.

"Kip said something about going to Gillette. Some business there, I guess. He was kind of vague about it."

"Back soon?"

The young man shrugged. His interest in the topic grew visibly dim.

Observing this, Pat changed the subject abruptly. She turned her incandescent smile back on the dimpled young man, asking, "I meant to ask—what's your name?"

The boy brightened. "Darn. Gordon Darn."

Pat's smile increased wattage. "That's a nice name, Gordon. What do you do when you're not watching your cousin's store?"

"I'm kind of out of a job at the moment. But I'm working on it."

"Good for you," returned Pat, finishing her drink and setting the empty bottle on the counter. "Let me have another for the road. Black cherry soda is something I can't get enough of."

"Happy to oblige," said the young man, digging out another bottle.

While they made the transaction, Gordon said hopefully, "If you're in town for a few days, Miss Dell, I could show you around. Maybe take in a movie."

Pat hesitated only a little. "I would like that very much. I'm staying at the Buffalo. Room 36. Call first."

"I'll do that, miss," Gordon Darn said, beaming. "Nice to meet you."

"Same to you," returned Pat, exiting with her unopened bottle of pop.

As she walked up the dusty street, Pat noticed that clouds were gathering. It looked as if a rain might be coming on. She decided that she had collected the only clue she was likely to gather in Bison, and so she made her way back to the hotel, where she lingered over her second bottle of black cherry soda.

Pat listened to the radio, paying particular attention to news broadcasts. She heard nothing new. The puzzling crash of the U.S. Air Mail plane near Devils Tower and the bizarre bank robbery in Casper were prominent, but no one as yet connected the two events. The bronze-complected girl had learned of the latter event listening to the radio earlier in the day and drew her own conclusions.

"I'll bet Doc is hot on the trail of that gang," she murmured.

Pat tried calling the Circle Bolt Ranch, but no one answered the buzzing telephone. She considered hopping into her private plane and returning to Long Tom's spread, but something told her to stay put. Perhaps it was the tantalizing nearness of her lost six-shooter.

The telephone rang about seven o'clock. It was Gordon Darn, calling from the general store.

His youthful voice had a bounce to it. "How about a movie, Miss Dell?"

"How about dinner first? I'm famished. Maybe a movie later."

"I know a top-notch place. I'll be over directly."

A FEW minutes later, there came a knock at Pat's hotel room door. Taking her automatic in hand, the bronze-haired girl went to the door. She always took precautions. Association with Doc Savage had taught her that hard lesson.

"Who is it?" she demanded.

"Me," came Gordon Darn's voice.

Pat still held the automatic, but it dangled at her side as she unbolted the door. She opened the panel. Gordon Darn walked in, holding a bright bouquet of bluebells in one hand.

"Flowers!" exclaimed Pat. "How thoughtful!"

Still smiling fixedly, Gordon Darn's other hand lashed out and knocked the automatic from the young woman's fingers.

Two other men appeared at Darn's back. They held two drawn guns, short-barreled Colt revolvers. Their faces were as hard and unyielding as if hewn from oak.

Gordon Darn lunged hastily and scooped up the automatic; Pat made no effort to beat him to the gun, because she was already covered by the revolvers of the other two.

Gordon Darn looked at Pat, then at the automatic and flushed, making his dimples look like matched strawberries.

"They forced me," he confessed. "I had to do it. They threatened to shoot me if I didn't cooperate, then shoot you as well."

Pat colored angrily, seemed about to say what she thought of the young man's actions, then subsided.

"It's all right," she said. Wringing her stung fingers, Pat demanded, "Who are these gentlemen? And I use the term gingerly."

"Friends of my cousin," the other returned sheepishly. "They stopped by, looking for him, and we got to jawing. The subject of your visit came up. When I described you, they thought they recognized you from my description."

One of the men had a face that was too large for his body. His eyes were round, glistening, feline. His ears were queerly pointed, and when he grinned tightly, showing two yellowed eye-teeth like fangs, his facial resemblance to a mountain lion was startling.

His voice was a sandpapery purr. "If you ain't Patricia Savage, cousin to Doc Savage, I'll bite down on a bullet and set off the primer with the tip of my tongue."

Pat tried bluffing her way out of the situation.

"Why, you gentlemen are gravely mistaken. My name is Darla Dell. From Boston."

The other gunman, a flat-faced individual with a nose that had been squashed by brutal force, laughed roughly and demanded, "Then why are you registered as Patricia Savage?"

Pat deflated. She would have registered under an alias, but she did not want to stir the suspicion of the new sheriff, who was likely to check up on the register book as a matter of routine.

The gunman with the bobcat expression wiggled the blued barrel of his Colt and growled, "Let's go for a ride."

"I would prefer dinner," sniffed Pat. "Preferably alone."

The other gunman laughed out loud. "We'd have it sent up, but none of us are going to be here for long."

Gordon Darn suddenly became agitated.

"Hold on! What are you mugs going to do with her?" he demanded hotly. "Don't you know you can't get away with this?"

Flat Nose grunted, "We have a lot of experience gettin' away with things."

The cat-faced one sneered, "And we're not gonna do anything *with* her. We plan to do things *to* her. *Permanent* things."

Malicious delight was a hot glow in his eyes.

Gordon Darn had been red of face. Now he paled as if all the blood had drained from him.

"What do you mean by that?" he demanded.

"What I mean is it would've been better for you never to have met this troublesome gal," purred Bobcat Face.

"Look," Darn stuttered, "I don't want to be part of any killing. I'm not a part of anything. I was just having a pleasant conversation with you fellows. I didn't know it would turn into something criminal!"

"Like it or not, you're part of the shivaree now."

"I want out," he said hotly.

Bobcat Face considered. "Your cousin Kip would probably wild up on us if you went and disappeared. O.K. Hightail it back to the general store and look busy. Slip out the back way. We'll give you five minutes. But don't look back. And keep your yap shut."

"Don't get our brands up with any hero hijinks, either!" warned Flat Nose. "We know where you clerk."

"Sure, sure," said Darn shakily. "I'll be mum. Don't you worry none."

Slipping out the door, he paused and looked stricken, his tone became contrite. "I'm powerful sorry we're not gonna have that dinner, Miss Dell."

"It's Savage," Pat flung back. "Just like my temper."

Gordon Darn winced, then he slipped away like a scolded cur.

"Coward," called Pat bitingly.

The other two kept their revolvers trained on Pat while the clock ticked away five minutes. Then they directed her toward the door.

"Get along, little doggie," one taunted.

"It's your misfortune and none of our own," laughed the other.

"You boys don't look bright enough to be your own bosses," Pat said archly. "Who do you work for? Quest?"

"Never heard of him."

"Mr. Calamity then," suggested Pat.

"Don't know who you're meaning," said Bobcat Face blandly. "We'll take the stairs down. Elevators remind me of the jug."

The trio walked down to the lobby, keeping their short-barreled revolvers deep in their coat pockets where the desk clerk could not detect them.

"Remember," reminded Flat Nose, "we can shoot you through our pockets."

"You boys don't surprise me one bit," snapped Pat.

"How's that?"

"You have low-down back-shooter written all over your faces."

"Our lady-killer instincts are what you need to worry about," sneered Bobcat Face.

OUT on the street, Gordon Darn looked miserable. He hesitated, seemed not to know what to do with himself. He started in the direction of the general store, stopped, seemed on the verge of reversing course, then stopped again.

In his hand, he still held the girl's flat automatic pistol. It seemed like a toy. Its pitiful smallness made him want to throw it away.

His eyes took on a queer light when he spotted the flashy blue coupé. It was the machine the gunmen had driven to the hotel. It was empty now.

Approaching, Darn tried the driver's door. It was unlocked. He opened it, threw the seat forward, and slipped the tiny gun into a door pocket in the rear, where he imagined they would place the girl. Perhaps she would come across it. He adjusted it so the butt showed a little.

While it was not much of a gesture in the direction of re-demption, it allowed him to feel like less of a heel.

Gordon Darn was closing up the auto when he heard footsteps rattling from the hotel entrance. Face going white, he peered back and spied the cat-faced man through the hotel window.

Frantically, he looked around, seeking a place to conceal himself from their view. His stricken gaze fell upon the coupé's rumble-seat lid....

Chapter XXIX
WILD RIDE

WHEN PAT SAVAGE stepped out of the hotel, it was perfectly gloomy. Fast-moving thunderheads packed the sky. There was a wind. It was whipping itself into a frenzy. No rain yet. But the smell of it was in the air. It was imminent.

Wind pushed against Pat's face, mussed her hair. Dust boiled like fog into the light before a nearby movie theater, a restaurant and some beer places. It had been a hot day, but the air turned abruptly cool.

A spear of lightning crawled jaggedly across the sky, adding to the ominous atmosphere. Thunder growled distantly.

During that interval, Flat Nose moved up the avenue, leaving Pat standing with Bobcat Face. The sound of an automobile engine came throatily.

Abruptly, Pat became aware of a light too steady for lightning. A flashy blue coupé drew up, swung in close, then stopped, headlights emitting glowing funnels.

Bobcat Face held Pat by the elbow to anchor her in place, which kept her from fleeing. The hard steel of the short-barreled Colt prodded her back forcefully.

"There's our ride," he growled. "Let's go for a nice long one."

The cat-faced crook opened the passenger door, threw the seat forward and pushed Pat inside. Then he took the restored passenger seat. With the flat-faced driver bulking behind the wheel, Pat knew she was boxed in thoroughly.

Flat Nose put the machine in motion.

In back, Pat sat perfectly still. She did not say anything, but her tawny brow furrowed. She was thinking furiously.

Rain began cascading down in great gray sheets, smearing the car windows and causing the tires to hiss and throw up water.

The coupé rushed through the Bison streets, heading for the outskirts of town and the open prairie country beyond, where habitations were few and far between. With each sharp turn, the car occupants bounced around on their seat cushions.

Headlights of another automobile appeared in the rear window. The following car stuck, but kept a respectful distance. Pat wondered if they were being shadowed, or were these confederates in another machine.

Pat's remarkably bronze hair began to curl, as it sometimes did when the weather was damp. Her exquisite lips were firm, golden eyes intent upon the driver and his accomplice.

"Doc Savage," she announced forcefully, "will move heaven and earth to find me. You boys should know that."

Neither man answered. But they seemed to have lost their ghoulish humor. Mention of Doc Savage often worked that spell of psychological sorcery upon evildoers. Newspapers had proclaimed his astounding feats for several years now. If the wicked men of the world feared an avenging angel, that angel was cast in bronze.

The car made a turn and headed north on the highway, the rain beating it, both windshield wipers going *swick-swick* furiously, headlamps blazing. Pat kept quiet, but her mind didn't, although the thoughts inside her brain went around and around. One fact did stand out though—she was certainly going to be murdered.

Glancing out the back window, she no longer spotted headlights of the trailing machine.

They hit a depression in the pavement which was full of water, and the water sheeted out from the car and up against its windshield. Lightning cracked the sky nearby. It made the interior of the coupé turn a ghostly blue-white, shocking them with its brightness.

Blinded by the flash, the flat-faced driver slewed wildly, but did not see-saw the wheel, as anyone the least bit startled would have done. Obviously, he possessed nerve.

"You don't need to go to all of this trouble," Pat said suddenly. "It is not necessary."

"What trouble?" growled Bobcat Face.

"The bother of doing away with me. It won't work. It never has. You're not the first to try. Don't forget my last name is Savage."

Flat Nose growled, "You seem to put a lot of stock in yourself. As well as in that damn cousin of yours."

"I know Doc Savage about as well as anyone. He doesn't seem hardly human at times. I've witnessed him take a Tommy gun in both hands and bend the barrel into a steel horseshoe."

Bobcat Face snorted with skeptical humor. The laugh was a little nervous around the edges, like a frayed shirt cuff.

"Why," continued Pat, "Doc Savage can practically read minds. I have accused him of that. He never gives me a straight answer. But I'll bet he's wizard enough to pin my possible murder on you both. And if Doc catches up with either one of you, I can't even say what will befall. You lads have probably heard the stories."

"What stories?" asked Flat Nose.

"Never mind!" snapped the cat-faced gunman.

Pat went on, despite feeling as if some of the cool rainwater was trickling down her backbone.

"Talk is that crooks who run afoul of Doc Savage disappear," she said softly. "No one knows what happens to them. They just evaporate. Even I don't know the truth. But I have my suspicions."

"What kind of suspicions?" asked the nervous driver.

Pat's tone dropped to a confidential whisper. "I think Doc

Savage captured some terrible weapon that he turns on crooks. It makes them turn into pillars of salt or something, after which they crumble like Lot's wife. Do you know that story?"

The cat-faced gunman snarled, "Don't listen to her. She's making up lies to scare us."

Sounding unconcerned, Pat inquired, "Mind telling me where you're taking me?"

"Yes, we do mind. Now shut up."

The bronze-haired girl was growing desperate. Her ruse to frighten the crooks into letting her go was not panning out. She started looking around the backseat a little desperately.

Golden eyes widened when she caught a familiar gleam.

Silvery metallic it was, sticking out from the seat pocket on her right side. Her own initials, *PS,* peeped out from the grip of a tiny gun. It looked too good to be true, so Pat did not immediately seize the object.

As her fingers surreptitiously groped toward the door pocket, Pat made her voice sound casual. Perhaps too casual.

"I take it that we are bound for some secluded spot where you intend to do away with me in the customary manner?"

"Orders is orders," Bobcat Face grunted. "Nothin' personal."

"Will I be offered a blindfold, and a last cigarette? Or do you boys prefer to back-shoot me like the desperadoes you obviously are?"

No one said anything.

"If I had a final wish," continued Pat nonchalantly, shifting in her seat to better reach the door pocket on the opposite side of the rear seat, "it would be for a last bottle of black cherry pop."

THIS time Bobcat Face did not voice what was on his mind. Suspicion had arrived as unexpectedly as the snap of a mousetrap in a kitchen cabinet. He wrenched his head around to see if his captive was up to no good.

Bobcat Face did not like what he saw, because his blunt revolver swung into view, and pointed directly at her head. "Sit still!" he barked. Mean eyes narrowing, his gaze shifted. He was staring through the back window, where the unfastened rumble-seat lid was bouncing loosely in the pummeling rain.

Imagining that this meant the end, Pat looked at him; her eyes flew wide. She cried, "No! No! Don't shoot—!"

"Shut up, you!" He reached back with his long arms. The coupé rear window was the type that lowered, and the cat-faced crook turned it down; now he could almost reach the handle of the rumble hatch by straining from his seat. The rumble lid stood open a fractional inch. Noticing this gap had aroused his suspicions.

Grabbing for the keys in the ignition lock, he got them. Most modern cars lock all doors and ignition with the same key.

Alarmed, Flat Nose stamped the brake. The coupé wrenched to a halt, tires squealing. Jolted unexpectedly, Bobcat Face lost his revolver. It slipped under the seat.

Seeing her opportunity, Pat's hands flew for the door pocket. She gripped the tiny automatic, pulled the weapon out.

The driver saw this in his rear-vision mirror. His eyes popped wide when he saw the gun's metallic gleam.

"Keep her from firing that thing!" he barked.

"Lost my damn gun!" Bobcat Face howled.

Panicked and unable to think of anything more constructive, Flat Nose put the car into gear again and roared off. He fishtailed the hurtling machine with wild swings, hoping to keep Pat from drawing a steady bead.

Bobcat Face had already squeezed his lean form half into the back seat. Pushing past Pat, he jammed his arms back through the rear window, shoved down on the rumble lid, got it shut; the key went in the lock and turned.

Pat cocked the tiny automatic gun. The sound did not go unnoticed. The cat-faced crook grabbed her, twisted her wrist. The gun fell onto the floor. They fought for it.

Inside the rumble seat, a man began to yell hoarsely and tried to force open the lid which Bobcat Face had locked.

The desperate driver promptly lost control.

The car eased off the concrete slab onto the soft shoulder, slewed around, then stood on its radiator in a ditch. The doors both popped open as the body sprung.

Pat Savage pitched out into the rain and disturbed the freckled water in the roadside ditch.

Bobcat Face had her weapon, the tiny automatic. The man trapped in the rumble seat fired a gun. The bullet came through the seat, leaving a hole that leaked upholstery stuffing. It broke the dashboard clock.

"Out!" Bobcat Face ripped at Flat Nose. They got out.

Pat was up and running; not up or down the road, but across a field. She kept low.

Inside the rumble, someone kept shooting. Not through the seat now, but through the car.

The frightened voice from the rumble seat yelled, "Damn guns! They scare me!"

More lead came out of the car. Trying to run a bluff, Bobcat Face shouted, "Cut it, guy, or I'll riddle you!" A bullet spanked out at him in answer.

Thinking that it would be smart business to show the man hidden in the rumble seat that he was trapped, Bobcat Face aimed at where he thought the fellow was situated, fired the girl's gun. The report surprised him. It sounded like a rotten egg. A blank! But on that point, he was wrong! Unfortunately, the cat-faced crook did not find this out until he started forward, and the gas out of the gun got in his face. Tear gas; potent stuff, too, which was like fire in his eyes.

Bobcat Face ran. No other sensible course was open because he was almost blinded. Flat Nose was wildly waving about a revolver of his own. A whiff of gas got him, too. His eyes began leaking tears. Naturally, he fled, encouraged by the zing of wild bullets coming from the coupé's trunk.

A great deal of commotion and yelling followed. Pat saw none of it in the drumming curtain of rain and murk. She kept out of sight for a time.

After a while everything died down, and the bronze-skinned girl crept back to the road. Approximately fifty yards along, she encountered a splashing that was Gordon Darn, who had blundered into a ditch half full of water.

The young man kept ducking his head under the surface, trying to wash the tear gas out of his eyes.

Pat yelled at him, "Whatever got into you?"

"I took a blind fling at salvation," he sputtered. "It came to me after I left the hotel. I spotted their parked car—unlocked. I slipped your gun into the seat pocket in back, figuring that's where they would stick you. Then I got into the rumble seat and pulled the lid shut. Found a loaded revolver there."

"Better late than never, I suppose," sniffed Pat.

"I overheard everything," Darn continued, splashing away. "So, I carefully raised the lid and would have gotten the drop on those two desperadoes except that one of them spotted the lid rising up. Then—well, you know what happened next."

"Whereupon," interjected Pat acidly, "you started flinging lead with wild abandon. To no useful purpose, I might add—except to scare the daylights out of me and everyone else."

"Tear gas seeped into the car and I broke out." Gordon Darn stood up, dabbing at his red eyes with his moist sleeves. "My eyes are working again."

Pat said, "Let's hike back to the coupé. It's shelter, at least. Maybe some Good Samaritan will happen along."

"And get shot up?" he said fervently. "Not much."

"Suit yourself," she sniffed.

Pat went back alone, cautiously following the ditch.

Inspecting the coupé, she noticed that Gordon Darn had broken out of the rumble seat by kicking the coupé seat-back loose. Tear gas was still a noxious presence in the interior, ruining it as a rain shelter.

On the ground, her flat automatic shone in the downpour, evidently dropped in the fuss. Pat picked it up, removed the magazine and saw that only one shot had been fired.

Returning to Darn's side, she advised, "We're safe now."

"They vamoosed, eh?"

The two of them crouched silently in the downpour, not certain what move was advisable. The coupé would never come out of the ditch without the aid of a wrecker; furthermore, the first passerby was sure to stop. The storm had halted traffic, but the fierce rain was slackening, the lighting blazing less frequently.

They stood in the soaking rain, Pat clutching her small automatic. She started off, Darn following meekly. "I wish you would put that gun in your pocket!" he murmured miserably. "Guns give me the jitters."

"Where is your spine?" wondered Pat.

Darn shrugged soaked shoulders helplessly.

Pat scolded, "You know you could have killed me with your reckless shooting back there. What got into you?"

"Blind, unreasoning fear," confessed Darn.

Pat squared her shoulders. "I suggest we give the road some attention. An automobile may come along at any moment. We might meet a Samaritan, good or otherwise."

INSTEAD, they came upon two men huddled by the side of the road. Bobcat Face and his flat-featured confederate. Apparently, they had flushed out of the sagebrush and were seeking to hitchhike their way out of the downpour. They kept pawing at their injured eyes and so failed to notice them.

Pat and Gordon saw them clearly after the rain slackened some more. Lightning flicker had become less frequent.

The men seemed to be waiting, as if certain of rescue. One kept putting a hand into his waistband and moving the butt of his short-barreled pistol around nervously.

"Guns!" Gordon muttered, squinting. "Here's where I walk back to town."

Pat reached out and caught him. "Take it easy. I don't cotton to being shot at any more than you do."

"You've been acting," Gordon Darn accused, "as if you enjoy being shot at. Those men have two guns between them. You have only one peashooter. I personally am not an odds fighter. I will go further and say I am no fighter at all."

"Save it!" suggested Pat. "They could be waiting on someone. Whoever it is may come by automobile. Let's watch."

A dark sedan cruised by and slowed to a stop. A man sprang out from behind the wheel and there was an excited exchange of words.

"What happened to you?" Bobcat Face demanded irately.

"Bald tires and rainstorms don't mix," the driver retorted. "What happened to your coupé back there?"

Bobcat Face snarled, "We were double-crossed by that milque-toast, Darn. He planted the girl's gun in the back and hid in the rumble seat. All hell broke loose when she found it."

"Not as much as it's about to," gritted Pat decisively.

Gordon Darn's eyes went wide. For Pat Savage rushed forward. She fired her small weapon twice, with the immediate result that a stinging cloud gushed toward the standing trio.

Howling painfully, the two who had been gassed previously retreated into the sagebrush to protect their eyes, their pistols momentarily forgotten.

The late arrival stood his ground, and so was unprepared when his eyes welled up painfully. He commenced cursing, and went stamping in blind circles.

Veering away from the spreading cloud, Pat made for the open door of the automobile.

Gordon Darn aimed his revolver on the choking man and yelled, "Grab sky!" at the top of his lungs. But the other was too busy floundering about blindly to hear. Darn fired his weapon skyward to get his attention, but the hammer clicked on empty chambers until it was obvious that the cylinder contained no unfired cartridges.

Otherwise defenseless, Darn got hold of a roadside rock. He held it cocked for throwing.

Gripping her silver automatic, Pat dived into the automobile. There was a man in the passenger seat. Pat had not anticipated that. His head had not been visible in the pelting rain.

Pat had bad luck with the unexpected passenger, for he saw her coming and rolled out of one door as she got in the other. His hand was hunting a gun in his coat.

Pat shot tear gas at the fellow. Her gun was loaded entirely with tear gas cartridges. He backed quickly out of the way. Then she fired more gas under the chassis, just in case the enemy should take shelter there.

For his part, Gordon Darn did not appear to have done well with his rock; he and his foe were going over and over in the mud.

"We're deputies!" Gordon yelled suddenly. "You're all under arrest!"

It was a foolish lie, but the effect proved almost all he had hoped for. The one who had dived out of the automobile now ran, got in front of the sedan, shot out the headlights, and continued running. When the fleeing man reached Gordon Darn's noisy fight, there was some violent commotion. It came to an abrupt stop. Then more than one person continued running—down the road and away from the late battle.

Exiting the automobile, Pat dashed toward the fracas in the rain. She had expected Gordon to follow her into the auto.

"Gordon!" she yelled anxiously.

Silence.

"Gordon!" Pat choked out.

"Sh-h-h!" Gordon hissed. "They may come back."

Lightning came then and showed him, a tottering scarecrow coated in mud. Not hurt, either, it appeared, but his gun was gone.

"I thought you were armed," Pat challenged.

"Ran out of bullets, so I threw it away," Darn confessed.

"Come on," urged Pat. "The tear gas has taken the stiffness out of their tails. Maybe we can capture one and get him to talk!"

"And them with guns? No, thank you."

Pat withered the young man with her golden glare. "What kind of son of Wyoming are you, anyway?"

Gordon snapped back, "Have you ever seen a man ventilated by a revolver? It's not like in the movies, where folks are grazed or nipped, and maybe have to wear a shoulder sling for a few weeks. Bullets will break bones, and put out perfectly good eyes. They will dash your brains out the back of your skull, if the caliber's large enough. A forty-five slug is large enough, believe me."

It was a sobering speech and Pat Savage took it to heart.

"Well," she said, "we rustled their automobile."

"Someone's auto," Gordon Darn pointed out. "We don't know they didn't steal it. We could get into a heap of trouble just by climbing behind the wheel."

"In my time," Pat said fiercely, "I've been wanted for murder, if not worse."

Gordon Darn eyed her dubiously.

"What charge is worse than murder?"

Pat stated with a vehement fierceness, "Whatever I do to this gang, if I catch up to any more of them, will be worse than murder, mayhem and whatever you want to add to the pile."

Gordon Darn looked suitably impressed. "Somehow, I believe you, Miss Dell."

"Savage."

"Eh?"

"It's my warpath name."

Chapter XXX

GHOST RANCH

DUSK MADE A spectacle of inflamed splendor of the Bighorns lying to the northwest. Darkly purple and frowning loomed their heights, Cloud Peak a greater knot, the treeless waste of rock above the timberline showing like pale bone piles above the fur of trees.

Riding at a distance-gobbling singlefoot toward the north, Doc Savage watched the fastnesses beyond the mountains swallow the sun. With the first racing streaks of black night, cold air gushed down from the heights like the breath of some weird, frozen jinni. He did not shiver. The bronze giant was inured to the cold. Also, his parachute harness served to insulate him from the wind. Not that it was very cold, for the chill from the mountains was cold only in comparison to the daytime heat of the range.

Doc's appaloosa whinnied nervously.

"Quiet," he whispered. His voice was gently reassuring, yet firm. The obedient animal fell silent.

The bronze man was studying the cloud cover, which obscured the moon, making for intense darkness, when he paused. A sound had reached his ears. Faint but familiar. Another sound soon arrived.

A bullet snapped by one ear. It whined away, fading from hearing. A rolling tumbleweed broke apart in the distance. Tumbleweeds abounded hereabouts.

Doc was out of the saddle by the time the second slug passed through the void he left behind. A bronze hand smacked the stallion, sending it charging away with a soft clamor of unshod hooves.

Fading in the opposite direction, Doc charged through the sage and around rocks with remarkable silence. Darkness concealed him. He collected a large tumbleweed on the fly and held it before him, moving low, somehow blending with his surroundings in a way that defied detection by eye.

By this time, he knew that a rifle was in operation. It was the cocking of a lever-action Winchester rifle that had first alerted him to danger. But he could not make out the rifleman in the smothering murk.

Removing an article from his carry-all vest, the bronze giant hurled it against a stone. It produced a loud report and harmless flash. That was enough to invite a third shot. The sniper was good. His slug struck the stone, ricocheting noisily.

The bronze giant spied the yellow fire-tongue of a muzzle flash. The sniper appeared to be mounted.

Doc Savage slipped headlong into a deep, level-bottomed wash and decided to use caution. He lay flat, listening. No sounds of approach came. But the next moment that changed. A Winchester cracked with unpleasant consequences.

The bulge of Doc's parachute pack stuck up above the lip of the gully. It made a convenient target. Bullets began plucking at it.

The bronze giant twisted until he was lying atop it. His reserve chute was not quite as bulbous. It did not collect any bullets.

The shooting stopped. Silence returned. Doc lay still, listening to the babble of a distant creek, the croaking of hoarse-voiced frogs and the buzzing of night insect life.

Doc crawled along, moving into the deeper portion of the crack in the earth.

From a pocket, he produced a tiny bundle of friction matches. With one of these, he set alight a clump of dried sagebrush. It produced an apricot-hued light, along with fragrant smoke.

A fresh spurt of bullets began knocking this modest bonfire apart.

Down the water-worn range gash, Doc strode. He went forward like the shadow of a wind-blown night cloud. After a bit, when he was well beyond the source of the rapid shots, Doc left the gully and trickled through the sage. He kept low.

Collecting another tumbleweed, the bronze shadow carried it to another specimen. He crouched behind the grouping, golden eyes alert and roving.

Lack of moonlight thwarted his vision, but Doc's hearing rivaled that of many wild animals. He waited patiently for something to disturb the evening quiet.

The clink of a horseshoe against stone soon came. It sounded quite near. The noisy croaking of frogs and the burring of crickets had drowned the sound of the bronze giant's stealthy approach. Doc popped up, holding something that gleamed clear and glassy in one metallic hand.

Suddenly, the horse halted. A creaking of saddle leather, along with the soft jingling of spurs, betrayed the fact that the rider was dismounting. He crept around, his boots squeaking with every step. Evidently, the stalker recognized this betraying fact, for he halted. Then came a slow mechanical sound, which Doc recognized as a Winchester lever being carefully worked. Whistling in imitation of the peculiar, halting cry of a killdeer, the rider paused, waiting.

After a bit, a similar sounding whistle answered. It came from a fair distance. Hearing this, the rider slowly retreated, evidently fearful of stalking his unknown foe in the dark. The scuff of boot heels on sandy soil came distinctly.

There was just enough light to make out the silhouette of a crock-headed horse, a man swinging onto it. He rode away amid a clattering of hooves, without knowing that Doc Savage had been within twenty feet of him.

Doc held the gleaming thing in one hand and did something unusual. He hesitated.

This object was a thin-walled globe of glass, small enough to fit into the palm of his hand. An oily liquid sloshed about inside. This was a liquid anesthetic with unusual properties. When crushed or shattered, the globe released the liquid, which immediately volatilized, producing a cloud of invisible gas that could knock out a man in seconds.

Doc Savage possessed the physical strength and skill to fling the glass bomb ahead of the fleeing horseman, but he knew that the cloud thus created would bring down horse and rider together. There was a danger in that the horseman might suffer a broken neck if his fast-flying horse suddenly collapsed in mid-gallop.

Hoofbeats were a volleying roar through the darkness. They clattered ahead, thundering pell-mell over loose stones. Soon, low sound grumbled in the distance, a pulsing clamor that steadily faded.

Doc made then, very briefly, a vagrant sound. It was the bronze man's strange trilling. Small and exotic, it seemed to come from no definite spot, but rather from everywhere, as if unknown, unseen insects were in chorus. The vocal emanation held a disappointed quality.

Reluctantly, the bronze giant pocketed the glass globe, returning it to the special container that would keep it from breaking accidentally.

Had it not been for the confining parachute harness, the bronze man could have gotten to the grenade more quickly and brought it into play ahead of the horseman reclaiming his horse. But that regret was something upon which Doc did not have time to waste.

With amazing swiftness, the rifleman had vanished. Not even the plod of his mount's horseshoes could be heard over the natural night noise of the prairie.

It was too dark to pick out freshly turned specks of mica disturbed by the horse's rolling hooves. That did not slow down the bronze man.

Removing a spring-generator flashlight from a pocket, Doc switched it on. It had been previously wound. Adjusting the lens, he made a broad fan of light, which he dashed about until shiny specks gleamed here and there. Mica.

Reclaiming his horse, Doc vaulted back in the saddle and proceeded as before. He paced the appaloosa carefully, not wishing to tire the animal, and not yet knowing how far he would have to travel. The bronze man rode slick-heeled, without spurs, and neither man nor mount made much in the way of noise.

Further ahead, a clump of buffalo grass had been pressed down and was still straightening. To Doc's acutely trained nostrils came the faint odor of burned tobacco. The fragrance helped guide him forward.

Not far along, the roving flashlight disclosed a discarded cigarette stub. Another butt was soon found.

All of these signs showed an intermittent trail.

The way took him through a thick pine woods. The bronze man was forced to dismount, and led his animal through the labyrinth of close-set trunks.

The odor of a person who had not washed himself recently soon drifted to his sensitive nostrils.

HALTING, Doc made the call of a killdeer, which seemed to be a range signal, a password without words.

The call was returned. Then a hissing voice demanded, "Who wants to pass?"

Doc made his voice sound tough. "Who's askin'?"

"Never mind my right name. I don't use it much. You come to join up?"

"What would I be doin' out in this forsaken spot if I weren't?"

"O.K., O.K. Advance and be recognized, pardner."

Doc had gotten a fix on the sentry. He sent his steed ahead of him, then circled off to the right, where he hoped he would not be detected.

The sentry was canny. He lay prone in a trench. He was armed with a snub-nosed .38 revolver—a modern weapon preferred by city gunmen. He appeared poised to shoot on sight. No doubt he had been warned of Doc's approach by the rifleman who had come this way first.

Hatred was in his eyes, murder on his mind.

Doc Savage came alongside the trench. His tall frame seemed to collapse. With the silent efficiency of a fly-catching bat, he enveloped the man who lay concealed there.

Landing astride the sentry, his powerful legs trapped the man's arms. Metallic hands, clapping over mouth and nose, were large enough to muffle the fellow's helpless attempts to raise an alarm. The captive flounced once without much noise, then quieted.

Doc struck a match, not wishing to betray his position with his powerful flashlight. The flare of light revealed his metallic countenance, eyes with their eerie inner stirrings resembling twin dust storms of golden flakes.

"Recognize me?" Doc demanded.

The gunman nodded as best he could. The bronze giant's grip was vise-like.

"Gunmen are assembling here," suggested Doc.

Another nod.

Releasing the cowed man's mouth, Doc asked, "Who is your leader?"

"I-I don't know his real name. Honest. But he put the call out through the grapevine that anyone who wanted a hunk of a million dollars to come hell-for-leather to the old E-Out-of-Hell Ranch outlaw hideout. He was about to start operations. I was the first to show, so he made me his straw boss."

"What does he call himself?"

"Calamity. That's all. I don't know if it's a nickname, but I suppose it's gotta be like Calamity Jane, you know. He keeps his face hooded, so don't ask me what he looks like, 'cause I got no honest notion."

"How many strong is this gang?" pressed Doc.

"Seven, but others are expected tonight. I just passed through a new hand not five minutes back." The man was perspiring freely now. He shook with a mounting fear. "Am I gonna disappear like all them other crooks you done caught?"

Instead of replying, the bronze giant transferred his grip to the man's neck.

Kneading a nerve center there, Doc put the man to sleep. Thinking he was being strangled, the fellow kicked wildly toward the end, but with no result. He was helpless.

Doc laid the slack body in his trench, removed the cartridges from his revolver and flung them in opposite directions.

Retreating to the appaloosa, Doc regained the saddle. He continued on. A break in the clouds allowed a scattering of lunar illumination to leak out of the close-packed nodular masses.

BEFORE terribly long, Doc came upon what appeared to be a deserted homestead, a little tract sitting a distance of two rods from an empty pole corral. Enough of a spread to graze a herd of saddle horses and a few milk cows, the necessary accoutrements of a family ranch. But this spread appeared to be a ghost ranch. Tumbleweeds lay scattered about, indicating disuse and neglect.

A sudden movement belied that judgment.

A puncher came to the ramshackle bunkhouse door, threw water from a water pan, then stepped back out of sight. Night breeze brought creosote smell from a dehorning chute. A locked-off windmill squeaked a faint protest.

Forking the horse, Doc retreated into the trees with such alacrity that pine branches clawed at his hat, almost knocking it off the metallic skullcap that was his hair.

The bronze man halted in the clump of sheltering pines, slid off his horse and left the reins dragging. The stallion straightaway began nibbling on succulent summer grass.

The appaloosa soon consumed his fill. Doc Savage left him tethered in a piney spot and, taking to the sage, neared the place with the easy stealth of a stalking bobcat. Doubled low, he felt his way ahead, pushing aside gray sage with long-fingered hands. He scouted the ranch house first. It appeared dark, although yards away two lighted windows were scarlet splashes on the cube of gloom that was the bunkhouse.

On a sun-bleached plank sign letters were burned, evidently by a red-hot branding iron: HLL RANCH.

"E-Out-of-Hell," in other words.

Doc drifted through the screening vegetation. As he went, moving with furtive haste, he inspected the place. The ranch house had the dilapidated look of being deserted, or, at best, occupied only as a winter line camp. Using his folding telescope, Doc studied it carefully. The squatting block of murk showed no window glowing. Then he eased out of the sagebrush and made for the ranch house, turtling forward.

Hovering outside, pressed against the log wall not far from the door, the bronze man listened a long time.

When he was convinced that the ranch house was unoccupied, Doc detached himself from the shadows. Stealthily, he circled the ramshackle building. A window in the rear wall was open. He waited there.

The window was not large enough to admit him, but Doc Savage played the beam of his flashlight around the interior of the structure. He did not use ordinary light, but rather infra-red light in conjunction with a set of red-lensed goggles, which he took from his many-pocketed vest.

There was only one room inside and it showed itself to be empty.

Moving with ghostly ease, Doc Savage made his way to the front door and slipped in, closing the panel behind him.

Faint moonlight slanting in through windows and door brightened the place a little. Two canned-tomato boxes nailed to the walls, a plank table also nailed to the wall and a rusty cookstove comprised the only furniture. Paper was loosening from the plastered walls and ceiling in great scales.

Doc Savage stood inside for several seconds, wondering just what he was up against. Voices seemed to be emanating from the lighted bunkhouse. It was difficult to distinguish how many. Horses were stabled in a rundown barn, but again, their number could not be discerned from their infrequent neighing and pawing. But the bronze man had trailed at least five horsemen, if he read the signs correctly.

Suddenly, there came the sound of booted feet outside. They came from the vicinity of the lean-to stable. The grunt of aging leather as someone dismounted was plainly audible. The twittering of birds in the thicket had stopped with the rider's arrival.

The door was closed. Doc moved quickly against the wall, in a position where the open door would form a temporary screen. He drove a hand into his clothing. It groped. Out came a tiny tin pillbox. Doc slid the lid aside and carefully extracted several small pellets. He set these before the door, retreated into the shadows.

Footsteps swished through the tall grass outside, and transferred to the plank porch. The door latch moved. The door swung open.

The man stepped in boldly, as if not expecting trouble. A Winchester hung down in one gripping hand. He clanked forward, spur bobs jingling. The sole of one boot compressed a pellet with explosive results.

Yelping, the man gave a wild jump, waving his arms in his confusion.

A huge dark ghost fell upon him, wresting the rifle out of his hand, jacking the lever so rapidly that shells spilled along the floor.

The new arrival began sputtering inarticulately.

Doc Savage found his neck, held him fast, lifted him off his feet to show how strong a foe the unfortunate one faced, and began squeezing sensitive nerves in the neck.

With a leaky sign of surrender, the fellow went limp.

Doc laid him out on the rude cabin floor. He picked up the rifle from where he had thrown it, and felt of the barrel. Cold to the touch. It had not been fired recently.

This did not appear to be the sniper he had encountered out on the prairie.

Kneeling beside his conquered foe, the bronze man fished about in the fellow's pockets, but produced very little in the way of information or identification. There was a drawstring bag of Bull tobacco and a book of Rizzes—the makings for cigarettes—loose coins and a brass money clip. The latter squeezed only three wrinkled dollars—less than a day's honest wages.

Doc took a few moments to stuff as much of the tobacco down the barrel of the Winchester rifle as he could. The strength of his fingers could be seen in the way he jammed in the dark stuff, despite the rifle barrel's narrowness.

After collecting the remaining pellets—they were harmless dime-store novelty gunpowder stuff that detonated under sharp pressure—the bronze man slid out the door and into the brush, crawling for a hundred feet until he reached thicker timber. He began a cautious semicircle around the meadow.

He was almost immediately shot at again. The slug carried off his hat, and the bronze giant felt a stab of emotion at the close call. Not fear, but annoyance. Sometimes his stature made him a more obvious target than was comfortable.

Sagging as if wounded, he faded to one side, a metallic phantom in the murk.

Chapter XXXI

UNLUCKY LUCKY SHOT

THE GUNSHOT HAD come, as nearly as Doc Savage could judge, from a spot directly opposite the cabin, not more than two hundred yards away. The pines offered fair concealment from that vantage point.

Doc rounded the end of the meadow, then used redoubled care, searching each tree and bush before exposing himself. A lifted tumbleweed served as conveniently portable camouflage.

At a point where the pines encroached upon the ghost ranch, Doc found the marksman. He was atop a small boulder, lying with his rifle rested over its edge.

Doc moved closer. Suddenly, a pine cone crushed gratingly underfoot. The man turned his head suspiciously, but apparently the bronze man was well screened, for he shifted his attention again to the cabin door.

Doc remained for some seconds without moving, then crept steadily closer. Once he narrowly missed discovery when the man on the rock turned his head to knock off a tremendous chew of tobacco. It was then Doc recognized the shotgun.

It was an antique, and two turkey-buzzard feathers dangled from the double barrels, one white as sun-bleached bone, the other black as coal. It had been lying to one side. Now the rifleman set down his Winchester and picked up the scattergun, which was better for close-quarters fighting inasmuch as its range was severely limited.

If the bronze man had been cautious before, his caution was

now redoubled. He fully understood the power of the weird weapon. Nor was the parachute pack on his back particularly reassuring under the circumstances.

Nevertheless, Doc Savage decided that he had to capture the shotgun before it could be discharged.

Doc had his flashlight out, and he wound it carefully. He watched until he could see the man's face. In the darkness, it had not been visible before. Now it was.

Or rather, what passed for his face was visible.

For the man wore a hood. It was no cheap flour sack, nor was it the coarse gunnysack favored by the rustler chief who called himself Quest.

This one appeared to be made of silk and was an emerald green. The color brought to mind the garish outfit worn by the fellow who styled himself Mr. Calamity.

It was not possible to tell if this was the same person, for the green-hooded man wore puncher duds—a faded flannel shirt over which a black-and-white cowhide vest lay. His hat was a nondescript thing the color of a tanned hide.

Doc waited until the man's eyes could be seen as a pair of gleams nestled in the carefully cut holes in the front of the hood. Those eyes were as hard and narrow as cactus thorns. Their color could not be distinguished.

Crouching down, Doc waited until both were clearly discernible. Then he clicked on his flashlight.

The power of the ray was intense and blinding. Doc dropped the torch immediately and lunged for the howling man, who was recoiling in shock.

The masked man had presence of mind. He had not suspected that he was being stalked. But he knew when he was under attack.

Blinded, he cursed, crouched down and stroked one trigger of the shotgun.

The awful maw was pointed at Doc Savage purely by happenstance.

The weapon discharged, but Doc was ready for it. The bronze giant threw himself to one side as the blast blew by him. Gunpowder smoke made a malodorous cloud.

The charge happened to strike a small tree. It was small for a tree, but it was not very small, being over eight feet tall. Shedding branches, the tree shuddered. Then something miraculous happened.

Groaning and cracking, the tree trunk jumped out of the earth, pulling the greater portion of its roots free, but leaving others behind.

Turning in place like a wounded scarecrow, the tree twirled skyward, its broken branches shaking as if in fear.

Doc Savage heard these things, but saw none of it. He was too busy trying to stay alive.

The bronze giant swung over to the left, while the sightless shotgun wielder attempted to fix his position using only his ears.

Speed meant sacrificing caution, for the ground was littered with pine cones and other debris. Doc could not help but step on some of these, although he avoided most.

After the echoes of the first blast died away, these sounds would give away his position.

Promptly, the bronze man froze, hoping to fool the other.

"Where are you, damn you?" the green-hooded one bawled out.

Doc was versed in ventriloquism. Opening his lips slightly, he spoke. "Over here. Behind you."

By artfully throwing his voice, Doc made it sound as if he was in fact behind the man. It would have fooled most adversaries. This one was wily.

"Nobody would give themselves away like that!" he snarled.

Doc realized that he was trapped now. If he moved, he might make a betraying noise. It was too dark to see the ground clearly. But if he stayed put much longer, the other man's eyes would clear and the bronze giant would be at his mercy.

Doc was slipping a hand into the pocket where he carried the tube holding the glass anesthetic bombs when the man started blinking rapidly. That was a warning that vision was returning.

Having no choice in the matter, the bronze giant made a desperate lunge, moving with cat speed.

On another occasion, he might have succeeded. But he was encumbered by his parachute pack, and the sound of its buckles clinking gave him away, as did the quick grinding of his heels in the sandy soil.

The ancient shotgun shifted suddenly. A frantic trigger finger compressed one trigger. The double maw was pointed directly at Doc Savage's chest when it exploded.

Instinctively, the bronze man flung both arms across his face to protect his eyes and features. This, too, threw him off.

The shotgun blast caught him full in the chest, ruining the reserve parachute dangling there. As if kicked by a donkey's hind feet, the bronze giant was thrown backward. The blast mashed him against a stout tree like a swatted fly. It was terrific. Despite all efforts to keep his feet, he fell.

His falling was queer.

Doc slammed to the ground, then bounced upward. He kept on going.

Once more, he found himself floundering in midair as the starry sky seemingly pulled him upward, his powerful form possessed of an uncanny and irresistible weightlessness.

Having no control over his body, Doc Savage surrendered to the phenomenon. This time he was better prepared for it. Up and up, he went. Higher, ever higher, into the chill of the night.

Doc took immediate inventory of the condition of his parachute harness. The reserve chute was spilling out of its canvas bag. With his knife, Doc cut it loose. It went billowing down, partially opened, and made a pale misshapen mushroom that blocked him from view of anyone on the ground.

That piece of luck possibly preserved his life.

DOC SAVAGE continued his helpless journey heavenward.

His great metallic hands were inspecting the buckles and straps of the harness, finding that they were all intact. That meant it would be safe to deploy his main parachute when the time came.

Safe to deploy, but not to land. For once the open parachute was visible, Doc would be a prominent target long before his boots hit the ground. His parachute bell this time was a regulation white, and not made of black material. As such, it would stand out starkly against the evening sky.

Time enough for that concern later. Doc studied the phenomenon of this helpless levitation. Compared to the previous encounter, he did not feel that he was rising as fast as before. He trusted that a single shotgun blast would not fling him all the way up into the stratosphere, where air conditions were inimical to life.

This proved to be correct. More than a mile up, according to his wristwatch altimeter, Doc Savage felt himself starting to slow. Gravity made his muscles feel heavy again.

No longer buoyant, he commenced to tumble earthward.

Now Doc faced a difficult decision. The sooner he cracked his parachute, the swifter he would become a target for any marksman on the ground. But to delay too much would risk a hard landing and possibly spraining or breaking ankles or knees.

In either event, the bronze man would be helpless until he could wiggle free of his parachute harness. And once unencumbered, there would be no safeguards against death should another shotgun blast rocket him back into the sky.

There were a few times that the bronze man wished that he had not developed a personal rule against carrying firearms. This was one such time. Had he been in possession of one of the supermachine pistols of his own invention, Doc could defend himself on the way down, and again upon landing. The compact superfirers could wither most groups of gunmen.

As it turned out, Doc Savage's regret soon proved to be misplaced.

The firefly lights of moving lanterns below indicated that others were coming out of concealment. Perhaps from the bunkhouse or dilapidated barn. It did not matter, either.

Doc yanked his ripcord ring, and the canvas bag on his back vomited a silken flower that blossomed into a mushroom which scooped quantities of air and acted as a brake for his tumbling body.

The bronze giant was yanked upright. He took hold of the shroud lines, and stared downward, his face impassive as flashlights licked about.

As he descended, dull shouting could be heard. Words could not be made out. But it did not matter. Rifles began working. They whacked spitefully.

The lobe of the parachute presented a large target, but not from Doc's present height. Bullets sought him futilely. The sounds of passing slugs warned him of their nearness. These sounds differed. Some were remindful of glass rods snapping, while others brought to mind struck tuning forks.

Doc spilled air from one side or the other by pulling on the shroud lines in order to make himself a more difficult target to hit. The disturbed canopy skidded along air currents, hiking left, then right.

The maneuver seemed to work, for no bullets punched through the ghostly pale bell. Nor was the bronze giant personally struck.

As he continued his descent, Doc reached into a pocket, pulled out a tube and unscrewed it. He dropped the lid, no longer needing it. Then he began dropping glass balls here and there. The tin-walled anesthetic bombs fractured upon impact with the ground, releasing their insidious contents.

The stuff might not get every rifleman. But it was enough to thin out the herd.

Here and there, a man collapsed, his rifle dropping from his grip. Anesthetic slumber had overtaken them.

Other riflemen scattered. Not all were aware of what was transpiring on the ground. They were too fixated on the bronze man floating back to earth to notice their brethren succumbing to the mushrooming invisible gas clouds.

Doc carefully poured out the last anesthetic bomb into his waiting palm when the lucky shot came. Or rather, the unlucky shot. For it was lucky for the rifleman who fired it, but not for the bronze man who was its recipient.

A blind bullet struck the tube, knocking it from Doc's fingers. But not before shattering the fragile glass sphere.

This happened so fast the bronze man did not quite comprehend what had transpired. His fingers stung and the tube was gone.

An interesting property of the anesthetic gas was that it was both colorless and odorless. When it struck down Doc Savage's foes, it was as if they succumbed to some stealthy sorcery. Doc sometimes considered adding a dye or a chemical odor to the gas to increase the terror it might inflict upon evildoers, but ultimately decided against this. Sometimes he was forced to use it upon people who were not necessarily bad and he did not want the stuff to be confused with poison gas.

Another property was that it volatilized so rapidly it usually turned harmless after a few short minutes. This enabled Doc and his men to hold their breath against the stuff until it dissipated while their foes fell all around them.

These were wonderful properties, but this was a case where they backfired on the man who devised them.

Doc had not realized the gas bomb had been broken until after he had inhaled the first whiffs of the stuff, unknowingly.

In fact, he was oblivious to all consequences. A strange flicker of something whipped his metallic features. And for a fractional instant, his weird trilling piped out, rather startled. His hand suddenly dropped to his side and his head fell forward, chin coming to rest on his collarbone. Golden eyes closed shut. So swiftly had the stuff overcome him that the bronze giant was unconscious before he grasped his peril.

Sagging in the parachute harness, Doc Savage completed his

return to the earth. Landing awkwardly, he folded up onto the ground while the parachute settled over him like a ghostly shroud.

A trio of riflemen emerged from the brush, approached with caution, prepared to shoot if the bronze man stood up.

He did not stand up. The shrouded form did not move. Night breezes played at the silken bell as it rippled and curled uncontrollably.

A man muttered, "He ain't gettin' up. Think he's dead?"

"I dunno. And I don't feel like bargin' in there and findin' out. Doc Savage is famous for playing possum."

So they hung back, pointing their rifles at the dancing silk.

Soon enough, the man in the green hood stepped up, antique shotgun in hand.

"I think we got 'im, Calamity," one of the riflemen said. "He hasn't moved a blamed muscle."

The hooded one grunted, "Better make sure. Fire into the hump. Empty your rifles. If he's dying, that will finish him off. If he's already dead, a few more bullets won't hurt him none."

No one hesitated exactly, although a few men swallowed hard and licked dry lips. They were cowboy enough to feel queasy about shooting an unarmed and helpless man.

"I've heard shootin' at that jasper is kinda like firin' into a brush pile," muttered one. "The lead may crack 'im up a little, but it don't change his shape none."

Calamity growled, "Get to it."

While Doc Savage lay helpless, they worked the levers of their Winchesters mechanically. One man brought out a six-shooter and fired into the silk.

The shapelessness of the billowing stuff made locating the body with certainty a trifle tricky. But they put enough bullets into the pile that all felt confident that they had penetrated Doc Savage's body several times.

Being smart cowboys, and not wishing to waste precious

ammunition, they finished unraveling their cartridges, then they stopped. No one reloaded.

The masked man asked, "Who wants to make sure he's dead?"

"Oh, he's defunct all right. How can he not be?"

"He's Doc Savage. He's got more lives than a damn cat. Somebody make sure. And make it snappy."

None of the killers appeared eager to execute the grisly task.

The wind-rippled parachute fabric commenced turning red. The color was quite distinct. It was a deep crimson, the exact color of blood.

"Look at that! He's only now started bleedin'!"

"Dead men don't bleed," intoned the masked man. "That means he's only wounded."

But the deep crimson kept on seeping, soaking the parachute fabric.

While this was encouraging, it also made for hesitation. Nobody was anxious to see what kind of red ruin the corpse of Doc Savage had become.

"Never mind," muttered the head gunman. "He's lost so much blood, it's just a matter of a few more minutes. We'll let him finish his bleeding, then we'll bury him deep once the others get here."

Every man looked relieved when those words came.

Without another word, they set off to collect such riflemen as had succumbed to the powerful anesthetic gas. These fellows they carried back to the ranch house, where, revived by redeye whiskey, they fell into riotous revelry as the night wore on.

Chapter XXXII

PROGRESS OF A SORT

PAT SAVAGE HAD plenty of time to think about matters in the steady driving which followed.

"By now," she was saying, "there can be no doubt that your cousin Kip is mixed up with these mule rustlers."

"Guess we should report all this to the new sheriff," Gordon Darn said unhappily.

Pat made a face that changed the entire topography of her tawny features. Turning back to town and enlisting the sheriff did not seem like a very smart idea to her.

"Too many complications," she told Gordon Darn.

His mouth poised to form a syllable, the young man seemed about to object. His heart all but jumped out of his throat when there came a loud report, and the sedan swayed and screamed its tires, once producing an ugly rubbery squeal.

"Whew!" he exclaimed. "A blow-out!"

"Maybe not!" said Pat hastily. "It might have been a gunshot."

In any event, the car was no good to them now. It was just worrying along on a wheel rim. Pat eased over to the shoulder and braked the machine. They sat in darkness, for the bronze-haired girl had swiftly extinguished all lights as a precaution against snipers. No bullets came.

Looking around, Pat saw nothing suspicious. "We should make a break for it," she suggested.

"If you think it's safe to do so," Gordon Darn said thickly.

"I don't," assured Pat grimly, "think any such thing. But I'm not sitting here waiting for hot lead to rearrange my hair."

Darn swallowed as they popped open the doors. Together, they plunged into the roadside sagebrush. No one shot at them.

"Maybe it was a blow-out, after all," Darn suggested hopefully.

"Doesn't matter," said Pat. "Follow me." She struck out through the woods, directly away from the roadway. Tall weeds in the timber were wet. Very quickly they got cold, but warmed up by running.

Unpleasant was the discovery that the woodland was surrounded by open fields. They would be excellent targets crossing them.

Pat and the young man skirted around the edge of the timber, seeking a safe avenue for flight. They came to a creek which had steep banks, its cool water approximately waist deep. They slid down one sheer bank, crossed, and clawed up the other side.

"Well," sputtered Darn, blowing water off his lips, "we couldn't get any more wet than we already are...."

Pat laughed merrily at his bedraggled garments. "At least you got rid of all that roadside mud you collected on your person."

Ahead lay another road, an occasional car whizzing along it. It did not look promising. But then Pat noticed that the road was favored by trucks.

"I wonder which one of us is the most foolhardy?" Pat grunted.

Gordon Darn regarded the golden-eyed girl quizzically.

"Never mind," said Pat. "Follow my lead. And try to keep up."

It would have been an all-night walk to the nearest habitation, except that they were fortunate enough to catch a stock truck, and crouch, unbeknownst to the driver, in back with a load of noisy sheep.

When they saw the lights of what appeared to be an eating establishment, they dropped off the back and moved in that direction.

THE ROADHOUSE had a bright neon sign out front which said, "The Hot Spot." The gravel parking lot was floodlighted; it was also crowded with automobiles. Music and the noise of people having fun came out of the place.

In the drizzling rain, Pat Savage and Gordon Darn studied the place with disapproval, deciding it represented an opportunity to get out of the rain, even if it was a dubious one. The roadhouse was likely to have a pay telephone. That was what they needed most.

"I don't like this," grumbled Darn. He had not enjoyed the long skin-soaking march which had preceded the finding of the roadhouse. He knew of the place. "By reputation only," he hastened to say. "It tends to attract bad hombres."

Pat considered this statement. She blew rainwater off her delectable lips. A flash of skyfire illuminated her pretty features. Distant detonation told that the storm was moving off.

"If we found this joint," she mused, "those footloose crooks might have, too."

Gordon shuddered. "If we barge in, we'll be spotted for sure. They won't be happy about that wreck of a coupé, or the sedan we stole."

"Let's see if we can find an unlocked car," Pat suggested.

"Brrrr! I'm not sure I like that idea any better."

"Feel free to offer your own suggestions," said Pat, squaring her jaw with determination.

They found one finally, a canary yellow roadster. Pat said, "You stick here. I'd hate to steal another car, but we may need it for a quick getaway."

Fully aware of the disreputable picture she offered, Pat noticed a side door of the roadhouse. She loitered there, waiting for the orchestra to take up another round of dance music.

Pat was just deciding they might pause all night when the music resumed. Furtively, she stumbled into the place and crept around cautiously. The joint—that was the best descriptive word for the sordid establishment—was hazy with tobacco smoke.

The atmosphere was so thick that Pat became less concerned about being spotted.

She found a man who looked as if he worked there and braced him.

"Have you a pay telephone?" she asked.

"Sure, toots," said the other. He pointed toward a booth in a back corner of the noisy place.

Pat looked around, and didn't like what she saw. Couples were dancing. They looked rough, even the women. Liquor flowed freely.

"Lord love a goose!" she murmured to herself. "This place looks like an owlhoot's conception of Valhalla."

Pat failed to spot Bobcat Face, or his confederate, Flat Nose. But that did not mean they were not concealed by the noisy throng.

A slightly inebriated individual bumped into her, lifted his hat straight off his head with one hand. "Say, bronze and beautiful!"

"Excuse me, please," said Pat frostily.

"Join me at my table, sister," he exclaimed mushily.

"I am *not* your sister," sniffed Pat indignantly, expertly weaving around him and throwing herself into the telephone booth. She pulled the door shut, began feeding the slot nickels.

First, she asked the local operator to connect her to the Circle Bolt Ranch. It was likely that Long Tom had returned from his visit to the Lynx Eyes spread.

The insistent buzzing of the line went on and on. Finally, the operator said impatiently, "No one is answering, Miss."

"Very well," said Pat. "Thank you for trying."

Pat again considered calling the Bison sheriff, but decided against it. She had had enough brushes with the law, although she still yearned to recover her grandfather's frontier six-shooter.

"Time enough for that later," she said, stepping out of the telephone booth.

Rejoining Gordon Darn outside, she announced, "I had no special luck."

Darn looked uncomfortably blank of expression.

"Kindly explain what that means, please?" he asked nervously.

"It means," returned Pat seriously, "we're going to have to become car thieves again."

"You say that like you have had vast experience!"

"More than I care to tell," said Pat, dropping behind the wheel of the unlocked canary-colored roadster.

Gordon Darn hesitated.

Pat ducked her head in order to catch his eye. "Are you coming, or are you just going to continue to impersonate a wet hen?"

Wordlessly, he flung himself into the passenger seat, slamming the door sharply. The entire automobile shook with the gesture.

Pat took out a nail file and ducked her head under the dashboard. She fiddled with the wiring a bit, and unexpectedly, the motor grumbled into life.

Grinning mischievously, the golden-eyed girl told her companion, "Monk Mayfair showed me how to jimmy the wiring to make any car start." *

"So you weren't fooling when you said that you were no stranger to trouble," Gordon Darn said in an impressed tone.

"Trouble and I are old friends." Pat put the machine into gear, and the car eased out of the gravel lot like a creeping mountain lion.

"Guess this makes me your accomplice," Darn murmured uneasily.

"Don't let it go to your head," suggested Pat. "I'm dropping you off as soon as we hit town. I have much to do."

"Such as?"

"Claiming my plane—and my six-shooter, if practical."

"Where is it at?" Darn asked curiously.

---

* The Wild Adventures of Pat Savage: *Six Scarlet Scorpions*

"Locked in the sheriff's desk."

"Oh."

Pat said archly, "You say that like you suddenly discovered that I'm notorious."

"Well, aren't you?"

Pat's grin was mischievous. "Only on my best days."

WHEN they reached Bison, Pat steered for the sheriff's office until Gordon Darn pointed out the fact that she was driving a car that might have been reported stolen by this point.

Pulling over to the curb, Pat frowned, "That gun means a lot to me."

The young man was seized by an idea. "Why don't you let me get it?" he asked suddenly.

Pat regarded him with a skeptical eye. "A fraidy-cat like you?"

Gordon Darn looked injured in an innocent sort of way. "I'd like to make it up to you for my earlier cowardice."

Pat considered. "O.K.," she said crisply. "Give it a whirl. But if you get into trouble, don't come running in this direction. I have a lot to do. Handcuffs will only slow me down."

Gordon Darn grinned crookedly and said, "Watch me."

Pat did. She watched the young man disappear around the corner and realized it would not be wise to be discovered sitting behind the steering wheel in a parked stolen car of such conspicuous coloring. So she got out and went for a stroll, doing her best to look nonchalant, if not innocent.

She came upon a corner newsboy hawking the evening paper.

The boy was crying, "Ranchers irate over ransom demand! Mail plane crashes in freak storm that causes lake to evaporate! Who is Mr. Calamity?"

"Let me have a paper, boy," requested Pat, handing him a nickel.

Pat took the sheet under the awning of a five-and-dime store, where she could read without getting further moistened. The thunder and lightning had finally passed, but the drizzle continued relentlessly. It was a dismal curtain with which to ring down the day.

Pat read the article. Her golden eyes got a little wide.

The gist of it was that an unknown person signing himself Mr. Calamity had been sending ransom notes to ranchers throughout Campbell County and elsewhere. He demanded that they leave money in their mailboxes after midnight. Otherwise, he was going to make their water disappear, as he had the lake near Devils Tower.

Glancing up at the rain, Pat clucked, "This Calamity character seems to have mighty poor timing. Either that or Mother Nature wants to show him up."

Reading further along, Pat wondered how the fellow had gotten so many ransom notices distributed in such a short span of time. She also wondered how he was going to collect. It seemed the easiest thing to set a trap at a mailbox after midnight.

But on further consideration, the bronze-haired girl realized that dozens, if not scores of mailboxes would need to be staked out. A difficult task.

"Must be smarter than I first figured," she murmured to herself.

Pat read further, keeping her eye on the stolen roadster in case she had to either claim or retreat from it.

To her surprise, Gordon Darn popped around the corner, his fingers stuffed into his coat pockets, his head hunched between his shoulders against the maddening drizzle. Despite his physical misery, he seemed to have a smile on his dimpled face.

He spotted Pat and sidled up to her.

"Reach into my coat."

"I beg your pardon," returned Pat.

"I collected your six-shooter. It's tucked into my coat. Go ahead and harvest it."

Reluctantly, Pat did as instructed. To her surprise and delight, one brown hand fished out the giant hogleg.

"How did you manage this feat of derring-do?"

Gordon Darn looked awkwardly self-conscious.

"I walked up to the sheriff's office and found the door unlocked. He usually leaves it open so folks can leave him notes. But he wasn't inside. So I rooted around until I found a set of keys and used them on the desk. This was the only antique six-gun."

"It's the only one I wanted," laughed Pat. "Gordon Darn, you have redeemed yourself in my eyes. Now I must bid you a reluctant *adieu*."

"Why is that? Have I not earned the right to—."

"Right now," said Pat, "I intend to climb back behind the wheel of that stolen car and hightail it to the airport and reclaim my plane. And I'm not going to allow anything—man or moose—to get in my way. I suggest you go back to your general store and count your lucky stars you didn't collect a bullet tonight."

"I would still like to catch dinner with you sometime."

"Don't remind me of my empty stomach," grimaced Pat. "I'll take you up on that another night."

"Promise?" asked Gordon Darn hopefully.

"Only if I live," admitted Pat ruefully.

With that, she jumped behind the wheel and took off without looking back.

Chapter XXXIII

THE DEVIL'S HEAD

LESS THAN AN hour later, Pat landed in the spacious north meadow of the Circle Bolt Ranch.

She noted no sign of the autogyro or Doc's big amphibian plane. Although disappointed, Pat had not truthfully expected to see either aircraft.

She landed beside Long Tom's silver ship, so that any arriving aircraft had room to alight. Shutting down the power plant, she stepped out and made her way to the ranch house, calling ahead of her in the Western fashion, "Howdy the ranch!"

Other than the mournful lowing of Gloomy the cow and whinnying out in the horse pasture, no human voice responded.

Pat stepped into the ranch house and saw that it was unoccupied. Her attractive face frowned like tarnished penny.

"I guess I'm back in exile until further notice," she murmured.

She went to her luggage and dug out two boxes of shells. Emptying the six-gun of mercy bullets, she began to reload. Her choices were unusual. She made every alternate bullet either a mercy bullet or a tear gas shell. Two chambers remained empty. Into one of these, she inserted an ordinary lead slug.

"For necessities," she told herself.

She closed up the revolver so that the vacant chamber lay under the hammer. It was an old Western custom, one taught to her by her father, who was wise in the way of firearms. Leaving one chamber unloaded was a safeguard against accidental discharge. Pat had removed the trigger from the weapon, so that only by hammer-action could it be fired. This was another old cowboy custom.

Satisfied that the weapon was in working order, she found her cartridge belt and filled the loops with fresh bullets. To her left, she inserted tear gas and to her right, mercy bullets. Into her pocket, she placed several lead slugs.

"Never know when you're going to need them," she told herself.

Only then did the bronze-haired beauty fix herself a hearty meal. She devoured it with a distinctly unladylike relish.

The sun was slipping behind the Bighorns when Long Tom Roberts rode up at last.

The golden-eyed girl rushed out to greet him. "Hello, you old electrophile. I was wondering when you'd turn up."

"Are you stealing words from Johnny?" demanded Long Tom. He was grumpy after his nocturnal ride. Distances in Wyoming were formidable.

"Any news?" Pat asked eagerly.

"Dug up some clues."

"Spill, my good fellow," said Pat jauntily.

Long Tom dismounted and led the horse into the stable.

"Several Lynx Eyes hands never came home last night. Sounds like they're part of the Quest gang. Or were."

Pat kept to herself the news that most of the gang resided in the Bison morgue. She didn't wish to get sidetracked.

"So, they *were* operating out of the Lynx Eyes spread?"

"Some of them, anyway," allowed Long Tom.

Noticing a grimness of feature, along with the subdued tone of his voice, Pat inquired, "Have you been spending too much time around that gloomy human derrick, Renny Renwick? You look positively bereaved."

Long Tom winced. "I found Hud Crater."

"His body, you mean?"

The puny electrical wizard clearly did not want to go into details because all he said was, "Somebody buried him by the side of the road west of Pumpkin Buttes. But that wasn't all they buried."

Long Tom was undoing the straps of one saddle bag. Once he had the flap up, he warned, "You might want to turn your head."

"On the other hand," said Pat gamely, "I might want to stare at it with all my might. Give."

Shrugging, Long Tom extracted a human head, pulling it out by its carroty hair. He said, "I need to find a sack for this. Doc will want to look it over."

Cringing, Pat emitted a revolted "Ugh!" and turned away.

"Does that—that head go with the body that parachuted down this morning?" she asked after regaining her composure.

"That's my thought," said Long Tom. "And it's got red hair. Just like Mr. Calamity. I checked one eyeball. Green as a lizard."

"So Mr. Calamity is dead."

"Sure looks like it."

PAT frowned, her tawny forehead wrinkling. She took her chin between fingers and thumb and worried it contemplatively.

"If that's so," she wondered, "then who robbed that bank?"

Long Tom blinked. "What bank are you talking about?"

"The one over in Casper. Masked robbers barged in, wielding shotguns. They blew a man clear into the sky. Another was plastered to the ceiling, so he lived. I heard about it over the radio."

Long Tom went paler than his usual pallor. "This development can only mean one thing. That rustler Quest got hold of that shotgun."

Pat nodded. "He must have culled together a new gang. Because someone's been sending messages to local ranchers, threatening their water. That scheme didn't pan out, so they moved up to banks. We have to tell Doc, pronto. He'll want to get on the trail of Quest."

"Knowing Doc," said Long Tom Roberts, "he probably already is. But he'll want to know one other thing."

"And what is that?" asked Pat.

"The foreman of the Lynx Eyes outfit is a bird named Buck Quane. He's one of the nighthawks who didn't come home last night."

Pat's eyebrows knit together, and her golden eyes got a little gleam in them.

"Are you thinking that Buck Quane might be Quest?"

"In my pocket is a gunnysack I found concealed in a Lynx Eyes sage cutter," said Long Tom. "It's got eye holes cut into it. That means Quest hangs out there."

"It sure means something," agreed Pat.

Long Tom was placing the dirt-caked head in a burlap sack which he tied up tight, then started toward the ranch house.

For some reason, the head in the sack made Pat shudder in a way that the exposed cranium had not.

"If Buck Quane is Quest, then who was Mr. Calamity?"

"That's another one for Doc Savage to figure out," muttered Long Tom. "This has got to be one of the most distressing mysteries I ever barged into."

Pat brightened, saying, "Actually, it's got my blood up."

"Good for you," said Long Tom sourly. "*You* can solve it then. I've had a belly full of death and destruction."

"We can jump into our planes and hunt up Doc," Pat suggested hopefully.

"Doc warned you to stay put. Besides, we don't know where he is—except that it's a safe bet he's on the trail of those bank robbers by now. The best thing we could do is wait for the phone to ring, or for someone to come back. Me, I'm going to get some shuteye. How's Laramie doing?"

Pat frowned. "Oh, I neglected to tell you. One of his wounds opened up. I had to fly him into Bison. The old boy's in the hospital. But he's on the mend."

"As long as you stayed out of trouble, Doc won't object."

Pat hesitated. "I don't remember saying I stayed out of trouble...."

Long Tom halted in his tracks. He turned. He had not slept all night. Only now did he recall spotting Pat's plane winging toward Bison.

"Now *you* give," he growled.

Pat offered a slightly sheepish smile. "Promise you won't tell Doc about any of my adventures?"

"Nothing doing!" snapped Long Tom. "What kind of disagreeable stew did you set to boiling this time?"

"Oh, nothing warranting capital punishment. I got kidnapped, but I wrecked the kidnap car. Then I stole another car. Two, actually. Then I got back my six-shooter from the sheriff."

"Any holes in the sheriff?"

"None that I put there," allowed Pat. "But I have a line on some desperadoes still on the loose. One in particular, who goes by the name of Kip Farr. He operates out of the Bison general store and may be connected to the Quest gang—or what remains of those mulenappers."

Long Tom looked perplexed. "If he's still alive, maybe he's Quest himself."

"How can Farr be Quest if, as you suspect, Buck Quane is the head rustler?"

"Search me," admitted the lean electrical genius. "If we put our heads together, maybe we can make sense of this range hash. You can fill me in over supper."

"I've already eaten," returned Pat crisply. "You'll have to settle for leftovers."

Long Tom made a disgusted sound deep in his throat.

"That Laramie *would* get himself all shot up! He wasn't much in a gunfight, but he sure knew how to cook."

Chapter XXXIV

SUNKEN SPRINGS

RENNY RENWICK WOULD not have found what they were looking for had it not been for the sheepherder.

The hulking engineer had attempted to plot a trajectory, using Fan Coral Island in the South Seas as a starting point and Great Salt Lake as a secondary one. Since Utah adjoined Wyoming, connecting these two spots and drawing a line continuing through the Bighorn Mountains should have narrowed the search. It did not.

"Wyoming," Renny complained at one point, "is a big bowl of emptiness."

Finding the sheepherder in question took all of a day and into the late summer dusk. Doc Savage had provided the sheepherder's name. It was Clem Spears.

This was the fellow who, while guarding his flock, had spied something roaring through the sky. Something that crashed to earth and then bounced back up again, continuing on in an easterly direction. This event had taken place a few years back.

The shepherd was out with his flock when Johnny and Renny caught up with him.

Spears had a good memory.

"I recollect it perfectly," he told them. "It was a-roaring like a flock of freight trains. It flew overhead and my sheep and I went flying everywhere. It was like we were tenpins, but there weren't no bowling ball—unless you count that thing in the sky."

"Where did this bolide impact?" inquired Johnny.

"The which?"

Renny rumbled, "He means where did the meteor land?"

"Oh. You mean where did it *bounce,* because that's what it did. Hit hard, and shot right up again like it was made out of rubber."

"Right."

The shepherd studied the horizon, and frowned. "I couldn't tell back then, but when that private detective sent by Doc Savage started asking me questions, and I couldn't answer right, I got curious. So I got to investigating later on."

"What did you find?" demanded Renny, his hollow voice thick with excitement.

"I found a place where the earth was stove in. Like a fist had rammed down out of the sky. A giant fist. Bigger than your mitts. See?"

"We get you," said Renny. "Go on."

The shepherd was still pointing. Fat white sheep were milling about. It was a placid scene, although the gyroplane stood out rather startlingly against the sinking red sun.

"It's about halfway between Pumpkin Buttes and Devils Tower, in the Belle Fourche badlands. A forbidding spot known as Sunken Springs. It's near the ghost town of Yarber Gulch. You'll know Sunken Springs because of the coal fires. They burn all the time. Stinks of fire and brimstone. Can't miss it, and you'll never forget the smell once you inhale a bracing whiff."

"Thanks," thumped Renny.

"Salutations," added Johnny as they reclaimed their gyroplane.

The gyro took off and its rotary wing beat in the direction the shepherd had indicated. Johnny clutched the complicated controls in his impossibly thin fingers.

As they passed low over the rugged terrain, Renny was saying, "No wonder Doc Savage's private Sherlocks didn't get anywhere. This place is as barren as the dark side of the moon."

"The lunar orb has no constant dark side," corrected Johnny. "For it rotates in the night sky. It is a childish myth to speak of a hemisphere that is never visible from earth."

"If you say so, Professor," grunted Renny.

Johnny, who was as much a geologist as an archaeologist, resumed his professional surveying of his surroundings. While the big engineer found Wyoming on the dismal side, the variety of natural wonders excited Johnny's rock-loving soul.

Before long, Johnny was expounding in his most professorial manner on the subject.

"These brown rocks scattered about are lava clinkers. But there are no active volcanos in this portion of the state. All are dormant. Now, the western portion of Wyoming is another matter entirely. The Yellowstone area with its superhot geysers is a cauldron of pyroclastic phantasmagoria...."

Renny pretended to listen for a bit, then yawned prodigiously. The noise thus generated sounded like a ram's horn being blown vigorously.

Johnny got the unsubtle hint and fell silent.

Evening was coming on and they started to worry about fuel. It would do little good to set down in the correct spot and not be able to take off again.

"Maybe we should turn back for the night," suggested Renny dolefully.

"Patience is the poor man's gold," said Johnny, using little words because the big-fisted engineer had more than once threatened to knock his block off if he didn't edit the worst polysyllabic enunciations out of his speech.

Renny was well educated, but Johnny's verbal jawbreakers tired him out every time he tried to translate or pick them apart.

DARKNESS had smothered northeastern Wyoming when the smoldering red glow caught their attention.

Johnny leveled a forefinger like a skeleton's digit slightly improved by a thin coat of hide.

"Lo!"

Renny squinted. "Holy cow, it looks like the earth opened up and Hell itself is bubbling up from far below!"

"Tartarus was never so fearful," commented Johnny, who picked up a device from the cabin floor and switched it on. The thing was a detector of invisible rays. It was particularly sensitive to what were known as "cosmic" rays.

"That the dingus?" asked Renny.

"It is," said Johnny. "It proved handy when we first encountered Repel."

Minutes later, the boxy thing emitted a whine like an injured dog.

Johnny jockeyed the gyro about in the sky, which caused the mechanical whining to become shrill.

"Thar she blows!" bellowed Renny.

Both men began scouring the ground with their eyes, seeking a safe place to land, but between the burning fissure and the darkness beyond it, no safe place presented itself.

It was just as well.

For a bullet snapped past the nose prop while Renny was hanging his head out the open door. It was a foolhardy thing to do, but the hulking engineer was accustomed to heights, inasmuch as he walked the steel girders of uncompleted skyscrapers as casually as most men navigated garden paths.

Renny boomed, "Holy cow!" He clapped the cockpit door closed. Another bullet arrived. This one bounced off harmlessly because the gyroplane hull was armored.

But the spinning propellers weren't, so Renny bawled, "Take us out of here!"

Johnny lifted the control yoke. The gyroplane climbed straight up, then canted, beating away like a frightened buzzard.

Johnny, proving himself to be very sharp-eyed, spied the rifleman on the ground.

"There are two assailants," he told Renny. "One armed with a rifle."

"Guarding something, all right," grunted the long-faced engineer. "And I'll bet it's not beef, mules or horseflesh."

Johnny had been looking at the instrument seated on his lap. "There are quite a few hotspots around here. That means pitchblende or radium ore."

"Maybe they're miners, staking a claim." Renny rubbed his jaw thoughtfully. "They were awfully quick to shoot. What do you say we beat it to the nearest town and rent some horses?"

Johnny was slow to reply. "I, for one, am not eager to pursue feral goslings—wild geese to you."

Renny returned, "This is about the place where that chunk of Repel slammed down to earth. We can't cover ground as fast as we can by air, but we can investigate more thoroughly by horseback."

Johnny considered. "It is not beyond the realm of possibility that whoever discovered pieces of Repel out here in the hills, might have placed sentinels to watch over the deposit."

"Now," rumbled Renny, "you're talking my language."

Chapter XXXV

THE UNSTOPPABLE FORCE

RENNY RENWICK AND Johnny Littlejohn had some ill luck with the gyroplane.

As matters developed, the bad luck ultimately turned in their favor. But at first it was a decidedly troublesome development.

The beating gyroplane was running low on fuel. They knew that. In their estimation, enough remained in the tanks to reach the nearest settlement, so they were not overly concerned.

So, it was distressing in the extreme when the gyroplane power plant started missing, and the forward propeller cut out.

In a conventional aircraft, this could have been catastrophic, inasmuch as they were over a desolate portion of Wyoming in the middle of the night. A safe landing would have been beyond the ability of most pilots under such treacherous circumstances. But the gyroplane was designed to land without power.

Once the propeller cut out, Renny disengaged the spinning rotor wing, rumbling, "Down we go."

No longer under power, the windmill blades continued turning freely, acting as a whirling parachute, retarding their unpowered descent in the fashion of the early autogyros. The gyroplane came in at a slanting angle, and Renny used his formidable strength to guide it toward open pasture under the whirligig craft's powerful hull lights.

The landing was surprisingly gentle.

Once settled on the ground, Renny got on the radio, saying, "Better let the others know where we are."

But neither the Circle Bolt Ranch nor the radio in Doc Savage's speed plane answered. The long-faced engineer finally gave up.

"Must be away from their sets," he muttered gloomily.

"Funny the ranch doesn't answer," Johnny Littlejohn murmured. "Pat was supposed to stay put."

"When have you known Pat to obey orders?"

Johnny did not have to think about that. "Never."

They popped open their doors, produced spring-generator flashlights and began searching the immediate surroundings.

The roving lights attracted the attention of a local rancher, who had wandered up to investigate the commotion on his back forty.

"Are you fellas O.K.?" he demanded. The man had a flashlight of his own. Not so powerful as theirs, but he dashed its light in their faces and decided that they were all right.

Renny replied, "We ran out of gas. How far to the nearest town?"

"Half a day's ride."

Johnny made a strangled noise in his throat. He was swallowing his long words. He decided they would be wasted on the rancher.

"Any chance we could rent a pair of horses?" Renny wondered aloud.

"To go to town? I don't know...."

"Now that you mention it," said the big-fisted engineer, "we want to finish our explorations. He's a geologist and I'm a civil engineer. We were doing work in our respective lines. We wouldn't mind getting back at it, if we had good horses, that is."

The rancher worried his long jaw in his reluctance. "You bein' strangers, I don't rightly know that I ought to."

Producing a billfold, Renny showed the hesitant fellow a pair of one hundred dollar bills. The rancher's eyes popped until they seemed twice their natural size.

"Last time I saw a hundred-dollar bill was never," he admitted, swallowing hard.

"Is it a deal?"

"For that kind of money," the rancher said fervently, "you can keep them crowbait nags. Except that I need them. But you're welcome to use them as long as you want to."

Quicker than they imagined, Renny and Johnny were astride a pair of swaybacked ponies and pushing due north. They let their mounts ride straight away until they were out of hearing of the ranch, then neckreined left. A canyon enwrapped them with sheer walls of sandstone and a blackness which seemed almost solid.

There, they donned their parachute packs, which they had salvaged from the stricken gyroplane. With the cumbersome harnesses firmly in place, they felt immeasurably better about their immediate prospects for survival.

This impenetrable darkness encouraged silence, so neither man spoke. From time to time, they used their flashlights, but sparingly. There was moonlight sufficient to get by.

They continued up the canyon. It pinched out in rugged breaks. These were marked by unnerving sandstone pinnacles and pencil buttes. Tottering hoodoos abounded. Wind and water had eroded everything, giving the landscape a haunted, forlorn aspect.

This forbidding expanse was Sunken Springs. No water seemed to percolate in it. It was as dry as an antelope skeleton left out in the elements.

Surveying the spot, Johnny commented, "As difficult as it is to envision, this area was once the bottom of a prehistoric sea."

"The moon's crust must look something like this," Renny grunted.

Johnny studied the fantastic surroundings and remarked, "If Doc Savage ever invents a rocket ship, I want to be the first geologist to study the lunar landscape."

"Be careful what you wish for," reminded Renny.

For all of an hour, they cantered along. Then one of the horses began throwing its head and snorting uneasily. A sulfurous reek came into the air, vague at first. It became stronger rapidly.

THE PAIR topped a hogback. A weird glow lighted the slope before them. Jagged red cracks rent the range. From these curled tendrils of bilious smoke. The sulfurous stench was now almost overpowering. It was as though the earth had cracked open to display a sample of the fire-and-brimstone Hell contained in its innards.

Both Johnny and Renny carried chemical gas masks that served as filters. They clapped these over their mouths and nostrils. Breathing became easier. They wetted bandana hand-kerchiefs with water from their canteens and, after pulling the coughing horses' muzzles around, affixed them to cover pulsing nostrils. After that, the animals quieted down.

His geological interest piqued, Johnny Littlejohn pulled to a halt and dismounted. He sidled to the crack gingerly, and craned his neck to look over the edge. The hot gash had a width of five feet or so and a depth of perhaps thirty. The bottom was a mass of scarlet, radiating terrific heat. A thick vein of coal burning underground!

Despite his filter mask, the bony archaeologist coughed explosively from the odorous sulfur dioxide thrown off by the smoldering coal. It made his rapidly blinking eyes smart.

Renny was suddenly beside him, a severely frowning tower of bone and gristle. Some awe was in his eyes as he cast glances about. He knew about such phenomena. The coal had been burning underground thus for years, probably. Rain, snow, cold, did not extinguish it.

Lightning might have set the bituminous seam a-smolder, or perhaps some Indian campfire or prairie blaze had initially ignited it. These burning coal fields were not unusual in north-eastern Wyoming. They burned perpetually.

Renny collected some dried wood lying about. He coughed

steadily while he tossed the bundle into the crack, careful to make them fall close together. They became glowing ashes almost instantly. Retreating, he came to a small pile of weather-whitened sheep and calf bones. He tossed them into the super-heated crack, atop the ashes of the wood. They also became crumbling ashes.

"Be too durn bad if someone were to fall in," he thumped.

"Indubitably," whispered Johnny. "Such fissures are intolerably hot. Yet in pioneer days, Indian tribes would camp by them in the winter, using their constant heat to keep warm. They would fry sage hen and jackrabbit by spearing them with sticks and holding them over the open crack."

Renny grunted, "I think I understood practically every word you just said."

Getting back on their horses, they continued on. Boulders loomed all about them, great towering obdurate masses. Small stones and little bushes made their progress stumbling. Scrub pine branches whipped their faces, the coarse pointed needles menacing their eyes. The air was better here, so they removed their filter masks.

After a time, they spied another glow, this one small and fitful.

"Campfire," breathed Johnny.

Renny nodded, monster hands tightening on the reins.

After removing their makeshift moist bandana nose guards, they left the horses, hoping ardently they would not take it into their heads to voice a betraying nicker.

Creeping closer, they did not use their flashlights. Visibility was poor. They could hear voices. Low and hushed. But it was impossible to tell the direction whence they originated.

Both Johnny and Renny had their supermachine pistols out. Renny now holstered his.

Climbing a needle-like spire of sandstone, he made a survey of the fantastic badlands until he spotted his quarry.

Returning to level ground, Renny produced his supermachine

pistol and used it to indicate the direction forward. Johnny followed, walking gingerly.

They walked within fifty feet of two men crouching among the granite boulders and lava rocks, keeping watch over their campfire.

One man cradled a Winchester in his lap. The other had a six-gun snug in a cartridge-belt holster.

The men were talking in low voices. Complaining, rather.

"I don't cotton to this stayin' awake all night," groused one. "I get up with the sun and I go down with the sun. Been that way my whole damn life."

"Knock it off, Bud. We got to guard the stash until the big boss gets here."

"I know that. Don't think I don't. I've been savin' my pay for some time and she comes in slow dabs. I'm ready to cash in like a king."

"Don't worry. There's millions in this. The boss has big ideas."

One man was smoking a cigarette. He blew out a long gust of smoke and tossed the butt into the campfire, creating sparks.

He searched the immediate vicinity with his eyes. "Keep an eye peeled for rattlesnakes, and I'll do likewise. I don't like rattlesnakes, and particularly sidewinders, which come out of their sand holes at night, crawling in all directions and still able to watch a given point. Some sidewinders can crawl forward, backward, port and starboard, and still keep lookin' at a man. I hate sidewinders, hate them with a righteous fervor."

"Shut up!" snapped the other. "You're making me fidgety with your loose talk of rattlesnakes slitherin' all over creation."

The two men fell into a long silence, during which Johnny and Renny slipped closer, undetected. When they stepped out into the firelight flicker, the quarrelsome pair practically jumped out of their skins.

"These are machine pistols," warned Renny. "They spit out slugs faster than you can whistle your favorite range tune."

The pair froze in mid-leap. The one with the Winchester

didn't seem to know what to do. But the other one was trigger-happy; his hand flashed to his weapon.

A dour glitter in his eye, Renny triggered the supermachine pistol. The compact weapon barked three times so swiftly the reports blended into vicious rolling thunder. The man lost interest in his fast draw. He was knocked backward and stretched himself out. He was soon snoring.

Johnny directed the muzzle of his weapon toward the rifleman.

"Expediency is imperative," he said.

The rifleman blinked twice. "Huh? Say again, mister?"

"What do you suppose he said?" Renny taunted.

The man let go of his Winchester reluctantly, and stood up.

Johnny seized the rifle and jacked the cocking lever until no cartridges remained in the receiver.

Renny barked, "Name your boss!"

"I don't know what he's rightfully named. Calls himself Calamity."

"We've heard of him," said Renny, nodding. "What's his game?"

"He's got a world beater of an idea. But he hasn't told us about it yet."

Noticing the man's accent, Renny observed, "You don't sound like a Wyoming waddy."

"I'm not any such article. I hail from Alliance, Nebraska. So did my buddy here. Is he dead?"

"You hear him snoring? Does he sound dead to you?"

"No. What kind of newfangled gun makes a man snore instead of kick the bucket?"

"Maybe it's a snore gun," grunted Renny. "What are you guarding out here?"

"A pit. That's all."

"A mine?"

"I guess you could call it that. All I know is our orders are to guard the pit until Calamity shows up."

"Ambulate," directed Johnny.

The dull-faced fellow looked blank.

Renny said, "Take us there."

Getting a good look at the rail-limbed archeologist, the cowboy from Nebraska remarked, "You're tall and thin enough to pass for a walkin' hoodoo, you know that?"

Johnny glowered at the other.

"This way," Renny urged.

Their supermachine pistols trained on his back, Johnny and Renny followed the fellow.

THE CRATER was large, perhaps sixty feet across. It lay among the foothills of the Bighorn Mountains, in terrain so rugged it was difficult to make sense of it.

It had qualities of a meteor crater, but also looked as if it might be a sinkhole. In the center lay a pit deeper than the surrounding depression. The crust around this was cracked, violently so. It was no alkali hole, but something more disturbing.

The cowboy brought Renny and Johnny up to the lip of the fractured depression.

"I don't know what's down there," he said. "But whatever it be, it's very valuable."

Johnny took a silver dollar out of one pocket and gave it a flip. It went flying into the crater. It landed somewhere. Johnny could not see where. But he had his flashlight out, its beam searching. Eventually, he found the silver dollar gleaming in plain sight and made a surprised grunt.

"What did you expect?" demanded Renny.

Johnny said, "I wanted to see if it jumped up into the sky."

"Well, it didn't. What does that tell you?"

"It tells me that the Repel deposit either lies very deep in the stratum, or has lost some of its propellency."

"It's what?"

"Force. Propellency is another word for force."

Renny nodded ponderously. He turned to the cowboy, who was standing with his hands held erect on either side of his downcast face.

"When's your boss due?"

The other shrugged. "Not sure. Tomorrow sometime. He gets here when he gets here. But I wouldn't stick around if I was you gents. He's got himself quite a gang. Men came from all over, interested in his game."

"We're interested, too," rumbled Renny. "Maybe we'll stick around until he shows up."

"Calamity won't like that much."

"He probably won't like that at all. But that's just too bad. We're sticking."

The Nebraskan's rather dull face fell, his expression turning slack and lifeless.

"I guess," he said slowly, "I can kiss my share of the million dollars goodbye."

Johnny stared into the crater mutely. Aided by his flashlight, he was searching its broken expanse with intrigued eyes.

"What is buried deep in that," he said slowly, using small words, "is worth many, many, many times more than one million dollars."

The cowboy's face quirked with sudden interest.

"Mister, you said that like you meant it...."

Johnny sighed. "The element buried deep down there, if it is still active, could be used to power aircraft such as mankind could only imagine—motorless, wingless vehicles. Possibly, it could fuel interplanetary ships capable of visiting other worlds."

The Nebraskan looked to Renny and asked, "Is he loco?"

"You know what gravity is?" countered Renny.

"Not exactly, but it keeps human's feet planted on the ground, doesn't it?"

"That's one way of saying it. Deep in that pit is something that's the opposite of gravity."

The dullard didn't know what to make of that.

"But gravity ain't a thing, is it?"

Renny said, "No, it's a type of natural force. Down in that hole is an element that gives off the opposite force."

"You mean what scientists call 'anti-gravity?'"

"Repel," said Renny. "It's called Repel."

The cowboy scratched his head. "I'm suddenly not followin' you."

Johnny said, "A bar magnet will push away another bar magnet's opposite pole. One can feel the repelling phenomenon at work, as if it were a tangible thing."

"That's my experience with magnets," agreed the other.

"Repel will push away anything and everything. Nothing can stand before it. It's the irresistible force some scientists talk about. Against it, there is no such thing as an immovable object. It's unstoppable."

The Nebraskan scratched his head some more and decided that his understanding was decreasing, not increasing. He went quiet.

While he was preoccupied, Johnny broke out of his reverie, turned and shot the man once.

Renny was so startled he bellowed, "Holy cow! What got into you?"

Johnny raked elongated fingers through his full hair.

"We are presented with an interminable wait," advised the gangling geologist. "It is my desire to investigate this pit, and I do not wish to be interrupted by anyone."

Renny shrugged. "I'll drag him over to the other one, and make a nice quiet pile. Looks like we have a long night ahead of us."

Turning his attention back to the crater, Johnny Littlejohn did not act as if he felt the same way. He was staring into the pit the way some men regard a thoroughbred stallion.

Chapter XXXVI

STRANGE SINKHOLE

AT THE CRACK of dawn, Renny Renwick took up the captured Winchester and went hunting. A single shot was heard. He came loping back, holding a jackrabbit by its long ears.

Using a knife, he dressed the dead animal and spitted it on a branch. He held the skinned rabbit over the crack in the earth that burned with disturbing vehemence, roasting it.

"Want some?" he asked Johnny Littlejohn.

Johnny was just waking up. They had taken turns guarding the prisoners. Shaking his shaggy head, the gangling archae-ologist and geologist declined breakfast and went to explore the great pit in the earth now that there was good light.

As he carefully walked around the circumference of the crater, Johnny paused from time to time to pick up gleaming shards of something. After a time, he found one that interested him.

"Eureka!" he exclaimed. "This is positively supermalagorgeous!"

Still holding his charred and smoking breakfast on the stick, Renny came bounding up, demanding, "Holy cow! Did you strike gold?"

"Better than gold!" Johnny appeared to be clutching something black in the bony basket of his hand. It resembled a diamond, if diamonds were ebony.

Renny frowned. "Looks kinda like anthracite."

"Obsidian."

Renny's frown deepened. "Volcanic glass?" he snorted. "Obsidian is hardly worth anything."

"You will remember," Johnny said loftily, "that when we were exploring the underwater base of the volcano on Fan Coral Island, we discovered a great rock that encased the original Repel element. The rock appeared to be composed of volcanic glass."

The big-fisted engineer grunted, "Funny, I thought the Repel stuff was encased in a metallic stone that blocked it from acting on anything."

"Correct. But the stone appeared to have acquired an obsidian crust from its volcanic immersion. The substance was entirely sealed within, except for a small crack in the stone, from which the force was streaming. When dynamite was detonated to dislodge the extrusion, it cracked the casing and the unleashed Repel force propelled the stone all the way to the United States from the South Seas, a distance of five thousand miles."

"That's right. We know from newspaper reports that the composite matter passed over the Great Salt Lake in Utah before landing here, then bouncing away like a rubber ball to drop into the Lake of the Ozarks, over in Missouri."

"Before that," interjected Johnny, "an excursion boat on the Great Salt Lake was buffeted by waves that were not produced by any wind—a disturbance undoubtedly generated when the jet of Repel force briefly pointed downward from the tumbling rock as it passed overhead."

The long-faced engineer had been picking at his barbecued rabbit as he spoke. Now he threw the remains away.

"Do you think this fragment of obsidian broke off when the hunk of Repel bounced?"

Johnny nodded sagely. "Obsidian is not found in this part of Wyoming. It is a glass, and the product of active volcanos. The outer Repel stone might have retained its obsidian coat in places.

This is further proof that the Repel stone impacted the spot—not that we required any such proof."

Johnny was again staring into the pit.

Renny rumbled, "What are you going to do? You've got a hungry look on your face."

Johnny was toying with his lapel monocle magnifier. "I am going to investigate this pit," he stated firmly. "You will remember that the samples of Repel that we recovered eventually lost their force. It may be that the specimen left behind is still potent."

"That means it's dangerous to venture into the pit."

"Unquestionably so. But my curiosity has gotten the better of me."

Frowning like a thundercloud, Renny started back. "Let me get a rope off one of the horses. In case I have to lasso you if you start floating off."

It sounded like a jest, but it wasn't. The big-fisted engineer returned with exactly that—a long length of hemp, with which he swiftly fashioned a serviceable lariat.

By the time he returned to the pit's verge, Johnny was scrambling down, pausing every so often, picking up pieces of detritus and applying his monocle magnifier to them.

At one juncture, he kicked something over—with comical results.

THE LONG-BONED archaeologist executed an unexpected somersault, but did not land on his feet. Nor on his head, nor upon his back. He floated about, elongated arms and legs kicking wildly. He let out a wordless screech of surprise.

That was when Renny cast the lariat, capturing Johnny by one loose boot. Had it not been equipped with a spur, the maneuver might have failed.

Johnny had been floundering about in midair not very high off the ground, as if the power acting upon him was undecided. His agitated kicking and arm windmilling caused him to drift toward the center of the pit. That was when he started to rise straight up.

Renny arrested his upward progress by hauling back on his rope.

"I'll be superamalgamated!" Johnny yelled out.

"You'll be super-stratospheric before you know it," thundered Renny. Giving the rope a two-handed yank, he pulled Johnny out of the zone of influence—with the result that the long-worded archaeologist landed like a pile of human cordwood, fortunately not breaking anything.

"I guess there's no doubt anymore that potent Repel matter was driven deep into this crater," suggested Renny as he helped Johnny to his feet.

Johnny was spanking buff-colored dust off his clothes and doing his best to recover his dignity. He turned, scrutinized the pit and said, "Not only is Repel present, but something else."

"What's that?"

"Pitchblende."

Renny knew what pitchblende was. "That stuff is kind of rare, too, isn't it?"

"It is not the rarity that concerns me," pronounced Johnny. "Rather, it is the significance of the blending of the Repel deposit and pitchblende."

"What do you mean?"

"The commingling of such unpredictable elements cannot be salutary. Indeed, I suspect they are dangerously problematic."

Renny made nervous fists with his monster hands. He gave his pants a defiant hitch.

"If it weren't for the fact that Repel loses its power after a while," he rumbled, "it would be the most dangerous weapon on earth. Anyone who controlled enough of it could become master of the world."

"Exactly," returned Johnny. "This deposit has not exhausted

itself as it should have. And Mr. Calamity is on his way to claim more of it."

Renny carefully folded massive fingers until they made something over a quart of fist, brought it up so that the other could study the horny, much-scarred knuckles that sprang into view.

"Over our dead bodies," he thumped gloomily.

Johnny turned to him, his bright eyes curious. "I take it you agree with me that we dare not leave this pit and report our findings to Doc Savage, lest Mr. Calamity show up in our absence."

"One of us might have to turn back," allowed Renny. "But let's give it a few hours before we draw straws. Are you finished poking around down there?"

Reluctantly, Johnny nodded his head. "This particular Repel deposit does not evince signs of its customary awesome force. If I were again hurled skyward, I might not rise far enough that my parachute would save me. One requires sufficient height for the canopy to fully open."

"That's my thinking, too," rumbled Renny. "Let's leave the durn stuff alone until Calamity gets here."

Johnny eyed him dubiously. "You mean Doc Savage, do you not?"

"Slip of the tongue," muttered Renny mournfully. He searched the early morning sky with troubled eyes. "Wish I knew where Doc was right about now."

"Ditto," echoed Johnny, his eyes equally clouded.

Chapter XXXVII

JERICO HOAN

THEY PUT OFF burying Doc Savage until dawn burned in the eastern sky with a scarlet smoldering.

The men who were assembled at the old E-Out-of-Hell ghost ranch did not appear to be faint-hearted individuals. Far from it. They were tough. They talked tough, and it wasn't the artificial toughness of a Hollywood gangster picture. It was the genuine article.

Their leader, who wore his green silk hood throughout the evening as the assembled men drank redeye and smoked and told grisly tales of their past doings, finally put a halt to the festivities by raising his hands. The sleeve ends of his flannel shirt were decorated by hand-tooled leather cuffs that looked expensive.

"We need to push out of this dump," he announced.

"Then let's roll!" barked a man.

Another skinned his revolver from a well-worn holster thonged low. He lifted it ceilingward, began popping holes in the roof. There was not much to the roof. No plaster. It was just cantilevered board. Dust and grit rained down, along with a single mouse that had been jarred loose from the rafters.

The trigger-happy one took aim at the mouse, turned it into a red smear with a single well-placed bullet. This brought a roar of approval from the owlhoot assemblage.

While holstering his smoking six-gun, he boasted, "I once shot both eyes out of a man with a single slug. I sent a bullet crashing into one side his skull and it came out the other, leaving two cavities in his eye sockets. He could've gone trick or treatin' without a mask. Except that he was dead."

Somewhat lubricated by beer, another proclaimed, "I bisected a jasper's breastbone with a single forty-five slug."

"Who hasn't done that a time or two?" sneered the mouse killer.

"Well, the ol' slug that split his breastbone also drove a segment out of his backbone. You could see right through him, if you wanted to."

The hilarity that followed was like something out of a ghoul's carnival.

When it settled down, the sound of a horse approaching caused everyone to go quiet.

"See who that is," directed the green-hooded man.

Two men went for the door and another sidled up to the broken window, his revolver lifted.

An approaching rider was skylined by the rising solar orb. There was not much more than a sliver of sun, so he was basically a big block of anthracite astride a horse.

The gunman at the window turned to his boss and demanded, "Are we expectin' another party?"

The hard eyes behind the green hood swiveled about. "I put out the word for any gunhand who wanted to join up with our outfit where to find us. Could be a straggler."

There was a solitary lit lantern. Someone picked this up and carried it out. Two others followed. They kept their big revolvers handy.

One shouted out, "What's the password, stranger?"

A hearty voice resounded, "I haven't heard that there was a password. No one told me about any password."

"That's because there ain't any password. But if you tried to bluff us with one, we would've perforated you from one direction and ventilated you from the other."

The green-masked leader stepped out then and demanded, "What's your name, big man?"

"Jerico. Jerico Hoan from up Montana way. In Bozeman, where I was brought up, they hung a nickname on me. Folks call me 'Big Sky.' Heard you're lookin' to take on extra hands."

The big man pulled to a halt and dismounted. He stood almost as tall as his mount, had the horse been rearing. It was a dark-faced appaloosa. The animal looked fatigued, as if from a long journey.

A gunhand said admiringly, "You must've been raised on bison meat, feller. To achieve so prodigious a mass of muscles, I mean."

The big man chuckled appreciatively. "Bison, elk and moose. I ate me an entire black bear one weekend. But I was extra hungry that time."

He stepped into the warm glow of the lantern and not a few of the hardened gunmen gasped.

For the new arrival was best described as a Goliath, a man-monster. His brawny shoulders, torso, arms and hands were huge and muscular. But it was his head that captured everyone's attention.

Plastered to his scalp was a black mop that looked as if it had been rearranged with axle grease. His features were dark, but that did not seem to be the natural hue of his hide. This last point was debatable, however. His complexion had a yellowish tinge that did not look like a mixture of trail grime and sweat. Sullen eyes were intensely black. There was no detectable difference between pupil and iris. His nose was slightly flat, as if it had taken more than one direct blow. The mouth was a hard edged rip in his substantial jaw.

He wore no shirt. He was bare from the waist up. His trousers, which were made of some thick material, were held up by a belt whose buckle gleamed like gold. But it was probably only polished brass. His exposed muscles were something to make other men feel inferior.

The leader asked laconically. "Are you good with a shootin' iron?"

The big man shook his head. "Dunno. I never carried one."

The emerald-hooded one grated out, "If you're not handy with the gun, stranger, then what *are* you handy with? We need experienced hands to do the kind of work we aim on doing."

"Dirty work, if you ain't got the trend of things," added a cowboy.

This comment garnered several guffaws. Someone emitted a war whoop, as if about to do violence.

"I can take any man who comes at me," said Jerico Hoan in an amiable tone, flashing a mouthful of snaggled teeth almost as yellow as his hairless bare chest.

And to demonstrate this, he noisily cracked his knuckles, first with one hand and then with the other. His arm muscles bunched like moving animals under his dark, yellowish hide.

The gentleman in the green hood pointed to the largest man in his outfit and said, "Start with him."

The indicated individual could not wait to be started on. Instead, he went charging toward Jerico Hoan. Closing in, he reached for one of Hoan's wrists, but by some miracle, he missed.

Registering mild surprise, Jerico Hoan took hold of the attacker's clutching hand and from his sleeve removed a young rabbit.

Astonishment registered upon the gunmen's features. There came a pop-eyed silence. A roar of laughter went up. The would-be attacker's mouth fell open.

Jerico Hoan immediately popped the little rabbit into the man's mouth. The mouth shut hastily. Patting the man with his hands, Hoan chased the rabbit down through the fellow's clothing and took it out of his left trouser leg.

There were gales of mirth now.

The rabbit continued to do impossible things for hulking Jerico Hoan. It vanished, appeared from the man's back pocket, vanished again and proved to be under a clump of cactus nearby.

Possibly a coincidence, but shortly afterward the rabbit turned into a clump of cactus which did amazing things.

One of the cowboys said drunkenly, "I thought you two were going to tussle?"

"We gettin' around to it," said Jerico Hoan good-naturedly.

This casual comment enraged the humiliated cowboy. Cursing, he unleathered a big six-gun, leveled it at the other. The hammer rocked back. But it never fell.

Although he had stood several feet away, Hoan seemed merely to reach out easily and clamp a gigantic hand upon the other's horny-knuckled fingers and the butt of the gun. The fall of the hammer was halted.

He tried to free his weapon, failed entirely, then stared down as though half convinced his hand was caught in a bear trap. The six-shooter came out of his fist as if it were a stick of striped candy being pried from a child's feeble fingers.

The cowboy looked Jerico Hoan up and down. What he saw didn't seem to sit well in his stomach. He became slightly green around the lower edge of his lantern jaw. He was unable to keep the awe out of his eyes. The big yellow-skinned man-mountain seemingly had not exerted himself in the slightest, but his gunhand felt as if a horse had stepped on it.

His gaze fell to the hand which the other had taken hold of. It was pale, as though all the blood had been squeezed out. He wiggled the fingers as if fearful they wouldn't function.

"Stand plumb gentle," said Jerico Hoan, breaking open the action and shaking five cartridges out of the cylinder.

One by one, using only the finger strength, he squeezed the brass tubes, popping the leaden slugs loose. They dropped to the dirt, useless. The giant threw the weapon into a clump of sagebrush.

More laughter came. It had a different quality now.

"You gonna take that kinda guff off a no-gun range bum, Butch?" one spectator jeered.

Against his better judgment, the gunman named Butch made

another pass at Jerico, who slapped him once. Butch went flying. Snarling, he bounced back onto his feet and tried to butt Hoan's midriff with his head.

The tricky Goliath grabbed hold of the head with both hands, then did something remarkable. Twisting about, he flipped the hapless fellow around in a helpless half-circle. Squawking, he careened wildly, yet landed perfectly on Hoan's saddle.

The horse reared and kicked and the confused gunman clung to its thrashing neck for dear life.

Striding over, the lumbering Goliath gentled the horse and helped the other man out of the saddle. He did it by grasping the man by his belt buckle and literally plucking him out of the saddle. He casually deposited him on the same clump of cactus that had previously been a rabbit.

Contact with the thorny plant caused the man to heave up, screech and go running off into the darkness.

"That was quite a performance," said the leader.

JERICO HOAN inclined his head politely and asked, "Who might you be, Mr. Green Sack?"

"Call me Calamity."

"O.K., I will. So are you hiring or not?"

"Sure. We're heading out to do a job up in Gillette. Ever been there, Big Sky?"

"Can't say that I have. But I'm game. If we're starting, let's start."

Calamity said, "Not so fast. We have to finish up something. It won't take long. In fact, you happened along at the right time. We're going to need your strong back to get it done."

Jerico Hoan nodded. "To get what done?"

"Dirty work. We got a corpse that needs burying."

"I've done that before. Anybody special?"

"Not anymore," laughed Calamity. "But you might have heard of the fellow. He used to be a big noise here and there."

"What's the unfortunate fellow's name?"

"Doc Savage."

Calamity and the others watched Jerico Hoan closely, noting his response. The black eyes blinked slowly three times, and his misshapen lips twitched a time or two. He made one fist, and then the other. Abruptly, he gave his dungaree pants a hitch.

"I heard he was almost as big as me. So it was good that I came along when I did."

"Fine," said Calamity. He pointed to the south. "He's out there under a parachute that didn't help very much. Just bundle him up in it and bury him deep."

Someone brought up a rusty old spade and handed it to Jerico Hoan. The thing looked like a spoon in his massive hands.

"Any of you boys going to help?"

"We'd only get in your way," said Calamity. "Think of this as your initiation, Big Sky."

"In that case," advised Jerico Hoan, putting the shovel over one shoulder as if it was a rifle, then turning on his heel, "consider me initiated into the club."

The human hulk strode off into the night, soon disappearing from sight.

Calamity turned to the man who had produced the shovel with which to bury the body of Doc Savage. The latter was the one the giant Jerico had manhandled so easily, the cowboy named Butch. Butch stripped off the calfskin gloves he had been wearing, and grinned evilly.

"I hope those gloves mean what I think they do," Calamity rasped.

The other's grin was like a skeletal slash of teeth.

"His fingerprints will be the only ones anybody finds on that shovel," Butch said flatly.

Calamity nodded. "That means if they ever find Savage's grave," he stated, "Jerico Hoan will hang for the slaying."

"Suits me just fine," the grinning Butch said with a chuckle.

The sound of digging came steadily and industriously. It was a John Henry kind of rhythm, almost as much machine as man.

After some forty minutes, Jerico Hoan ambled back, pitched the shovel ahead of him, where it speared the soft ground to land upright, quivering.

"Doc Savage is dead and buried," he announced.

"Did you check to make sure the body was dead?" asked Calamity.

"Didn't have to. The parachute was soaked clean through. Nobody bleeds that much and keeps breathin'."

"Then the deed is done," Calamity decided. "Doc Savage is behind us. We'll all mount up and head off to Bison, where we'll meet up with the other crew. They have cars. Then it's off to Gillette."

"What's in Gillette?" asked Jerico Hoan.

"The start of one million simoleons, maybe more."

"Sounds good to me," said the big brutish Hoan.

After they saddled up, they wended their way out of the desolation of the forlorn ghost ranch, and struck due north.

Calamity had donned a black-and-white calfskin range vest which matched the gaudy markings of his piebald horse. His hat was an enormous black custom creation, a more flamboyant thing than John B. Stetson had ever dared manufacture. The showy hat helped to keep the silken hood from shifting around on his head.

Lastly, he set in place a pair of smoked goggles, which covered the eyeholes in his green silk hood, to protect his eyes from the sun and dust of the day ahead.

"Are you going to wear that hood all the way to Gillette?" wondered Hoan.

"No, but right now it suits me."

Noticing the old shotgun in the other's saddle boot, Hoan added, "Kind of an antique scattergun, ain't it?"

Calamity patted the hammer gun and said, "This is the most powerful weapon currently on the planet earth."

"Is that so? What you got it loaded with?"

"Fire and brimstone, and worse besides that."

"Sounds like a real devil gun."

Calamity laughed roughly. "You don't know the half of it."

"Mind if I have a look at it?" Jerico asked casually, one huge hand drifting out toward the worn butt.

A wrist reinforced by a tooled-leather cuff snapped out, blocking the big man's reaching fingers.

"Nobody can handle it except me," Calamity said sharply. "You see, an old Crow medicine man gave it to me. With his dying breath, he said that I was the one the Great Thunderbird Spirit had selected to wield the weapon. If anybody tries to fire it in my stead, the Great Thunderbird Spirit will strike them down. Strike them dead."

Withdrawing his hand, Jerico Hoan said, "Sounds like you got hold of some mighty powerful medicine."

"You'll see it in action before long, Big Sky. And you'll marvel."

The sun continued coming up and they rode single file, with Calamity taking the lead and Jerico Hoan following in the rear. He had somehow recovered the rabbit and was playing with it, making it scamper about the saddle, and doing other tricks.

Laughing, Hoan remarked, "You're so clever I ought to give you a name. Think I'll call you 'Dagnabbit.' Dagnabbit the rabbit. How does that sound, little feller?"

The other horsemen soon tired of watching the performance, clever as it was, and kept their eyes turned to the way ahead.

Noticing this absence of interest, Hoan captured the rabbit, and flung it into the brush, where it scampered away. He seemed to have become bored with the little creature.

The terrain they rode through was monotonously empty. Tumbleweeds rolled about, a few rotating as if being examined by invisible hands. But it was only wayward winds spinning them in place.

As the morning wore on, they came across only one interesting landmark. It was not natural.

In the middle of nowhere, they happened upon a slab of concrete that had been poured into the shape of an arrow. It pointed west. It stood out from the monotonous ground by virtue of having been painted yellow. The paint had faded and the concrete cracked here and there, but its yellowness glowed.

There was an automatic beacon tower nearby, but it did not seem to be in use.

In the lead, Calamity pointed at the yellow concrete arrow, which was several yards long.

"That," he proclaimed, "is pointing toward a pot of gold the likes of which you gents have never imagined."

"What is it?" asked one gunman.

"I'll tell you when the time is right."

They rode past the marker, which was drenched in Wyoming sunlight.

Taking up the rear, Jerico Hoan studied the concrete arrow with interested eyes. He said nothing. Nor did he ask any questions. He seemed to be content to follow the others, a new man hopeful of fitting in.

The blazing Wyoming sun did not appear to bother him in the least. His darkly yellowish hide looked as if it had progressed well beyond the stage of burning and peeling long ago. No doubt Jerico Hoan had spent a great deal of his life in the out-of-doors.

His only concession to the sun's rays was a cream-colored hat, which he kept pulled low to shade his unreadable eyes. He had not been wearing it before. It could be seen that the crown had been pierced by a bullet in the recent past.

None of the gang thought this was anything special and so did not remark upon it.

Chapter XXXVIII

GOLIATH MAKING MAGIC

THE RIDE THROUGH the sweltering morning sun was devoid of incident. Penetrating alkali dust sprouted from under the horses' pounding hooves as they cantered across the glaring sinks, making the animals sneeze and powdering their coats.

The desolation was littered with the scattered bones of antelope and elk that had been shot, skinned and butchered by hunters in years past. They did not encounter any live specimens.

In time, they left the rolling range behind and drifted into the badlands with its craggy canyons and sandy draws arranged into a haphazard labyrinth. At the rate they were plodding along, they would reach the city of Gillette nearly an hour before the late summer dusk.

Having rid himself of the juvenile jackrabbit, Jerico Hoan pulled a silver dollar out of a pocket and began fooling with it.

The silver dollar walked across his knuckles when he wiggled them, hopped into the opposite hand when he let go of the reins, and repeated the performance.

Hoan did this several times for practice. Each time the silver dollar tottered toward the end knuckle, he switched the hand clutching the reins and captured the coin with his newly freed fingers.

Perhaps it was the boredom of the journey, but the big brute showed every sign of enjoying the amazingly flexible dexterity of his own much-scarred hands.

307

The rider directly in front of him happened to look back, saw a portion of the performance and whistled in low admiration. This attracted attention. Soon, other riders forked their horses back to allow the big man to catch up.

Three riders were soon riding either side of him, enjoying the nimble-fingered display of legerdemain.

"Bet you used to be a pickpocket," chortled one.

"With finger magic like that," crowed another, "you musta been a whiz!"

The Goliath snorted. "Used to be? Still am!"

Evidently becoming tired of making the silver dollar walk across his knuckles, Jerico Hoan suddenly gave the coin an upward flip with a dark thumb.

Three pairs of eyes jerked skyward, seeking to follow the coin's trajectory.

They were more interested in where it would land, but since it was traveling upward, they naturally followed its glinting progress.

Or they thought they did.

For the dollar coin never came back down to earth.

They shaded their squinting eyes, craned their heads about futilely. Jaws began dropping.

"Where the blue blazes did it go?" exploded one man.

Another claimed, "I know I seen it spinnin' up there."

Eventually, they realized the silver dollar was not dropping back to earth.

"Where did it go?" a man demanded.

Grinning brokenly, Jerico reached behind his ear and made it appear. He spun it a couple of times to make it flash in the sun.

"How'd you work that trick, Big Sky?" one rider demanded suspiciously.

"You know that a conjuror never tells," returned Jerico good-naturedly.

SCOWLING like a thunderhead cloud, the rider yanked out a silver-mounted six-gun and gave the hammer a slow, menacing cock.

"Never ain't hardly ever when you're facin' a bullet. I'm findin' you kinda tricky. Cough up some truth."

Expression bland, Jerico said, "I gave the silver dollar a flamboyant flip upward, and your attention naturally shot ahead of it. Before it hardly got off my thumb, I snagged it with my other hand. You didn't see that part. It's called misdirection."

"Don't fib! I saw it spinning high up."

Hoan chuckled. "Well, you thought you did. That was your imagination. It got ahead of your brain. Because the coin never went any higher than my collarbone."

Reluctantly, the gunman took his pistol off cock. He holstered it again.

"O.K.," he said grudgingly. "I'll buy it. But I don't want to be flimflammed like that again, so stow your fool tricks."

Shrugging, Jerico Hoan pocketed the silver dollar and assumed a more sober mien.

The others hurried ahead of him to resume their single-file trek.

The hotheaded one caught up with the hooded Calamity, who led the column atop the piebald mount who matched his flashy calfskin vest. "I'm startin' to not cotton to the new hand," he drawled in a casual voice.

"What's wrong with him?"

The rider scowled while his rough hands made a cigarette with the smooth efficiency of a machine. He struck a match on the saddle pommel, got the cigarette end glowing red.

"Acts like he hasn't a care in the world. And here we are, ridin' off to do some mean business. A lot of folks are gonna die maybe. All he does is fool and clown around."

"Hoan's the type who'll come in handy in a brawl. And if he's tricky, he might perform some magic for us. Leave him be."

The other drew deeply on his cigarette and trailed smoke out through his nostrils. "Sleight of hand don't win any gunfights," he drawled. Taking the cigarette off his lips, he squinted at it.

Instead of replying with words, Calamity gave his right arm a shake, as if a hornet had stung him. Suddenly, a two-shot derringer was in his hand and pointing at the other rider. One hammer made an audible click in cocking.

"Good thing we're with the same outfit," drawled Calamity. "Otherwise you'd be lying in the dirt, your six still in its holster."

The rider blinked in the face of unexpected death. His cigarette dangled from his lower lip, then fell.

"Slick move! Got a hideout gun tucked into your cuff, huh?"

Restoring the derringer to the tooled-leather cuff, Calamity said, "And another in the opposite one. That's why I wear them."

"O.K. You're the boss, Calamity. But I'm gonna keep an eye on that big yeller devil."

Calamity snorted. "Keep both eyes on him, if it suits you. But I like a man who is cool in the face of trouble. He looks like that sort. I could use three more like him."

The rider took hold of the butt of his six-shooter and said, "And that's another thing, when the shootin' starts, what's he gonna do? Throw jackrabbits?"

"We'll see how handy he is, once trouble pops. Maybe we can collect the first million without any bloodshed."

"I never heard of that much lucre falling into a man's hands without there being a fuss. The more dollars, the greater the fuss."

Calamity slapped the antique percussion shotgun stock protruding from his saddle boot and said, "That was before. We have a world beater. A world beater of a plan and a world beater of a weapon. But we're going to need more than one devil gun if we're going to make good on our threat."

"We headed for the place you talked about?"

"Gillette? Sure. But first we're bound for Sunken Springs."

"Ain't never heard of Sunken Springs. Is it up in Montana?"

"No," said Calamity slowly. "It's on the other side of Scalped Man Canyon, right next to Tophet."

"Never heard of no town called Tophet, neither."

"It goes by another name you surely heard of. Hell."

"You sayin' that we're ridin' into Hell?"

"No, but we'll skirt it reaching Sunken Springs."

Chapter XXXIX

CHANGE OF PLAN

THE DAY WORE on, and the heat grew sweltering. The horses became thirsty and exhausted. There was little water with which to quench their thirst. Gray alkali dust coated them from the crowns of their hats to the toes of their boots.

The followers of Calamity, riding through the Wyoming prairie, passed a bottle of redeye up and down the line. Only two riders abstained. One was the hooded leader of the outlaw gang. The other was Jerico Hoan, riding in back, seemingly unfazed by blinding sunlight, heat or thirst.

From time to time, he fell to whistling. His mouth music was without tune, but pleasant in an aimless, wandering way.

For an outlaw, he appeared to be an amiable sort. Or perhaps he was not very bright.

As they grew increasingly inebriated, the Calamity bunch began wondering about Jerico's state of mind.

The prairie began to crack open in canyons about them. Sagebrush grew ranker, the buffalo grass scrawny and less succulent. Ranches were not seen. And small wonder. These breaks were not good range.

They soon came to Scalped Man Canyon, the mouth of which was marked by a great weird rock with a rounded white top that had struck some long-dead cowpoke's imagination as looking like the scalped head of a man.

Sheer, forbidding heights of sandstone jutted up around them, and sandy soil ground mushily under plodding horseshoes as one rider rode up to the head of the line, falling into low converse with his boss. His face was sallow and drawn. Several days' growth of dark beard gave him an unkempt appearance. It was Butch, the outlaw Jerico Hoan had humiliated at the start of the trail. He appeared to have recovered his gumption.

"The new gunhand strikes me as a peculiar sort."

"No argument from this quarter," returned Calamity blandly. "But leave him be. I have a hunch he'll come in handy."

"Kinda oafish, if you ask me. Not much to 'im except beef."

"Beef," expressed the other, "was how men got things settled before the invention of guns. It's still a right handy thing to have at your disposal."

Butch took out the makings and got a cigarette working. "If you say so." His ratty voice grew softly dismissive. "But a man who ain't even Colt-broke… hate to think he's the chicken-hearted kind."

"Just because his hide is on the yellow side," said Calamity carefully, "doesn't make him any less of a rooster."

"Some of the others are talkin'—"

"Don't waste your breath or my patience with idle trail talk!" rapped the flashy leader, air-puffs of his words driving little clouds of alkali dust off the gaudy green mask. "You're just sore because on account of the way he manhandled you. Now put a hackamore on that loose jaw of yours and get back there. Warn the others to do the same."

Disgruntled of face, the scruffy rider fell behind, resuming his place in line.

From time to time, it could be seen that the masked Calamity reached into his pocket and brought something up to his mouth. Whatever it was, he kept it concealed until he slipped his fingers under the green silk hood and took it into his mouth.

It was assumed that he was chewing something. Perhaps nuts. Or berries. His mouth made squeaking sounds, as if he had wooden teeth or something.

EXITING the great gash of a canyon, the fatigued and be-draggled riders clattered along, picking their way over loose stones, between impressive boulders, in and out of gash-like draws and around hair-width ledges.

Big buttes stood about, great masses of gumbo, sandstone and lava boulder conglomeration. They avoided these obstacles.

After a spell, they came upon another of the yellow concrete markers formed to resemble an arrow pointing west. It sat forlorn amid the sagebrush and buffalo grass, which encroached upon it.

No one commented, but Jerico Hoan studied the flat thing intently. He said nothing this time, either.

Under the blazing sun, the horses eventually showed signs of faltering. They struggled. Stopping to permit them to chew on grass helped with their stamina. But water was hard to come by. And they were not built for endurance.

Jericho Hoan took it upon himself to ride up to the head of the column and warned, "These horses won't make it all the way to town. Something's gotta be done."

Calamity did not respond for some time. He was obviously thinking. His chewing motions stopped gradually, and his head pulled up.

He paused to roll something on his tongue. Lifting the bottom of his hood, he turned his head away from Hoan and spat something out into the grass. Jerico could not see what it was. The horses kept plodding along.

Finally, Calamity said, "I expect you're correct, Big Sky. Not a lot of ranches in these parts. Not big ones. We need to change modes of conveyance."

Jericho nodded. "These poor cayuses are about done."

Suddenly, Calamity squared his shoulders, brushed a powdering of alkali dust off of his smoked goggles and announced, "I have a notion. It's a good one."

"Well, spit it out," encouraged Hoan. "Let us all look it over."

"I know of a ranch where they keep at least one plane, maybe two."

"Do you know how to fly an airplane?"

"No. But the folks who live at the ranch do. We'll take them prisoner. Make them ferry us to Gillette, where we'll hook up with the others."

Jericho Hoan grinned. The grin was exceedingly wide and showed his yellowish broken teeth alarmingly. It was the crooked grin of a bear.

"Now you're talking! What's the name of this ranch?"

"It used to be the old Split-C spread. Now it's called the Circle Bolt. And it's not so far ahead we can't push these flagging horses straight up to it."

"Well, tell that to the horses," laughed Jerico Hoan, forking his mount and returning to his place in line.

After he had settled in, his dark features took on an increasingly sober cast. The amiable whistling did not resume. There was something deep in his intensely black eyes, an uneasy gleam that might have been worry.

Chapter XL

STRANGE SURPRISES

LONG TOM ROBERTS awoke to discover that Pat Savage had already been up for an hour.

Emerging from his bedroom while adjusting his arm sling, the undersized electrical wizard saw Pat pronging the ranch telephone handset and grimaced. "If you're making long-distance calls, you're going to reimburse me for every one of them."

Pat sent a scornful glance his way. "Oh, hush, you miserly tinker! I was just talking to the F.B.I. office in Cheyenne. They haven't heard a word of or from Doc Savage since he took up the trail of those bank robbers in Casper."

"What about Doc's speed ship?"

Pat shrugged carelessly. "It's still hangared at the Casper airport."

Long Tom looked around. "No word from Johnny or Renny?"

"I tried to raise them on the gyro radio, but without any luck."

"Sure wish Monk and Ham were here," muttered Long Tom. "We're short-handed, seeing as how we're spread out over half of Wyoming."

Monk and Ham were the missing members of the Doc Savage outfit, Colonel Andrew Blodgett Mayfair and Brigadier General Theodore Marley Brooks, respectively. Monk was an industrial chemist and Ham one of the most prominent attorneys in the long and distinguished history of the American Bar. At present, they were on an ocean liner bound for England, and unavailable.

"Are you hungry?" Pat asked suddenly.

"Starved to the bottom of my backbone," said Long Tom feelingly.

"Good. You put the flapjacks on the stove. I'll milk Gloomy."

Long Tom's face fell. "I don't usually do the cooking around here. Laramie does that."

"That reminds me," said Pat, heading toward the door. "I called the hospital. Laramie is on the mend. He requested I tell you not to let things run too far downhill until he returns."

Long Tom's tone turned irate. "Who owns this spread, anyway?"

"It's not who owns it," said Pat cheerfully. "It's how it's run. Now get to cooking while I go a-milking. I haven't done this since I was in pigtails."

After breakfast was consumed, Long Tom burned up the telephone wires calling Bison, Casper and other localities.

This activity accomplished exactly nothing. Banging down the receiver, Long Tom turned to Pat Savage and complained, "The F.B.I. won't return Doc's plane. They say they can't get into it. It's locked up tight."

"Shouldn't we leave it at the Casper airport so Doc can reclaim it?" countered Pat.

"We're down to two airplanes, yours and my private bus. They'll do in a pinch, but neither is armored and they're not suitable for diving into trouble."

"Speaking of trouble," said Pat thoughtfully. "I think I will go outside to get in some target practice. Being without my grandfather's Frontier Six for a day, I fear I might have gotten rusty."

Long Tom bestowed a skeptical glance in Pat's direction. "That hogleg will get rusty before you do."

"You flatter me," said Pat, laughing as she exited the ranch house.

Long Tom suddenly thought of something and called after her, "You know, there are plenty chores to be done around here."

"I'm a guest," returned Pat. "But don't let me get in the way of your chore doing."

"Females!" Long Tom groaned.

WHILE the slender electrical genius went about the ordinary work-a-day chores of his modest spread, Pat Savage slipped behind the barn, where she filled her six-shooter with lead slugs. Setting a number of tin cans on the top rail of the pole fence constituting the horse corral, she began detonating cartridges noisily in their direction.

The empty cans hopped off with alacrity. As they struck the dirt, Pat ventilated them for extra measure. She did not miss once.

After she had burned through every can, Pat found one that was relatively undented, gave it a heave upward. Her hand flashed down to the six-gun, which had gone back into her holster. The pistol jumped out again.

The heavy weapon pointed skyward in a flash. Pat began firing methodically. Her method of doing so seemed unusual if one did not know frontier pistols and their proper handling.

She wrapped her thumb around the big spur of the hammer, and rocked it back each time she fired. This was not fanning in the dime-novel sense of the term. Nor did she use the ball of her thumb, knowing from deep experience that the hammer could slip under a fast-moving thumb.

Enwrapping the spur with her crooked thumb ensured both reliability and accuracy.

The tumbling can jumped around, performed a somersault once, and pretended to defy gravity, except that it was the work of well-placed bullets that kept it banging around up in the air.

Five times Pat Savage fired, and five times the tumbling can rang under her unerring lead hurricane. When it was hammered beyond recognition, she allowed it to strike the ground.

When she got bored with her gun wizardry, the golden-eyed

girl picked a suitable horse and went for a noontime saunter. Pat wore her parachute pack as a precaution.

This waiting did not agree with her. Pat had every confidence that Doc Savage was on the trail of the bank robbers. But until her cousin resurfaced, she was a prisoner of the Circle Bolt Ranch, pending instructions from the Man of Bronze.

Her perambulating took the bronze-haired girl to the main trail cutting through this portion of Wyoming.

Pat was more than a little taken aback to see two motorcars approaching in a whirl of reddish dust. The first one she did not recognize immediately. But the second was unmistakable.

"If that isn't Long Tom's long-lost station wagon," she vowed, "I will eat my gun belt, cartridges and all."

The two vehicles pulled up and Sheriff Easy Gates stepped out of the lead machine, his old jalopy.

"Howdy, Miss," he said in greeting.

Dismounting, Pat asked, "Where did you find Long Tom's wagon?"

"It had been run into a ditch. Since it was reported stolen, it's my duty to return it."

Out of the station wagon stepped another familiar figure.

It was Gordon Darn. Despite his engaging smile, the sight of his dimpled face made Pat nervous.

"Hello, Miss Savage," he said, doffing his hat.

"We meet again," said Pat dryly.

"I had hoped you'd stay in town longer," the sheriff said without rancor.

Pat looked to Gordon Darn. "Did you have any more questions for me, sheriff?" she asked lightly.

"No, can't say that I have. I see you are still wearing that parachute rig."

Pat smiled a little sheepishly, but offered no comment.

"Gordon was kind enough to offer to drive the stolen car

behind me," explained the lawman. His canny gaze went to the well-worn butt of Pat's six-shooter, jutting up from its holster.

"Quite an antique you got there," he remarked.

Now Pat was perspiring slightly. Her eyes went to Gordon Darn and back to the sheriff, seeking signs of suspicion or betrayal.

"Thank you," she said. "It was handed down from my grand-daddy to my own father and then to me. It accounted for a lot of hostiles back in frontier days. In fact," added Pat, "the town of Savageton, over in Campbell County, was named after him."

The lawman seemed impressed and said nothing about the six-gun that had gone missing from his predecessor's desk. Perhaps he knew nothing about it.

Sheriff Gates asked, "Did Doc Savage ever turn up?"

"Not yet," said Pat.

"Well, I'll want to talk to him about those dead rustlers when he does."

"I'll convey the message, sheriff."

Sheriff Gates glanced back at his flivver. "I reckon Gordon can complete the delivery. I got business back in town." He lifted his hat, and said, "Nice to run into you again, miss."

"Same here," said Pat with relief.

She wandered over to Darn and watched the lawman wrestle his machine around and disappear back in the direction of town.

"You had me worried for a minute there," she told him.

Darn grinned. It was rather a goofy grin, due to the deep dimples that sprang to life under its pressure.

"Shucks, when I heard about the station wagon being found, I volunteered my services. It was the best way I could contrive to see you again. Maybe we can have that dinner, after all."

Pat looked at the sun, which was hovering at the noon hour.

"It will have to be luncheon," rejoined Pat. "And we'll need to take it at the ranch. I can't leave just yet."

"Suits me," said Darn.

Mounting her horse, Pat fell in behind the station wagon. It rocked and jounced its way up the dirt road to the Circle Bolt ranch house.

Long Tom looked as elated as Pat Savage had ever seen him when his station wagon trundled into view.

"Hot damn!" he ejaculated. "Where did you find it?"

"It found me," returned Pat lightly.

Pat made proper introductions, and into the ranch house they repaired to investigate the possibilities of lunch.

"Are you hungry?" asked Pat, doffing her parachute harness.

"I'm always hungry," joked Darn. "Except when I'm famished, which is half the time. Lunch sounds super."

Pat said firmly, "We're not having lunch. When I make it, it's called luncheon."

"Must be an Eastern custom," said Darn, taking a chair around the circular kitchen table.

Luncheon was consumed with a seasoning of pleasant conversation. Yet, underneath it all, Pat Savage grew increasingly concerned while Long Tom Roberts fretted wordlessly.

Lack of word from Doc Savage, Johnny and Renny was becoming worrisome. Particularly was the silence from the latter two puzzling. The gyroplane was equipped with a short-wave set, but neither man answered repeated radio calls.

To pass the time, Pat asked Gordon Darn, "What are the papers saying about this Calamity business?"

"There's talk that he's coming up in the world."

"Oh? What type of talk?"

"Some of the national airlines have been receiving letters. These letters are demanding a powerful lot of money, else this Calamity character will start interfering with passenger airplane operations."

Hearing this, Pat Savage got a little pale. Long Tom's neck turned red.

They were thinking of the U.S. Air Mail plane that had flown into a wall of water that had been levitated up to the sky. The thought of a big transport craft filled with passengers encountering the same fate was alarming.

"This Calamity fellow thinks big," Gordon Darn was saying as he chomped his way through an overstuffed ham sandwich.

"If you ask me," returned Pat, "he's getting too big for his britches."

A strange look passed between the bronze-haired girl and the slender electrical expert. They were thinking of the as-yet-unidentified mortal remains lying in the barn, the one whose head lay separate. They still did not know the identity of the corpse, and these most recent developments were adding to their concerns.

"I meant to ask you," said Pat, giving Long Tom a look that suggested he stay quiet. "The cousin of yours who owns the general store. Any news of him?"

Gordon looked sheepish, and a little guilty. "Haven't seen or heard from cousin Kip since he took off the other day."

"Imagine that," quipped Pat. "My cousin Clark is similarly misplaced."

Gordon Darn blinked his confusion. "I didn't mention to the sheriff about how his friends tried to murder you, if that's what you're driving at."

"It wasn't, but thanks for volunteering. By now, your cousin knows that his hired guns failed miserably. Bison is too hot for him now. He won't be coming back. And once Doc Savage catches up with him, that will be his finish. Doc will punish him severely for attempting to murder me."

Gordon Darn swallowed uncomfortably. He knew that Doc Savage was a terror to criminals the world over.

AROUND the shank of the afternoon, the drumming beat of horses' hooves came distantly.

This was not an unusual thing to hear in Wyoming, but the Circle Bolt Ranch wasn't situated close to any other spread. Nor was it on the way to any place in particular.

The rolling clamor drew near.

Naturally, Long Tom stepped out to investigate.

"Are you forgetting something?" reminded Pat.

Hesitating at the door, Long Tom went blank of expression.

Pat indicated a parachute pack sitting in a corner.

Long Tom hesitated but decided that Pat was making sense.

Grumbling, he went over to the contrivance and meticulously buckled it on.

Darn watched this procedure with increasing incredulity.

"Long Tom likes to take precautions," suggested Pat dryly.

This did not take away from Darn's puzzlement. Long Tom exited the ranch house and stood on his veranda.

Like a dusty storm cloud, a posse of rough-looking riders boiled for the spot where Long Tom stood.

"Who's calling?" he demanded.

There was no response from the riders, other than a horse snorting noisily. They were an unlovely band, their hats dusty and range duds looking starved for a wash tub.

Long Tom stepped off his veranda. For his pains, he was catapulted straight up into the sky.

It happened suddenly, unexpectedly, the way lightning strikes.

The puny electrical wizard was trudging in the direction of the approaching riders. He lifted a hand in greeting.

Too late, he saw the emerald hood on the head of the lead rider and the dark smudges of his smoked goggles. Also too late, he noticed the side-by-side shotgun gripped in the man's hands.

The double maw was pointed directly at him. It blew out fire and noise, and Long Tom's breath went out through his gold front teeth like air from a thrown steer. He was suddenly hurtling backward, but only briefly.

With a long howl of surprise and a desperate flailing, he began climbing into the sky entirely against his own will.

Chapter XLI

TRAGEDY

PAT SAVAGE HEARD the shotgun blast, followed by Long Tom Roberts' weird howling.

The golden-eyed girl did not have to look out the window to deduce what had transpired. But she did peek. One glance was enough. Booted feet kicking, good arm windmilling, the helpless electrical expert was moving away from the terra firma rapidly. Going straight up.

Swiftly, she threw Gordon Darn an extra parachute pack that had been lying about. "Put this on, pronto. And don't ask questions! It might save your life."

Darn did as he was told. Pat had to help him with the buckles, then she swung about to put on her own parachute harness.

"Stand in the front door and keep them occupied," she rapped. "Whatever you do, don't leave the ranch house. *Comprende?*"

"Got it," returned Darn shakily.

"Good," said Pat, slipping out the back door.

Exiting, she did not have a plan. There was no time to formulate one.

While sneaking behind the ranch house, she peered up into the sky expectantly.

Long Tom Roberts was a dwindling dot against the blue bowl of the heavens. A pair of startled turkey buzzards hastily flapped out of his way.

Pat bit down on one of her knuckles as she watched Long

Tom seemingly depart earth's comforting gravitational field. He ceased to be visible. Breathless minutes dragged past.

After what seemed like an eternity, a pale mushroom blossomed high in the sky.

Long Tom's parachute had opened. He was descending in a much more leisurely fashion than he had gone up.

It was not a windy day, but Long Tom did not come straight down. He appeared to have been caught by some upper atmospheric drafts, for the canopy was pulling to the south, drifting away from the Circle Bolt spread.

"I guess it's up to me," Pat told herself.

Opening the little gate of her frontier revolver, she broke a rule and inserted a sixth cartridge. Closing the action, she listened. At the open door frame, Gordon Darn was demanding what the new arrivals wanted. He tried to sound confident, but came across as nervous.

The harsh voice called back, "We want your planes. Can you fly one?"

"Can't say that I can," said Gordon Darn truthfully.

Those were the last words the young man uttered. A six-gun cracked once. There followed an ugly thud.

Hearing this, Pat Savage did not have to paint pictures in her brain. Gritting her teeth, she stepped out into the sunlight, and pointed her six-shooter in the general direction of the arrivals.

"When this dog barks," she called out loudly, "strong men quake in their boots."

She said it so forcefully that the assembled gunmen hesitated.

"Want to bet that I can drop most of you before you can plink me?" Pat added.

No one rushed to take up that bet. There was a general hesitation.

Then a man growled, "If you don't get a doctor for that sorry excuse for a gunfighter, he's liable to bleed clear into the evening."

Someone else laughed. It was a cruel laugh.

Pat hesitated. She could not let poor Gordon Darn bleed to death. But she knew if she surrendered, her goose was cooked.

"Can you fly a plane?" one of the gunmen demanded.

"I can. What is it to you?"

"Fly us to Gillette and we'll let the young feller live."

Again, Pat hesitated. She did not trust these men. They were desperadoes—killers.

Then the matter was taken out of her hands.

FROM behind her, stepped a shadow. It was monstrously large and moved with the silence of a lamb-stealing coyote. Pat failed to notice the looming presence in part because she was concentrating on holding off the raiders with her intimidating weapon.

A massive hand swept around, captured her six-shooter and relieved her of it. It was gone before she realized she had been accosted.

An arm that felt like the trunk of an oak tree wrapped around her waist and Pat was lifted off her feet. Struggling, she was carried out into the open.

Turning her head, Pat gasped.

The man who captured her was a giant. A fulvous monster. He was not so much ugly as he was unlovely. Between his disorderly black hair and his broken teeth, he was about as uncouth a specimen of primitive manhood as she ever laid eyes upon.

The hooded leader called over. "Nice work, Jerico! She fell for it."

Pat was helpless as she was dragged forward. The man shifted her from one meaty hand to the other and tucked her underneath an overpowering arm. Pat tried beating at him and kicking, but nothing seemed to faze the mute man-monster.

"Let me go, you—you roughneck!" Pat demanded hotly.

Unbothered by her flailing fists, Jerico the giant sagged down beside Gordon Darn sprawled across the threshold of the ranch house door. With one massive paw, he turned the man over and studied him.

With a discouraged grunt, he said, "This feller up and died."

Hearing this, Pat Savage flew into a rage. "Murderers! You'll pay for this! Don't think you won't!" she vowed.

Neither harsh words nor her pounding fists accomplished anything. Jerico stood up and carried Pat over to the assembled horsemen. They had their hands full of artillery. Their hardware ran to revolvers of impressive caliber.

"That," Jerico told the rider in the green hood, "wasn't wise."

Calamity shrugged negligently. "He couldn't fly a plane, so we didn't need him. And who are you to be giving me orders?"

The Goliath was unmoved. "I know who is boss," Hoan said slowly, replacing the bullet-punctured cream Stetson back on his huge head. "I also know murder's nothing to monkey around with."

"Maybe you're right," he returned. "But don't get the idea that you're telling me what to do, Big Sky. Drag that body out of sight. And we'll take off in the plane."

Jerico met the other's hard gaze unflinchingly. "Just understand that I ain't taking any chances for a murder rap."

Calamity paid no attention to that comment. "Two of you grab the girl."

A pair of gunmen dismounted, swiftly captured Pat Savage. Wrenching wildly, she tried to break free. But the pair were determined and not at all respecters of the fair sex. She struggled in their hands, kicked out and was tripped.

Pat landed hard.

"Don't break her," warned Jerico. "She's supposed to be our pilot, remember?"

Lifting limp Gordon Darn in his brawny arms, Jerico marched over into the barn, and deposited the body next to Gloomy the cow. He studied the man's blood-soaked trouser leg. Removing

Darn's belt, he tied a tight tourniquet, adjusting it until he was satisfied.

Hoan was about to turn to go when he noticed the other body wrapped in a horse-blanket shroud.

Curiosity quirking the corners of his eyes, the big man stepped up to the shrouded form and undid the wrappings. This disclosed the corpse's head. It also showed that the head was not attached to the body.

Brutish face stiff, he examined the head carefully, noted the color of the hair, along with the shape of the face and other details. One eye lay open. It was the color of a faded leaf.

From his mouth, a sound escaped. It started off a little like the call of a songbird, but when he realized he was emitting the trill, Jerico pursed his lips and blew out a little low whistle of astonishment instead.

Replacing the shroud, Hoan exited the barn, his expression bland as a cow's countenance.

"All set," he proclaimed. Jerico said nothing about his grisly discovery.

Riding over to the transport plane, they released the exhausted horses and climbed aboard, after first forcing Pat in at gunpoint. Assorted revolvers were directed at her head and spine, so there was no possibility of resisting. Then she was made to sit down behind the controls. Calamity sat in the copilot seat to keep her in line. He removed his trail dust-smeared smoked goggles, disclosing sharp gray eyes.

"Fire up your engines," he commanded.

Pat did as she was told. Her lips were a bloodless line and her bronze face held a strangely determined expression.

"Is it too much to ask where we're going before we take off?" she inquired.

"We're going to Gillette to pick up some friends of ours, but first we're going to make a little stop."

"Where are we stopping?"

"A place where we can pick up fresh ammunition."

"And where is that?" demanded Pat.

"Just head northwest. It's a wasteland called Sunken Springs. Can't miss it. It will look like a crack in the badlands showing the bowels of Hell itself."

"Sounds charming," murmured Pat, getting the engines going and turning the plane into the wind.

The aircraft seated everyone comfortably. All except Jerico Hoan. There wasn't a seat available for him. As the new man, he sat in the rear, on a packing case. His dark face was pensive, intensely black orbs reflective.

From time to time, one meaty paw went to the handle of Pat Savage's six-shooter, which he had stuffed into one pocket after disarming her.

After bumping along rather alarmingly, the plane took off without trouble, its wheels drawing up electrically.

As the trim ship sought altitude, Pat Savage's bleak golden eyes searched the ground that was falling away beneath them.

She saw Long Tom Roberts' parachute collapsing as the puny electrical genius landed safely in the horse pasture. Shrugging off his harness, he shook an enraged fist at the departing aircraft.

Under her breath, Pat murmured, "At least one of us is still on the loose."

"What's that?" demanded Calamity.

Pat replied, "I hope this isn't a wild *goose* chase."

Calamity spanked the checkered grip of his percussion shotgun meaningly. "Just fly where I tell you to, and *your* goose won't be cooked. Get me?"

"I get you," Pat said evenly, her white teeth clenched tight.

"And if you're thinking that Doc Savage is going to come along and pull your lovely fat out of the fire, think again. He's gone west."

Pat's brow furrowed up. "How do you mean, west?"

"I mean west as in he's seen his last sunset. Get me?"

Pat's pretty mouth twisted grimly.

"Doc Savage," she asserted confidently, "does not die easily."

"You got that straight," a gunman scoffed. "Took damn near all of us to ventilate him properly. Ain't that right, Big Sky?"

In back, the silent yellow-skinned Goliath was fiddling with Pat Savage's revolver. His actions demonstrated that he knew nothing about pistols, for he was peering down the barrel, squinting rather stupidly.

"I wasn't with this outfit when Doc Savage was murdered," Jerico muttered distractedly. "I only buried him later on. Get me? I ain't no killer."

Pat took her lower lip between perfect teeth. She felt hot emotion rise in her throat. She choked back a rising sob, only half succeeding.

From the rear of the plane, hulking Jerico Hoan asked, "Is this old hogleg loaded? I can't tell."

Chapter XLII

HOODOO OUTPOST

THE TWO GUNMEN from Nebraska were awake and complaining.

They were homesick. Both expressed a strong desire to return to their hometown of Alliance. The one who was afraid of rattlesnakes returned to the subject periodically. He appeared to be obsessed with the subject of sidewinders.

"Rattlesnakes," he was saying, "will sink their poison fangs into a man's ankles at slightest provocation, or none at all. There's just a cussed meanness to the critters. And don't get me started on the subject of bedrolls. Sidewinders adore slitherin' into bedrolls, so that when you stretch out for the night, they're already in your blankets, waitin' on you."

The other Nebraskan barked, "Will you lay off that scare talk?"

The first man rattled on unpersuaded. "Happened to a buddy of mine. Went to bed one night, and he could hear the rattlin' around midnight. The cussed snake was in the blankets with him. He didn't dare move all night. That morning, his friends found him, covered in his own sweat and shiverin' despite the heat. Someone put a bullet in the bulge where the sidewinder was coiled up, killin' it. My pal never got over it. Me, I still get the shakes thinkin' about it."

Renny had enough of the unhappy pair grousing the morning away.

"Knock it off, you!" he thundered.

"How long you gonna keep us prisoner here?" demanded one.

Johnny Littlejohn answered that. "Interminably, if your confabulation persists through the diurnal cycle."

"What did that fella say?" the rattlesnake hater asked the other one.

The second man shrugged. "Search me."

It proved to be a long morning and a longer afternoon. Renny and Johnny considered flipping a coin to see which one of them would ride to the nearest ranch in hopes of finding a telephone. This was a chancy proposition, however. It cost good money to string a telephone line out to an isolated spread, and many self-reliant ranch owners preferred to do without.

The droning of an approaching airplane brought all heads turning to the south. Necks craned and eyeballs searched the unclouded sky.

Renny's distance eyesight was better than Johnny's. He spotted the approaching plane first.

"Looks like Long Tom's bus," he thumped.

"A Pythian augury," the gangling geologist chortled. Johnny was pleased. He had exhausted all of the geological opportunities the landscape presented.

Long Tom's plane was not an amphibian like Doc Savage's speed ship. It was an outdated two-engine transport, larger than a private plane, and therefore handy for hauling some of the complicated apparatus that Long Tom experimented on, but it was no air giant.

The plane scooted overhead, silvery wings flashing. It banked, entering into a slow approach turn.

Renny grunted, "Finding a safe stretch to land is going to be a chore."

Shading his eyes with one long-fingered hand, Johnny nodded. "Without a doubt."

The chore of finding a landing spot took the better part of an hour. Both Johnny and Renny grew noticeably worried. The plane turned and banked, dropped and climbed again. It circled like a lazy buzzard.

Finally, the pilot found a spot that seemed promising and slanted down for a landing.

Johnny and Renny held their breaths. Both men were experienced pilots. They understood that all that circling meant that there was no obviously safe place to put down. The pilot was about to take a long chance.

Renny found a high hoodoo and climbed it, the better to see. The expression on his horsey face was worrisome. Noticing this, Johnny realized that the big-fisted engineer was half expecting a crack-up.

The plane touched down, bouncing along a level stretch of stony wash. At one point, the aircraft bounced back into the air, but finally got settled in. It rolled for a long time before the pilot threw the aircraft around and set about shutting down the motors.

Renny squinted at the plane whose silvery surface reflected the dazzling sunlight with blinding intensity. After a bit, a door popped open. Someone stepped out, peered about uncertainly.

When Renny saw who it was, he gave a whoop of pleasure and dropped back to the ground.

"I just spotted Pat!"

Johnny beamed like a happy skeleton. "Who else was with her?"

"Didn't wait to see. She's a fair hike away. Maybe we should ride out to meet her."

"One of us needs to guard the prisoners," Renny reminded.

"Right. They are plenty goosey."

"Match you for the privilege," said Johnny.

Renny shrugged, flipped the coin. Johnny called heads before Renny could ask his preference.

The coin came up heads. So Johnny saddled up, and rode off to greet the new arrivals.

Disappointment showing on his long face, Renny Renwick settled in to guarding the prisoners.

"I don't want to hear any more talk of rattlesnakes from you two sidewinders," he warned them.

"Who are you callin' a sidewinder?" one demanded indignantly.

"When was the last time you had an honest job?" countered Renny.

The two men looked uncomfortable. Their eyes rolled up in their heads as if they were doing calculations.

"Thought so," rumbled Renny. "Just stay coiled up like you are, and we'll be moving on soon."

"Did he say coiled?" undertoned one.

"He's just rubbin' in his insults, ain't he?"

At a withering glare from the hulking engineer, the two subsided.

QUITE a spell passed. Nearly an hour.

"Shouldn't be taking them this long," Renny muttered to himself.

Scaling the towering hoodoo, he searched the stretch of badlands between himself and the silver aircraft.

Renny spotted Johnny's horse, but the elongated archaeologist was not astride it. In fact, he saw no persons approaching.

The mournful-faced engineer decided that something was amiss and saddled up. He rode out toward the plane, but did not get very far.

The area abounded with lofty hoodoos, lava rocks, boulders and other detritus of the badlands. Renny rode through these things, picking his way carefully. He was alert, and sensed something was wrong.

So he should not have been greatly surprised when men suddenly popped out from behind sandstone spires and granite boulders, brandishing assorted revolvers, as well as other deadly weapons.

One of the men wore a green silk hood, over which was clamped a flamboyant black Stetson hat. He held a shotgun before him. The shotgun was not new, displaying the curled tumblers of a percussion hammer gun. Dangling from the twin barrels were two buzzard feathers, one white and one black.

"You know what this devil gun can do, hatchet face," the shotgun wielder called out. "Climb down off that saddle or take an elevator ride—without an elevator."

Another voice yelled, "And while you're at it, elevate those big meathooks up into the sky where they belong."

Renny's eyes went to the second voice. He saw a man who brought to mind a darkly yellow human mountain with muscles. His hair was black and plastered to his scalp in such a way as to make one think he was unfamiliar with the comb. He was bare to the waist and his musculature was unnerving to behold.

"Name's Jerico," the big monster said. "But you can call me Big Sky, if you have a mind to."

Jerico held an antique frontier six-gun. Studying it, Renny was reminded of Pat Savage.

"Holy cow!" he exploded. "Where'd Pat get to?"

A ruffian roughly shoved Pat Savage and Johnny into view. A long-barreled Colt revolver menaced them.

Pat stared in defiant silence.

"It was a trap," said Johnny, thick-voiced. "They ambushed me before I could pull out my superfirer."

"Holy cow!" Renny repeated. He seemed not to know what to say. But he put his hands up as high as his head. The expression on his long features made it look as if he wanted to laugh at the absurdity of life, which meant that he really wanted to cry.

Jerico stepped up, took the reins of the horse and said, "Out of the saddle, you. We're claimin' this nag."

Having no choice in the matter, Renny dismounted slowly and carefully. The man-monster reached in and harvested his supermachine pistol. Then he was prodded in the direction of the other prisoners.

For a moment, the long-faced engineer looked as if he wanted to take a poke at Jerico Hoan. The tenseness of his elephantine muscles and a bunching of one blocky fist communicated that intent.

Jerico growled, "I can take you, buster. Don't think I can't."

Renny met the other's gaze. Although constructed very differently, they were of a similar size. Both were big men, and looked as if they knew their way around a fistfight.

"Put down that gun," invited Renny, "and we'll see who's the better man."

"Another day, mister. Now shove along or I'll mow you down with your own pistol."

"It's a date," rumbled Renny. He moved along, joining the other captives.

"Expect a proper larrupin'," Jerico promised.

Renny thundered a rough, dismissive laugh.

Pat Savage said uneasily, "We are not doing so well without Doc, are we?"

"Where's Long Tom?" Renny asked suddenly.

Pat said, "These brutes shot him up into the sky. The last I saw of him, Long Tom was coming down by parachute."

"What about Doc Savage?"

Pat hesitated. Some emotion made bright flecks in the tawny slits of her eyes.

Finally, she said, "They claim that Doc Savage is dead."

Face working, Renny said, "I'll believe that tired old tune when I see it, not hear it."

The Goliath calling himself Jerico said boastfully, "The only way you'll see it is if we plant you next to him." He dug a big thumb into his bare chest, adding, "You're lookin' at the guy who buried him. And I buried him deep."

No one knew what to say to that. Renny swallowed his holy

cow expression before it passed his lips, and Johnny formed the words, "I'll be superamalgamated," but the syllables were not audible.

The man in the green hood and outrageous black hat suddenly said, "In case you don't know who I am, I'm Calamity, and this is the Calamity outfit. Now let's go and see what's what."

They started off on foot, although Calamity claimed a horse. Another gunman did the same. Jerico Hoan took charge of the prisoners and kept them moving along.

He did his prodding with Pat's six-shooter. The supermachine pistol he kept tucked into the waistband of his pants. No doubt he was more comfortable with the old pistol. The rapid-firer looked complicated.

As they marched along, Johnny asked Pat, "Is that your six-gun?"

Pat nodded.

"What's in it? Mercy bullets?"

"Assorted shells," Pat replied softly.

"Any lead?"

"I can't vouch for its current contents."

The comment told Johnny and Renny that if they made a break for it, anything might happen. It was not a comforting prospect. So they marched along, faces downcast, prospects appearing bleak.

Chapter XLIII

AUDACIOUS SCHEME

A S THEY WERE marched through the fantastic terrain, Renny Renwick noticed something.

His eyes had been going to hulking Jerico Hoan, who was whistling tunelessly, as if oblivious to the grimness of the general situation.

The big-fisted engineer elbowed Johnny Littlejohn. His voice became a husky whisper.

"Take a close look at that man-mountain," he undertoned.

Johnny did. His mouth became a pucker of distaste.

"A ruffian of the lowest order," he commented.

"Take a gander at his belt. Recognize it?"

Johnny blinked rapidly, then blanched. "I'll be superamalgamated!" he hissed. "I *do* recognize it. That is Doc Savage's belt. The special one he wears that—"

Renny's sharp elbow came into play again. "Don't let anyone hear you. Do you know what I'm thinking?"

"If you are contemplating what I am cogitating," Johnny said glumly, "the fact that that oaf is wearing Doc Savage's belt is further proof that the bronze man is deceased. He took it off the body before burying it."

Renny rumbled, "I'm thinking ahead of that. I'm thinking if I can get hold of that belt, I can make good use of it."

Johnny considered. "That belt has special properties, I grant you. But how will you take it off him? He's half as big as a house."

Renny blocked and unblocked his monster fists. "He doesn't look that tough to me. In fact, he's kind of sappy. Listen to him whistling like he's walking through Central Park."

"You may be correct," ventured Johnny. "But a fellow that Brobdingnagian in stature has little to fear in the world."

Renny thumped, "If I get to see my chance, I'm taking it. Let Pat know, so she's prepared."

Johnny nodded. His eyes went to Pat Savage. The tawny girl looked grief-stricken. Her own eyes were rimmed in red, but they remained stubbornly dry.

Johnny saw no point in letting her in on Renny's observation. Not just now. Jerico Hoan was hovering close by her side, and might overhear.

They continued along and eventually they came to the great pit that was the object of the trek.

There they discovered the two cowboys who hailed from Alliance, Nebraska. These men were swiftly untied and their gags taken off. They promptly got to their feet cursing.

Their violent expostulations were as much about their fear of hidden rattlesnakes as their recent captivity. Evidently, the first ranny had spent so much time fretting about sidewinders lurking in the neighborhood that his confederate had caught the phobia.

Both men were shaking in knock-kneed fashion.

The emerald-masked leader walked up to them and snarled, "A fine pair of guards you two turned out to be."

"We did our best," said the first one.

"Your best wasn't good enough," returned Calamity fiercely.

They looked crestfallen, downcast and miserable. They inspected the toes of their boots wordlessly. Eventually, their gaze lifted and they noticed Renny and Johnny towering over the others.

One jabbed an accusatory finger in their direction.

"Those are the cultus hombres who ambushed us!"

"Those no-good no-accounts," spat the other.

"Don't worry about them," said Calamity. "Get your nerves assembled. We have a lot to do."

The nervous pair looked relieved.

Calamity then turned and faced the others.

He took a moment to pull from a pocket some matter, which he slipped behind his green silk hood. He commenced chewing. It distorted his speech some, which appeared to be intentional.

"Now most of you men are new, and I've made some mighty tall promises. Now is the time to hear about what lies ahead."

There was a general murmur from the assembled outlaws. They had ridden a long, monotonous way, and they were hungry for diversion.

Raising the antique percussion-style shotgun, Calamity became boastful.

"I am holding in my hand what may be the most powerful weapon ever devised by man."

General skepticism greeted this pronouncement. Several of the men made faces suggesting they were trying to keep their expressions under control. A narrowing of eyes and a thinning of lips plainly told this. A few faces twitched.

"I took this off a greenhorn who had not much in the way of brains, and even less in the matter of imagination. This man discovered the pit you see before us. He was, in his way, a prospector. But he wasn't prospecting for gold, or any of that typical stuff. He was after what scientists call rare earth. Pitchblende. Radium. And an even rarer form of matter called uranium. He found some of that stuff in this pit. It's the yellow matter. But he found something more. Something that he was learned enough to have read about, and recognize when he came upon it."

Now Calamity had the attention of his men. They lost their skeptical demeanors.

"This greenhorn discovered that some of the uranium had absorbed the property of a buried element known as Repel. Repel does what its name suggests. It pushes things away. It pushes them away in a manner that doesn't take no for an answer. Somehow, the uranium took on some of the properties of the Repel. But only when it was ignited. This man discovered this by accident, and mixed the Repelanium—which is what he called the composite matter—into ordinary shotgun pellets loaded with rock salt. The pellets blew out bursts of the Repel force.

"One day while experimenting, he discharged his shotgun by accident into a swimming hole. The water went straight up, taking everything in the swimming hole with it. That was when he got ideas about getting rich. But he thought too small. He thought if he threatened ranchers with the loss of their well water, he could make a killing and go back to where he came from. Instead, he tangled with my old crew, and he tried to scrag me. He put this very shotgun to my head and threatened to pull both triggers."

This tale by now had everyone rapt.

WITH his free hand, Calamity gave a violent shake and his fist came up holding a fat derringer that had not been there a second ago.

"Before he could pull the triggers," he said squeakily. "I had my holdout gun in hand and I threatened him with both barrels. Had them pressed right into his gut, where they would do the most damage."

Someone laughed crudely. "Sounds to me like you had yourself the makings of a Mexican standoff."

"You aren't far off," barked Calamity. "But he wasn't much of a hand with a scattergun. He up and surrendered on me. I got the scattergun, as well as the diary in which he had recorded everything he had done in Wyoming. When I finished reading it, I was seeing dollar signs in the sky. I'll tell you about that in a minute. But first, I feel it is important to demonstrate the power of this weapon so that there are no doubts as we undertake the work before us. You see, I intend for every man of my Calamity bunch to pack a similar weapon."

The masked gang leader let that sink in, then he directed the shotgun toward the prisoners.

Renny, Johnny and Pat Savage barely had time to react. Nor did they.

Hulking Jerico Hoan was hovering beside them. Prudence would have dictated that he step away from the imminent shotgun blast.

Instead, he did the opposite, lifting hands as large as hams.

"This is wholesale murder," the yellow Goliath said simply. He did not make his voice hard, or contrary. He simply stated a fact.

"What if it is?" Calamity retorted. "We may be getting into the wholesale murder business. These three are small potatoes."

"But every one of 'em is famous the wide world over. You'll bring down a lot of fury on our heads. By killin' them, I mean. Maybe you want to think it over some."

"Careful, Big Sky. You're a little too free with your talk."

A deep concern registered on the gargantuan fellow's broad features.

"Told you before that I want no part of a murder rap. I don't mind muscle work, or even a little dirty work. But this is too dirty for me."

The colorless eyes of Calamity were hard thorns nestled in the silk of his mask. The Damascus steel barrels of his shotgun did not waver. Nor did huge Jerico Hoan flinch from its empty cavities of doom. Calamity continued chewing whatever was in his mouth. Soft squeakings could be heard. In the open space, it sounded like mice at play.

Standing behind Jerico Hoan, Pat Savage's hands suddenly flew to her lips. She started. "I recognize that sound! I think I know who this man is!"

"It may not do us much good," murmured Johnny, "given our present predicament."

Jerico Hoan suddenly turned. "You dry up and blow away, you animated collection of beef jerky."

Johnny was sometimes sensitive about his meatless anatomy. He could have put on twenty pounds and still been considered as thin as a rail. He expressed his indignation by puffing up his sunken cheeks like a bullfrog and blowing out angry air.

Pat lifted her voice. "I know who you are now. You had me abducted in Bison!"

This meant nothing to the assembled group.

Calamity seemed unconcerned by the accusation. He shrugged rather negligently and lowered the shotgun, unfired.

"Maybe you're right, Big Sky," he told Jerico. "There's still one of them that might be alive back at the ranch. And a couple more not in evidence. As long as one is breathing, the Doc Savage outfit will try to hunt us down. But having a hostage squares matters."

Abruptly, he spun in place, and then unloaded the scattergun in the direction of the two cowboys from Nebraska, who were expecting nothing of the sort.

The double charge blew them backward, in the direction of the pit. Traveling horizontally for several yards, they suddenly veered upward, as if caught by invisible hooks. They kept going. Their ignominious flight became completely vertical. If they uttered any outcry, it was lost in their rapid ascent.

All faces lifted as eyeballs followed the unfortunate pair.

Not a word was spoken. Jaws were dropping, but everyone was otherwise frozen in place.

"You are witnessing," announced Calamity rather vaingloriously, "the awesome power of Repel. The power each of you will soon control with me."

The two men did not quite become lost in sight as they hurtled upward. But they came close to it. They were a pair of dots that might have been turkey buzzards flying particularly high.

After what seemed like several breathlessly long minutes, the two dots commenced their sickening return to earth.

Now heads were turning away and eyes were being shielded.

Some of the witnesses placed their palms over their ears to block out the sound that they knew was coming.

Both men were screaming at the top of their lungs as they returned to the barren expanse dubbed Sunken Springs. That sound would have drowned out the ugly thuds of their demise except that they did not exactly land in the normal fashion.

The screaming stopped. Rather abruptly. But it turned into a kind of baffled howling instead of the silence that would normally follow the impact of two human bodies striking solid ground.

This weird alteration of expectations caused the bravest among the group to wrench their eyes toward the strange crater.

The pair were floundering about, not ten yards above the center of the crater, where the pit made a huge pock mark in the cracked crust.

The two men squirmed and twisted like worms snared on fishhooks. Except that there was no visible hook. There was only empty air, and an unseen force keeping them from striking the earth.

"Holy cow, will you look at that!" Renny Renwick's booming exclamation was deafening. It jarred the fearful to peek.

One of the outlaw band cried out. "If that ain't the most stupefying thing I ever did see!"

"Damnation! What's holdin' them up?"

Calamity answered that nonchalantly. "The same force that was packed in the shotgun shells. Repel. You can send a man screaming into the sky, or hold him off the ground almost indefinitely."

Someone wanted to know, "You just gonna leave them up there? They're caterwaulin' to beat the damn band."

Calamity said, "It is not possible for any man or any power known to man to rescue them. Deep in that pit lies Repel. Anyone attempting to step into the center of the crater will encounter the force. It will defeat him every time."

"You can't let them die howlin' like coyotes, can you?"

"I'm used to hearing coyotes howl," said Calamity coldly. "If anyone wants to put them out of their misery, have at it."

One man seemed to relish the prospect. Butch. He had his revolver out, and began triggering it. Tongues of leaping flame and clouds of gunsmoke erupted. He emptied the entire cylinder at the pair, who were flayed by hot lead but could do nothing about it.

They ceased screaming, however. Blood began leaking from their bodies. Instead of dripping downward, it formed globules of varying sizes which streamed out like air bubbles from two fish, and floated around the two corpses. The way they hung in midair, bleeding yet lifeless, was gruesome.

Pat Savage cried out, "How ghastly!"

No one else had much to say.

CALAMITY gave instructions. "You men scoop up the yellowish deposits. Don't stray too close to the center of the pit. We'll make our bullets later. But get all you can. Fill sacks. Saddlebags. Pockets, if you have to. We're going to need a lot if we're going to pull off what I got planned."

Jerico Hoan had been staring at the floating corpses with a kind of controlled horror etched upon his features. Now he tore his deeply black eyes from the horrific spectacle and asked, "So, what have you got planned?"

"Remember those yellow concrete markers we came across?"

"Sure do."

"Those are old airplane route markers. They were used to guide mail planes and the like. They're falling out of use with modern radio navigation, but some cross-country pilots still rely on them. They're kind of like milepost markers for highways in the sky—skyways they call them."

"So?"

"When I first got to experimenting with this scattergun, I made a lake levitate right up into the sky. A whole lake. It just so happened that a U.S. Airmail plane ran smack into this water, and came to pieces. That gave me the idea."

"What idea?" asked Jerico, drifting up quietly.

Calamity was reloading the percussion weapon, and he snapped it closed. He pointed it at big Jerico Hoan.

"The idea of blackmailing the airlines in this country. Letting them know if they didn't pay one million each, I would levitate bodies of water for their planes to plow into. My gang in Gillette already sent out the demand letters. But I'm thinking they're not going to believe it until I demonstrate what I can do."

Jerico growled, "So you figure to knock down a passenger plane?"

Calamity chewed a moment squeakily. "Bigger than that. I'm thinking about lifting Great Salt Lake into the sky, just as an airliner is flying toward it. Between the lifting and the destruction of the plane, the airline companies are going to fall all over themselves to send us cash. Bales of it. And it will not stop there. Once we collect, we'll do the same thing next year and every year. We'll collect a cool million a year from every one of those big corporations."

Jerico Hoan's grin was a little fierce. "That's a lot of jack to split up."

"Now you understand why killing a few folks here and there doesn't amount to much," drawled Calamity.

"Yeah," said Jerico. "I can see that now."

Calamity was still holding his shotgun generally in the direction of the stupendous Goliath from Montana.

"Any objections?"

Jerico shrugged. "None that I can think of just right now."

"Good," said Calamity. "I would hate to have to send you shooting up to the topmost floor without an elevator car."

"I don't like elevators much anyways."

The men finished collecting as much of the yellow stuff as possible. They filled every container they could.

Calamity watched them, chewing thoughtfully, his mouth making strange squeaking noises.

"What's that you're chewin'?" wondered Jerico, who was keeping an eye on the prisoners while the others collected the yellow deposits lying on the surface of the fractured crater.

"I got bum teeth," said Calamity abstractly. "Chewing on things helps with the discomfort."

As if the question had reminded him of his habit of chewing, Calamity lifted the lower part of his silken hood and spit out what was in his mouth.

Jerico's eyes went to the matter that had been expelled. They showed faint surprise when they saw the moist tangle in the dirt.

He grunted two words.

"Rubber bands?"

"They are the only things I can chew that don't come apart in my mouth," said Calamity dryly.

Behind Jerico, Pat Savage was whispering to the others.

"I'm positive I know who that hooded crook is. It's that general store proprietor, Kip Farr."

Jerico's ears pricked up the whispering, but he did not react to the name. Evidently, it meant nothing to him.

Calamity was saying, "We'll get back to the plane now and fly on to Gillette to pick up the others. They're waiting for us."

"What about these prisoners?" Jerico wanted to know.

"They're coming with us. We'll figure out what to do with them later."

Turning to the trio, Jerico made his voice harsh. "You heard the boss man. You're being spared. For now. So march!"

The march was not far along when there came a buzzing to the south. A plane. They began searching the heavens for the aircraft.

Soon enough, it showed up. A small private job, ivory with golden wings and trim. Pat Savage identified it for everyone.

"Oh, that's my plane," she cried out. "Long Tom must be at the controls."

"Maybe if he lands," Renny interjected, "he can take control of the bigger plane."

This whispered idea evidently occurred to Calamity because he was suddenly whipping his men into action.

"We'll make a run for the other plane. We can't let him get to our ship. Without it, there's no way out of this forsaken landscape, except on foot."

Since most of the Calamity bunch were cowboys born and bred, the prospect of traversing the badlands on foot was anathema to them.

There was a concerted run toward the descending craft.

Jerico shouted, "Want me to guard the prisoners?"

"With your life!" Calamity raged, rushing off along with his men.

Chapter XLIV

THE BURNING BELT

THE PRIVATE PLANE presumably being piloted by Long Tom Roberts buzzed about for a bit, then slammed down onto largely level ground.

The landing was abrupt, hasty and more than a little reckless. The pilot was in a violent hurry. By all rights, the little aircraft should have done a wingover or experienced some similar aerial mishap. But it did not. It did bounce twice, causing Renny and Johnny to take sharp indrawn breaths. Pat gasped.

It was not possible to see the aircraft taxiing to a halt, owing to the many hoodoos and sandstone spires studding Sunken Springs. But it did not blow up in a ball of fire and smoke. So they knew that the pilot had made it.

"That flyboy sure knows his onions," remarked Jerico Hoan with no little admiration.

"He does," said Pat frostily. "And if you're smart, you'll let us go. The law will never rest until the killers of Doc Savage are hunted down and punished."

The golden-eyed girl's warning caused Renny Renwick to stiffen. His eyes went to the bronze belt buckle that the big man wore.

Blocking his fists, the gloomy-faced engineer decided to make his move.

Perhaps it was those fists doubling up to their robust size that caused Jerico Hoan's flat black eyes to snap in Renny's direction.

Hoan had been gripping Pat's six-shooter in one hand. Now

he directed it toward the big-fisted engineer, who was on the verge of springing at him.

"Think twice, Horse Face," Jerico warned him.

But Renny was in no mood for warnings. Hands knotting into mallets, he charged.

Jerico backpedaled suddenly and seemed not to know what to do with the six-shooter. Apparently forgetting it lacked a trigger, he squeezed the trigger guard in vain. Then his thick thumb went in search of the hammer.

Renny's roundhouse right would have taken the head off another man. Somehow Jerico managed to duck and weave to one side and come up behind Renny. Renny blinked. It happened so fast it was as if the mild-mannered Goliath had evaporated.

Giving up on the six-gun, Jerico pocketed it and growled, "I guess you want that larrupin' after all."

Renny swung with his other fist, bellowing, "I can lick you any day of the week."

Jerico's fist connected first. Somehow. By some legerdemain of fisticuffs, Renny felt rock-hard knuckles connect with the side of his head. Renny's skull snapped around, taking his entire body with it. He staggered off, dazed.

"I guess today must be *Moonday*," chuckled Jerico, " 'cause it ain't any of the other seven days of the week, and I just licked you one-handed."

By this time, Johnny came charging in. Jerico spun, took hold of the gangling archaeologist with both sweeping arms and lifted him off his feet, sending him spinning away. Johnny ended up in a tangle of awkwardly bent limbs. He did not seem to be particularly injured.

Out came the big six-shooter again. This was directed at Pat Savage. "I think I got this contraption figured out. You pull back on the hammer and look for a fight. Is that right?"

Pat gave him a withering look. "You wouldn't shoot a woman, now would you?"

"I wouldn't shoot anybody," countered Jerico coolly. "If I didn't have to. Don't make me have to."

While Renny and Johnny were getting themselves organized, collecting their scrambled senses, the moan of a superfiring machine pistol came from far away. Answering shots rang—the crack of assorted revolvers. Their bark and bite made it sound like mechanical dogs snapping at one another.

The superfirer croaked like a monstrous bullfrog, occasionally hooting like a spooked owl. Eventually, it fell silent. All firing did.

Jerico turned his attention toward the landed plane.

"Sounds like that dogfight has been settled." He looked worried.

Abruptly, the yellow-skinned Goliath clambered up a fifty-foot mass of stone and peered over the crest for some minutes. Then he slid back to earth with careless disregard for his own person. His eyes appeared clouded and unfocused.

They waited. Renny and Johnny climbed to their feet, but neither seemed to be in a fighting mood. Renny particularly appeared to have borne the brunt of it.

Calamity and about half of his men showed up with Long Tom Roberts walking in front of him, both hands upraised, his sling gone, looking perfectly defeated. The dispirited electrical genius sported two black eyes, a leaking nose, and appeared to have lost one of the gold incisors that he wore in the front of his mouth.

"Oh," said Pat. "They knocked out one of Long Tom's gold teeth."

Jerico grunted. "That doesn't look like the worst of it."

"You don't understand," said Pat firmly. "Long Tom has a temper. Anytime someone knocks out one of those teeth, he finds a way to repay the favor."

Jerico Hoan did not look impressed. "He looks more than a little outnumbered, now don't he?"

Pat studied the big bruiser. Her aureate eyes widened when

they caught the gleam of his belt buckle. "I recognize that belt! It belongs to Doc Savage."

Without taking his eyes off the approaching group, Jerico nodded. "Took it off the man myself. Fits almost as good on me as it did on him."

"You're a monster, a cold unfeeling monster," snapped Pat. "Doc Savage is—*was*—one of the greatest men who ever lived." Then catching herself, she began to be wracked by sobs.

Jerico Hoan favored her with a glance that harbored a particle of sympathy. "Don't cut up so. Everybody's gotta die someday."

Calamity came up and stared at the looming giant speculatively. "I was half afraid you might've done something foolish when we were out hunting."

Jerico blinked. "Foolish? Like what?"

"On account of you're kind of queasy about killing. I was afraid you might let the prisoners go."

"And get myself shot into the sky for a turncoat?" Jerico shook his slovenly head. "Thank you kindly, but no thank you. I'm no rat, but a member in good standin' with the Calamity bunch. I aim to keep it that way."

Calamity nodded his head so that his emerald hood rustled softly like the muffled slithering of a sidewinder. His eyes were flinty as arrowheads.

"Glad to hear it. Now let's all take a walk. The sun is starting to go down. It's going to get right cool. We could all use with a little warmth."

Jerico blinked again. "Walk? Walk where?"

"Just follow me."

Long Tom was roughly shoved into the small clot of prisoners that included Renny, Johnny and Pat.

Renny rumbled, "A fine rescue party you turned out to be! Getting yourself captured."

Long Tom snapped back, "Look who's talking! You all got yourselves captured."

The wiry electrical expert looked around, counted heads and mused, "This would be a good time for Doc Savage to show up."

Jerico Hoan chuckled abruptly. It was a little bit of a cracked chuckle, perhaps even a nervous one.

"I guess he ain't got the telegram yet," he said to no one in particular.

Long Tom regarded him dubiously.

Johnny offered in a tired voice, "They claim Doc Savage is dead."

Long Tom seemed not to take the news very seriously. "I've read those exact words in the top newspapers, and they proved to be bunk."

"Buried him myself," said Jerico. "Took his fancy belt as a souvenir. Now let's get a move on. We got some walkin' to do."

Long Tom noticed the belt then. His eyes fell upon the bronze buckle and they flew wide. Then he flew into a rage.

Yelling something incomprehensible, Long Tom Roberts jumped Jerico Hoan without thinking of consequences. One consequence was when his bloody nose acquired a second leak. The hulking Goliath simply lifted a fist in front of him and the overmatched electrical expert ran directly into it, rebounded hard, then landed on the seat of his pants. He shook his head like a dazed dog.

Without seeming to make any effort, Jerico sagged down, bundled Long Tom Roberts under one arm and toted him as if he were in fact a canine pet.

DUSK was darker than the immediate surroundings when they came to the edge of the burning coal seam. The heat was terrific. It evaporated the sweat off their faces and made their suddenly-dry eyes blink furiously in response.

When Jerico saw this, he remarked quietly, "We're not down here to warm up, are we?"

Calamity eyed him with flinty challenge. "What do you think, Big Sky?"

"I think I'm going to be a little sick," muttered Jerico, his hearty voice suddenly wavering.

The prisoners were made to sit down. While Calamity and his men conferred, giant Jerico loomed over the miserable quartet.

Renny was snapping out of his punch-drunk stupor while Long Tom suddenly sat up, took hold of his head and groaned interminably.

"Did a truck hit me?"

A gunman laughed. "No, you hit the truck!"

Johnny said in a thick, dispirited voice, "It is increasingly evident this marks the exordium of the ultimate terminus."

Renny looked blank.

Long Tom offered, "Johnny means the beginning of the end. In other words, they plan to do us in."

Studying the blistering crack in the earth, Pat asked, "Do you suppose they'll just toss us over like so much cordwood? Or will they do us the mercy of putting a bullet in our heads beforehand?"

Renny was slow to realize their immediate peril. He looked around the group, studied the flames leaping up from deep below, and said, "I'm not ready to die just yet. But if I have to go, I'm taking a few outlaws with me."

"I'm taking them all," vowed Long Tom.

Suddenly, the puny electrical wizard looked up at big Jerico Hoan. His pale eyes got crafty.

"If I'm going to die, then I'm going to die. But before you pitch me into that hot crack, you might want my wristwatch."

Long Tom raised his shirt sleeve and exposed a watch that was obviously expensive and perhaps custom-made. The casing was substantial, indicating that it housed inordinately complicated works.

"Why would I want that thing?" Jerico grunted. "The band is too small for my wrist."

"It's an expensive watch. There isn't another one like it in the world. You could hock it. It's probably worth a hundred dollars."

Jerico almost laughed. "One hundred shekels for a watch! Are you funnin' me?"

Long Tom dangled the watch, saying, "Take it or leave it."

"You don't fool me," said Jerico. "I get caught wearin' that watch after you're dead, they'll try to pin your murder on me. Thanks for nothing."

"In that case," interjected Johnny, "you might want to get rid of that belt."

Jerico did not have to think about this very long. "You must be a mind reader. I've been thinking those exact same thoughts myself."

Without further ado, he unbuckled the belt and yanked it out of its loops. The belt was substantial, the leather thick, and evidently constructed from two straps hand-stitched together.

Drifting close to the burning gash, Jerico peered down, contemplated its fiery maw for some moments, never once taking his eyes completely off the prisoners seated nearby. He seemed to be thinking long and hard.

Reaching into one pocket, he drew forth what appeared to be a fishing line. To the end of this was affixed a device of some sort—a knot of steel. He began plucking at it. A single hook popped out. He hung the bronze belt buckle on this, then slowly he lowered the belt down into the fiery fissure.

Jerico concealed his actions with his broad back, so the others did not see it. But it would have been evident to anyone observing him closely that he was attempting to burn the evidence of Doc Savage's death.

Yet something caused him to hesitate. He dangled the belt well above the burning coal, just enough to cause tendrils of smoke to appear as the high heat singed the edges of the leather.

When this happened, he pulled the belt higher, so that it did not fully ignite.

Jerico seemed indecisive about this. Calamity soon came back with some of his men. They had drawn their revolvers anew.

"It's time for the dirty work to commence," he said loudly.

"Well, then, I guess it's time," Jerico said morosely. "No sense avoidin' the inevitable."

Striding forward, Calamity demanded, "Any objections?"

Jerico did not completely turn around. "Just one."

"What is that?"

"You got to spare the gal."

Instead of answering, Calamity stuck out his jaw, causing the lower portion of his green hood to jut out.

"In another minute, you're going to push me too far, Big Sky."

"I told you I don't cotton to killin', Calamity."

"Do you want trouble?"

"It won't be the first time I've had it," Jerico said, glancing down into the burning coal bed.

They stood almost boot toe to boot toe. Calamity was tall, but Jerico Hoan seemed to belong to another order of human being. He was more than a head taller than the masked man, but also broader of beam and deeper of chest.

The two men glared at each other, and there was something in Jerico's gargantuan size, the impressive quietness with which he stood his ground that was menacing. For Calamity held his shotgun pointed downward, toward the other's boots. There was no mistaking what would happen to the big man from Montana if either trigger was pulled.

"Unless one of you learned to fly a plane since we landed," Jerico went on casually, "we're going to need a pilot. The gal will be the easiest one of the lot to handle."

The face of Calamity could not be seen. Visible through the slits in his mask, his colorless eyes were coldly expressionless. But from the way his body stiffened, decision gripped him abruptly.

CALLING over to the others, he said, "Two of you pull the girl aside and keep her alive."

This was done. Pat was roughly seized and dragged off. She resisted. A gun butt was raised in warning.

"Go with them, Pat," Renny encouraged. "There's no need for you to die, too."

Pat hurled back, "I'm no coward. I'm a Savage through and through. Right down to the ground."

Calamity regarded Jerico. "You got brains in that muscle, Big Sky. Brains are the only commodity in the world that could be worth one million dollars a pound, or not the thin dime. Once you learn to take orders, you'll be valuable."

Jerico turned his attention back to the hot coals frying before him. "Then what do you say—suppose we quit gettin' in each other's hair."

"Suits me."

But neither of the two strange hard men made a move to shake hands.

Calamity noticed that Jerico seemed to be in the act of fishing.

"What are you doing?" he asked suspiciously.

"Gettin' ready to burn the evidence that Doc Savage is dead. I don't want no tie-up to that. Even in his grave, Savage probably has ways of gettin' even with folks who cross him."

"Good thinking. When you're done, you can pitch the three prisoners into the furnace."

Jerico Hoan stiffened. His eyes grew narrow. "I told you how I feel about murder."

"Sure you did," sneered Calamity. "That's why *you're* going to do the deed. There's a lot worse ahead of us. We may have to slaughter a few hundred people to make a point and collect our first million. You've got that old six in your waistband. It's time you learn to use it."

Jerico continued to stare down into the coal seam. His eyes grew clouded.

In time, he shrugged one enormous shoulder, then the other, and said quietly, "If you say so, boss."

"I say so," said Calamity in a cold voice.

Jerico emitted a good-hurt sound like a man who had just pulled a cactus sticker out of himself. The big brute began lowering the leather belt. Once again, it took to sizzling and gave off tendrils of black smoke. Half under his breath, Jerico began speaking. The words were unintelligible.

Hearing the unfamiliar syllables, Calamity demanded, "What's that? What's that you say?"

Without taking his eyes off the belt, Jerico Hoan remarked, "Just sayin' a little Indian prayer. I'm half Shoshone myself. Guess I never told you that."

"Just make it snappy."

"Snappy it is," said Jerico, returning to his muttered prayer.

Sitting on the ground, the three Doc Savage men became unnaturally animated. Their eyes started to get round, and they turned pale. Renny's severe mouth twisted in a way that might have been a smile or a grimace. The way the long-faced engineer's dour countenance was arranged, it was hard to tell.

As Jerico concluded his Indian chant, the leather belt he sent into the yellow flames was suddenly afire. Tendrils of smoke turned into a sudden gush of intensely black, malodorous vapor.

The uprush of smoke was startling in its abruptness, and before anyone could remark upon that, Jerico Hoan suddenly twisted his great body and brought the burning belt swinging up and out at the end of the fishing line.

The burning belt went careening through the air, landing in the middle of the group holding Pat Savage. Upon impact, it produced a great upwelling of black smoke, which caused an immediate and understandable uproar.

Pat recognized the acrid smell right away. *"Tear gas!"*

The bronze-skinned beauty sounded positively giddy with excitement.

Chapter XLV

HELL AND DAMNATION

ALMOST INSTANTLY, THE startled gunmen were pawing at their eyes, groping for their weapons. They milled about, bumping into one another, cursing the stinging cloud, each other, and the world in general.

Whirling, Pat slipped around and industriously kicked shins with her riding boots, dropping anyone she encountered with her surprisingly hard brown fists. The tawny beauty moved fast, paying no attention to the fact that she could not see clearly and was having trouble breathing.

The masked Calamity was fast on his feet. His mental processes were not sluggish, either. He took one look at the confusion that had befallen his men, and swung the clumsy-looking shotgun on gargantuan Jerico Hoan.

"You double-crosser!"

Calamity had previously lowered the antique scattergun. That was his mistake. Jerico Hoan was moving on him, closing with a blinding speed that defied easy description.

The feather-decorated hammer gun lifted. One great hand shot out, knocked the double muzzle aside, simultaneously wrenching off the emerald hood.

The face that stared back at him was unfamiliar. Strong emotion may have rendered it unrecognizable. For the revealed visage was very surprised. Shock eddied across his square, sunburnt features.

Calamity felt the shotgun leave his suddenly-numb fingers.

Howling in pain, he shook both hands. Out of the tooled leather cuffs on his wrists dropped a matched set of palm pistols. Double-barreled derringers.

Snarling, he brought these up, triggering one. Jerico Hoan narrowly evaded the first coughing shot. The slug whistled harmlessly past his burly bicep.

Backpedaling, Jerico reached into his waistband and yanked free Pat Savage's formidable six-shooter. Showing a sudden and unexpected familiarity with the weapon, he cocked it with his thumb, firing in Calamity's direction.

The first bullet seemed to surprise both shooter and his target. It struck one arm, high up, drawing blood and causing Calamity to jerk half around, crying out in pain.

Queerly, Jerico made a sound that was either a mutter or a sigh. It was impossible to tell which because shock or surprise at having nearly blown his boss's head off twisted it up in his throat.

Thumbing open the smoking revolver's loading gate, he gave the cylinder a quick spin, noted five still-unfired cartridges, then snapped the weapon back to proper working order.

Aiming at Calamity, he rocked the hammer back and dropped it on a fresh cartridge. The barrel gushed out bitter tear gas. Jerico was forced to backpedal even further. He apparently had expected something other than tear gas.

By now the swelling smoke cloud was creeping in from the other party, the tear gas mixed with it filling the immediate vicinity. Eyes began smarting and leaking prodigious tears.

Still clutching his matched derringers, Calamity fired wildly in almost every direction. His lead struck nothing mortal. When the hammers clicked futilely, he flung the useless pistols aside.

There was a frantic rushing about, in which Doc Savage's men fully participated. They had been knocked around quite a bit and were not at their best. Now they employed their fists, using them with relish.

A gun came up and released a clap of powder noise. Again,

the weapon coughed. The wielder yanked a second pistol from a belted holster, and attempted firing two-gun style. He was not very good at it.

A cloud of hastily-aimed slugs hit a towering hoodoo, causing sections to be knocked off. Sandstone splinters sailed away, swirling like reddish snowflakes. A bullet sang off a boulder.

Before that furious storm of lead, most combatants ducked or froze in place.

Both smoking cylinders ceased revolving. The foolish gunman had emptied them in a useless display.

Renny pounced, struck the man in the nose with monster knuckles. The paralyzing blow knocked him loose from his guns.

The long-faced engineer scooped up both, threw one to Long Tom Roberts.

In the haze of smoke and stinging gas, they reloaded from the prone man's cartridge belt while the other gunmen got themselves organized.

The big six-shooter looked like a toy in Renny's giant fist. Eyes leaking, he hunted foes and swiftly located one of the Calamity bunch shifting about with an old .38-55 carbine rifle, trying to draw a bead on a suitable moving target.

Unable to insert his huge trigger finger into the guard properly, Renny found the hammer of the gun, rocking it back. It jumped in his massive fist. The roar of the exploding weapon threatened to deafen him.

The rifleman yelped and stepped back, clutching at the place where his left arm hinged strangely between elbow and shoulder. The carbine clattered to the ground, discharging from the abrupt jarring.

The tumbling .38-55 slug found lodgment in the face of a stalking Calamity gunhand. It created a kind of keyhole where the fellow's nose had been. He dropped, stone dead.

Another gunman stepped up, aimed. Long Tom's six-gun

blew out loud, smoky noise. The second gunman's right hand and revolver became a shattered tangle. He yodeled in pain.

From somewhere in the smoke, another six boomed out. Bellowing, Renny felt of the top of his head where a bullet put a part in his hair—a part in the wrong direction. It was that close.

The hulking engineer spun to throw roaring, enraged words. He sounded like a longhorn bull on the prod. Renny could not see who had shot at him through the smoke.

But Johnny Littlejohn had. He rushed forward and managed to kick the revolver out of the aiming man's hands. It flew away.

Johnny pitched against his disarmed foe, causing him to lose his hat. They staggered about, struggling, went down in a pile. Over and over on the ground they tumbled, Johnny swinging bony fists with arms as long as fishing poles.

The would-be killer bit at Johnny's throat like a mad animal. Straddling the tangle of flailing limbs, Renny pulled the fellow's head away with both huge hands gripping hair and ears.

They separated. Everyone got to their feet. The gunman clawed for another pistol somewhere inside his clothing. Producing a short-barreled Colt, he pointed it at Johnny.

"Holy cow!" yelled Renny. "A live one!"

The gunman switched the bulldogged blue barrel back and forth, as if uncertain whom to plug first. A mistake.

Hampered by his injured arm, Long Tom was winding the stem of his oversized wristwatch. He slipped up behind the gunman and pressed a small electrode that was suddenly jutting out against the nape of the man's neck. A slight buzzing sound came.

Shaking strangely, the victim flounced once after the jolt hit him. The impact threw the jittering man off his feet. His limbs quivered a little, then spread slackly as he measured his full length on the ground.

"Shock watch," puffed Long Tom. "It generates a stinging

electrical charge. Kind of on the order of a miniature cattle prod."

Renny felt of his scalp and brought his huge hand away sticky with blood. He blinked. "You tried to jolt that Jerico with it, didn't you?"

Long Tom shrugged. "Before I knew what was what." He peered around. "Where did he get to, anyway?"

Renny shrugged enormous shoulders helplessly.

THE EXPANDING pall of black smoke had spread out fully, making rushing about particularly dangerous, owing to the frightening nearness of the burning coal seam.

Eyes blinded half-shut, Calamity showed presence of mind. He dropped to his knees and began groping about for his fallen shotgun.

Seeing this through the increasing haze, Jerico fired the six-shooter into the smoke, seemingly wildly. Not all of the cartridges exploded were tear gas shells. When he realized this, a strange expression came over his brutish features.

Pocketing the gun, he lunged for Calamity, whose frantic fingers finally found his weapon.

Striving to his feet, Calamity brought the shotgun to bear, but he was almost completely blind. Stamping around in a circle, he prepared to unleash both barrels in no particular direction.

Realizing the danger, Jerico shouted, "Looking for me? I'm standing over here!"

Then he moved to one side like a streak of yellowish lightning. The silence of his fleeing was uncanny.

His voice, too, was different. It was stronger, more powerful. It sounded not like that of an ordinary human being. Such a voice might have thundered down from Mount Olympus in ancient days.

"Who is that?" Calamity rasped.

The powerful voice replied, "Doc Savage."

Hearing this, Calamity became enraged. He fired once, then set himself to unleash the second barrel in a completely different direction. He must have believed this would achieve his murderous aims. The first shot cleanly missed his target.

But the blast did not miss entirely. It struck someone who was running around aimlessly in the evil eye-stinging smoke. That person was blown off his feet. He bawled out of shock and surprise. Then, with a helpless caterwauling, he went straight up into the sky.

"Well, did I get you?" howled Calamity.

Instead of receiving a reply, the outlaw leader found unbreakable bands of steel gripping his tooled-leather cuffs. He was trapped. He could not move. He knew this. Calamity tried kicking, but to no avail. He attempted slamming his forehead against his foe. Painfully, he encountered nothing less than an unmoving obstacle that might have been made of solid brick.

"You can't be Doc Savage," Calamity screamed. "You can't be!"

Abruptly, he ceased to struggle.

Holding his foe firmly, Doc Savage forced the man's arms up, the long shotgun barrels pointing skyward, all while keeping his Herculean body out of the way of the double muzzles. The tear gas was getting into his eyes, and it was soon going to be difficult not to flee the vicinity to escape its stinging bite.

Calamity mustered his courage somehow. "You had better let me go."

"Why is that?"

"Because I have a third hideout gun. It's mounted in my belt buckle. All I have to do is stick out my stomach and pressure will trigger the release. The gun will snap forward on a pivot, and fire automatically. You probably know what that will do to your bare belly."

"I do," admitted Doc Savage.

It might have been a bluff. It could have been the truth. Doc Savage could not see clearly enough to tell. He released one of the man's cuffs. Wrenching his entire frame, Calamity pulled loose from the other, leaving the bronze man clutching its mate.

No derringer report sounded. It had been a bluff, after all.

The bronze giant snapped out a hand, missed his foe, but captured the shotgun. Finding the trigger by feel, Doc sent the remaining charge exploding harmlessly upward. Cracking open the action, he twisted the scattergun in two in his mighty hands, sending each half flying in opposite directions.

Thinking his own weapon was hunting him, Calamity broke and ran. Doc charged after him. Amid the smoke and the confusion, he collided with Renny Renwick, whose grunting bellow of surprise shook the night.

They grappled briefly, Renny thumping, "Who have I got?"

"Doc Savage."

Realization sinking in, Renny let go. "You were Jerico. You spoke Mayan, not Shoshone."

"Calamity is trying to flee."

Renny grunted. "He won't get far. Not in this tearful soup."

The two men broke apart and continued searching. Doc Savage rapped out additional instructions in the Mayan tongue, which all of his aides knew. Pat Savage understood a smattering, too.

Hearing the familiar tones, Pat suddenly yelled, "Doc? Doc! Am I dreaming?"

"I was Jerico," the bronze man returned in English.

Pat Savage was struck speechless. It took a moment for her to recover. And when she did, she coughed out, "I don't know whether to laugh or bawl my eyes out, but when this is over with, I'm going to give you the tongue lashing of your life. You let me believe you were dead, you—you brass-faced Indian."

"It was necessary to locate the Repel deposit in order to smash the scheme," returned Doc Savage. "I could not allow the Calamity gang to suspect who I was."

Then there was no more time for talk. Six-guns blazed here

and there, and it became dangerous to move around. The smoky air all but seemed to fill with vicious wasps and hornets chasing one another in anger.

In the Mayan language, Doc Savage called out for everyone to drop prone to the ground. His men were well-trained. They obeyed instantly.

There came a horrible sound—a piercing wail of pain. Then a hoarse, tearing screaming resounded. The frenzied screaming kept going on and on. Mortal terror was thick in its vibrations. This vocal pandemonium was accompanied by a sickening hissing and sizzling that sounded as if a side of beef had been thrown into a campfire.

But it was not a side of beef. A human being had blundered through the tear-gas cloud and over the lip of the fissure in the earth and fallen to his destruction amid the unquenchable flames. Death was not instantaneous. It was accompanied by a wordless howling, a spurt of profanity, and then a prolonged, agonized groan that died even as the horrible sizzling cooking sounds continued unabated.

Eventually, the smoke cleared and their eyes became functional again.

Bronze features fixed, Doc Savage went among the fallen.

One man had died from a gunshot wound, evidently fired by a confederate. Others were dazed. Doc and Renny rolled them over so their faces could be seen, and knocked them out with their fists.

The metallic giant picked up weapons dropped by the defeated gunmen. With a quick blow from the barrel of each on the breach of the other, he shattered off the hammers. Most were single-action guns, nearly impossible to use without the hammers.

After this was done, they counted heads.

Long Tom said, "There's a bunch of them I mowed down back at the landing spot. We'll have to load them into the plane."

Still in his Jerico Hoan disguise, Doc Savage nodded.

"I do not see the man who was back of the scheme—the unknown individual who borrowed the name of Mr. Calamity, but called himself simply Calamity."

"The first bird is dead," Long Tom snorted. "I dug up his head. Bright red hair, lizard-green eyes—no mistaking it for anybody else."

Doc advised, "I found the head in the barn, Long Tom."

Renny grunted without sympathy, "You don't suppose it was Calamity that fell into the hot-coal crack, do you?"

Doc nodded somberly. "That is my conclusion. Unpleasant as it may be."

Renny looked sanguine. "Maybe not as unpleasant as it could have been. If his scheme had taken off, that is."

No one showed much inclination to gaze down into the burning coal seam. But the sizzling coming from below was all they needed to know. That, and the smoke which carried a horrid stench none of them would ever forget.

Eventually, Long Tom Roberts drifted to the edge, braving the heat. He peered downward, but what remained of the man was hardly recognizable as such.

Rejoining the others, he muttered, "Talk about ending up in everlasting fire."

"Guess he got a head start shoveling coal in the hot place," snorted Renny.

Spreading out, they looked over the fallen, paying particular attention to their features.

"I do not see the unmasked gang leader among the survivors," Doc said grimly.

"That settles it, then," rumbled Renny.

Pat Savage walked up to Doc Savage and said with tears in her eyes that were not entirely the result of stinging gas, "I don't know whether to hug you or smack you silly, you big bronze lunk."

"I will settle for a smile," said Doc Savage rather wearily. Then he asked, "Pat, what was loaded in your six-gun?"

"Oh, a combination of tear gas and mercy bullets. Why?"

"I had expected mercy bullets. The tear gas came as an unpleasant surprise."

"You sound disappointed."

"Mercy bullets would have accounted for more of the gang humanely."

"I'd say in your case, the gas came in right handy."

"The first shot I loosed proved to be lead," said the bronze man. "That was the most unpleasant surprise of all. Normally, you leave one chamber empty in order to avoid an accidental discharge."

"This was a special circumstance," explained Pat. "I was going into battle."

"Someone might have been killed by accident," admonished Doc gravely.

Pat glanced around the now-quiet battlefield. "It appears to me," she said levelly, "that they brought this on themselves."

Doc made no reply. The fact that his smoke screen of potent tear gas had led to at least two deaths was sobering. But criminals who went up against the Man of Bronze often had a way of destroying themselves in the end.

Doc began removing the black glass eye-shells which concealed the true color of his orbs. His flake-gold eyes were thus revealed. Next, he extracted a set of dental plates that had distorted the natural appearance of his teeth. The facial appliances that contorted his regular features would have to wait. While he did so, the metallic giant explained for Pat Savage's benefit the secret of the leather belt that had burned up with such spectacular and distressing effects.

"The special belt consisted of two segments, each holding a different substance pressed between the leather layers. One side contained a compound which, when burned, produced black smoke. The other housed a chemical mixture formulated to generate tear gas through ignition. Between the two halves of the belt, there were sufficient noxious gases to overcome the Calamity gang and its leader."

Pat averted her gaze from the superheated coal seam. "I wonder if we'll ever learn who the original Mr. Calamity really was...."

Doc Savage said nothing. The look in his metallic eyes suggested that in his mind the violent matter was not entirely concluded.

Chapter LXVI

THE EARL OF TROUBLE

"HIS NAME WAS Henry Hemstead."

The speaker was the Special Agent in Charge of the Cheyenne, Wyoming, office of the Federal Bureau of Investigation. He and his subordinate had driven in to the Circle Bolt ranch from Gillette. Special Agent Heflin was giving a report of all F.B.I. activities after they had parted company with Doc Savage in the aftermath of the spectacular Casper Bank robbery.

"Which?" rumbled Renny. "The first Calamity, or the second one?"

Doc Savage answered that. "The peculiarly-dressed individual calling himself Mr. Calamity was the aforementioned Henry Hemstead."

The F.B.I. chief nodded. "We did a checkup on all dude ranches in this area. There were only two, the Broken Circle and the Lazy-C. It was at the Lazy-C that we learned of a greenhorn who had gone missing. He was this Henry Hemstead, although he had registered under a highfalutin alias, Sir Jennifel Boniface-Lacey. We were able to identify the body through the fingerprints Mr. Savage provided."

The second agent added, "Hemstead was an Englishman, and a member of British nobility. He was the Earl of something or other. He lost a pile of wealth during the Depression, and came to Wyoming to strike it rich and restore the family fortunes, bringing along an heirloom percussion shotgun manufactured in London during the reign of Queen Victoria. Unfortunately,

Hemstead had read too many Western thriller novels. He dressed all wrong and affected a ridiculous accent. This made him a laughingstock at the dude ranch. But he did locate the Repel material. It seems to have gone to his head. He decided to turn Jesse James and take advantage of the local ranchers. But he got in over his head."

"And lost it, too," rumbled Renny Renwick without sympathy.

Doc Savage produced a thick diary that he found in Long Tom's plane. It had been carried in the saddlebag of the second Calamity, the master mind of the grand scheme to blackmail the airline industry.

"This book contains a complete account of the man's prospecting activities while seeking rare earth elements. From this, the second Calamity got his nefarious ideas."

"So who is the second Calamity?" asked Johnny.

"I can tell you his name," announced Pat proudly. "It's Kip Farr. I know because Farr liked to chew on something that made his mouth squeak. I don't know what it was, but the sound was unmistakable. The Calamity who died so horribly made such squeaking noises with his mouth."

Doc Savage advised, "He was chewing on rubber bands."

"Oh!" said Pat. "That explains it."

"But it does not explain the true identity of the second Calamity," stated Doc. "He was not Kip Farr, who was merely the Calamity lieutenant in charge of shipping stolen mules out of the state, using his general store as a blind."

Agent Hale interjected. "That rustler bunch has been wiped out. We arrested a second group, including Lion Needers and others, in Gillette. They were waiting for the Calamity gang to catch up with them. They were bad actors, all of them."

Pat frowned. "Did Lion Needers have kind of a bobcat face?"

"That's him," said the F.B.I. man.

"Well, he's the one who tried to kidnap me. I hope he doesn't get out of the penitentiary until he's in a wheelchair."

"Needers may be facing worse than a penitentiary stretch,"

the federal agent pointed out. "He has a murder record in other states. But he made out better than Kip Farr. His body's in the Bison morgue."

Pat asked, "Did he resist?"

"No. He was one of the rustlers who were hurled into the sky over by Pumpkin Buttes that time the original Mr. Calamity let loose on the Quest rustler gang. His body lay unidentified in the morgue the whole time because the new sheriff hailed from Sheridan, so he didn't know him by sight. Not that it would have helped much. His face was pretty well stove in."

"Ugh," said Pat.

Long Tom had a steak over one eye and was transferring it to the other. His knuckles were skinned raw, but he appeared satisfied. He had pounded away at the man who had knocked out one of his gold teeth, all but demolishing him.

Long Tom wondered, "Why was Alta Crater killed?"

Doc Savage answered that one. "She was slain for the same reason, approximately, that Lord Hemstead was. Gunnysack fibers were found under her fingernails. This is surmise, but Miss Crater was by reputation a headstrong and direct young woman. When she was inadvertently carried off in the car in which she had secreted herself, she presumably attempted to unmask Quest, the culprit who was rustling her mules. Perhaps she recognized his voice, despite attempts to disguise it. Quest was forced to do away with her. An autopsy has shown that she perished from drowning."

"How cold-blooded," said Pat, shuddering.

"The original Mr. Calamity, Henry Hemstead, no doubt also saw Quest's true face," continued Doc. "Thus, the need to eliminate him. Fibers were evident under his fingernails as well, but these were the result of a struggle."

Long Tom muttered, "A lot more would have died if the devilment had been carried out to its planned conclusion."

"So who was the second Calamity?" asked Pat.

Doc Savage produced one of the tooled leather cuffs that had been worn on both wrists by the criminal master mind.

"The second Calamity went by many names. We first knew him as Quest. At the Lynx Eyes Ranch, where he was foreman, he was calling himself Buck Quane. But that was not his real name, either."

Everyone looked at Doc Savage expectantly.

Before the bronze man could give answer, Pat snapped, "Wait a minute! How could Kip Farr not be the master brain if he was the one who squeaked?"

"This is only theory," said Doc Savage, "but it is my belief that the true master mind chewed rubber bands to make it seem as if his lieutenant, Kip Farr, was the actual head of the gang. The second Calamity went to great pains to conceal his real name. He wanted some of the gang to think Kip Farr ran the Calamity bunch, when in fact he was merely its straw boss."

"Sounds tricky of him," murmured Pat. "Almost as tricky as a certain Jerico Hoan of my recent acquaintance." Pat looked around the ranch house. "Anyone see where he got to?"

Doc Savage looked slightly uncomfortable. Then he went on.

"Pat, do you remember the man who gave you a ride into Bison after you were stranded on top of that butte?"

"You mean Oakley Wood?"

"Yes, Oakley Wood. Do you recall his chief characteristic?"

Pat made thinking faces. "He didn't have very many."

"His forearms were covered in thick white hair. Surely you remember that?"

"I do," allowed Pat. "I thought it odd since he didn't look particularly old." Pat's golden eyes went to the tooled leather cuff in Doc Savage's metallic hands. "Hold on! Do you mean to tell me that—"

"Oakley Wood wore these things to conceal his profuse forearm hair when he was operating as Quest. Wood was his actual name, by the way. Quest and Buck Quane, not to mention Calamity, were all aliases."

Long Tom murmured, "That explains why no one knew of him at the Lynx Eyes spread. He was Buck Quane to them."

"I'll be superamalgamated!" exploded Johnny. "Pat was the only one who ever encountered him without his various hooded disguises."

Doc nodded. "When I pulled off his hood, I did not recognize Wood. It was rather disconcerting. We might never have figured out the truth, except that I found specimens of white hair in the leather cuffs he wore. This brought to mind your description of him, Pat."

"Well," said Pat cheerfully, "it was my mystery to start with. I'm happy to contribute what little bit I can."

Doc Savage said, "I know you wanted to be more involved in this adventure than you were."

Pat smiled. "Oh, I think I did all right under the circumstances. I had more happen to me than I care to count. Being stranded on top of a mesa all night. Jugged. Kidnapped. Nearly killed. Almost murdered again. Come to think of it, I believe I've been almost murdered during this mystery more than any other mystery I can recall."

Doc Savage regarded her fixedly. "Perhaps you understand now why I prefer that you stay out of our adventures."

"I'm starting to. But let me remind you. This was *my* adventure from the start. You and the others horned in on my shindig."

A slight smile touched Doc Savage's firm lips. "If you will search your memory, you will recall that you invited us in."

"So I did, so I did. And I got the scare of my life twenty times over. Not the least of which was thinking that you were dead. Why didn't you whisper in my ear that it was you?"

"I could not risk it," said Doc. "The most important thing was to tag along with the gang until they took me to the Repel deposit. Also, I was unarmed and significantly outnumbered after my supposed interment."

Pat laughed shortly. "I guess you went through a lot, too, didn't you?"

"More than usual," confessed the bronze man.

Pat grew thoughtful. "You know, you never did explain how you convinced the gang to assume that you were dead so that you could turn up as Jerico Hoan."

Doc Savage looked abashed. "I told you that I was overcome by my own anesthetic when I parachuted back to earth during the hectic encounter at the ghost ranch. After I landed, I was covered by the collapsing parachute canopy, whereupon the gang unloaded their weapons at me."

Pat said fervently, "It was a miracle that you weren't killed."

"Not a miracle, but the result of foresight. And precautions. Thanks to the billowing lobe, very few bullets struck me as I lay insensate. And those that did were turned by the chain-mesh undergarment I wear into battle. Still, I was entirely vulnerable. I was carrying extra vials of mercurochrome to treat my injured hands, and bullets struck the vest pockets containing these vials, releasing a realistic semblance of blood. This convinced Calamity's men to stop wasting ammunition on me.

"Fortunately, the gang did not feel it necessary to bury me until the next morning. By that time, I had recovered from the gas and employed the disguise kit in my equipment vest to transform myself into Jerico Hoan. It was necessary to leave my shirt and vest behind. I was unarmed, except for my folding grappling hook and line, as well as the belt containing the compartments that generated tear gas and black smoke when burned. None of these would have given me away if I was searched. Nevertheless, I was severely handicapped in joining the gang. It was necessary to play along to discover their goals, as well as to locate the Repel deposit."

Long Tom had been listening with interest.

"Why did Quest or Wood cut off the first Mr. Calamity's head and blast the headless body up into the sky to land here?"

"To confuse us, as well as obscure Lord Hemstead's true identity," explained the bronze man. "Wood hoped that we would consider the matter of Mr. Calamity closed, and further expected that our focus would be on ascertaining the dead man's actual name. Wood did not imagine that his victim's fingerprints would be on file anywhere. Or that Long Tom would later stumble upon the buried head."

Johnny spoke up then, "What about that Repel deposit?"

Addressing the two F.B.I men, Doc Savage said, "The disposition of the remaining matter is something that should be handled with utmost secrecy, and by qualified experts.

"I cannot think of a more qualified expert than you yourself," said Special Agent in Charge Heflin.

"I heartily concur," added Agent Hale.

"Thank you both," said Doc Savage.

That left the matter of the body of Henry Hemstead. When a hearse arrived to convey it away, Pat Savage was gripped by sudden twisting inner emotion.

"Excuse me," she said thickly, retreating to the ranch house as the headless corpse was removed by solemn undertakers.

"What's eating her?" Renny wondered.

Long Tom answered that. "Pat and young Darn were getting friendly, if you know what I mean."

"Oh," said Renny. "But he's going to pull through, isn't he?"

"Sure. Doc Savage saved his life when he tied Darn's belt around his wounded leg. But it was a near thing. Pat's pretty cut up about it still. She thought he was dead, and kinda blamed herself a little. When she called the hospital to talk it over, Darn wouldn't come to the phone."

Renny closed one eye and regarded Long Tom with the other. "Wouldn't, or couldn't?"

Long Tom felt of his gold front tooth, which had been replaced after the battle hard by the hellish coal seam.

"Sounded like a little of both to me. Either way, Pat's idea of treating him to dinner went bust."

Chapter XLVII

THE EXCAVATION

DOC SAVAGE GAVE the matter of the buried Repel considerable thought. After the F.B.I. men had departed with the body of Henry Hemstead, he assembled the others to advise them of his decision.

"We will attempt to excavate the pit and salvage the chunk of Repel buried there. It is too risky to leave to future generations to rediscover it."

Renny thumped gloomily, "That durn stuff is a handful. Once we disturb it, there's no telling what could happen."

Fingering his monocle magnifier thoughtfully, Johnny remarked, "It is too valuable, as well as too volatile, to simply let be."

Hearing this, Pat Savage perked up. Her eyes were a little red, but the bronzed beauty had regained her composure. "I expect my rightful share of any gains," she said sternly. "After all, this was my mystery before any of you fellows barged in."

Doc Savage shook his head gravely. "Repel is too dangerous. In the wrong hands, it could become the most destructive weapon mankind has ever known. Aside from that fact, breaking it up into chunks and dividing it amongst ourselves is simply asking for more trouble. Our objective is simple, brothers. We will capture and contain it. Perhaps one day Repel will be understood sufficiently that it might be properly harnessed. Until that day, it is best stored at my Fortress of Solitude high in the Arctic Circle."

Folding her arms defiantly, Pat Savage frowned. "Just my darn luck! I come all the way out to Wyoming to seek my fortune, and I have nothing to show for it."

Long Tom pointed out unkindly, "You have your skin. Be thankful for that."

"Believe me, I am," said Pat with conviction. "I would just like a sprinkling of wealth to adorn it."

The preparations to excavate the Repel matter took several days. Doc Savage had a crane and an excavator trucked out to the pit site, something that cost nearly a thousand dollars.

One truck carried a band of an alloy steel and chain. Doc explained that this was to be used to encircle the element, if possible, prior to lifting it with the crane's hook.

They never got to the point of using the steel band, however.

Renny Renwick naturally handled the excavator. Once he disturbed the earth, and after four or five shovelfuls of soil were removed, the crane toppled over and he had to leap from the cabin.

Everyone who had been standing about watching was knocked off their feet. They stayed there for a time, until Renny decided to stand up.

He found that he could not. His bellowing "Holy cow!" made the turkey buzzards high overhead suddenly fluster their feathers and take off with a mad beating of pinions.

"I can't stand up!" he complained.

"Verticality is prohibited," added Johnny.

Long Tom Roberts put that in simple terms. "The Repel influence is keeping us from pushing back against it."

"Remain calm," instructed Doc Savage. The bronze man was crawling along the ground. He reached the truck containing the steel band. He did not go to it, however.

The truck had been pushed sideways away from the pit, the sides of its tires making broad sweeping gouges in the sandy soil.

There was a case of dynamite in the front seat, carefully packed in sawdust and cotton batting. Doc Savage opened the crate, made sure the dynamite was dry, and then he started the engine.

The motor ran well enough. The bronze man drove in the direction of the pit. He made reasonable progress until he reached the zone of influence.

The motor started complaining as the big truck slowed down. It continued crawling forward, but at a much slower pace.

Doc Savage wedged the gas pedal to the floor and leapt out.

The truck kept going, but it crawled with agonizing slowness. Motor straining, it crept along. There was just enough horsepower to reach the edge of the pit, but not penetrate further. The laboring truck stopped dead, its motor growling. Smoke poured from the hood.

While the truck had been in motion, Doc Savage went among his men and pulled them back to safety. Most of them had already started crawling. Doc simply finished the job.

When they all reached a place of safety where they could stand on their own feet, Doc Savage told them, "Stick to the shelter of the hoodoos and big boulders. Get behind them. Retreat as best you can."

"What about you?" Pat asked anxiously.

"Never mind about me. I have a plan. Now go."

The bronze-haired girl was reluctant to leave her cousin's side. Renny scooped her up and bore her off.

"No foolish heroics!" Pat called after the bronze man.

Doc Savage did not reply. He plunged back into the zone of force created by the buried Repel.

Among the items he carried with him were small grenades resembling smooth steel eggs. They were activated by tiny lever-actuated timers. They were quite powerful for their size, since the largest was only the circumference of a pigeon's egg.

Reaching the stalled vehicle, Doc Savage crawled into the dump-truck bed and crouched down behind the band of alloy steel. He took from a pocket one of the small grenades, armed it and flung it as high overhead as he could.

The grenade got only so far. It encountered the powerful force. It literally floated in the air, fixed. This interesting phenomenon proved brief. For the grenade let go.

The detonation did not seem to accomplish very much in the way of destruction. After an interval for allowing grit and debris to settle, Doc Savage pitched two more grenades. They fell closer to the center of the pit. They, too, exploded with great force. Since they were not packed with shrapnel, the bronze man was in little danger. The windows of the truck blew out of course, forcing Doc to plug his ears each time in order to protect his eardrums.

The fourth grenade managed to hit the ground, with the immediate result that there was a violent upheaval in the crater's center. Something had evidently shifted deep down in the pit.

Coughing malodorous smoke from its exhaust pipe, the truck lurched forward again.

Doc Savage pitched himself off the back with alacrity. He raced with great speed, flashing for the nearest shelter. It was not close. The nearest hoodoos had been knocked over by the persistent force emanating from the crater.

Eventually, Doc reached such shelter as he deemed sufficient for what was to come. But it was a near thing.

Throwing himself behind a granite boulder, the bronze giant called out, "Cover your ears, all of you!"

"Holy cow!" boomed Renny. "What gives?"

Doc rapped out, "Dynamite!"

No one had to be told twice. Fingers were inserted into ears. All eyes squeezed shut.

Everyone waited. No one quite saw what transpired next.

The rumbling truck pitched into the crater, and grumbled along for a short while.

From his pocket, Doc Savage removed the compact radio transceiver which he used to communicate with others. It had several other purposes, one of which was that it functioned as a radio detonator. The bronze giant made the proper adjustments to the device, then he sent a signal to the detonation device packed in with the dynamite.

Results were instantaneous.

Bar-r-r-room!

The truck flew to fiery pieces, the blast hurling fragments in all directions. One intact tire went hopping merrily along, while the engine struck a hoodoo resembling a primitive totem pole, toppling it. The crater actually collapsed inward from the force of the blast.

Almost immediately, there was a roar followed by a whistling. The whistling trailed off so swiftly they were not sure they actually heard it.

Only one person saw what happened. And then only briefly.

Doc Savage looked up. Into the heavens flew the fragment of Repel—the unknowable, unstoppable element that could never be tamed. It went straight up. And kept going.

Doc Savage had out his pocket telescope and attempted to follow it. But to no avail. It had already vanished into the stratosphere before he could get the slender tube orientated.

The bronze man waited for the element to tumble back to earth. It continued to climb.

For several minutes Doc Savage deeply regretted having attempted to disturb its resting place. If it crashed back to earth, he knew, the mass could land anywhere, including on top of them, with catastrophic results.

Having no ability to foresee the future, Doc Savage simply waited, flake-gold eyes fixed upon the heavens.

But the fleeing Repel did not drop back to earth. It simply departed the atmosphere, it seemed.

When it was safe to do so, Doc Savage stood up and collected the others.

"It is gone," he told them.

"Where will it land, do you suppose?" Pat asked fearfully.

"It is not expected to land," advised Doc. "The force of the blast liberated the full potency of the element. It appears to be well on its way to escaping earth's gravitational influence."

Johnny blinked owlishly. "I'll be superamalgamated! Do you mean it has gone into outer space itself?"

Doc nodded. "That appears to be the case. While it cannot be recovered by human hands, neither will it be a danger to the human race in the future."

Long Tom added a sour note. "Unless of course there's more of that weird stuff buried underground somewhere else on the planet."

Doc Savage said nothing. It was a sobering thought.

THEY salvaged what they could of the equipment and made their way back to Long Tom's ranch.

Laramie awaited them there. He had been released from the hospital and was cooking away, supported by a proper crutch.

Finding him in the kitchen, Long Tom scolded, "I don't think any of us have appetites right now."

The old cow nurse glowered. "No? Where'd you lose them?"

Renny grimaced. "They all went straight up into the sky—along with the pits of our stomachs. Not expected back for a day or two."

"Suit yourself," muttered Laramie, returning to his hot stove.

"So you can stop frying all those steaks," Long Tom chided.

"Don't you worry none, Long Tom. After all that hospital food I et, I'll just treat myself."

"Do you know what steaks cost?" Long Tom exploded.

"Take it out of my pay, if you're gonna be miserly about it!"

Long Tom's face grew raw. "What pay? You haven't worked in days!"

"And I ain't eaten decent in all that time! Now go tickle a dynamo or something and let an honest cowboy make chuck."

In the adjoining room, Renny closed the door on the argument and grunted, "Those two are getting to be worse than Monk and Ham."

Pat said, "I suppose you boys are heading back to New York now that all the excitement is over with."

"There is nothing keeping us here," advised Doc.

Pat looked thoughtful. "Speaking for myself, I think I will stick around. Laramie was telling me how to find gold dust and nuggets in the ruby sands around here. Maybe I will strike it rich, after all."

Long Tom stepped out of the kitchen, red of neck and miserable. Hearing Pat's comment, he made a disagreeable face.

"You're welcome to stay as long as you need to, just don't make it a habit."

Taken aback by the annoyed electrical wizard's apparent rudeness, Pat demanded, "Are you hinting that I've overstayed my welcome?"

"No, but I've had a bellyful of this neck of Wyoming. I came here for peace and quiet to conduct my electrical experiments. Between local rustlers, unwanted trouble and unexpected strife, I'm giving up on this place."

Renny asked, "You're selling out?"

"As soon as I can find some sap to buy the dump. It doesn't suit me."

Pat considered. "Maybe I will purchase it. If I strike it rich, that is."

Doc Savage offered a suggestion.

"If it is peaceful solitude you want, consider Jackson Hole. It has a reputation for quiet living. Perhaps you could buy a more suitable spread when you dispose of this one."

Long Tom brightened. It was evident that the idea appealed to him.

"I might investigate that possibility once I get this place squared away," he allowed. "I like the idea of ranch living. I've just had it up to here with Pumpkin Buttes."

With that problem apparently settled, Johnny Littlejohn drifted over to stand with Doc Savage. His long thin face was thoughtful.

"I have been wondering," the bony archaeologist mused, "if there might not be more deposits of Repel scattered around the globe."

Doc Savage regarded him steadily.

"Are you proposing that we seek out any undiscovered examples?"

Johnny nodded eagerly. "The samples we found on the Calamity bunch were Repelanium—which is neither pure nor stable. It would be a benefit to mankind if we could tame the awesome element."

Doc Savage said, "Twice Repel has gotten loose and wrought havoc. While the element's potentials are conceivably fabulous, it has proven too intractably dangerous for human purposes. It would be better to let any such deposits remain buried where they lie. Perhaps future generations will acquire the requisite scientific knowledge and wisdom to harness Repel. But the present Twentieth Century lacks either quality."

Johnny looked as crestfallen as a skeleton the day after Halloween.

"You are unassailably correct," he decided. "But think of the possibilities inherent in the element. As a means of propulsion, mankind could reach the moon, and go beyond it."

Pat Savage appraised the bony archaeologist skeptically.

"Why on earth would you want to go to the moon in the first place?"

"Because," replied Johnny, "it is not the earth."

Pat's skepticism made her tawny features dubious.

"What's wrong with this planet?" she challenged.

Johnny sputtered, his tongue tangling up.

"Why," he said after gathering his injured dignity, "I would go to the moon for its selenite."

"It's what?"

"For its rocks," explained Doc Savage. "Johnny has ambitions to be the first geologist to explore the moon."

Renny asked, "Is that another way of saying he's got rocks in his skull?"

"Anyone who says such a thing," proclaimed Johnny in his most dignified tone, "suffers from acute cranial calcification of a cubistic configuration."

The blank expressions all around prompted Doc Savage to translate the injured archaeologist's incomprehensible words.

"Another term for what Johnny means," explained the bronze man patiently, "is blockhead."

At that, the group broke into laughter. Doc Savage did not join in their merriment. But the dust-fine golden flakes in his arresting eyes seemed to dance humorously.

Noticing this, Pat placed her hands on her hips and demanded, "Would it hurt you to crack a smile once in a while? Or did the gaggle of experts that raised you include a wooden Indian?"

In response to that playful dig, the bronze giant did display his strong white teeth. He made a conscious effort to do so. No one was fooled.

The Valley of Eternity

Chapter I

LETTER FROM YESTERDAY

DOC SAVAGE WAS hiding.

It was not the fear of danger, nor threat of sudden death, that caused the bronze man to lock himself in the fastness of his skyscraper laboratory in the center of Manhattan. As far as Doc knew, no enemy was on his trail. A stealthy assassin was not stalking him. It was nothing like that.

He was engaged in an experiment that could only be understood by less than a dozen other learned men, all of them experts in nuclear physics. But that was merely something to do while he ignored the incessant pounding on the laboratory door.

A squeaky voice demanded, "Doc! Are you in there?"

The bronze giant refused to reply.

Another voice demanded, "Don't think you can fool us, cousin. We know you're in there. And we know why you're hiding."

The voice was tart and very female. Doc ignored it.

A cultured voice asked, "Do you think you can avoid us all day long?"

That was Theodore Marley "Ham" Brooks, the attorney of his organization.

The bronze man switched on a complicated apparatus that only a qualified nuclear scientist could operate. This produced an electrical humming noise, punctuated by crashing sounds resembling electrical discharges.

Doc knew the crashing sounds would be heard through the

steel door, and he intended that they be understood as a polite but firm admonition to go away.

The trio outside the heavy laboratory door would not go away, however.

The frustrated group resumed their insistent banging and shouting. It was difficult to say if they were simply exasperated, or angry. But they certainly were noisy.

Doc Savage gravely ignored them.

The reason was a surprising one. Today was his birthday. It was also a day he preferred to skip over.

An innate modesty lay behind this sentiment. But there were other, deeper reasons. For one thing, Doc Savage had never really known his mother, the long-deceased woman who gave birth to him. He did not like to be reminded of that missing piece of his growing up.

Most of Doc's birthdays had not been celebrated in a family way. Early in life, he had been handed over to a succession of scientists and other experts for the arduous regimen of training that ultimately produced the superman of science that he became. They did not celebrate his birthday, except in rare circumstances.

Doc's own father had done this to him. The reasons for this were confoundingly obscure. He had not gotten to know his own father well until he had fully entered manhood. Less than a decade later, Clark Savage, Senior, had been murdered, thereby cheating Doc out of getting to know his male parent as deeply as he would have liked.*

So the idea of a family celebration of his natal date was something foreign to the bronze man's upbringing.

The truth was, birthday celebrations, along with the attendant cake, heaping of praise and inane revelry, embarrassed him. Consequently, he did not know what to do with himself when his few close friends took it upon themselves to celebrate his natal day.

---

* *The Man of Bronze*

Doc Savage had decided to lock himself into his laboratory until his birthday had completely passed.

Eventually, the noisy assault on the door died down, and the insistant entreaties to join the festivities soon abated.

"You don't know that you're missing!" the saucy feminine voice called through the heavy portal.

The bronze giant enjoyed nearly two hours of solitude after that. Solitude, as much as any other experience in life, had molded him. Doc had not been completely friendless growing up. But the frequent relocations around the globe—during which he had been placed with groups as diverse as cold-blooded scientists to hot-blooded African hunters—had prevented close friendships from forming, or lasting for very long when they did.

It had been an extraordinary two decades of training. But it had had its drawbacks. One of which was that Clark Savage, Junior, as he was known during his youth, had formed very few personal attachments.

Even after he had become the remarkable man the world knew as Doc Savage, he had recognized the value of solitude. To that end, he had built in the Arctic a retreat that he dubbed his Fortress of Solitude. It was there that he made many of his greatest scientific discoveries. There, too, the bronze man periodically revisited the solitude that had sculpted and honed his mental machinery. The polar refuge had been his father's idea.

Peace and quiet enabled him to think along scientific lines. But it was also a way to avoid an excess of human contact, which he sometimes found uncomfortable for reasons he could not entirely explain.

Long after Doc had assumed the birthday celebration had broken up, a note was slipped through a narrow notch in the laboratory door resembling a mail slot.

The note was brief:

Visitor. Benjamin Ellis Ross, esquire. Shall I send him away?

The note was signed "Ham."

Very briefly, Doc Savage's parted mouth emitted an ethereal sound, a vocalization he did not often make in these serious times. It was one he had acquired in his youth, from a Hindu yogi. This sound was a trilling, musical and yet devoid of tune. It started low, rose like a cresting wave, and broke into a not-unpleasant cascade of crystalline notes that defied description. This was an expression of emotion, practically the only one he ever manifested, for part of his training involved the steely repression of emotion.

A newspaper reporter, once overhearing the trillation, had described it in print for his readers as "the kind of a sound you could imagine a Martian making as he whistled in astonishment upon encountering his first Earthman."

It was an awkward turn of phrase, but nonetheless fitting. The sound was unearthly in its way. Doc's trilling soon drifted off into the unutterable nothingness that belonged to the ineffable.

Getting control of himself, the bronze giant moved to an intercom, keyed it and said simply, "Inform Mr. Ross that I will be out presently. And let's put the celebration aside, shall we? This may be important."

A squeaky voice said, "If you say so, Doc. But we saved you some cake."

Removing his laboratory smock, Doc Savage put on a conservative tie the hue of a chestnut mare, and donned a brown coat jacket that harmonized with it.

They complemented the deep bronze of his skin, which had been baked brown by decades of exposure to solar radiation in myriad climes. Yet there was a metallic quality to Doc's epidermis that was not explainable by action of strong sunlight. This uncanny quality, along with his skullcap of even darker hair, had earned him the cognomen "Man of Bronze."

Doc stepped out into a library that was fabulous in its massive elegance. A veritable university library set up on the eighty-sixth floor of Manhattan's tallest skyscraper, and occupying more square footage than the Grand Central Station concourse. Despite its size, almost every volume was scientific in nature. Doc Savage passed an impressive globe that would have been perfectly at home atop a midtown newspaper building. It, too, was enormous.

Set on a low table on the other side of the vast sphere were the remains of a birthday cake. Chocolate, with white frosting. It was one of his favorites, the other being vanilla with cocoa frosting. He did not understand why he preferred such stark contrasts. It was another of his mental quirks.

ARRAYED around the table were five of the most unusual individuals ever assembled together in one room since the Potsdam conference.

One was a human skeleton who wore his hair so unfashionably long that he looked as if he might take up the baton and commence conducting an orchestra at any moment. His pinched, studious face regarded Doc Savage with benign inquisitiveness. This was William Harper Littlejohn, one of the most learned archaeologists and geologists of his or any other generation. Despite his professorial bearing, he was known informally as "Johnny."

Next to him, standing equally as tall, yet more ponderous in stature, was a dour derrick of gloom with fists so large they exceeded the size of his head. John Renwick, mechanical genius and civil engineer extraordinaire. "Renny" was the name that his friends called him.

Standing next to him and looking like a young-old youth was Long Tom Roberts, the electrical engineer. Long Tom was the least impressive of Doc Savage's tight circle of comrades in purely physical terms. But his unimpressive build belied his punishing fists and fighting spirit.

No doubt people had named Andrew Blodgett Mayfair "Monk" shortly after his birth. No other nickname could possibly apply. Monk resembled a human gorilla furred with rusty red hair stuffed into a garish green suit. His arms were so freakishly long that his coat sleeves had to be specially tailored in order to fit properly. Even so, his thick wrists jutted beyond his cuffs, showing bristled forearm hair resembling stubby rusted nails. Monk was stocky, broad of beam, with a nose and ears which fists had damaged in the past.

Contradicting his brutish appearance, Monk was a leading industrial chemist, whose efforts had helped win the Second World War for the Allies.

Lastly, there stood an enchanting young woman whose skin, eyes and hair all but matched Doc Savage's own. She was a symphony of color from her luxurious bronze hair and skin to her enchanting golden eyes. Her features approached perfection, and her shape not far behind. A gold foil gown made her look like something you'd find under the Christmas tree.

The bronze giant's dominant flake-gold orbs softened slightly as they fell upon her. This was Patricia Savage, his only close living relative, and paradoxically Doc's most complicated relationship in life.

"You all may continue the celebration without me," stated Doc. "I will be conferring with my late father's attorney in private."

Pat laughed throatily. "Like fun we will! We are saving a piece of cake and we are going to watch you eat it, whether you like it or not."

"We will see about that," said Doc flatly, striding on to the reception room.

Passing through the door, he found his own attorney, Theodore Marley Brooks, engaged in polite conversation with an elderly man who looked as if he might have voted for William McKinley in his youth. He held a neat dark Homburg hat in his lap.

Both men arose, breaking off their conversation.

Doc allowed a semblance of a smile to warp the metallic mask that was his features when in repose.

"Clark! Or should I call you Doc? I remember you so vividly as a young man."

"It has been many years," said the bronze man politely. He did not know Ben Ellis Ross well, but recalled that his father had trusted him unreservedly.

The two shook hands. Doc waved the elderly attorney into a comfortable leather chair while he took a seat behind a desk that was actually an inlaid table of Oriental workmanship that his father had bequeathed him and could have served as a director's table but for its exotic touches.

Once they were comfortable, Doc asked, "What brings you here?"

"The date."

Doc looked blank.

"Your birthday, to be exact."

"This is a rare occasion, but I have a birthday every year. I have not seen you in a very long time."

"Not all birthdays are equivalent," reminded the attorney. "In this case, I am operating under instructions from your father, who long ago directed me to present you with a sealed letter upon this specific occasion."

A flicker of interest came into the bronze man's flake-gold eyes. A quality of perpetual animation made them seem as if the aureate particles contained within each iris ebbed and flowed with Doc's inner thoughts, like tiny autumn leaves stirred by wayward winds.

Rising, the attorney proffered the letter. "I do not know its contents. Only that you are to receive it on this day."

"Thank you for remembering," said Doc.

The oldster all but bowed, saying, "With my duty done, I will take my leave. I can only imagine that the letter is personal and private, and I do not wish to pry."

"Thank you," said Doc.

Ham Brooks showed the fellow out and said, "I will rejoin the others while you peruse the missive in question."

Picking up a letter opener, Doc Savage nodded and began the process of excavating the envelope's contents.

Ham shut the connecting door between the reception room and the library, taking along a fashionable black cane which would probably go to the grave with him, for he was rarely seen without the stick.

Traffic sounds came very faintly from Fifth Avenue far below as Doc Savage extracted the letter. He hesitated. His father had been gone a good many years now. Murdered by criminals. It was this slaying that launched the career of Doc Savage back during the early years of the Great Depression. Doc and his five men had already organized themselves to do important work, but had not become public figures in their early endeavors. The death of Clark Savage, Senior, physician, explorer and humanitarian, had thrust his son into national prominence, something the bronze man would have preferred to put off as long as possible.

In the intervening years, the Doc Savage organization had become a worldwide entity. Its humanitarian work had been the salvation of thousands of unfortunates, while its growing financial power had uplifted foundering businesses crippled when the stock market crashed, and performed wonders in keeping criminals and even greater international rogues in check.

During the Second World War, Doc and his men had become willing instruments of the U.S. War Department, but now, with that horrific global conflict behind the victorious peace-loving nations, the Doc Savage enterprises had resumed ordinary operations. He was looking forward to a long stretch of welcome normalcy.

The letter in hand, Doc hesitated before unfolding it. A faint and familiar odor came from the paper. It struck him with great force. It was the vaguest hint of his father's cologne. Waves of memories came flooding back. A lump came into Doc's throat as he realized how much his father had been the architect of his formative experiences—and how little the senior Savage had personally figured into the cascading rush of those successive years.

The linen stationery unfolded in metallic fingers. Flake-gold eyes scanned the handwritten lines, inscribed in flowing India ink with his father's favorite fountain pen—a long-discontinued brand called Remex.

The address was the present one, for this suite of offices had belonged to Clark Savage, Senior, before his untimely passing.

"My Dearest Clark," it began.

> First, allow me to congratulate you upon achieving the lofty age to which you have ascended. I have no doubt but that you have by this time made your mark upon this trouble-beset world.
>
> I am writing in this year of 1928 A.D. in the event that I am not among God's children populating the planet Earth in the future decade in which you presently inhabit. I would prefer that we confer personally on this matter, but inasmuch as no man is the complete master of his fate, as both precaution and insurance for the Savage heritage, I must take pen in hand.
>
> Now, as to what is on my mind. Having achieved my 60th birthday, I am reminded of certain poignant lines from my favorite poet, Robert Burns. As a kind of preamble, permit me to share them with you.

> *The wan Moon is setting*
> *beyond the white wave.*
> *And Time is setting with me,*
> *oh!*

Doc Savage read the paragraphs that followed with deliberate slowness, acutely conscious of the fact that this was his father's final communication. The minute golden flecks that made his eyes so uncanny began to churn and give the impression of picking up momentum, like twin dust storms forming.

When at last he came to the familiar paternal signature, those gathering storms had frozen, and from his lips escaped the uncanny trilling that signified an inner, emotional tempest had broken loose. It sounded like a hurricane of wild notes unleashed by a thousand tropical songbirds stirred into unified voice.

Chapter II

QUEER QUEST

IN THE SPACIOUS library, Doc Savage's aides, along with Pat Savage, were discussing the unexpected visit by lawyer Benjamin Ellis Ross.

"I do not think it is betraying any confidences to reveal that Mr. Ross came bearing a letter from Doc Savage's father," Ham Brooks was saying.

"A mysterious letter!" exclaimed Pat. "How intriguing."

"From beyond the grave, it sounds like," grunted Renny of the monster fists.

"Whatever could it contain?" murmured Johnny, who spun a monocle he wore attached to his coat lapel by its black ribbon.

Monk scratched the back of his bristled neck as if trying to dig a hole.

"Could be it's a birthday greeting," he offered squeakily.

Ham favored Monk with a withering glance of disapproval.

"If Doc's father desired to wish him a happy birthday," he sneered, "he would have made arrangements to make it an annual event."

"There you go again, jumpin' to false conclusions," Monk snarled back. "Maybe it's kind of a special birthday."

"Possibly," allowed the lean and elegantly-dressed Ham while examining the polished sheen of his black cane. It was really a sword cane, the wood the finest Malacca and the concealed blade forged of Damascus steel. "But I doubt that the elder Savage would or could have anticipated his own untimely demise. No doubt this missive bears tidings of greater importance."

"Do you think Doc will share its contents with us?" wondered Long Tom, tugging on an oversized ear suggesting a jib sail.

"Good question," said Pat. "If I know my cousin, probably not. Not if it's personal, which it surely is."

While they were chewing over the matter, a hairy paw reached up from under the table, closed around a piece of half-eaten cake that had been set down, and withdrew covered in frosting.

This stealthy act did not go unnoticed. Monk spotted the disappearing fingers and let out a howl of complaint.

"That was my cake!" he yelled, small eyes blazing in the direction of Ham Brooks. "Your sneaky chimpanoutang stole my cake!"

The hairy chemist got down on his knees and one overlong arm lunged for the thief.

Stepping up, Ham Brooks unsheathed his thin blade and warned, "If you harm a hair on Chemistry's head, you dumbskull, I will scalp you and hand the pelt to him for safekeeping."

"Give me that, you miserable monkeyshiner!" gritted Monk.

The thief flew out from under the tablecloth, looking like a ball of reddish fur. This was a diminutive ape of unknown species which Ham Brooks had acquired during a hair-raising adventure in South America many years back.*

Ham was by reputation a fastidious dresser and it staggered the imagination to conceive that he would associate himself with such a creature. But the dapper attorney loved squabbling with Monk Mayfair almost as much as he enjoyed landing on the annual best-dressed lists, so he took possession of the creature he dubbed "Chemistry," knowing that its resemblance to a miniature Monk would vex the simian chemist.

It worked like a charm. Monk routinely threatened to drown Chemistry in the handiest sink.

---

* *Dust of Death*

Climbing to the top of a ponderous bookcase, Chemistry squatted and began licking frosting off his hirsute fingers. Then he spied a sleeping form on a settee.

It was a runt pig. This was Monk's pet, Habeas Corpus, whom the apish chemist had picked up to rankle Ham, who detested his nickname in addition to despising pork in all forms, cooked and otherwise. This made Ham's adoption of Chemistry more understandable. The two animals served as annexes of their ongoing friendly feud. When they were too tired or busy to squabble, their respective pets could be counted upon to pick up the slack.

Spying the sleeping shoat, Chemistry opened his fist, regarded the hunk of crushed cake in his palm, and his eyes grew sad. Then they became mischievous as he made up his monkey mind.

With a screech, he flung the cake downward, striking Habeas on his snuffling snout. The pig jumped up on long legs, and distended ears flew up like flapping wings. He jumped off the settee, racing around the labyrinth of bookcases in search of his tormentor.

Monk was now boiling. He tore in Ham's direction, squawling red rage and bloody murder all at once.

The elegant attorney unsheathed his sword cane and took up a fencer's position, seemingly prepared to run Monk through— or perhaps allow him to impale himself on the glittering blade during his headlong charge.

"Oh, for Heaven's sake!" cried Pat in exasperation. "Somebody please prevent those two homicidal maniacs from ruining Doc's birthday."

Renny Renwick got between the pair, kept them apart and showed each antagonist one of his gargantuan fists. The much-scarred knuckles were intimidating.

"Chemistry started it!" Monk yelled.

Ever the lawyer, Ham attempted to upend reality.

"Which would never have happened had you not carelessly

left your cake unattended," he sniffed. "You should have re-membered that Chemistry has a sweet tooth."

"Nice try, shyster!" growled Monk. "But no soap. That flea circus up and slapped Habeas with cake for no reason."

"On the contrary, he had ample reason. It was in retaliation for Habeas nipping at his ankle that time."

"What time?"

"Oh, it was about three or four years back," drawled Ham.

"Knock it off, you two!" bellowed Renny, shoving them apart effortlessly.

"Don't you boys ever get tired of roughhousing?" Pat wondered aloud.

"It's in my blood," said Monk. "Like iron."

Sheathing his sword cane, Ham said thinly, "Remind me to let out some of that rambunctious fluid at my earliest oppor-tunity."

"You two," scolded Pat, "need to find saner hobbies. Why don't you acquire a set of wives, or something?"

"Monk would only try to steal her from me," sniffed Ham.

"Excuses, excuses," observed Pat. "You're just a pair of over-grown adolescents who should have settled down ages ago."

WHILE Pat was attempting to cool frayed tempers, the two animals, Chemistry and Habeas, got into another fight. Their owners hastily separated them, then stood glaring at each other as if they were tempted to throw their pets down and take up the hostilities between themselves.

Pat seemed to take such pugnacious behavior as a matter of course. She paid it scant attention.

Doc Savage's trilling suddenly came into being. It possessed a weird, shocked cadence unlike anything they had ever before heard during their long association with the bronze man.

Monk and Ham abruptly called off their glaring and face making.

Through an intercom speaker concealed in an air vent, the unmistakably resonant voice of Doc Savage came.

"Come in here, please. All of you."

His voice sounded strained, as if barely under control.

Rushing through the connecting door, they assembled before the massive ebony table. An opened letter lay before the seated bronze man.

Doc Savage stood up. His face was strange. Normally, he held his expression under rigid control. His metallic countenance possessed an innate immobility that was at times unnerving. It gave the impression of a thinking machine formed like a man.

Now it was different. The contour lines had lost their unyielding firmness, and the natural impassivity of his features gave the appearance of strong metal approaching its melting point. His facial poise was wavering.

That told them all that the bronze giant was having difficulty with his self-control.

"Let me go directly to the point," he said stiffly. "My father has instructed me to undertake a quest, possibly the most important quest of my life to date."

"Holy cow!" exploded Renny. "Where will it take us this time?"

"That cannot be determined for certain. But to the ends of the earth, if need be."

Johnny piped up. "Is this a quest for treasure? Or a lost city?"

"Nothing like that. But I will need your help in this undertaking."

Monk beamed, displaying large teeth like white stones. "Count on us, Doc."

"I guess that lets me out," murmured Pat, folding her attractive arms. "I'm always left behind to swallow your dust whenever you get to gallivanting around the globe."

The bronze giant's remarkable golden orbs found and held those of his cousin.

"All of your help," he amended. "Perhaps especially yours, Pat."

"Somebody take my temperature," sighed Pat. "I'm hearing hallucinations."

Doc Savage shook his head gravely. "I am in earnest. For I cannot do this thing alone."

Ham's dark eyes sparkled with curiosity.

"What is it you are seeking?"

"A woman."

"What is this woman's name?"

"I have no idea at present. That is what makes the problem so perplexing."

"Did your father provide any clue as to her present whereabouts?" pressed Ham.

"None whatsoever. I have absolutely nothing to go on. That is why your assistance will be crucial to the success of this quest." His voice had a vaguely shocked quality, like that of a man who had been told that his dog had died.

They stared at him, realizing that for one of the few times in their long association, Doc Savage was confronting a challenge that truly baffled him.

Their stares turned into open-mouthed gawking when Doc abruptly announced, "My father has directed me to find a wife."

Monk proved a little slow on the uptake. His simian brow wrinkled up. "Whose wife?"

"A wife of my own," stated Doc.

No one spoke until Pat Savage gave Johnny a poke in the ribs with her elbow.

"If you're not going to say it, I will."

Johnny blinked owlishly. "Say what?"

"I'll be superamalgamated!" shouted Pat with exaggerated boisterousness.

"Holy cow," rumbled Renny in a shocked whisper.

"Those were going to be my next words," added Pat dryly.

Chapter III

SAVAGE DILEMMA

DOC SAVAGE AND his men milled around the reception room with the dazed expressions of individuals who had been struck by lightning and whose brains had not yet registered that unhappy fact.

No one spoke. It was plain they did not know what to say. Looking at them now in their consternation, a stranger would have been astounded to know that here were five of the greatest brains ever assembled in one group. They were eccentric, to be sure. Genius and eccentricity often go hand-in-hand, as any study of great men in the fields of science, literature, or the arts would conclusively demonstrate.

Only Pat Savage seemed to have held onto her wits. Moviestar face firming up, she grabbed Doc by the elbow and said, "Follow me."

The bronze giant permitted himself to be led into the depths of the library. Pat found a quiet corner where they could not be overheard. The library's stupendous spaciousness aided in that aim.

"Now listen to me carefully, cousin," she began. "You may be a howling success in everything that you undertake, but this is a different sort of endeavor. Seeking a matrimonial partner is not in a class with going after Blackbeard's treasure, the lost silver of the Inca kings, or any of your other wild adventures. You can't start with the proposition that there is a special damsel sitting at home waiting for you to call. It's not that simple."

His self-possession returning, Doc Savage said, "Of course I realize that. But I can't very well undertake a quest without recognizing that this is what it is at its heart—a search."

"Yes, a search. But not a quest. You're not Sir Lancelot seeking the future Lady Lancelot. So get all those highfalutin romantic ideas out of your idealistic head. Women are more like tigers than you imagine. You've got to think of yourself as a hunter, not a suitor."

Confusion returned to Doc's voice. "I don't think I care for your analogy."

"Please remember that I run a beauty emporium and listen all day to women and their frank talk of men. Think tiger. Be a hunter. Otherwise, the she-tigers are liable to eat you alive."

Doc touched the perfect knot in his tie uncomfortably. "How do you propose I start?"

"By dating up a storm. If you knew what you wanted in a wife, you would probably have acquired one by now. That means you haven't the first clue as to who might be compatible with you."

"You are starting to make sense," replied the bronze man. "I will begin by going out on dates."

"Excellent. Just don't think you can capture a wife this season. You've fallen a few decades behind in your socializing. Dating isn't something you are good at."

Doc took slight umbrage at this remark.

"I have dated several women in recent years."

"I know you have. You take them out. You wine them and you dine them properly. It may be at the end you kissed one or two politely. But that's as far as it ever went."

Doc advised, "Some of them grew too serious too rapidly, others did not hold my interest."

"Let me ask you, Doc. These women you've taken out. Did any of them ever get a second date with you?"

"No," confessed the bronze man. "Something always came up."

"I know, I know," said Pat, throwing up her hands. "There's always a new damsel in distress to rescue. And Heaven knows, with all the women you attract, it can get a little overwhelming." Pat made thinking faces. "Let me ask you this: Of all the beautiful women who threw themselves at you over the years, were there any you would have considered keeping around?"

Doc Savage pondered the question.

"One or two."

"Name them."

"I'd rather not."

"If we don't have somewhere to start, then we have nowhere to go," lectured Pat. "And if you're going to be stubborn, you'll need another nursemaid to get you through this alive and unclawed. I hereby resign my commission."

"There was a woman named Rhoda Haven once."

"Oh, yes. Monk told me all about that fiasco. You were in some kind of cockamamie disguise and she didn't know you were Doc Savage. You almost fell for her, didn't you?"

Doc's metallic brow shot up, then down again. "I was glad to extricate myself from the situation when I realized I'd gotten in too deeply." *

"You don't know what deep is until you sink up to your neck in matrimony. That reminds me: Did your father tell you why you had to get hitched to somebody?"

"My father had feared that I might not have married by this point in my life. It was important to him that the family name be carried on and the Savage heritage continue through the Twentieth Century and beyond."

"In short," said Pat, "he wanted you to sire a child."

"The letter stipulated a son."

Pat made a delightful face of polite disapproval. "Of course it would. Your father was old-fashioned, right down to his boot heels. My father was the same way. And since they were broth-

---

* *The Freckled Shark*

ers, we can skip the proverb about apples falling close to the paternal tree. So, you must acquire a proper wife in order to produce a son, and then all will be right in the world."

Doc nodded. "You make it sound peculiar, when it is a perfectly natural pursuit."

Pat eyed her cousin sternly. "Except that you never quite got around to pursuing it. And now that you're getting up in years, you are being commanded from beyond the grave to step up and throw off a few fresh branches on the old family tree."

Doc's voice became slightly queer. "I always imagined I would get around to it. But the years went by so swiftly...."

"If you intend to make up for lost time, you're going to have to get even more busy. What do you think about looking up Rhoda Haven?"

"I would not know where to find her."

"Don't hand me that stalling routine. You have an army of private detectives working for you. If you want her located, she'll be found. And while you're at it, you should make a short list and put your gumshoe snoops on every name on the list. Just in case Miss Haven doesn't work out...."

Doc hesitated.

"He who hesitates has to marry an old maid," warned Pat. "Every year that has gone by, some of your choices have no doubt acquired suitable husbands. Knowing you, you'll have to start from scratch. But you could at least give this approach a valiant try."

"I will," agreed Doc.

"Promise?"

"Solemnly," said Doc.

"If that's the attitude you're going to take plunging into this," countered Pat, "you'll be lucky to wed by the time you're sixty. Solemn doesn't ensnare many maids. Unless you count old maids."

"I will talk to Mike Durwell."

MIKE DURWELL had run his own private detective agency until the business depression of the previous decade had all but put him out of business. Doc Savage had acquired the agency, set it up on the eighty-fifth floor just beneath his own head-quarters suite, and over the years had expanded it in scope of operation until nondescript offices were scattered worldwide.

So it was a simple matter for Doc to take his private elevator down one flight and meet with Durwell.

"I have a list of names," he said. "I want these women found as soon as practicable."

Durwell said agreeably, "I'll get my best men right on it."

Doc wrote out the list from memory, along with the last places he had seen these women. Then he handed it over.

The names meant nothing to Durwell. "This is a pretty far-flung group you've handed me," he remarked.

"When you find them, determine their marital status. If any are married, cross them off the list and do not proceed further."

Mike Durwell cocked a weather eye skeptically. "If I did not know better, I'd say you're casting about for a wife."

"You do not know better," said Doc, rising to his feet. "Keep this under your hat."

With that, Doc Savage left the office and Mike Durwell, who could read between the lines as well as anybody, attempted to pick his jaw up off the ink blotter and set it back in place.

Rejoining the others in the eighty-sixth floor reception room, Doc Savage took his seat at his ebony desk, lifted the letter from his father off the blotter and requested, "I wish privacy for the rest of the afternoon."

"Is there anything we can do to assist?" asked Ham.

Doc shook his head. "Thank you. I would like to be alone with my thoughts."

"O.K.," said the dapper attorney. "Please don't forget another shipment of gold is due in tomorrow. You will need to attend to the consignment."

Doc nodded somberly. He seemed to only half hear the reminder.

Ham, Monk and the others filed out and sought the private elevator at the terminus of the corridor.

Monk spoke for all of them when he said, "I hope this don't mean the end of our adventures together."

Renny rumbled, "Doc would never give up his life's work."

Long Tom added sourly, "There's many a husband who thought he could keep up his hobbies after marriage. Most of them learn otherwise—the hard way."

The elevator door opened and they stepped aboard. The car sank so rapidly Ham clutched at his Borsalino hat for fear it was a lifting straight off his head.

"What type of woman do you suppose Doc Savage would choose for a wife?" wondered Johnny.

No one answered. None of them had any inkling. They realized that for as long as they had been associated with the Man of Bronze, they did not truly know him very deeply. Perhaps no one did. In his earliest adventuring days, the newspapers had called him the "Man of Mystery." It was still true. Doc Savage rarely revealed his inner workings to others. Over the years, they had caught sufficient glimpses of his mental and emotional makeup to become convinced that they understood what type of man he was.

Those glimmerings of insight had fooled them. Revealing his outward character, they now realized, was not the same thing as imparting his innermost being.

As they stepped off the elevator car at the lobby level, Monk squeaked, "One dang thing is for sure. Things around here ain't never going to be the same again."

They all wore long faces as they exited the building.

Chapter IV

DISAPPOINTMENTS

THE FIRST REPORTS were not long in arriving. To say that they were discouraging was to put it mildly, if baldly.

Mike Durwell began his recitation. "India Allison has been married for a few years. Two kids, a boy and a girl. We crossed her off the list on the first day.* Sanda McNamara, on the other hand, has been married, divorced and remarried. She's still a big wheel down Cristobal way. Do you want more details?" **

"No, scratch her off the list," said Doc.

"Consider her scratched." Durwell went on. "Then there's Retta Kenn. We've been watching her for a long while. Runs a successful private detective agency, and doesn't seem to be too particular about who her clients are." ***

Doc cut him off. "Never mind that one."

The discouraging truth grew even more dismal. Name after name was crossed off. Prospects were diminishing rapidly.

"Tip Galligan is another one that got hitched," Durwell recited. "Add Barni Cuadrado, as well as that war correspondent, Carla Trotter, to the matrimonially-occupied list. And Miss Angelica Carstair-Flinders snagged herself a loose specimen

---

*   *The Terror in the Navy*

**   *The Dagger in the Sky*

***   *The Roar Devil*

of faltering European royalty, a Count Gerling. She's a countess now." *

"Just as well," Doc said dryly. "Annie Flinders was a skyrocket in female form." Wearily, he asked, "Did you dig up anything on Rhoda Haven?"

"No. That one has proven elusive. But we're still working on it. Same with that other adventuress, Kit Merrimore. No sign of her, either." **

There were yet others whose whereabouts were still to be determined. After the conference concluded, Mike Durwell asked, "Are any of these names to be given special attention?"

"No," said Doc. "Continue working your way down the list."

With that, Doc Savage returned to his headquarters suite.

The bronze giant was back in his laboratory smock and had returned to the experiment that he had left off the day of his birthday. An imposing cyclotron crackled and hummed as he scrutinized gauges and dials.

LATER in the day, one of the many telephones scattered around the big laboratory began buzzing. Doc moved to answer it. It was a unlisted number known only to his aides.

He was not surprised when Pat Savage came on the line, asking, "How goes the quest, Sir Clark?"

"So far the direction is circular."

"Usually circular activity precedes the mating dance. Dating anyone yet?"

"My private detective agency has yet to locate a suitable party."

"Good. It occurs to me that I am in a perfect position to play matchmaker."

"Be specific."

"Here at my beauty salon, I meet all classes of women. Perhaps

---

* *The Man Who Shook the Earth, Violent Night, Jiu San* & *The Screaming Man*

** *Ost*, also known as *The Magic Island*.

if I keep my ears open, I could find you a suitable but fetching bride."

"How would you know who was suitable?"

"Frankly, I could only take a wild fling at it. But if I start flinging women in your general direction, would you treat them gently?"

"The way you put it," remarked Doc, "makes me entirely uncomfortable."

"Think of yourself as a brave stalker of she-tigers, and I as your faithful servant beating the brush, driving the striped possibilities in your direction."

"I still do not care for your analogy."

"Well, believe me, it is preferable if you do the hunting. If word of this ever gets out, the she-tigers will come stampeding in your direction. More than you can count. You're famous, you're rich, and you're what gals today call a 'gorgeous hunk of man.' You could collect a harem, if you were so disposed."

"I am not," Doc said flatly.

"Good. Have you done any serious thinking about what type of woman you would find compatible?"

"I have."

"Swell. Let's hear it."

"Hear what?"

"The list of qualities or attributes you would find desirable in a potential spouse."

Doc considered briefly. "She must be healthy, beautiful, but not too young. Intelligent. Athletic. Adventurous. Comfortable in the city, as well as in wilderness. Willing to travel at the drop of a hat. But prepared to settle down and start a family."

"I can think of only one woman who qualifies," said Pat.

"Who is that?"

"Her first name is Jane. I can't bring to mind her last name. But it doesn't matter. She's taken. A hairy-chested he-man named Tarzan snapped her up. Sorry."

"Your attempts at humor," said Doc Savage firmly, "are not helping the situation."

"Admit it," said Pat. "If this was a lost gizmo, or a kidnaped heiress, you'd have solved the riddle by now and be onto your next caper. Since women are not normally up your alley unless you're performing surgery on them, you're lost at sea. Up a stump. And generally bamboozled."

"Bamboozled," Doc Savage said heavily, "perfectly fits my present mood. That is why I am working in my laboratory."

"Hiding in your laboratory, you mean. You might as well be holed up in that austere retreat you call your 'Fortress of Solitude,' where you hide from the world."

The bronze man's voice took on an edge. "I am not hiding."

"Then go out on the town tonight and meet somebody. Date them up. Paint the town red. Just don't marry the first girl who kisses back."

With that, Pat Savage hung up.

Fuming, Doc Savage returned to his experiment. He was self-aware enough to realize that he was throwing himself into his scientific work out of sheer frustration. He was getting nowhere. And he was accustomed to always getting somewhere.

In the absence of progress in his assigned task, he was making progress elsewhere. Yes, it smacked of procrastination. But Doc Savage was not interested in aimless efforts to no clear objective. It went against his deeply disciplined grain.

After a bit, a thought occurred to him.

Returning to the telephone, he called Pat Savage and asked, "Why is it you have never married?"

"You know I get proposed to practically every other month."

"Yes, and you turn them all down. Why?"

Pat's voice seemed to shrug. "Why, simply I haven't met anyone exciting enough to entice me into settling down. I'm young yet. There's a lot of the world I still want to see. A husband would only be an anchor around my neck."

"You sound the way I often feel."

"Maybe it's the Savage curse. To be a magnet to the opposite sex, and never feeling quite the same attraction in return."

"That is an interesting way to put it," Doc said thoughtfully.

"Before you get any ideas," reminded Pat, "go back and reread your father's letter. You have been commanded. I am under no such duress. Besides, eagles don't mate with lesser avians. You have yet to meet another eagle. You might think in those terms when you get serious about your tiger-hunting."

Once again, Pat disconnected without warning.

Doc resumed his experimentation. But when the sun started going down, the bronze man changed into a coat and tie and went out into the night, a determined expression on his metallic features.

Chapter V

UNFUNNY BUSINESS

THE SHRILL RINGING of a telephone wrenched Renny Renwick out of a sound sleep.

His giant fingers fumbled for the instrument, which was a modern and more substantial version of the old-fashioned candlestick telephones. Renny once had it custom made by Long Tom Roberts because the commercial instruments provided by the telephone company were too small for his whopping hands.

Seizing the candlestick portion, he pulled the horn of a handset off its hook and brought both to his sleepy face.

"What's doing this time of night that you would roust a man up out of a sound sleep?" he roared.

The phone roared back in Monk Mayfair's voice. "Renny! You gotta hoof it over to the Stork Club. There's a riot goin' on down there. And Doc's in the middle of it!"

"Be right down," said Renny, hanging up.

Renny was still tucking in his shirt when he stepped out of a midnight cab and saw what Monk had described.

Prowl cars were parked catercorner all around the famous nightclub. Patrons had spilled out of the long awninged entrance and onto the sidewalks, creating an uproar the likes of which the big-fisted engineer had not witnessed since V-J Day.

Monk shouldered his way out of the crowd when he saw Renny's massive head sticking up like a frowning lighthouse.

"Renny, we missed him. There's talk he's over at the Copacabana."

"What's going on?" demanded Renny.

Monk shoved Renny back into his cab and climbed in the other side. "Copacabana nightclub, driver. And make it snappy." To Renny, he panted, "I don't have it all straight, but it sounds like Doc Savage strolled into the joint and, before you could say Cary Grant, he was being mobbed by autograph hounds and bobby-soxers."

"What was he doing here?" grunted Renny as the cab careened through midnight streets.

Monk shrugged slopping shoulders. "Sounds to me like it started when Doc asked some hot number to dance, but it turned into a ruckus when he ended up waltzin' with Sinatra's girlfriend of the moment."

"*Frank* Sinatra? The singer?"

"The one and only. And, man oh man, is he steamed! He's tellin' everyone from Walter Winchell to the mayor that Doc Savage stole his girl. But from the people I talked to, the dish wouldn't let go of Doc once she got her hooks into him. When he finally tore loose of the place, she was followin' right behind."

The taxi took a hard left turn and went up on two wheels briefly.

"You'd think Doc would know better," grumbled Renny.

"Go easy on the poor guy; he's kinda new at this dating racket."

"God knows it's not easy being Doc Savage," agreed Renny. "He knows he can't even patronize a restaurant without causing a commotion. What made him think he could go dancing with any different result?"

Monk's wide mouth opened, but he never replied. They were pulling up before the Copacabana. The situation was no different, just noisier. Patrons were milling about the vicinity. Bottles were being flung wildly, and two women were tearing each other's hair out, calling one another some extremely unladylike names.

"Such language!" exclaimed Renny primly.

"I've heard worse," growled Monk.

"Where?"

"I've dated me a mess of chorines," replied Monk nonchalantly.

Accosting a police officer who was trying to separate the two combatants, the hirsute chemist demanded, "Where did Doc Savage get to?"

"I don't know, but I hope he has the good sense to go home and hide under his bed. These dames have gone wild over him."

Returning to Renny's side, Monk said, "I don't think he's here anymore. Do you want to try another night spot?"

Renny rumbled disconsolately. "I'd like to go home and pull the covers over my head. It must be near to three o'clock in the morning."

Nevertheless, they made the rounds of the nightclubs, jazz clubs and juke joints. But they found no trace of the elusive bronze man.

Finally, Renny said, "I'll bet he turned in."

"Unless he's under protective police custody," muttered Monk.

DOC SAVAGE was not in official custody.

He finally had shaken off the sugarcoated blonde who had deserted a famous crooner for his company. Since he was not far from Pat Savage's apartment, the bronze man hurried there on the theory that no one would look for him at his cousin's place.

Pat lived not far from her beauty salon, a solid-gold-and-black-marble emporium off fashionable Park Avenue. There was a snooty doorman on duty twenty-four hours a day. Doc had some difficulty convincing him to buzz Pat but, when he did, she said through the building intercom, "Tell the mental giant to come on up."

When she answered the door, Pat was wearing a bathrobe that looked as if it was spun out of crushed pearls. Her head was encased in something like an emerald turban, evidently to protect her exquisite hair while she slept. Her tawny features were sans make-up, but it mattered not one iota. Pat was a natural beauty.

Seeing her cousin's disheveled state, the bronze charmer asked with a puckish grimace, "Who is gunning for you now?"

"Half the women who like to stay up half the night," returned Doc morosely.

Closing the door behind him, Pat asked, "What about the other half?"

"Sleeping peacefully in their beds, I imagine. Which is where I wish I was right now."

"Since I'm up, I might as well listen to the whole sorry story. Unless you'd rather flop on the couch?"

"Might we do both?"

"As long as you hurry along with your recitation. I'm a working girl and have to be up early."

Doc Savage told his tale. It began with his attempt to go dancing at the Stork Club. He was immediately besieged by admirers and autograph seekers.

"I did not know that the blonde woman had come with Mr. Sinatra," he confessed.

Pat's mouth warped with undisguised glee. "I'll bet anything this yarn has a smash finish. If it starts with Sinatra, the only direction left is up."

"Her name was Lile Bobbs. She wanted to slip away to another night club. Mr. Sinatra saw her leaving, and took umbrage. Matters escalated from there."

Pat laughed shortly. "Matters! Is that what you call a blazing Manhattan scandal? Do you have any idea what the tabloid newspapers are going to be printing in the morning? Not to mention the radio commentators? 'Doc Savage steals Frank Sinatra's date.' I'll bet you ten smackers someone is concocting that headline right this very minute."

Doc Savage looked as miserable as a man of his dignified stature and bearing could appear.

Dropping his massive frame onto a tasteful couch, he stated, "I managed to ditch the blonde bombshell after we changed night clubs twice. However, I left quite a commotion in my wake."

"I can hardly wait to hear the casualty count of fainting femmes. What has gotten into you? You know that you're as conspicuous as a jack o'lantern in a goldfish bowl. And wearing that gleaming metallic armor you call skin, feminine eyes see you as a cross between Sir Galahad and Sir Lancelot, forsooth."

Doc raked his slightly-disheveled hair with metallic fingers. "I thought I should brush up on my dancing. It is not one of my strongest skills. I had no sooner stepped onto the dance floor when the trouble erupted. Perhaps next time I should wear a disguise."

Pat lifted her elegant eyebrows as far as they could go. "I'm sure *that* will impress the girls. Will you take your false face off before or after giving the lucky ladies a good night kiss? Or do you intend to put off any necessary unmasking until you reach the altar?"

Doc sighed. "I feel as if I'm a million miles from walking down the aisle."

"You will get no contrary argument from me," said Pat frankly. "Honestly, sometimes I wonder if in back of those arresting golden eyes lurks a brain of dense brass. Well, I suppose it's partly my fault for suggesting that you start dating. Hilarity ensued, and Lord knows I should have seen it coming. But it was worth a try."

Doc Savage offered no rejoinder.

Pat regarded her cousin with something akin to pity. "Why don't you simply turn in for the night? Try not to frighten the maid while you're at it."

"Thank you, Pat."

"She's not your type, by the way. Trust me on that."

WHEN morning came, Doc Savage was still sleeping. Pat called down to the doorman and had every available newspaper sent up. When they arrived, she tipped him handsomely and sat down to examine the headlines.

"Hmmm," she murmured appreciably. "These are choice."

When she found the inevitable one that screamed "Doc Savage Steals Sinatra Date," Pat rolled the paper tightly and used it to rouse Doc, swatting him on the head as if aiming at a fly.

The bronze giant snapped to his feet, looked around and saw Pat. She was grinning. She held the ten-point headline in both hands under her grin.

"What did I tell you? Cough up."

Reading the headline, Doc Savage groaned.

"Well, cheer up," said Pat. "This isn't even the worst one. Some of the wild yarns these sob sisters concocted would make a swell screwball comedy. I can see Clark Gable playing your part—sans metropolitan mustache, of course. Sinatra would play himself, naturally. It doesn't matter that he probably can't act. The bobby-soxers would be too busy swooning in their seats to notice. Too bad Carole Lombard shuffled off this mortal coil when she did. This would have been perfect for her...."

Doc groaned. "I will refrain from delving any further."

"It won't do you any good. No doubt Ham Brooks' office will be fielding telephone calls once it opens."

A startled light came into Doc's eyes. "What do you mean?"

"Sinatra's blind date gave the *Blaze* an interview. She's hollering breach-of-promise and is fingering you as a bronze plated cad of the lowest sort."

"It will never hold up in court."

Pat shrugged negligently. "No doubt Ham will quash it before it gets very far. But it will be a long time before you go dancing in this town again. The cops will clap you in protective custody before they let that happen. Gadzooks, Sir Clark, the complica-

tions you bring to the gentle art of pitching woo and whispering sweet nothings!"

Doc Savage rubbed his features dry before he spoke again.

"Are you having breakfast here?"

"No time. But I'll have the maid fix you up whatever you'd
like. Then you need to skedaddle. Go out the back way so you're
not seen. Otherwise, the headlines will read 'Doc Savage Love
Nest Discovered,' or some other travesty. Tah-tah!"

After consuming his breakfast in steely silence, Doc Savage
called a cab and all but vaulted into the back seat.

He gave the address of his headquarters, but no sooner had
the cab started off into light traffic than he changed his mind.

"Driver, take me to the Hudson River waterfront."

Shrugging, the cabbie obeyed. They soon drew up before an
enormous covered pier, a warehouse constructed of grimy brick.
The sign at one end read: *Hidalgo Trading Company.* The sign
was very old. The building was elderly. The bricks were a sooty
red and cracked in spots. Despite the sign, the thing was virtually a vault. But it was no ordinary warehouse. This was Doc's
combination boathouse and aircraft hangar.

The bronze man entered at the landward door, and turned
on the lights.

In years gone by, the place had been crammed with aircraft
ranging from streamlined trimotors to a small dirigible. The
dirigible was no more. But there was a small blimp floating
high under the rafters. A large amphibian plane stood near the
river doors, each wing sporting two powerful motors. There
were other aircraft, including a very modern helicopter that was
probably a decade more advanced than any commercial or
military model. There was even a submarine, but that was very
old and looked as if it had not been put into the water in years.

Doc glanced at a wall clock and noted the time. He was early.
So he walked around the vast space, making sure that all was
shipshape. He gave special attention to an express cruiser that

was overdue to be taken out into the water. If the rakish vessel stayed in dry dock too long, it was not good for the hull.

The bronze giant moved around the spacious interior with a studied restlessness, testing alarms and performing other routine checks. He had felt consistently unsettled over the last few days, and working like the devil did not seem to make much difference. He had grown introspective, falling into a distressing habit of taking his mental machine apart and examining the pieces. Too much of that, he was aware, is not good for anyone. But something entirely new, wonderful and yet terrible, had thrown the metal machinery into a jumble. Doc failed to quite understand it.

As the hours passed, an acute sense of nostalgia crept over him. From this decrepit-looking hangar of a warehouse, he had sallied forth to virtually every corner of the globe, a modern Galahad on a succession of miraculous winged steeds, solving the problems of the world, setting wrongs aright, and earning a reputation as an indestructible nemesis to the wicked. There had been a soaring freedom in that endeavor. Now Doc Savage wondered how much of that splendid calling he would be forced to abandon.

He felt absurdly like a young man forced to leave behind the toys of his carefree youth as he sets out on the path of manhood....

NOON was almost nigh when the radio set suddenly broke into song.

The song was a fragment of an old sea chantey, "Stormalong John," but it carried special meaning. Doc went to the radio, took up the microphone and said, "You are early."

"I made good time," said the author of the ditty. His voice was nondescript. It belonged to one of the guards who watched over the warehouse when no one was around. The man had been in Doc Savage's employ for a very long time. He was trusted.

But even he did not know the nature of the cargo he was bringing to New York City.

Doc Savage opened the great riverward doors electrically and before long a twin-engine plane set down on the Hudson chop.

The aircraft taxied in, its motors blooping, and veered toward the concrete ramp that dropped sharply into the water. The aircraft surged, motors gunning, and climbed up onto level concrete.

After he shut down the engines, the sunburned pilot stepped out and said, "Another cargo successfully delivered, Mr. Savage."

"Difficult trip?"

"Long and tedious. If you call that difficult, I suppose it might be. But I can stand it, Mr. Savage. By the way, one engine started missing. The port. You might look into that."

"Thank you. You may take the rest of the day off. With pay."

"Thanks, Mr. Savage!"

The watchman-pilot exited the warehouse and claimed his parked car. He was a loyal employee. But he never suspected that in his youth he had been a desperate criminal. Doc Savage had captured and reformed him, incidentally erasing from his young brain any memory of his previous identity and past misdeeds, which had been very black indeed.

The man had brought his cargo from the Republic of Hidalgo, in Central America, through special arrangement with the national bank in the capital city of Blanco Grande.

Taking up a short crowbar, Doc Savage entered the plane and started breaking open a stack of wooden crates. He had expected an even dozen crates, but only eight were in evidence. This was enough to give him pause. Then he attacked the first container. It opened under his pry bar, revealing gleaming ingots of gold.

The stuff was pure. The pry bar happened to nick one corner and it instantly deformed. It was very soft gold. Soft and lustrous. The ingots looked to be hand-formed, not machine-made.

In one of the crates, Doc Savage found something like a scroll.

He had not expected such a thing. Unrolling it, he saw writing in the pictographic language of the Mayan Indians. For this was Mayan gold.

The message was terse.

"I am deeply sorry. This will be the last shipment."

It was signed by a glyph representing the Mayan rain god, Chaac, a frowning face made distinctive by an upturned nose resembling a striking serpent.

Doc Savage's tuneless trilling came, swelled until its rising notes touched the rafters and then meandered about aimlessly until finally extinguishing itself.

The bronze giant returned to the task of uncrating the gold and discovered a folded piece of bark-paper inserted between two flat ingots. On the smooth side was inscribed a poem. The poem was not in English, but Doc could read the Mayan language fluently and translated it in his mind without thinking.

> *Ixchel's wan face,*
> *rises over the Western cliffs.*
> *Stealing my future,*
> *one sunset at a time, ay.*

The bronze man's trilling piped up at once. It had an eerie, wondering quality. When it finally trailed off into nothingness, Doc Savage's face was as fixed as if cast in living metal.

Chapter VI

BEDLAM

A **RAGGED LINE** of humanity wound around the block, beginning at the main entrance to Doc Savage's skyscraper headquarters.

Monk and Ham arrived separately in their own vehicles, and almost collided with one another as they jockeyed toward the concealed basement garage entrance behind which Doc Savage kept his fleet of motor vehicles.

The line happened to snake past the door. Since the entry was disguised to look like a segment of the building's masonry façade, the women forming the line did not realize that they were blocking it.

Braking, Monk popped his apish head out and howled, "For the love of Mike! I haven't seen a riot like this since nylon stockings came off the rationing list."

Ham found a parking space and emerged, clutching his ever-present black cane.

"What is going on here?" he demanded of Monk.

The gorilla-like chemist shrugged sloping shoulders and confessed his ignorance. The act of shrugging seemed to make his short neck vanish.

Being the take-charge type, Monk strode up to the line, and asked, "Is there some kinda sale goin' on here?"

An attractive red-lipped brunette said, "This is the line for Doc Savage."

Monk blinked. "Is he givin' away money, or something?"

"Better than that. He's on the marriage market. We're here to put in our applications."

Another woman added, "Of course, the lucky girl will expect a proper courtship, and none of this fast stuff that men like so much these days."

A rather overdone blonde remarked pointedly, "I don't mind if he's a little fast. As long as we get somewhere in the end."

This comment brought jeers and booing. A hand reached out of the milling throng to yank at the blonde's hair. She whirled, and brained the wrong woman with her purse. The epithet "hussy!" flew from several carmined lips.

A riot would have broken out, but a beat officer happened upon the incipient melee and shook his billy club in the general direction of the noisy gaggle of femininity.

"What's goin' on, Finnerty?" demanded Monk.

"Ah, word got out that Doc Savage painted the town red last night. And all these gals have jumped to the same conclusion, namely that he's looking to settle down. The line is going all the way up to the fourth floor and that screening room Doc Savage maintains there."

Monk knew the room. Doc Savage set it up long ago to manage the seemingly endless parade of private individuals seeking his help with one problem or another.

Periodically, Doc moved the room from one floor to another in the hope that it would cut down on pests. But that never seemed to work for very long. Only those who got through the screening process were allowed to meet with the bronze man on his eighty-sixth floor headquarters proper.

"Any sign of Doc?" demanded Monk.

"If he was smart," growled the officer, "the big bronze fellow would go on vacation. I wouldn't want to face this pack of howling females for all the tea in Singapore."

"I get it," squeaked Monk.

"I'm glad of that. Now would you kindly get your vehicle out of city traffic?"

"I don't know where to put it," complained Monk.

"If you felt up to the challenge," growled the cop, "I might suggest you stack it atop any handy vehicle. But I suppose that would cause further complications."

"You're in a rare mood, Finnerty."

"I'm in a blue funk, and I don't care who knows about it!"

Reclaiming his jalopy, Monk pulled back into honking traffic and drove two blocks until he found a parking spot. When he walked back, there was no sign of Ham Brooks.

The hairy chemist availed himself of a side door, and took the private elevator to the fourth floor.

The corridor was packed, but he bulled through as best he could—a difficult procedure inasmuch as Monk was almost as wide as he was tall.

Holding forth in the screening room was a man named Jim Lubbock, who happened to be Mike Durwell's chief assistant. The employees of the investigations business handled routine inquiries, but sometimes Monk, Ham and the others spelled them.

Jamming himself sideways into the office, Monk shouted, "I'm looking for Doc Savage! Any word?"

Lubbock yelled back. "Tell him to kindly come to my rescue. I'm being mobbed. I never knew there were so many single femmes in Manhattan."

"I'm from Jersey City," a redhead corrected.

"Philadelphia," another volunteered.

A loud voice lifted above the others, demanding, "Who said anything about being single? This is Doc Savage we're talking about. No woman's husband can compare."

"Sez you," a Bronx voice retorted. "My husband's just as much a man as Doc Savage. He just ain't rich and famous, that's all."

Craning his bull neck around, Monk said, "Any married dames need to make themselves scarce. Doc ain't interested."

No one took the hint. So Monk retreated to the elevator and

took it all the way to the eighty-sixth floor, after first shoving a couple of pushy ladies off the car.

"Private elevator. Sorry."

"Send Doc Savage down, will you?" one implored.

"Don't stay up all night waitin'," Monk said gruffly as the doors rolled shut.

Arriving on the eighty-sixth floor, Monk found Ham already seated in the reception room. The elegant lawyer had a respectable newspaper under one arm. Unfolding it, he showed Monk the headline.

DOC SAVAGE SOUGHT!

Under the black scarehead was the following:

By Womanhood Everywhere

His features scarlet, Ham declared, "Can you imagine a dignified sheet such as this making light of the matter?"

"Did you read about what happened last night?" countered Monk.

"Why do you think I arrived this early? Doc will need legal representation in these unfortunate matters."

Monk flopped down in a comfortable chair and tried to rub his eyes to keep awake.

"Renny and I scoured the town looking for Doc. Finally, we gave it up. No telling where he got to."

"This uproar is unprecedented."

Monk rolled his tiny eyes ceilingward. "Uproar is kind of a weak word for it. I call it pandemonium. Blind pandemonium."

OVER the next hour, Renny, Long Tom and Johnny filtered in, waving newspapers like hapless birds whose wings were soaked in oil.

"We are going to have to rescue Doc from this muliebrous ensnarement," proclaimed Johnny.

"Huh?" grunted Renny.

"Female mess," Johnny translated.

Long Tom grunted, "Which mess do you mean? The fire he stoked last night, or the conflagration his late father got him into?"

Ham announced, "I will handle the complications created last night. None of the lawsuits have a leg to stand on. The courts will not even entertain them."

Monk groaned. "You'd better be on the beam. Doc could go broke just fightin' off the ambulance chasers." He cocked a suspicious eye at the dapper attorney. "Present company excepted."

Ham was so upset he failed to hear or respond to Monk's sly dig at his professional ethics.

They sat around the reception room for several hours before there was any sign of Doc Savage.

To their astonishment, the bronze giant emerged from the library and said casually, "I imagine you fellows have been reading about me in the newspapers."

"Holy cow, have we!" boomed Renny. "Where did you spend the night? Or is that a personal question?"

"I managed to bunk at Pat's apartment. I thought it more prudent than trying to make it all the way here. I have somehow become a magnet for the opposite sex."

"Nothin' new there," muttered Monk, who was sometimes jealous of the way women swooned at the bronze giant.

DOC SAVAGE looked weary. He lowered himself into his customary chair and explained, "I took the subway to the nearest stop, and employed the secret tunnel that leads to our sub-basement garage."

Ham snapped his fingers. "We should have suspected that. It has been a number of years since it was necessary for you to use the one-man elevator concealed in a basement pillar. Since it lets off into the laboratory, we did not hear you arrive."

"I have not been eager to face you all," admitted the bronze man. "In my own defense, I had no inkling of what my explorations of the city's nightlife would bring about."

Ham remarked dryly, "Well, at least you know what *not* to do."

"Yeah," agreed Monk. "If you wanna find a nice girl to date, this ain't the town to start anything in."

Renny suggested, "It might be a good idea to leave Manhattan for a while. Until all this rhubarb blows over."

Doc Savage let out a rare sigh. "That is an appealing idea. Especially since my private detective agency has failed in their search to find me a suitable mate." Doc paused and looked rueful for a moment. "But we may have to depart the city for another reason."

They stared at him, expectation tramping over their faces with tentative feet.

Doc advised, "I've just returned from our warehouse on the Hudson, brothers. The latest shipment of gold has arrived. It was shy four crates. In one of the crates was a message from King Chaac. He stated sorrowfully that this would be the last gold shipment sent north."

This news stunned the five aides. Since their first great adventure together long ago, their activities had been funded by Mayan gold. This wealth came from a secret valley deep in the Republic of Hidalgo, in Central America. Doc Savage's father had discovered it a generation or two ago. The place was known as the Valley of the Vanished. Kindly King Chaac ruled over this enclave that had survived untouched by civilization since before the days of the Conquistadors.

Sometime after Doc Savage had been born, his father had made an arrangement with King Chaac. The agreement stipulated that when his first-born son came of age he would have unlimited access to the treasure, which after all did not do the Mayans much good since they did not treat with the outer world, which knew nothing of them to this day.

This was the legacy Clark Savage, Senior, had left to his son.

Doc had learned of it only upon his father's death and, following certain clues, visited the Valley. There they had been wel-
comed by kindly King Chaac.

For many years the gold had flowed to Doc Savage's worthy
hands as uninterrupted as a river. It was his to expend as he
wished, so long as it was in the service of good.

That it had finally trickled down to nothing astounded them.
The store of gold had been vast. The wealth of successive Mayan
kings. It was expected to last generations.

Ham Brooks said in his best courtroom voice, "It has been a
few years since we've visited the Valley, but there was plenty of
gold then."

"There was," agreed Doc. "But we had been tapping the
treasure rather heavily in order to finance the Allied effort
during the war. We may have miscalculated, although I do not
see how."

Renny rumbled, "Maybe there's some trouble brewing down
there. Could be the durn message is a fake."

Doc nodded. "That thought had crossed my mind. There was
also another message enclosed with the gold. It was a poem."

Johnny lifted his monocle reflexively. "A poem? Who composed it?"

"Princess Monja," replied Doc quietly.

The room was very still. No one spoke. This was a sensitive
topic.

Doc Savage had encountered the lovely princess during their
first sojourn in the Valley of the Vanished. The beautiful daughter of Chaac had fallen in love with the big bronze adventurer,
fallen in love to no avail. Doc had pledged himself to his work,
and early on realized that to marry would be to place any wife
and offspring in the path of unending danger. For even in the
beginning of his career, the bronze giant understood that he
was bound to make mortal enemies. And so he had.*

---

* *The Man of Bronze*

Twice since that visit, Doc and his men had returned to the Valley of the Vanished, each time to protect the gold from raiders. Each time Princess Monja had grown more mature and ever more beautiful. Her interest in the bronze giant, if anything, had only been fortified by his long absences.*

It was a problem with no solution. But matters now were different. Everyone realized that.

"What did the poem say?" inquired Johnny quietly.

Doc recited it from memory.

> *"Ixchel's wan face,*
> *rises over the Western cliffs.*
> *Stealing my future,*
> *one sunset at a time, ay."*

The faces of the others grew perplexed. Except for Johnny Littlejohn.

"I have never before heard that verse, yet it sounds familiar...."

Taking his father's letter from a receptacle of the ebony table, Doc Savage recited the paragraph in which his father had evoked the poet, Robert Burns.

> *"The wan Moon is setting*
> *beyond the white wave.*
> *And Time is setting with me,*
> *oh!"*

Renny muttered, "They're kind of alike, aren't they?"

"In spirit, they are identical," admitted Doc.

Johnny offered, "Ixchel is the name given to the Mayan moon goddess. It is remarkable that this woman expressed the same sentiment as the long-deceased Scottish poet."

Doc was thoughtful as the silence returned.

"We have an arrangement to communicate by radio with the Valley on every seventh day, if gold is needed. We have only

---

* *The Golden Peril* & *They Died Twice*

another twenty-four hours before that day. I will radio King Chaac and, depending upon his answer, we may pay him a visit."

"What are we going to do if the gold did run out?" asked Monk.

"There are other ways of making money," said Doc Savage. "But a free flow of gold is indispensable to our post-war plans."

Ham Brooks was polishing the gold head of his cane with a monogrammed handkerchief of pearl-gray silk. When the gleaming ball was clean enough to return his reflection, he inquired, "Do you suppose that this unexpected cessation of cooperation has anything to do with your father's letter?"

Long Tom snapped his fingers. "We should've thought of that! It's a funny coincidence."

Doc Savage said, "If King Chaac was aware of my birthday milestone, there might have been arrangements made long ago, but somehow I do not think so. My father did not engage in subterfuge or psychological blackmail. I'm sure he trusted me sufficiently to be confident that his letter provided all the motivation I required to fulfill his last wishes."

That seemed to settle the matter.

Monk asked, "Are we all going with you this time?"

"That will depend upon King Chaac's response. But this time Pat is coming along."

Ham's eyes were suddenly bright. "So you *do* expect trouble?"

"Not the kind of trouble you were thinking of, Ham. But the kind that might involve Princess Monja."

Monk grimaced. "She oughta be married by now. Probably has a pack of papooses, too."

"That remains to be seen. This poem she composed suggests otherwise."

The room fell silent again. It was as if they were suddenly attending a wake in their own minds. A wake not for a dead person, but for a way of life they had enjoyed over many years and by which they greatly profited in ways that were not monetary, but spiritual.

Each man in the room understood that the fate and future of the Doc Savage organization, something as solid in substance as a bronze bell, was hanging in the balance.

Since no man could predict the future of the events that had already been set in motion, worry rode their faces. Only Doc Savage's metallic countenance did not reflect that fact. The bronze giant had seemingly reverted to his customary stoic self.

Chapter VII

GLOOMY CONSULTATION

IT WAS THE morning of the seventh day. Sunday morning. Doc Savage rose early, as he always did. It was his habit to rise with the sun, a practice ingrained upon him by his father.

Before taking breakfast, he performed his usual morning ritual. Early in life, Clark Savage, Senior, started him on a routine of daily exercises. It had been modest at the start, for he had been a toddler. Over the years, this regimen expanded to include a variety of exercises for the brain, the senses, and not merely the muscles.

Doc began with the routine of calisthenics, switched to a mental puzzle-solving interlude that involved doing advanced mathematical calculations in his head, returned to the physical, and concluded with a number of apparatus which engaged the senses. There were sealed bottles containing subtle smells that he was required to identify blindfolded. Next came a portable device to push the limits of his hearing to nearly superhuman extremes.

Returning to the blindfold, the bronze man navigated his maze of a laboratory successfully, without bumping into or brushing against any standing object. In order to make the test as difficult as possible, Doc spun in place before embarking. He could not use his sense of touch to help guide him. This restriction aided in keeping sharp his memory.

Two hours passed. Doc showered off the coating of perspiration that made his metallic body gleam and then prepared himself a simple breakfast. All of this took place in a nook off the big laboratory where he had set up a modest living quarters.

The sun was a glorious body streaming light through the banks of windows on all three sides of the laboratory, displaying a panoramic view of Manhattan and New Jersey. Inasmuch as the walls were hospital-white enamel, the place brightened up amazingly.

The laboratory was subdivided into sections, each one given over to a specialty which Doc had mastered. There was a chemical corner, portions dedicated to atomic research, metallurgy, and other scientific disciplines.

In one corner stood a powerful all-wave radio. It was always switched on, but Doc turned the volume up to its maximum, so he could hear any transmissions of interest. Not that he expected any. All of his aides were in New York. But it was a habit, a precaution, one of the many examples of his disciplined mind, which prevented him from forgetting necessities in the course of a demanding and hectic existence.

It was over the big radio transceiver that the bronze man intended to contact the Valley of the Vanished when the appointed hour came. That was not for some time yet.

His breakfast concluded and the dishes cleared away, Doc strode through the laboratory, passed through the labyrinth that was his scientific library and into the comparatively modest reception room.

There was a device next to the desk telephone that was in the nature of a robot. When a call came in, an armature lifted the telephone receiver while a steel-wire recorder captured the voice of the caller after a record played, stating that the bronze man was not in his office.

A steady amber light signaled that a recent call had come in.

Doc rewound the steel wire on its spools, and made it play back by switching the control in the opposite direction.

"Mr. Savage, this is Jim Lubbock with Mike Durwell's office. We have located one of the women you inquired about. Her name is Willia Hannah, and she is still living down in the Caribbean on an island called Geography Cay. We have not contacted her, as per your request. But we know where she can be reached if you wish us to go forward on this matter."

Doc Savage shut off the recording device and his flake-gold eyes were reflective.

He remembered Willia Hannah vividly. She was a salty daughter of a line of pirates and had been involved in a violent scrape in the Caribbean back during the war. Doc had found her to be quite unlike most of the women he encountered. She was adventurous, knew how to scrap, and was self-reliant to an unusual degree. These exceptional qualities he had noticed at the time, and many of them were to be admired. She had also shown a noticeable interest in the bronze man, but in those days Doc studiously avoided feminine entanglements.*

Looking back on the brief association in the light of his father's injunction to marry, Doc considered that Willia Hannah possessed sufficient out-of-the-ordinary qualities that she might make a suitable wife. It was a startling thought. And it scared him a little. He was evaluating women in an entirely different way than before, and it bothered him that his thoughts ran along such practical lines.

In his mind, Doc had naturally thought that someday, in some future he did not permit himself to imagine, he would settle down with someone he loved. But he had never sought love from a woman. The truth was, he spent a great deal of time thwarting and evading their interest in him.

Now that the shoe was on the other foot, he was not certain how to conduct himself. It was disconcerting.

His thoughts drifted to other women from the past. There was Elma Champion, who had a ranch in Wyoming. There had been some sparks there, but no fire. Consequently, Doc did not ask Mike Durwell to check into her present whereabouts. Doc

---

* *Mystery on Happy Bones*

was reasonably certain she was still holding forth in her Wyoming ranch. Perhaps he should look her up at some point.*

Doc had asked his men to assemble in the morning prior to their consulting old King Chaac in the Valley of the Vanished. Monk and Ham showed up first. Contrary to their usual demeanor, they were sober-minded upon arrival.

"How are you, Doc?" said Monk in his incongruously squeaky little-boy voice.

"Good morning," said Ham elegantly, twirling his cane like an ebony propeller.

They took comfortable chairs, sat down and avoided any appearance of mutual antagonism.

"Where are your pets?" asked Doc.

"We decided to leave them at home," volunteered Monk.

"In the event that we take off for Hidalgo today," added Ham.

"It is not like you two to be so agreeable," Doc pointed out.

"These are serious times," said Ham.

Monk's small eyes wrinkled up. They became like tiny twinkling stars in the gristle pits rimming his simian orbs.

"We're worried," said Monk. "Worried about you. Worried about everything."

"This directive from your father," added Ham, "threatens to upend our association. It concerns us. Greatly."

"Massively," said Monk in a mild tone.

Doc regarded the pair steadily. "I am beginning to wish," he said, "that one of you would pull a ripe tomato out of his pocket and belt the other with it. I never thought I would feel this way. But neither of you is acting like your normal selves."

Ham and Monk exchanged concerned glances. Monk nodded slightly and Ham took the cue.

"We are wondering if you are aware of what you are getting involved in," he declared.

"Matrimony ain't what the storybooks make it out to be,"

---

* *The Man Who was Scared*

added Monk. "It's kind of a tough stew to swallow every dang day."

"Scalding," agreed Ham. "When it is not merely simmering."

"What would you two know about matrimony?" Doc shot back. "You chase every skirt that flutters by. Yet when they chase back, you skedaddle for the hills."

"We're smart," grinned Monk. "We know enough not to be ensnared by love."

"We are afraid," said Ham frankly. "Marriage terrifies us, and it should terrify you as well."

Doc steepled his metallic fingers and gave them careful attention.

"This entire proposition unnerves me," he admitted. "And it is not going well. I am at a loss as to how to proceed. I wish there were a scientific book I could consult, but insofar as I am aware, no reputable scientist has ever penned a volume on the subject of winning a wife."

Monk was suddenly grinning. "Hey, do you remember that time in Tibet where we all got whammyed by the radiations off that Blue Meteor? When we woke up, they convinced us that you'd gotten engaged to that babe, Rae Stanley." *

"Fortunately for all concerned," said Doc, "that was a ruse."

Ham chuckled. "We were all fooled for a time there. Imagine if it had been true? You would have been married all of these years."

"Incontrovertibly inconceivable!" proclaimed a new voice.

Johnny Littlejohn had entered from the corridor. He took a seat like a granddaddy longlegs spider gathering his elongated limbs together preparatory to climbing into his hole. In his ill-fitting suit, he might have been a scarecrow constructed out of odds lengths of pipe and rail. Only his hair possessed any thickness.

---

* *Meteor Menace*

"We were discussing my immediate problem," Doc told Johnny.

"I have nothing to offer on the subject of women," Johnny said dismissively. "I have not studied them in depth."

It was typical Johnny Littlejohn. If it was a rare rock or a hieroglyphic, his fascination was almost hypnotic. Where women were concerned, he appeared indifferent.

"On the other hand," continued the bony archaeologist, "I would not listen to either of these two on the subject. All they have learned is to flee the very thing they are continually chasing. They are like a pair of magnets whose polarities are constantly reversing."

Neither Monk nor Ham responded to that. It was an uncomfortable truth, and they knew it.

Renny popped his head in next, and wondered, "Who died? Looks like a wake in here."

Monk grunted, "Our collective futures may have kicked the proverbial bucket."

Doc Savage interjected, "I have every intention of continuing our association, and the work that we do. My father would want it that way. Raising a child is a significant expenditure of time and effort, but it is not exclusive of other activities."

Renny dropped his bulk into a chair and his face took on the character of a grimacing smile. That actually meant he was morose.

"It's not raising a child you should be worried about, it's managing a wife. Me, I'd rather have a pet lion. It would be less trouble."

Doc sighed. While his men were perhaps the most accomplished individuals in their lines of work, as confidants in affairs of the heart, they were all but hopeless.

Just as the desk telephone began ringing, Long Tom Roberts arrived lastly.

He was sitting down in a big leather chair that almost swallowed his puny frame when Doc took the call.

It was Pat Savage. She got right to the point.

"Mind if I drop by?"

Doc said, "I was going to invite you to participate."

"You're just saying that."

"On the contrary. I may need you."

"Hah! Now I know you're fibbing. When did you ever need me? Scratch that. Let me rephrase myself: When did you ever realize that you needed me?"

"I have been discussing my predicament with the others, and we are accomplishing nothing helpful toward the fulfillment of my father's wishes. A woman's point of view might be illuminating."

"That sounds more like the truth," snapped Pat. "Hold on. I'll be over in a jiffy. I may have some ideas—not that you will cotton to them."

"I would be grateful for any advice you could offer us," said the bronze man sincerely.

After Doc Savage hung up, Long Tom said, "My advice would be to find someone who can cook and clean and otherwise keep house while you pursue your own interests."

Doc observed, "I cannot imagine a modern woman who would stand for such an old-fashioned proposition."

Renny rumbled, "Don't listen to that woman-hater; he's all wet where romance is concerned."

Long Tom took umbrage. "I don't dislike women, I just don't have time for them."

"Same difference," said Renny, folding his massive arms.

Ham remarked, "We are getting nowhere on this subject. I look forward to Pat's arrival. She may have interesting ideas."

A silence fell over the group of six men. It was a painfully uncomfortable silence. The morning was fully developed now. None of them seemed to know what to say. This was a situation unlike anything they had ever before encountered. Had the objective required fists or guns, or even the application of nitroglycerine, they would have probably settled it by now.

All concerned realized they were out of their depth. It was as unsettling as if yellowjacket wasps had gotten trapped in the crowns of their hats.

To fill the conversational void, Ham remarked, "I have quieted the fires around that blonde woman and the singer. In fact, I am pleased to report that they are an item once again."

Doc Savage looked intrigued. "How did you engineer that miracle?"

"I happen to know Mr. Sinatra's attorney. It was all rather discreet. But it is done."

"Thank you," said Doc.

"Also," added Ham, "I sent Miss Bobbs a bouquet of roses in Sinatra's name. He knew nothing about it, of course. But it greased the wheels of romantic reconciliation, as intended."

The silence returned. It was prolonged. They all but stared at the walls.

PAT SAVAGE showed up in less than an hour. Her entrance immediately brightened the room.

The bronze-haired beauty was like that. She was practically incandescent. Her smile could melt anything from butter to dry ice.

"It is good to see you, Pat," said Doc Savage.

"I feel as if I should take your temperature," returned Pat skeptically. "Usually you're trying to trick me into departing the premises as rapidly as possible."

"Not in this case," admitted Doc.

Pat looked around the room. She noted the silence and the gloomy expressions on everyone's faces.

"I feel as if I walked into a wake. And not an Irish one, either."

"You are not the first to observe that," said Doc quietly.

"Well, I may have good news."

Everyone brightened slightly.

"If anyone can pull a hare out of a hat," said Ham gallantly, "it would be you, Pat."

"I may have found Cousin Clark a bride."

"Just like that!" exclaimed Johnny.

"Let me pull up a chair and regale you with some juicy gossip."

Pat took a seat near the oversized steel safe that had belonged to Doc Savage's father. A jeep could be stored inside with room for four spare tires.

"I'm sure I do not need to remind you of my erstwhile accomplice in misadventure, namely Miss Hornetta Hale." *

"Not on your life!" said Doc sharply.

"Hear me out," insisted Pat. "Since we went our separate ways, Hornetta has been busy as a bee in a florist's hothouse. She's quite the adventuress, you know, and is as free as a bird."

"You cannot be serious, Pat," said Ham Brooks. "Hornetta is trouble, although interesting trouble, I will allow."

Pat smiled. "That's why I got along with her. Trouble is her favorite dish, the same as mine. We just happen to be incompatible in other ways. Hence our association drifted in different directions. But consider this: Hornetta is one of the few women—other than yours truly that is—who could keep up with you, Doc."

"She's a daggone gold-digger," snorted Monk.

"Actually she's made her own pile. She's done well for herself. Perhaps you should consider it. Go out on a date, or better yet, circle the globe together. Since she's an accomplished pilot, you could spell each other at the controls."

Doc said frankly, "I cannot tell if you are making fun of me or not."

Pat smiled broadly. Her teeth were dazzling. Her golden eyes grew mischievously warm.

"Just testing your nerve. You're holding up just fine. I've been worried about you."

"So I hear from my other friends," said Doc dryly.

"What I is mean is," continued Pat in a more serious tone,

---

* *Phantom Lagoon*

"sometimes you appear as devoid of emotion as an oyster. If some gal took you firmly in hand and remade you into a normal human being, I'll bet you'd be a swell sort of husband to have around. Speaking strictly for myself, I'd like to gouge the emotions right out of you, so they will get air and come to life and learn to feel things." Her eyes flashed. "I wasn't serious about Hornetta, by the way. She's too much of a zany. Have you any prospects otherwise?"

"One or two," said Doc, "but nothing serious."

"Do tell," invited Pat.

"Not now," said the bronze man. "We have another matter to discuss. A rather serious one. The most recent shipment of gold from Hidalgo contained a note from old King Chaac, saying that the gold reserve has run out."

Pat knew about the gold supply. She had never visited the Valley of the Vanished, but in years past she had sometimes brought shipments in from Cuba or the Hidalgoan coast on Doc Savage's behalf. The Federal laws against ownership of significant quantities of gold had created certain complications, and Pat had to be let in on the secret in order to assist in circumventing them.

Pat blinked. "Well, aren't you as rich as Midas even without your strange inheritance? Don't you have a raft of scientific patents? Haven't you invented wonderful inventions?"

"The gold supply ensures that my life's work continues on uninterrupted," reminded Doc.

"What did the note say?"

"That King Chaac was regretful, but this was the end of the supply. We are considering dropping in to make sure. There was also a note from Princess Monja. A cryptic one."

Pat's golden eyes gleamed. "I've heard about her. She's had a crush on you going a long way back."

Monk laughed heartily. "Shucks! That babe has been carryin' a torch for Doc Savage since this whole thing started. Last time we were there, it was still smolderin'."

Pat looked interested. "What did she write?"

Doc Savage removed the patch of bark-paper from his desk and offered it to Pat, who leaped up and tried to read it. Her Mayan was shaky, at best. But Johnny helped her with certain words.

"This is a poem!" she exclaimed. "Is this a Mayan maiden's notion of pitching woo?"

"I do not know what to make of it," admitted Doc.

Pat absorbed it, then exclaimed, "You wooden Indian! Can't you read between the lines?"

Doc winced. "I was struck by the similarity between her sentiments and those of the poet, Robert Burns. Particularly my father's favorite verse."

"That may be," said Pat firmly. "Let me translate this for you. This is a woman in love saying that she can't wait for you forever."

Doc Savage's trilling floated out and around the room very, very briefly. He suppressed it.

"I had an inkling of that," he confessed.

"Inkling! She merely dropped an anvil the color of a Valentine heart on your thick skull. And you call that an inkling?"

Doc looked at his hands. He said nothing.

"How do you feel about her?" Pat pressed.

"She is very beautiful."

"I'm cheered that you noticed that much," said Pat tartly. "But I asked how you felt about her."

"Each time I see Monja, she seems more beautiful than before. But she is the princess of a faraway land. Our destinies seem very different."

"Would you marry her?"

Doc Savage actually lost a shade of bronze. "I confess that I don't know. Her frank interest has always made me uncomfortable. I do not know if it was the work that I do, or the temptation she represented."

"If this were anyone else," sighed Pat, "I would say that you were a lost cause. But we might be able to do something with you."

"We?" asked Doc.

Pat smiled like the Cheshire cat. "By we," she said lightly, "I mean the Princess Monja and I. I think it's time you hie to the Valley of the Vanished and investigate."

"We were planning to look into the problem of the exhausted gold."

"Not that!" exploded Pat. "Investigate Monja and this unrequited love you feel for each other."

"I am not in love with Princess Monja," Doc returned hotly.

"Men are sometimes the last to know," Pat said vaguely. "And don't be so shirty. It ill-becomes you. But you better take me with you. You're going to need a courtship navigator, and if it was up to you and your usual gang of associates, I would expect the ship of romance to go up on the rocks and sink like a stone."

Doc glanced at a clock on the wall.

"I lost track of time. It is the agreed-upon hour."

They followed Doc into the laboratory, where he picked up a microphone and dialed the big all-wave radio to the frequency used in the Valley of the Vanished.

An aged voice offered greetings in English. It was King Chaac. He sounded older than their last encounter, but no less dignified. *"I am pleased to hear from the son of my great friend, Clark Savage, Senior. I have been expecting this communication. No doubt you read my message."*

"It came as a surprise," admitted Doc. "Since there have been problems with the gold in the past, I thought it prudent to hear from your own lips what has happened."

"The mines have been exhausted. This was not foreseen by your father, although he knew that the gold we guard is not without limit."

"I'm sorry to hear this," said Doc.

"I am deeply distressed to convey this news to you," said King

Chaac. *"But until the gold was gone, I saw no reason to warn you. The agreement with your father was unequivocal. The gold was yours to do with as you saw fit for as long as you needed it. It was also understood that any son of yours would be equally entitled to draw upon its stores. Alas, the gold ran out before you could father a child."*

Doc Savage said nothing. While the tone of the old king was friendly, he detected a note of regret and possibly disapproval in his quavering tone.

Doc said, "We would like to pay our respects at your earliest convenience."

"I anticipated as much. Of course you are welcome. No doubt you will want to see with your own eyes that all is well in my kingdom, and that the gold is truly gone. Call upon me when you are able."

"We intend to leave this afternoon," advised Doc Savage. "Expect us tomorrow morning."

King Chaac replied, *"I will inform my people. Expect a celebration upon your arrival."*

"Thank you," said Doc. "Until we are face-to-face again."

Doc Savage switched off the big set and turned to the others.

"I see no point in wasting any time. Gather your things and rendezvous at our warehouse hangar. Pack for a week. We will leave as soon as everyone is assembled there."

Monk and Ham and the others left quickly to prepare for the trip.

Pat Savage lingered behind.

"So I'm invited on this little shindig?" she ventured.

"Yes."

Pat elevated an eyebrow that cost a small fortune to maintain. "I hesitate."

"Why?"

"Oh," said Pat airily. "I remember that time you told me to fly to Montreal on an important mission. Only to have me cool my heels for a week while you and the boys went tearing south to Peru without me."

"That particular adventure was too dangerous for you," said Doc. "It would not have been necessary to decoy you to Canada, but you eavesdropped on our conversations and would have followed."

Pat set her hands upon her hips, golden eyes going slightly molten. "Then there was that time you gave me an important package to guard and I spent another week in the mountains guarding it. It turned out to be a photograph of a billy goat."

Doc looked uncomfortable. "In this instance, there will be no trickery."

Pat charged on. "I'm thinking that if I leave your sight, you and the others will take off within the hour, instead of waiting for Cousin Patricia."

Doc looked more than a little abashed.

"This time, your presence will be indispensable."

Pat studied her cousin. Years of close association enabled her to pick up subtle clues as to his state of mind, the true feelings that lay behind the resolute and impassive bronze mask that Doc Savage showed to the world.

"I'm half tempted to believe you."

"You should."

"But not entirely convinced. Here's what I offer. You will kindly accompany me to my place, and I'll grab my overnight bag. Then we're off to the fabled vale of Maya."

"It is," said Doc, "a deal."

"And if you dare renege on me," warned Pat, "I'll sick Hornetta Hale on you. Don't think I won't!"

"Heaven forbid," said Doc fervently.

Chapter VIII

SUBTERFUGE

DOC SAVAGE WAS unusually pensive as he drove through midtown Manhattan traffic.

The bronze man had escorted Pat Savage to the sub-basement garage of the towering skyscraper. As soon as the bronze-skinned girl entered the vehicle, he sent the powerful sedan up a concrete ramp and swerved it into light Sunday traffic.

Instead of turning toward Park Avenue, where Pat maintained an expensive apartment, he drove directly toward the Hudson River.

Noticing this, Pat Savage turned vehement. "Don't tell me you're welching on our deal already!"

Doc shook his head firmly. "You can pick up new clothes in Havana when we refuel there."

"This better not be a trick," Pat warned.

"No trick," said Doc, depressing the accelerator and pushing the vehicle past the speed limit.

Doc Savage had cultivated a certain quietness of manner. He rarely made idle conversation, spoke sparingly, and often withheld his opinion, even when asked.

Over their long association, Pat Savage had learned to read the big bronze man despite his seemingly-impenetrable psychological armor. He had something on his mind, but was not ready to divulge it.

As Doc pulled up to the Hidalgo warehouse on the Hudson River, she asked, "A penny for your thoughts, milord?"

Instead of replying, Doc said simply, "We are the first to arrive."

"The wild way you hoicked this armor-plate chariot through the city, how could it be otherwise?" Pat countered. "Where's the fire? Other than in your fevered brain, that is."

"I'm sure the others will be along directly, Pat," Doc said quietly.

The sedan slid into the landward side, through a garage-type door that opened once the hood intercepted a photoelectric beam. The bronze giant braked, then stepped out, Pat doing the same.

The interior always took Pat's breath away a little. There was no such enterprise as the Hidalgo Trading Company. It was a blind. Few New Yorkers suspected that a formidable fleet of air-and-sea craft were housed here in its cavernous confines.

Doc moved with a studied swiftness toward the portion of the vast barn of a place where aircraft were hangared. He went to a two-motored amphibian airplane, and fell to inspecting it. It was the craft the trusted watchman had ferried the Mayan gold in.

"Call Monk or Ham," Doc directed. "See what is keeping them."

Frowning, Pat returned, "They could hardly have gotten to their places and back here so quickly."

"Ask them to hurry."

Shrugging, Pat went into a modest corner office, closed the door and made telephone calls. No one answered.

Stepping out, she called over, "No answer. They're already on their way, I presume."

Doc did not reply. He was busy inspecting one motor of the aircraft.

Climbing down, he said, "I've decided that we are going on ahead of them."

Pat stamped her foot suddenly. "Now I know it's a trick. Why would you want to do that?"

"I will explain once we're in the air," said Doc.

"You will not! How do I know you're not going to boot me out over the Catskills or some such wilderness, leaving me to parachute to safety?"

Doc displayed a slight edge in tone. "How many times do I have to reassure you that I am not pulling a stunt?"

"Remember that candid picture of the goat you gave me to take up in the mountains to guard? Well, I haven't. In fact, I will never forget it."

"That was a long time ago," said Doc. He looked genuinely contrite.

Pat folded her sinewy arms defiantly. "Nay, I say. Nay and ix-nay. I'm going to need a notarized statement before I climb into any airplane alone with you."

Doc Savage was normally gentle with his cousin, but suddenly a bronze hand reached out, grabbed her by the upper arm. Without speaking, the metallic giant marched her to another plane and put her aboard.

Pat attempted to resist, but it was as if a mechanical man had seized her in its steely grip. Doc Savage was completely irresistible. Pat had never felt his power to that degree before. It made her shiver a little inside, realizing how strong he truly was.

"Do you have your six-gun in your purse?" he asked.

"I wouldn't try knocking you over the head, if that's what you mean. I know better."

"That is not what I mean," Doc said firmly.

Soon, Pat was seated in the co-pilot seat, and Doc was warming up the engines of a four-motored seaplane. Their synchronized thunder made the warehouse interior echo resoundingly.

"What's wrong with the other plane?"

"I will explain once we are in the air."

"What about the others?"

"They can follow us," said Doc.

"Now you're really being mysterious. This isn't like you. This isn't like you at all. Should I fear for my safety?"

In the middle of revving up the engines, Doc Savage turned to Pat and said earnestly, "You will have to trust me. I have come to a realization."

"Do tell."

But Doc Savage simply firmed his lips, pressed a button and radio-controlled doors opened on the riverward end. The plane lurched forward, exhaust pipes belching smoke, rolled down the concrete apron and slid into the water. The flying boat turned into the wind and began shaking and howling. Soon it was moving forward. It got on step, and clawed into the air on four glittering propellers.

Down below, Pat could see two cars pulling into the warehouse and several men pointing fingers at the climbing plane. They were visible for only an instant, but one seemed to be Renny. His mouth was hanging open.

Swinging south, Doc Savage leveled out the plane and flew in silence for a few minutes.

Monk's squeaky voice soon came through the radio receiver. *"Doc! What gives?"*

Doc keyed his throat microphone and said, "There has been a change in plans."

"Where are you goin'?"

"To the Valley. You'll follow in the second plane."

"What for?"

"Purely as a precaution," advised Doc.

"O.K., but it sounds like you're expectin' trouble."

"Trouble is always to be anticipated," said Doc, ending the conversation.

THEY flew along for a little while, and Pat Savage studied her unruffled cousin. Long years of association had not made him any less mysterious than he was when they first met in the wilds of British Columbia, more than a decade before.

Monk's voice was soon back on the radio.

"Doc! There's something wrong with this plane, one engine won't fire up."

Doc did not seem surprised. But then, he rarely did. Pat noticed that his trilling did not issue forth.

The bronze man said, "Endeavor to repair the bad engine and follow when you can."

Renny's booming voice cut in. *"Holy cow! That could take half a day."*

To which Doc replied simply, "Do the best you can. Pat and I will size up the situation in advance of your arrival."

Pat was wearing a throat microphone of her own. She asked, "Which engine won't work?"

Renny thumped, *"The port engine. Why?"*

"Oh, no particular reason. Just curious."

Doc signed off. Pat eyed him skeptically.

"Wasn't that the engine you were tinkering with while I was making those unnecessary phone calls?"

"It was," admitted Doc.

"So what are you trying to pull? And don't tell me you didn't sabotage that engine. I know you, even though I don't, really. You're tricky, tricky like a fox. A sly and sneaky one. Give."

Doc Savage appeared reluctant to engage the subject, but finally he did.

"The port engine was already problematic. For what I may have to do, Monk and the others might prove to be a hindrance. You, on the other hand, are wise in the ways of women, having to deal with them professionally as you do."

Pat wrinkled up her pert nose. "Are you implying that Monk and Ham don't know women? Don't tell them that. They think they do."

"Not in any way that will be helpful," stated Doc. "We had a long conversation before you arrived at my office, and I realized how conflicted they are about my father's directive to me. I'm afraid they may sabotage this trip, even if unwittingly."

"So you decided to ditch them?"

"Delay them," corrected the bronze man. "They will have that faulty engine repaired in a few hours."

"Hmm," said Pat. "None of this is like you, except the tricky part. You're plenty tricky."

"You might," suggested Doc, "put on your parachute."

"And risk getting booted out the door? I'll take my chances."

"Suit yourself." Changing the subject, Doc asked, "I trust your six-shooter is filled with mercy bullets."

"It is. What kind of trouble are we barging into?"

"Perhaps no trouble. The last time we visited the Mayan valley, we encountered difficulties. We were seized upon our arrival. And subsequently learned that, unbeknownst to us, there were hidden powers above King Chaac. A group who lived apart from the main city, who called themselves the Clan of the Very Highest. In fact, they represented the ultimate authority. There were misunderstandings, but they were rectified." *

"So you're worried that this Clan of the Very Highest might be behind the turning off of the golden spigot?"

"I cannot discount the possibility. There seemed nothing in King Chaac's voice suggesting tension or subterfuge. But we will not fly into this situation blindly."

"Which situation—the exhausted gold or the pretty princess?"

"Both."

Pat favored the bronze giant with her golden regard. "I would say insofar as the latter situation goes, you're flying pretty blindly even with your eyes wide open."

"That," said Doc Savage evenly, "is why you are here."

"I," said Pat, "am starting to believe you."

Sincerity made Doc Savage's voice resonant as he said, "It is

---

* *They Died Twice*

important that you do. Vitally important. For I have realized that, as close as I am to my friends, this is a family matter. One that requires the kind of advice that only a blood relative can provide. You are the only family I have left, Pat."

Pat let out a long breath filled with unspoken emotion.

"Coming from you," she said breathily, "that's really something."

Doc nodded. "Something very important. The branch of the Savage line that you and I represent will go extinct unless measures are taken."

"Well, don't get to thinking that I'm ready to settle down. Not just yet. I've been a free bird a long time. My wings aren't tired yet. And I have yet to meet the male who can clip them."

"You cannot avoid facing this decision forever, Pat."

"Look who's talking! Mr. Fraidy-Cat around females."

"I wish I could say that that has changed. It has not. I am probably more terrified now than at any point in my life to date."

"You darn well should be," sniffed Pat. "You're talking about setting out to circumnavigate the globe without having done more than sail around a nice placid lake."

"That's why I've decided to rely on you as my navigator."

Pat Savage folded her sinewy arms. "I never thought I'd live to see this day. Finally, I'm going to visit this fabulous vale of plenty that has kept you in clover and chemicals all these years. That's something to look forward to."

Chapter IX

TURBULENCE

OVER THE SYNCHRONIZED drone of supercharged radial engines, Doc Savage warned, "Brace for a little wind."

In the co-pilot bucket, Pat Savage nodded. She had control of the aircraft. The bronze-haired girl was an expert pilot. She had flown her own sport plane for many years, winning a nice collection of racing cups before the war. The big four-motored job was a different matter, however. But she showed herself to be a capable and adaptive pilot. Doc Savage had taught her to fly.

They were over the section of Hidalgo that was heavily jungled. Below, the rain forest canopy was a shivering mass of lush greenery over which the shadows of scudding clouds passed like prowling phantoms.

Tropical birds darted about above the branches, tiny specks of riotous color like living sparks, momentarily troubled by their passing.

They had taken on fuel in Havana, and then again in Blanco Grande. Now they had settled in for the final leg of their thousand-mile hop.

Pat was wearing a cream-colored tropical shirt and tan slacks with boots suitable for jungle trekking, purchased at in one of Havana's ritziest women's shops. Her vitality appeared undiminished by the long flight.

Doc Savage had changed into a fresh jute shirt and whipcord

riding pants and boots in anticipation of their arrival in the Valley of the Vanished. Now he was back in his bucket seat.

"Better let me take the controls, Pat."

"I can handle turbulence."

The air had been bumpy for some time, but now the powerful aircraft was being sucked down by downdrafts that Pat fought stubbornly.

"It will be worse when we near the Valley," warned Doc.

An updraft shot the amphibian skyward and Pat was suddenly fighting to keep the ship level. Her face became bathed in perspiration and strain got into her manner.

Seizing the dual controls, Doc brought the aircraft into trim. He sat like a bronze statue, his mighty arms rigid against the growing turbulence.

Unexpectedly, they were in a mad hurricane of winds. Pat was almost tossed out of her seat. She grabbed at anything she could, held on tightly.

"What's happening?" she asked with a trace of panic sharpening her voice.

Doc Savage sounded unnaturally calm when he replied, "We are over the Hidalgoan mountain range."

Craning her head to look down, Pat spotted the mountain peaks. They were numerous. But that was not all. Great gorges and gashes tore the ground between them. Some of these cuts were exceedingly deep. Then Pat understood. The wind whipping through the mountains and charging down into the numerous rents in the earth created a kind of perpetual turbulence. One that made knowledgeable pilots avoid the area.

Looking about, Pat asked, "Which horrid gash is the Valley of the Vanished?"

"The one with the worst turbulence," said Doc.

"In that case," returned Pat, taking her hands off her wheel, "be my guest."

Even with Doc Savage's powerful hands on the controls, the

approach to the Valley of the Vanished was an ordeal. Despite her safety belt, Pat was tossed about. She turned a little green. But she gamely kept her lunch down.

Something like awe came into her golden eyes as she watched Doc Savage hold the wind-buffeted plane on course. She doubted there was another human being on earth who could do the same so effortlessly.

"What are the odds that we'll live?" she gulped at one point.

"This is the time of day where the winds are least fierce," replied Doc. "I've landed safely three times in the past, flying aircraft less advanced than this one."

"Just the same," gasped Pat, "my last will and testament is in the custody of Ham Brooks. Just in case."

Doc said nothing. His remarkable flake-gold eyes were searching the terrain ahead.

The Central American jungle may change with the seasons, but not greatly. The towering mountain ranges were eternal, however. Not even avalanches and rockslides greatly altered their forbidding heights. The thundering plane became a puny speck surrounded by their massive peaks.

Abruptly, the plane plunged into a nosedive, and Pat thought they were about to crash. She clung to the edges of her seat, endeavoring to stay in place. When she looked over, Doc Savage seemed unperturbed. Despite everything, he was fully in control of the aircraft.

"Are we landing?"

Doc nodded. "Unless we crash."

"That's still landing, isn't it?"

"Technically speaking, I suppose."

"Yet they still call a crash landing a landing, don't they?"

The plane was suddenly flying sideways and Pat held on wordlessly. Panic was on her face now, like smeared make-up. The bronze of her face took on a greenish patina.

Doc jockeyed the rolling plane level and suddenly steep rock was on either side of the sweeping wings. The sheer walls whipped past in a blur, mixed with a scattering of disturbed howler monkeys clinging to jungle vines.

Pat noticed the pyramid then. It dominated the clearing ahead. Perhaps a hundred feet high, it seemed to gleam like solid gold. There was a single staircase, and beside it a flow of water that ran down the steep front to feed a narrow lake.

It was toward this lake that Doc Savage pointed the nose of the amphibian craft.

The turbulence was abruptly gone. Doc smacked the plane down with one abrupt jar, following by sheeting water, after which it glided placidly toward the white sands of a modest beach. Wildly colored birds flushed from ground cover, a riot of hues on beating wings.

SHUTTING down the engines, Doc announced, "We have arrived."

Pat unbuckled her safety belt, and winced with all of her face. "Do you practice chiropractic manipulation?"

"Why do you ask?"

Pat felt of her back. "I think my entire skeleton has been knocked out of joint. I need an expert to put it back together."

A slight smile touched Doc's firm lips.

"You'll feel better once you stand on solid ground."

Doc Savage did not leave his seat immediately. His intent eyes were watching the approach to the lake. It was not long before a knot of people showed up.

Pat had out a pair of binoculars and studied them carefully.

The people pouring out of a nearby village were surprisingly light-skinned for Indians. Well formed, stocky, with a pronounced golden cast to their smooth skin and a slightly hooked Roman nose. Both men and women dressed elaborately. Some had short mantles over their shoulders, a network of leather, woven and gold-plated. Leggings, wrist and ankle guards were of woven silver. Many wore hide sandals, the backs of which came high up on their calves.

The women of the tribe were dressed more modestly than the men, and their skirts practically touched their feet. Others wore short aprons from waist to knees and something resembling turbans. Sea shells and jade seemed to be a favorite ornament with everyone, and there were so many feathers stuck in their glossy black hair that the women appeared almost avian in their finery.

Pat let out a surprised gasp. "Why, these people look as if they were poured from molten gold."

Doc nodded. "When this valley was first inhabited, the settlers were members of the highest Mayan clan of their era. They have been cut off from the civilized world for hundreds of years. There has been no intermarrying with the outside populace."

Studying the approaching group anew, Pat noticed that the Mayans were not by any means svelte, but rather short, and on the thick side. "They remind me of Polynesians or Hawaiians," she remarked. "Not Indians."

"Do not be fooled," advised Doc. "They may look soft of physique, but those men are strong and powerful warriors."

"If I could get some of these Mayan women into my gymnasium," mused Pat, "I could do a lot with them. Especially if they paid in gold."

Doc continued scrutinizing the feathery welcoming committee without stirring to meet them.

Pat wondered, "What are we waiting for—the band to strike up a tune?"

"I want to be sure none of them are wearing blue war paint on their bodies," advised Doc.

"What's wrong with blue?"

"It signifies that they intend to make a sacrifice to the gods. But I don't see any blue-dyed warriors, so it should be safe to deplane."

"You first, great bronze hunter," invited Pat. She pulled her six-shooter out of her rather large purse, but Doc interrupted the gesture with a staying hand. "Better keep that hidden for now."

Reluctantly, Pat did so. She stowed it in her purse, but held onto the oversized convenience.

"If they start throwing spears," she sniffed, "I will count on you to throw yourself in front of me, since you're the one who wears a chain-mail hauberk instead of an undershirt. Er—you are wearing your knightly nightshirt, aren't you?"

"Always."

Doc Savage went first. He opened up the plane and stepped out, Pat following.

The reception committee was a serious-faced lot. That by itself was not significant. The Mayans, especially the menfolk, were not given much to smiling gratuitously.

Studying the faces of the assemblage, Doc Savage was able to read beyond their fixed expressions. There was no malice, nor any animosity written there. Their dark eyes shone. A warm and welcoming light danced in every pair of orbs.

Recognizing this, Doc said to Pat, "There will be no trouble."

"I'd feel better if I had my trusty Colt in hand."

Advancing, Doc Savage approached the welcoming party, raising one bronze hand. Other hands were raised in a return salute.

They were empty of weapons.

Doc Savage addressed them. "Greetings, I see Kax and Chen, whom I know well. But I do not see King Chaac, your ruler."

"He is coming," said one man. "He does not move so quickly these days."

Doc and Pat were surrounded, and glad hands clapped them on the back and shoulders in hearty welcome.

Pat murmured, "Rather familiar, don't you think?"

"It is their way," Doc advised. "Try not to offend them."

"If this happened back in New York, I would be slapping male faces right about now."

A minute later, King Chaac appeared. He was attired in a complicated robe, purple about the neck and arms. His bobbing headdress was like a peacock's tail, but the long feathers belonged to various local birds, chiefly the quetzal and macaw. The regal old man was more stooped than Doc Savage remembered, and he walked with the aid of a hardwood cane cut from some tropical tree.

Arthritis was not much of a malady in the tropics, so Doc knew that his difficult and halting gait and stooped posture were products of advancing age. As the old ruler drew near, the bronze man was struck by how feeble he appeared. On either side of his hooked beak of a nose, his dark eyes were a little sunken. Age had done that.

Striding up to him, Doc Savage said, "It is good to lay eyes upon you once more, King Chaac."

Still-strong hands reached up and took Doc by the shoulders and the bronze giant reciprocated the welcoming gesture. Mustering up his dignity, the aged sovereign stated, "And it warms my heart to once more behold the son of my great friend, your father. May he take pride in the knowledge that his son has achieved earthly greatness."

"Are you well?" wondered Doc.

"I am old," said Chaac. "I will never be as hale as I was in my younger days." Then his eyes went to Pat Savage curiously.

Doc said, "May I introduce my cousin, Patricia. Her father was my father's brother."

"You are welcome here, Patricia Savage."

"You speak excellent English," commented Pat.

"My friend Clark Savage, Senior, taught me well. I, in turn, have taught many of my people the English language. We also know some Spanish, as well as our own tongue."

Doc Savage's flake-gold eyes searched the retinue of King Chaac.

"I do not see your daughter, the princess Monja."

"She could not come at this time."

A flicker of something queer touched Doc Savage's ordinarily impassive face.

"She is well?" he inquired.

"She, too, has grown older, but not in the way I have grown older." Chaac hesitated ever so slightly. "She is with the man who wishes to marry her."

Now Doc Savage's countenance truly twisted. His trilling seeped out, but he suppressed it instantly. His metallic hands became bronze blocks at his side, and Pat Savage thought that his great forearms trembled slightly. But perhaps that was just her perception.

"She is betrothed?" asked Doc when he got full control over himself.

"Not formally," allowed Chaac. "But the hour draws near when she must make her decision. She should have long ago, but something held her back. I do not quite understand what."

King Chaac's kindly eyes held a flicker of something that communicated to Doc Savage that he was feigning polite ignorance.

"I was hoping to spend some time with her during my sojourn here," said Doc frankly.

Chaac nodded. "My daughter will be interested to hear those words. Even if they come years too late. But I thought you have journeyed all this way to see to our welfare, and to behold with your own eyes the sad state of our treasure vault."

"All of these things are on my mind," admitted Doc Savage.

"Then let us show you the gold vaults so that you may see the truth with your own eyes. My daughter can wait." Then the king added more softly, "She has been waiting a long time. A few more hours will not matter."

So saying, Chaac turned. His retinue swung about with him and they commenced the trek toward the great pyramid dominating the center of the valley that was shaped like an immense egg whose sheer sides blocked all horizons.

As they walked along, Pat Savage drew near Doc Savage and

whispered, "It could be worse, you know. Monja could have been married already, and surrounded by little barefoot brats."

Doc Savage said nothing. The bronze of his face seemed just a shade lighter than normal. His eyes were strange. The gold flakes in them were hardly moving. Pat decided that this meant that the metallic giant had experienced an emotional shock.

"Buck up, Ivanhoe," said Pat. "All is not lost. Not while Lady Patricia is your second...."

Chapter X

VOID

THE COLORFUL RETINUE marched through the blistering sunlight toward the imposing pyramid that shone with its own golden light.

Pat studied this as they approached.

"Is that rock pile made of solid gold?" she asked Doc in a hushed tone.

The bronze man had been studying King Chaac as he walked along. "No. It's formed from dressed quartz blocks that contain considerable wire gold. The pyramid is not part of the treasure. It is sacred to these people. Therefore, the gold wire will never be extracted, having less material value than the spiritual meaning of the structure itself."

Pat frowned. She had expected to see pyramids like those in the ruined Mayan cities scattered throughout Central America, such as Chichen Itza and the recently discovered ruin of Bonampak. Absent were the stepped sides that made the other pyramids resemble square wedding cakes with each successive layer being smaller than the one below. This was more like an Egyptian pyramid, except that a long line of stone steps climbed its face. Alongside the steep staircase flowed a gentle cascade of water that was undoubtedly artificial.

Shading her golden eyes with a bronze hand, Pat saw that the top of the pyramid was flat and supported an open stone temple which housed a bulky shape she could not make out amid the shadows of the square roof.

When they came to the staircase, the royal guard got down on their knees and they began ascending, remaining on their knees with every step.

"We will be expected to do the same," explained Doc.

Pat frowned. "Thank goodness for these slacks. But what about King Chaac? He can barely walk, much less climb up on his knees."

Doc Savage turned to King Chaac and asked, "Is it permitted that I assist you in the climb?"

Old Chaac hesitated. His expression quivered slightly. He was a proud sovereign, but now the mounting years had made his limbs gaunt and stringy, rendering his former strength frail.

"I am able to mount the steps," he said firmly.

Then he got down on his knees and showed his inner strength. He used his cane differently now, holding it in the middle instead of at one end for balance, but he began his ascent without hesitation or complaint.

Doc and Pat knelt behind the man and followed suit. It was no pleasant experience. The knees were not made to bear a grown person's weight in such a manner, and a hundred feet makes for a lot of steps, but they managed to reach the top, Pat only whispering, "Remember what I said about needing chiropracty, or whatever it's called."

Doc Savage remained solemnly silent.

Reaching the top, all involved stood up with uncomplaining stoicism. There was no mistaking their pain. Faces were sheathed in sweat.

The group assembled in solemn silence. Before them stood a temple with a stone roof and pillars at every corner, but no walls or door. The pillars were carved out of hardwood, and each depicted a fantastic figure facing outward to the four points, each garbed in ornate armor, heads adorned with astoundingly complex feather headdresses, yet no two alike.

"What are those?" Pat whispered to Doc.

"The Bacabs," replied the bronze man. "They represent the

four primordial brothers who hold up the sky so that it does not fall."

"Four Mayan Atlases, huh?"

"Exactly. Strangely enough, this style of anthropomorphic pillar is called by archaeologists Atlantean, after Atlas. The Bacabs are the Mayan equivalents to the Four Sons of Horus in Egyptian myth, the Four Dwarves of Norse legends and the Four Heavenly Kings of the Buddhist religion, each of whom represents the four winds, as well as the cardinal points of the compass."

"Have you been eating the same breakfast cereal as Johnny?" hissed Pat. "Because you sound more like him than you do your own self."

Inside the open enclosure was a convoluted image carved from a black material that was neither dull basalt nor glassy obsidian.

The effigy was a grotesque amalgam of a boa constrictor and some species of avian. It stood perhaps fifteen feet high and was half again around. The thing was coiled like a rattlesnake, but each thick loop was piled upon the one beneath it, so that the winding figure formed a fat cone that dwindled toward the head. Instead of scales, overlapping plumes ran in orderly rows along the muscular loops of the snaky body. The uppermost portion reared up. Around its serpentine throat was a crest of stony feathers, spraying outward in a manner reminiscent of a cobra with an inflated hood.

The jaws of the monstrous image were distended. Instead of revealing a cavernous mouth, a human face was framed by fanged teeth. The face had an unearthly cast. It was as if the giant serpent were about to vomit forth a human being. Or perhaps had swallowed one, and its jaws were on the verge of closing shut, sealing him in.

This grotesque statue was the loftiest totem of the Maya.

The stone from which this had been fashioned in ancient times long before Christopher Columbus was dark, but flecked with green. Doc Savage had seen the statue before. But the nature of the stone puzzled him. He was geologist enough to recognize virtually any rock or stone set before him. This was like nothing he had ever seen, but the Mayans possessed no knowledge or records of where the stone had originated. Doc wondered if it might not have been shaped from a fallen meteorite. The scientist in him would have greatly enjoyed conveying the carven mass to his laboratory for rigorous analysis, but the idol was sacred to the Maya. They would never permit it to leave the Valley. So Doc had abandoned all hope of studying it scientifically.

Yet each time he beheld it anew, his flake-gold eyes whirled with interest.

"Kukulcan," said King Chaac in a low voice.

"He is their great culture hero," Doc told Pat. "The Aztecs called him Quetzalcoatl. The name means 'Feathered Serpent.' It is recorded that Kukulcan was a redheaded white man who came from across the sea and brought civilization to the Indians of Central America. No one knows who he really was. But fabulous legends surround him. When I first visited, these people honored me by making me an ordained son of Kukulcan."

Pat Savage was impressed. But not in a positive way. The image of Kukulcan was a hideous, barbaric grotesquery, but she had the good sense not to voice her honest opinion.

SEVERAL burly Mayan men took hold of the stone temple by its pillars and pushed hard, grunting with the effort. The structure rolled aside with an agonizing grinding noise, exposing a rectangular hole, and revealing another flight of stone steps.

These, they were allowed to walk down in the normal fashion. The steps were ancient. Generations of bare feet and soft sandals had worn them until the stone showed depressions at each step. The deeper they descended, the darker it got.

The Mayans had brought their own light. Ceramic bowls

with floating wicks were lit. Also strange lanterns containing huge tropical lightning bugs, which glowed a pale electric blue.

Doc Savage took out one of his special flashlights that ran off a spring-generator that could be recharged by winding. This provided the most powerful illumination. He sprayed the beam around liberally so that they might descend safely.

At the bottom was a tunnel. Along the tunnel ran a stone viaduct that carried the water artesian-style to the top of the temple pyramid to flow down to the central lake. The air smelled strange—musty and old. The walls were chipped and cut and showed signs of veins of gold that had been mined in the past.

Doc recalled that these veins were intact during his last visit. That meant that the Mayans had dug in and cut out the yellow trace ore that previously had not been considered worth mining.

King Chaac led the way to the great underground treasure store house, and once Doc Savage entered, he directed his flash beam around, searching stone shelves and detritus that remained on the ground. Roosting bats squeaked, and a few flapped off, seeking to flee the darting illumination.

The emptiness of the stone vault astounded him. This had once been the greatest mine of the ancient people of Maya, before their extensive civilization had collapsed. When the bronze man had first laid eyes upon it, the space had been heaped with gold vessels, plate, statues and crude ingots. All gone now. Not a trace remained.

Doc Savage said frankly, "I have no words."

"No words are necessary, esteemed son of my old friend," Chaac said warmly. "The gold was for your use, and you have used it well. Let there be no regrets on your part, for there are no recriminations on ours. Great works have been accomplished. I only regret that we have no more yellow gold to supply you. For your work on behalf of mankind must go on."

"Thank you," said Doc sincerely.

There came a long silence and King Chaac's obsidian eyes appraised Doc Savage, measuring him, noting the changes that had been wrought by the passing years. Obviously, this caused him to consider the future in a new way.

"Why have you not sired a son?"

The question startled Doc. Not only due to its personal nature, but because it cut to the heart of his present troubles.

"Why do you ask?"

"It was your father's desire that you carry on his work, and that his grandchildren would do the same. Alas, that he did not live to see any of what he inspired. But since there are none, it may not matter."

Doc shook off the mild shock the question had occasioned.

"It was my father's wish that I bring a son into the world and do exactly that," he allowed.

"Then why have you not?"

Doc hesitated. His thoughts were tumbling.

"Perhaps I waited too long," he said at last. His voice had a low, almost wistful quality, entirely unlike its usual resonance.

Pat Savage absorbed this exchange and saw the look that passed between aging King Chaac and Doc Savage. She was not a mind reader, but she did not need to be. Unspoken between the two men was the question of Princess Monja.

Clearing her throat, Pat spoke up.

"Since we've cleared the air on the missing gold, I would like to meet your daughter, the princess. I'm sure my cousin would also like to renew his acquaintance with her."

A stark look came into Doc Savage's eyes. He said nothing.

"Wouldn't you, cousin?" pressed Pat.

"I suppose it is time that we did so," said Doc in a voice much less confident than his usual confident tone.

Hearing this, Pat Savage stared gilt daggers at her cousin. She looked as if she wanted to upbraid him like an unruly child. But she mastered the impulse and instead smiled sweetly—too sweetly. Her teeth might have been coated in treacle.

"We've had an exhausting flight," she explained to King Chaac.

"I'm sure Doc will start feeling like his usual sunny self before very long. Shall we seek fresh air? It's rather stuffy down here—and I do not confine my remarks to the stale atmosphere."

Pat Savage was staring rather pointedly at her cousin when she made that observation.

Chapter XI

HUN BALAAM

TO THE SURPRISE of Doc Savage and Patricia Savage, King Chaac guided them to a far portion of the rock vault near the aqueduct carrying water to the top of the fabulous golden pyramid.

A rock wall stood there. There was a glyph cut into the raw stone. King Chaac took an ornament from his girdle and inserted it into what appeared to be a slash of a fissure in the rocky face. There came a click as of some simple mechanism unlocking, then at the old ruler's hand signal, two burly Mayans stepped in and put their shoulders against what proved to be a cleverly dressed stone panel.

It went inward with a grinding sound. The thing was not hung on hinges, but was simply a thick block of dressed stone that could be shoved inward. This disclosed an opening through which it was possible for persons to pass, provided they went one at a time.

"Permit me," said Doc. "I will lead the way. My light is stronger."

The snowy-haired sovereign inclined his head in silent assent.

Turning on his flashlight, Doc squeezed through. And beheld an ancient tunnel carved out of the living rock. There appeared to be no danger ahead, so he kept going, confident that the others would follow close behind.

It was soon evident that they did. Doc swung his flashlight about, making sure Pat was part of the retinue. When everyone had entered the tunnel, the two stocky Mayans pushed the stone panel back into place.

King Chaac said with a trace of regal humor, "It is not necessary to wear out one's legs at my age."

Pat hurried up and declared, "My poor knees are grateful, if anybody is wondering."

Doc understood that since they were not descending the sacred pyramid, passing by the idol, the usual solemnities did not need to be observed. It was a relief. Even his iron knees ached from the climb.

The valley floor above had a pronounced slope, which was mirrored in this tunnel. The direction of the slope indicated that they were passing near the narrow lake.

The sloping floor explained why modern aircraft had not intruded. Unless it were a seaplane, no aircraft could safely land. This was a natural feature of the valley, but it served to safeguard the Mayan enclave in these days where exploring pilots could easily stumble upon it.

The tunnel terminated in what appeared to be a stele—a carven pillar, fabulously ornate in its decorative furbishments. This was as large as a truck standing on end. It did not seem to ever have been moved.

A fearsome figure was cut into the stone stele. Doc recognized him as Yum Cimil, the Lord of Death, who ruled the Mayan underworld, Xibalba. He was skeletal in his appearance, with hollow eyes and a necklace of eyeless sockets. Any Mayan Indian coming upon this monstrous depiction would naturally retreat from it in superstitious fear.

Seeing this stone specter looming in the flashlight glow, Pat shuddered and said, "Brrr! Is this a tomb?"

To their astonishment, King Chaac walked up to it and, using only a single weathered digit, pushed at one side of the figure. It pivoted as if weightless. When it had made a quarter turn, the stele showed that its far surface had been dressed to depict

Kukulcan in his human form, resplendent in a plumed headdress cut into the stone.

Turning, the Mayan ruler smiled thinly. "Our engineers may not be up to the standards of yours, but they are nevertheless clever in their own right."

Doc smiled back. "This turns on a balanced pivot, doesn't it?"

Chaac nodded proudly. "A pivot of jadeite."

Doc recalled that the mineral was one of the hardest substances known to the Mayans historically. Not being metal, it would never corrode.

King Chaac led the way forward, this time up rough-hewn stairs that came out in a clump of ferns and foliage that sheltered them from view. Behind, they could hear the pillar rolling back into place with a teeth-jarring grinding, like bones being pulverized into grit.

"Daylight!" Pat exclaimed, putting her tawny head up and taking a deep breath. "Thank goodness. I felt as if creepy-crawlies were eyeing me every step of the way."

Doc ascertained that they were not far from their beached aircraft. Hovering near the plane, her back to him, stood Princess Monja, her black tresses flowing in a cascade of hair.

SOMETHING seemed to kick out his heart and make his stomach drop to the ground. Monja had had that effect on him before, but the bronze man had mastered it.

Now, under different circumstances, he felt the urgent emotion of seeing her again.

Doc hesitated, momentarily paralyzed by indecision. King Chaac lifted his voice and proclaimed, "My daughter! Come! Come here and greet our old friend from days gone by."

The princess had been conversing with a burly man wearing only a broadcloth and sandals whose coarse black hair looked as if he had placed a gourd onto his head and cut away the excess with a sharp knife. Scarlet woodpecker feathers stuck out at his crown. Both turned. The broad features of the man seemed to gather into a scowl while Princess Monja's exquisite face showed waves of emotions that were difficult to decipher.

Her dark liquid eyes widened, and a smile made her lips resemble an exotic flower. But something troubled her comely features as well.

She started forward. Her companion reached out to take her by the hand. Then they came forward, all but arm in arm.

Beside him, Pat Savage gave her cousin a shot in the ribs with a sharp elbow and hissed, "If you remember how to smile, this would be the perfect time to hang a happy one on your kisser."

Doc shook off his shock and his face relaxed. His smile was slow in coming but it was genuine when it arrived.

When they were face-to-face, Princess Monja bowed her head without speaking.

Doc told her, "I am gratified to see you again."

"And I, you," she said softly. Her voice was like her face. Demure.

Doc Savage found himself groping for words. His thoughts bogged down, unable to rise to speech.

Old King Chaac inserted, "Permit me to introduce you to Hun Balaam, one of my bravest warriors."

Eyes flinty, Hun Balaam grunted out a greeting in Mayan. Doc replied in the same tongue. The two men stared at one another, like unfamiliar stallions meeting by chance. It was obvious that they did not know what to make of one another.

Princess Monja volunteered, "Hun Balaam has asked for my hand in marriage."

Doc Savage covered his surprise nicely. "Congratulations then. I'm sure that you will both be very happy."

A flash of anger showed deep in the golden woman's obsidian eyes. A shadow crossed her face that was not created by a passing cloud.

Hun Balaam did not notice this. He was absorbed in Doc Savage, sizing him up with sullen eyes. At Doc's words, he seemed to relax physically.

Pat Savage slipped behind Doc. "You darn fool! Can't you see that she wants you to rescue her from him?"

Doc Savage had sensed this, but the situation was unbelievably awkward. He struggled inwardly.

With a stiffness in her voice, the Mayan princess added, "I have not yet made my decision. But I must do so soon. I am not a girl anymore. I have not been a girl in many *tun*. Today I am still a princess, but one day I will be queen." Her dark eyes veered self-consciously toward her father and looked away again. "I do not look forward to that day, of course, but when it comes I will need a strong man to rule beside me."

King Chaac watched the bronze man and his aged face appeared conflicted. It was evident that the bronze man's words baffled him.

Doc Savage simply stood there, as tongue-tied as he ever had been in his life.

"Don't just stand there with your face drooping like a palm frond," whispered Pat in perfect French. "Do something!"

Doc mouthed, "But what?"

"Pick a fight with him, you dolt. Make a pass at her. Do something. Anything. This may be your last chance."

Doc Savage struggled with his inner turmoil. His flake-gold eyes flicked from the face of Princess Monja to the man, Hun Balaam. Finally, he said, "Permit me to introduce my cousin, Patricia Savage."

Pat stepped forward and turned on the charm. She offered her hand to the princess, who took it. Executing a polite curtsy, Pat said, "I've heard so much about you. Doc talks about you all the time."

The princess' gold-dusted features brightened.

"Oh?"

"Indeed. Why, many is the time when he's remarked that you are the most beautiful woman he's ever laid eyes on. And believe me, he's encountered beautiful women by the score. And you're not the only princess, either. Just the most entrancing one."

Smiling sweetly, Pat turned to the big bronze man and said, "Isn't that right, cousin?"

Before Doc could formulate an articulate response, Hun Balaam stepped forward and demanded, "Have you come all this way to claim the woman I intend to marry, eagle-eyed one?"

This was a blunt question and by nature Doc Savage was a direct individual. He answered it honestly, without equivocation.

"I came for many reasons, Hun Balaam. The Princess Monja is high among them."

To Monja, he said, "I received your poem. It was very touching, but also quite sad. I believe I comprehend its meaning."

Her lips trembling, the princess said softly, "I could not wait for you forever."

"I did not mean for you to. The life I have chosen, rather the life my father chose for me, created many obstacles. But now he wishes that I wed."

With trembling voice, she asked, "Are you here to ask to be my husband?"

Doc hesitated. "I do not know. Yet."

This was too much for Hun Balaam. He stepped forward belligerently, growling and scowling, his strong jaw outthrust, clipping off his words with his strong white teeth. "If you desire to fight me for the princess' hand, I stand ready to accept that challenge."

"Should that not be her decision?" inquired Doc calmly.

Pat was suddenly behind him, whispering again. "If you want to wed a princess, you sometimes have to smash any toads and frogs crowding around her. It's old-fashioned, I know. Even a bit ridiculous. But that's how it's been done since the days of the cavemen."

Firming his jaw, Doc Savage said, "I accept your challenge."

At those simple words, Princess Monja and her father grinned broadly. Hun Balaam scowled anew. But no fear roosted on his broad features.

Lifting his arms, King Chaac proclaimed, "We must repair to the ball court to settle this matter once and for all."

He turned and led the group away, the sumptuous feathers of his high headdress dipping and bouncing with each step.

Princess Monja detached herself from her would-be suitor and joined her father. She walked on the side of the proud sovereign closest to Doc Savage. But she clung to her father.

Grumbling wordlessly, Hun Balaam followed at the rear.

Walking just behind the bronze man, Pat Savage undertoned, "This is going to be nice if it works."

"I do not yet know if I want to marry her," whispered Doc.

"It might be too late to back out now," cautioned Pat. "Stow your natural male hesitancy for the nonce. You have a dragon to slay, Sir Clark."

The speed with which matters were moving caused Doc Savage to muster up his buried sense of humor.

"Zounds!"

Chapter XII

CONTEST

THE BALL COURT was one that was common among the Mayans and Aztecs in the days before the Conquistadors.

It consisted of a narrow stone-flagged courtyard, at either side of which stood sloping walls topped by a stone ring set high up and hung at a ninety-degree angle from the playing field. The game was one played throughout Central America in the Precolumbian era. To the Aztecs, it was known as *tlaxtli*. The Maya called the game *pokolpok*.

The purpose of the bruising game was similar to that of basketball. The players would roughhouse in the center trying to get control of a ball made of hard rubber, and weighing about eight pounds. Unlike modern-day soccer or basketball, it was forbidden to use hands or feet. However, padded hips, shoulders and elbows were allowed. Knocking the ball through a hole in one of the stone rings was the object of the game. That goal was made devilishly difficult by the stonecutter, who deliberately fashioned the aperture to be only inches wider than the weighty five-inch diameter ball which, in addition to its right-angle placement, made scoring a goal a rare event.

Centuries in the past, it was believed that the losing team was sacrificed to the gods. Doc was not quite sure if that was the case, and he doubted it was true among this peaceful-dwelling Mayan colony. But he also knew that *pokolpok* was a team sport, so he was a little nonplussed when King Chaac

480

brought him face to face with Hun Balaam in the center of the ball court.

A runner brought up two pairs of impressively large conch shells. When Doc saw them, he understood the nature of the contest. It was to be a kind of boxing match. But instead of boxing gloves, hard spiral shells were to be used. With their ridged protuberances and horny spire tips, they resembled fist maces.

Princess Monja was given the honor of tying them into place. She tied Hun Balaam's shells over his hands with tapir-hide thongs. Then she did the same for Doc Savage. Her face was impassive. She had control of her emotions now, and was trying not to show favoritism. The matter would be settled between the two men.

She withdrew. Doc and Hun Balaam squared off.

The bronze giant naturally towered over the short stocky Mayan man, whose name in English was "One Jaguar."

While they were squaring off, someone blew a conch shell horn. Its long, low note brought other Mayans from the buildings that comprised the city squatting in the shadow of the sacred pyramid. Soon there was a sizable crowd, perhaps three hundred people, standing at either end of the court.

Old King Chaac lifted his hands over his head and clapped them twice. That was the signal to commence.

Hun Balaam wasted no time. He shot his right fist toward Doc Savage's chin. Doc wavered on his feet, and the spiral conch point missed.

Doc drove his right-hand shell into the man's paunch. Hun Balaam let out the contents of his lungs, not to mention any air that was in his stomach, and flew backward.

Doc had pulled his punch, but not by much. He did not want to injure the man, but simply knock him off his feet. A flicker of surprise touched his metallic countenance when he saw Hun Balaam stumble backward on his sandals and yet keep his feet.

They went at each other again. Doc Savage had been trained

in boxing during his rigorous upbringing, and he had forgotten nothing of the art of fisticuffs. But during a lifetime of adventuring he painstakingly avoided using his fists as much as possible. He had a secret horror of injuring his hands. This because he frequently conducted delicate surgery and finger dexterity was essential to his medical practice.

This concern put him at a slight disadvantage. The fact that the conch shells protected his fists did not overcome his natural caution. Should either one shatter, the resulting lacerations would be something fierce.

On the other hand, Hun Balaam suffered from no such inhibitions. The way he danced around on his feet, keeping his shell-encased fists raised, showed that he had been fighting in this manner since childhood. And was good at it.

Hun Balaam showed this when he feinted with his right, and tore up Doc Savage's forearm with a sudden left hook.

Blood flowed. Doc was taken aback. A boxing glove would hardly have bruised him. But the horny ridges of the spiral shell were another matter.

STEPPING back, the bronze man realized that he was troubled by a psychological disadvantage as well.

Hun Balaam was motivated. His emotions were written large on his face, in the way his breath came whistling out his bull-like nostrils. He saw Doc Savage as a mortal enemy. Perhaps not someone he wanted to kill, but someone he desired to soundly defeat.

Doc Savage, on the other hand, had been goaded into this fight and was not yet certain that he truly desired the princess' hand in marriage. That was something Pat had clearly engineered. Mentally, he berated his cousin.

On the sidelines, Pat was doing an excellent impersonation of a Bronx fight fan, yelling, "Sock him in the chops! Smash him in the ribs. Don't just stand there! Demolish him!"

Frowning, Doc Savage realized he didn't want to demolish anyone.

That's when Hun Balaam jabbed him in the jaw.

Caught off guard, the bronze man reeled backward, stumbled, almost lost his footing, but recovered. Then he did something that showed that he was upset.

Stepping back, the steeply-slanted stone wall behind him, he slammed the conch shell on his right hand against the masonry blocks. It split, but did not crack. He stripped off the lacings, shook his fist free, and started forward. His golden eyes were twin fires.

Hun Balaam never knew what hit him. The bronze man's bare fist floated out like a metallic thunderbolt and connected with the square jaw at its exact point. There was science behind the blow. Doc knew exactly where to hit.

Hun Balaam was driven back, his eyes going unfocused. Miraculously, he kept his feet, but all the fight was knocked out of him.

Seeing this, Pat Savage yelled, "He's out on his feet! Finish the job, Doc!"

"No need," said Doc, unlacing the other conch shell casually.

As if the bronze man's confident words held power, Hun Balaam crossed his knees and collapsed where he stood. Air blew out of his open mouth raggedly. His eyes rolled up in his head, showing bloodshot whites.

Princess Monja came alive then.

"Doc Savage, you have won. You are once again a hero to all of my people. And most of all, to me," she added softly, lowering her lashes modestly.

Doc stood there, his normal self-control reasserting itself.

Then it sank in.

"What have I done?" he asked Pat Savage.

"Oh, I don't know," said Pat jauntily. "Looks to me like you won the fair maiden. Congratulations. I must say I had tall doubts. I wasn't sure you had it in you."

"This is your doing," Doc said. And the tone of his voice was neither a compliment, nor an accusation. It was flat, as flat as his facial expression was blank.

When he looked to King Chaac and Princess Monja, their faces were aglow. The bronze giant's stomach felt like an elevator car racing to a bottom with no end in sight. The sinking feeling went on and on….

Chapter XIII

STRUGGLE

THAT EVENING, PRINCESS MONJA and Doc Savage took a moonlit walk by the narrow lake that lay like a silvery mirror in the heart of the Valley of the Vanished where winking blue pinpoints signified lantern bugs at play.

They were not alone. Pat Savage had appointed herself chaperone, a word she had to explain several times to old King Chaac.

"I'm calling myself a chaperone," she confided to him, "but between you and me, my real job is matchmaker."

The white-haired ruler knew what a match was. But here was another term where his command of English proved deficient.

"I'm going to steer Doc in the direction of matrimony, assuming he's cooperative," she clarified.

"Do you think Doc Savage is reluctant where my daughter is concerned?"

"As reluctant as a tabbycat stuck on a rickety barrel about to go over Niagara Falls. But don't worry. If he can't take the leap for himself, I'll push him. Hard."

It was one of those extraordinary tropical evenings when the air was warm and inviting, a soft breeze stirring the natural perfumes of the countless wildflowers growing in profusion.

The sky overhead was a starfield packed with what resembled diamond dust. Owing to the sheer sides of the valley, the moon was tardy in appearing. When it crossed the open sky above the great crevice, a shooting star appeared. It made a thin green streak in the sky.

485

"Behold!" exclaimed the princess. "It is a feather of Quetzalcoatl. He sheds his plumes the way serpents shed their skin. It is always a beneficent omen."

Doc Savage watched the streak fade. He remarked, "That is a meteor. Its green glow means nickel is present. A yellow meteor signifies that the falling rock consists largely of iron. Calcium yields a violet glow, while meteors containing significant sodium glow orange."

Listening to the scientific analysis in the middle of an obviously romantic moment, Pat Savage wanted to tear her hair out. She swallowed the impulse. She also resisted an even greater urge to go up to Doc Savage and give him a good swift kick somewhere memorable.

Instead, she switched to Pig Latin, which the princess would be unlikely to understand, given that her English was so formal.

"Iss-kay the ench-way, you big ummy-day."

Doc had to roll the words around in his mind until he realized he was being encouraged to kiss Princess Monja.

It was a nervous moment. More nervous than he thought it could be. The bronze giant had kissed women before, but it never had much significance. Nor did it seem to be so important that he do it correctly, as now. He felt a kiss would be premature. His own feelings were in chaos, lurching from an unfamiliar exhilaration to cold apprehension.

"What are your feelings toward Hun Balaam?" Doc asked quietly.

The princess shrugged exposed shoulders that gleamed duskily in the moonlight.

"If there were no other," she murmured, "he would have to do, I suppose. Among my people, he is highly regarded. I can find no fault with him. I could love him, or learn to love him in time, were Hun Balaam to become my husband."

Doc Savage absorbed this in thoughtful silence.

"So you do not love him?"

"No, but he loves me. In my innermost being, I cannot deny such strong feelings toward me. But my heart is torn."

"It distresses me to hear this," said Doc.

Pat whispered, "Onja-may is aiting-way. Ucker-pay up-yay."

The last really threw Doc until he grasped that Pat was encouraging him to pucker up. So he did. He wasn't sure if he meant to. It just happened.

Taking the princess in his strong arms, he began awkwardly, but it soon felt as natural as sunbathing. But infinitely warmer. He lifted her chin, applied his lips, and any hesitation or uncertainty evaporated once they melted into a passionate embrace.

"Ray-hoo! I mean, hooray!" cheered Pat.

The two strolled along in the moonlight, not saying anything for the longest time. But their eyes met often. They offered one another no words. No words were necessary. No words seemed large enough, or significant enough to express what was swelling in their hearts.

Pat Savage decided to fade into the background.

"I may have found my calling," she grinned. "If I can get Doc Savage hitched, I can move mountains. Mountains would be easier to move, actually."

Pat went strolling by the edge of the narrow lake, watching the pale blue phosphorescent fireflies dart and flash over its placid surface and so failed to take full notice of her surroundings.

FROM out of a cluster of lakeside cattails something slipped silently. Even in the brilliant moonlight, the shadows were etched deep, and the crawling thing was stealthy and cunning as it insinuated itself toward the preoccupied girl.

Before she knew it, something had looped around Pat's legs, and that something showed its muscular might when it brought her down with a sudden wrestling maneuver that took her by surprise.

For a moment, Pat thought she had tripped over a branch,

but something heavy was slowly dragging her into the water. Heavy, and *alive*. In her stunned brain she wondered if octopuses lived in lakes. Then she saw the triangular head, decorated with beady amber eyes. A slick black tongue slipped out, showing a devilish fork, then retreated.

She let out a scream. The scream included a word. Pat kept repeating it.

"Snake! Snake-snake-*snake*."

Pat felt helpless as she was dragged into the water. Suddenly, her mouth was bubbling wordlessly. She fumbled for the oversized purse she had prudently brought along. Groping fingers found her Frontier revolver, yanked it free.

Finding the hammer with one thumb—the weapon was triggerless—Pat cocked it and attempted to direct the long steel muzzle toward the coils enwrapping her calves. The hammer dropped. The six-shooter failed to discharge. By this time, the weapon was immersed.

Immersed in the beauty that was Princess Monja, Doc Savage noticed none of this until Pat's repeated screams reached his ears.

He turned, flake-gold eyes scanning the surroundings. Almost at the last second, he saw Pat's moon-burnished bronze hair vanish into the water, and on the turbulent surface spied a cream-colored muscular loop he recognized by its reddish-brown markings.

"Boa!" he said sharply.

"*Chij-chan!*" hissed the princess.

Then Doc Savage was moving. He pelted toward the water, plunged in.

The boa constrictor was a long monster of a serpent, easily nine feet in length. It possessed plenty of coils to enwrap Pat Savage. The writhing reptile was intent upon dragging her to the bottom, with the cold-blooded objective of drowning her. The golden-eyed girl was frantically beating its scaly sides with her heavy revolver, but accomplishing very little in the way of positive results.

Metallic hands clamped around the snake's sinuous tail, and the bronze giant was suddenly in battle.

The silent reptile possessed sufficient scaly length to wrap around both of them, and the constrictor did exactly that. The thing was powerful. Doc battled to keep it from wrapping around his waist, and only succeeded in pushing it off so that it snapped a leg instead. The constricting power of the closing loop was bruising, cutting off blood flow.

All three combatants—man, girl and serpent—thrashed about the water, battling for their lives.

On the little white beach, Princess Monja was calling for help, voicing her wretched helplessness. A great fear was in her eyes and this rising emotion was turning into anguish.

Doc Savage fought strenuously. Through the moonlit water he could see Pat Savage succumbing to the powerful serpentine muscles that had her legs firmly trapped. Water bubbled out of her mouth and nose. Her golden eyes were rolling back into her head.

Groping, Doc found a little container in a pocket and popped it open with a thumb. Three white tablets were revealed. Doc pinched them in between two fingers, and with a mighty wrench of his body, struggled to reach his drowning cousin.

He forced all three pellets down Pat's throat. She swallowed them. She still struggled in the throes of drowning and muscular constriction.

Then Doc Savage began beating the snake's scaly sides with his punishing fists of bronze.

The powerful serpent began convulsing. It released Pat a little, but not enough for her to pull free. One leg was still caught up in a looping tangle of snake. But she was no longer being crushed. Strangely, Pat's face became strangely composed, her mouth closed and her golden eyes came back into focus. She did not appear in danger of drowning any longer.

Doc Savage seized the serpent by its pulsing sides and began squeezing its ribs, causing it great distress. The boa's jaws distended. Writhing weakly, it began to struggle for air. Doc punched it hard, driving air out of its laboring lungs.

Squirming and contorting, it lashed its head about, attempting to strike at the bronze giant with rows of recurved fangs. Doc batted the wedge of a head away with smacking force. The serpent was swiftly discouraged by its inability to clamp down on its foe's warm flesh.

During his youth, the bronze man had mastered the art of holding his breath underwater from the pearl divers of the South Seas. He had continually practiced the skill over the ensuing years. True, he had not had time to fully charge his lungs, saturating them with reserve oxygen. But his ability to hold his breath was prodigious.

Not so fortunate was the boa constrictor. With metallic fists, Doc smashed the air out of it time and again, his muscular arms working like tireless pistons.

As it attempted to struggle free, the boa's reptilian energy flagged. Like a python or any similar crushing snake, it counted on its prey succumbing without much of a fight. A fighting demon such as Doc Savage was beyond its ken.

Doc wrapped his powerful legs around the serpent. Steel-hard fingers stretched out, found Pat Savage and, with irresistible force, wrested her free of the weakening coils.

Pat struck toward the surface, soon breaking into open air. She opened her mouth as if to take in reviving air, but then shrugged as if it were no longer necessary.

Beneath the lake's surface, Doc Savage and the boa grappled together. But the battle had shifted. The flailing constrictor was no longer attempting to hold its prey underwater in hopes of drowning it.

Doc Savage now had it by the scaly throat, fought to keep it from surfacing. Great jaws yawned as air rushed out in frantic bubbles. The serpent's amber eyes slowly closed. Its frantic thrashing about lost force, then subsided. Air bubbles gushed from nostrils and open maw, then subsided to a trickle that soon ceased.

Doc Savage waited until the thing was limp in his hands before releasing the inert reptile.

When he was satisfied that the monster snake was dead, he rose to the surface and took in fresh air.

Doc and Pat Savage found themselves facing one another.

"I don't think I would've made it without you," gasped Pat.

Doc nodded. He had expended much of his prodigious strength, but lacked the energy for words.

Pat went on. "You gave me all of your oxygen pills. You should have saved one for yourself."

Doc shook his head. "I didn't think it was necessary. And I couldn't take the chance of you drowning before I could over-master the boa."

The oxygen tablets were something Doc had devised long ago. Their unique chemical constituents permitted someone to subsist without oxygen for as long as the tablets held their potency—typically twenty minutes if the person was active.

After fishing around and locating Pat's water-logged six-gun, Doc helped his cousin reach shore. Princess Monja stood there waiting for them. Relief was on her face like reflected moonlight. Her eyes still held the fading echoes of terror, however.

"There is no other man in the world like you, Doc Savage," she said sincerely. "A warrior fit to wed a princess, and protect a future queen. I would be proud to the end of my days to be your wife."

Doc simply stood there, a little stunned.

Pat was still being guided by the bronze giant, and their bodies were close. That enabled the tawny-haired girl to give him a concealed nudge in the ribs and whisper, "Princess Pocahontas practically proposed to you, I think. If you don't take the ball and run with it, you sap, I will never speak to you again."

Swallowing hard, Doc Savage said, "I would be honored to be your husband, Princess."

Moisture began seeping out of Monja's dark eyes.

"Upper-puck," hissed Pat, mangling her Pig Latin. "Am I going to have to be your romantic navigator 'til the day I drop?"

Doc Savage took the hint.

Throwing herself onto the white sand to recover from her dual ordeal, Pat stared up at the silvery moon high above and implored the night sky, "The things a gal has to endure to get a stubborn man to do the natural thing...."

Chapter XIV

BLACK FLOWER OF WARNING

THE FOLLOWING MORNING, Doc Savage and
Princess Monja went to petition old King Chaac. Pat
Savage accompanied the couple.

They stood before him in what passed for a throne room in
the old ruler's private dwelling. It was not large, but it was the
largest building in the Valley. By the standards of the modern
world, it would have been called modest.

Not that there wasn't a throne. There was. It consisted of a
rosewood platform inlaid with jade and silver. A jaguar-skin
mat covered the pallet. A spray of quetzal-bird plumes, symbol-
izing the Feathered Serpent, Kukulcan, formed an iridescent
halo behind him.

Doc Savage explained, "I have asked for Monja's hand in
marriage and she has consented. Now I ask permission of you,
her father."

The ancient sovereign smiled and his wise face wrinkled up
with delight.

"I have long despaired that I would never live to see this
joyous day. Of course, you have my blessing."

Doc and the princess broke out in broad smiles—not that
they had any doubt about wise old Chaac's decision. But sleep
had eluded them as they worried about his reaction.

The biggest smile belonged to Pat Savage. She had visions of
being a bridesmaid.

"Wait until the boys finally show up," she proclaimed. "Better let me break the news, Doc. It won't be so stupefying."

"How do you plan to accomplish that, Pat?" asked Doc.

The bronze-haired girl shrugged unconcernedly.

"Oh, I'll have them wrapped around my little finger, don't you worry."

Chaac raised both hands to quiet the room.

"I have given my permission," he announced, "but other permission is also required. My daughter is my only heir to the throne from which I rule. You must go, both of you, to meet with the Clan of the Very Highest. In order to marry royalty, you must have the consent of Lord Chi-Ahpuch as well."

"Oh," murmured Pat. "A snag."

"We will go at once," said Doc forthrightly.

"Yes, go now. And with you take my hopes for a safe return."

From somewhere in his robes, old Chaac removed a turquoise dagger. It was a beautiful thing, if excessively wrought. The handle was silver and complicated in its design. The blade itself was polished turquoise. In ancient times it might have been a sacrificial knife. But it appeared to be a votive trinket now.

King Chaac offered this to Doc Savage, hilt first. The bronze man took the thing and found it difficult to grasp comfortably, owing to the ornate nature of the silver handle. It did not seem designed to fit the hand, which was puzzling.

"This is the key to the upper valley," intoned Chaac in a solemn tone. "Without it, you cannot pass into the preserves of the Clan of the Very Highest. You will remember Lord Chi-Ahpuch, the high priest."

"Vividly," said Doc.

"He awaits you there. The final decision is his."

"Thank you," said Doc, tucking the blade into his belt.

As the bronze man and the princess turned to go, Pat took Doc aside to inquire, "Didn't you once tell me that this Clan of the Very Highest are a bunch of tough customers?"

"They are," allowed Doc. "But they are also fair. I am not overly concerned."

"Well, you should be. You're marrying into the biggest family in these particular woods. Such matters aren't taken lightly. Watch your step."

"I will," promised Doc.

THEY went out into the splintering sunlight. A crowd had gathered, expectantly. Whispered word had spread of the betrothal. There was a kind of joyous energy to the milling Mayans. They did not display it very openly. But it was there. The feeling was palpable. It was as if they were electric torches whose batteries had been exchanged for fresh ones. They stepped more briskly, and the songs they sang aloud or hummed to themselves were more uplifting than the everyday tunes of their folk.

It was not a far walk to the entrance to the other valley. Doc and Monja took their time. They had all day. They held hands as they walked. And their hearts were full to overflowing anticipating what fate had in store for the two of them.

Monja's dark eyes went to the morning sky.

"Behold, Kinich Ahau smiles upon our journey. He is our sun god, you know."

Doc nodded. "I know."

"*Kinich* means 'sun-eyed.' When I first laid eyes upon you, Clark Savage, I thought to myself, how like the Sun-Eyed Lord is that giant stranger with golden eyes. He must be a god among men. My heart knew then what yours did not. That we were meant for one another." She squeezed his hand with surprising strength. "You are mine, now. And I am yours."

The Mayan maid's words brought an uneasy feeling. Doc Savage brushed aside his inner qualms. Perhaps it was only his scientific mind rejecting any talk of sun gods. He felt a deep urge to correct Monja on the subject of solar deities. Ancient Mayan astronomers were amazingly accurate in their heavenly calculations, and their calendar system superb, even by modern standards. Yet they failed to distinguish between the fixed stars and the wandering planets, holding Venus to be *Xux Ek,* the "Great Star." These were the beliefs taught since childhood. They would have to be addressed carefully, Doc knew. Time enough to educate Monja to the celestial truths later.

"Clark, do you remember what you called me when we first met?" asked Monja suddenly.

A slight frown crossed the bronze man's countenance. "I confess that I don't."

"You said that I was a brick. Do you recall it now?"

"Yes."

"I did not understand your meaning then," said Monja. "I still do not. My father told me what the word meant, but its meaning confused me."

Doc smiled gently. "To call someone a brick in those days was to compliment them for being brave and dependable. A trustworthy person, in other words. It's a slang word, now out of date."

"Oh."

Doc felt the heat of embarrassment overtake his face. He had long ago foresworn the use of slang, and realized what a foolish compliment it had been to offer someone so lovely.

Again, he drank in her beauty. Monja had put on her best *huipil*—a deep blue embroidered dress that left her golden shoulders and arms bare. At her earlobes, earrings of amber fixed in silver danced. She swung along with an easy grace that was flowing, almost as if she floated along the ground.

A fragment of a folk song the bronze giant had first heard in his youth suddenly popped into his mind, surprising him. Doc had not thought of the ditty in many years. Indeed, he had not believed it had made much impression upon him.

> *The girl was sweet and fair to view,*
> *Hoodah, to my hoodah;*
>
> *Her hair was so brown, her eyes so blue,*

Hoodah, hoodah day.

The tune reminded the bronze man of his strange childhood, when he had been a lonesome lone wolf of a boy. A child knowing no mother, whose father was a distant and often absent figure, roaming the world for impenetrable reasons while Clark—he had not yet acquired the nickname that marked his adult renown—was shunted about the same globe, being passed from teacher to scientist to tutor in furtherance of his father's ambition to make of his son an all-around superman, fit for any kind of challenge.

As an adult, Doc often pondered what a severe price he had paid in service to his father's single-minded vision, and frequently wondered what unexplored paths his personal life might have taken if he had had a normal childhood.

Gazing at Monja floating beside him, he realized that he was on the threshold of reclaiming part of his lost self, and another fragment of that inane song popped into his head.

My love is young, my love is true.
Hoodah, to my hoodah!

Their progress took them to a portion of the Valley that was forbidden to the common folk. It was sacrilege to trespass here, even for Princess Monja. Outwardly, there was nothing remarkable here. It was simply a grove of trees in which green parakeets and brown *piam-piam* birds cavorted in their aerial dances, squawking noisily at the unusual intrusion. The only indication of its taboo nature was the profusion of cactus plants lurking about, primarily prickly pear cactus, whose pads and pears could be eaten once denuded of its spines.

Conceivably, those stickers were intended to mark trespassers not otherwise discouraged from invading.

A yellow butterfly clung to one of the cactus plants. Spotting it, Monja rushed over and, with practiced ease, captured the creature between both hands.

Kneeling before a flat rock that appeared shaped by rude

tools, she set the butterfly on it. The insect stood there, working its wounded wings, testing them preparatory to flight.

To Doc Savage's horror, Monja calmly picked up a rock and smashed the unsuspecting butterfly against the tiny stone altar.

Standing up, she returned to his side, beaming like a child.

"Why did you kill that butterfly?" asked Doc.

Her response was carelessly casual. "I merely sacrificed it to the moon goddess, Ixchel. It was an offering to her, made in order to appeal for her intercession in the matter that lies before us."

Seeing the shocked look on the bronze man's face, the princess quickly added, "We Mayans long ago abandoned the practice of human sacrifice, you know. Only butterflies and small creatures are sacrificed now."

Doc Savage said nothing. Words failed him. Taking her hand firmly, the bronze giant continued on.

FINALLY, Doc and Monja came to the entrance to the other valley and passed through. It was a passage cut through the living rock comprising one of the surrounding cliffs. There was no door, no barrier. But such was the esteem in which the Mayans held their laws, no one entered without permission.

Doc Savage had been here once before, but he had not penetrated far. He had explored only the portion adjacent to the Valley of the Vanished. What he had found was in the nature of a garden. He knew of course there had to be more to it than that. People lived here. There should be houses somewhere in this verdant paradise.

"Have you ever been to the other village?" asked Doc.

Monja squeezed his hand, shook her head and said, "No. Never. It is forbidden."

"You appear nervous."

"This is the beginning of a new life, for you and for me. Of course, I am nervous."

"About being here in this other valley, I mean," said Doc.

Monja considered. "My father has had the deep honor of visiting from time to time. But even he is not permitted to come and go as he wishes. There are secrets here. He has whispered this to me. But I do not know any of them. The Clan of the Very Highest are the true lords of the two valleys. The one that you know is called the Valley of the Vanished. The other one that you do not know is called by my people the Valley of Eternity."

"Why is it called that?"

"It is said that the people of this higher valley came from far away, and settled here so long ago that no one can count the *baktun* since their arrival."

"I see," said Doc.

They walked through the garden and the smell of the tropical flowers filled their senses. Doc watched for wild animals, especially boa constrictors. Ocelots and jaguars were common in these jungles, but the scent of either cat Doc Savage could read from a significant distance. He smelled neither. The perfume of countless flowers all but overpowered his acute sense of small. Hibiscus and philodendrons mixed in the humid air, commingling delightfully. Orchids bloomed in profusion, many white as ivory.

They crossed the length of the lush garden, across an open glade where towering kapok and breadfruit trees drowsed in the sun, finally coming to the place where this smaller valley pinched off.

Doc stopped and turned around. "Where are the people? I see no dwellings."

"I do not know," admitted the princess, sounding uneasy. "My father never discussed life in this valley."

Doc Savage began moving around, looking for something, even if he did not know what it was. The encircling walls of rock were covered in vines, moss and other greenery. Buzzing insects whirled about lazily. Hummingbirds hovered amid a stand of calabash trees. A trilling quetzal bird flashed past, trailing its amazingly long train of blue-green tail feathers.

A glint of sunlight gave back something that caught Doc's eye.

Doc moved toward it, pushed aside some lianas to expose what appeared to be a plate of black obsidian fixed in the cliff. The volcanic glass seemed to be naturally a part of the rock, yet it also showed signs of having been smoothed or shaped.

Ripping down more foliage with his strong fingers, Doc uncovered a carving in the black glassy surface. A design stood out in sharp relief.

What he saw caused his trilling to come eerily.

Princess Monja knew Doc Savage well enough to understand that this was how the bronze giant expressed certain emotions, particularly astonishment.

"What surprises you, Clark?"

"This carving. It is a flower."

"I do not recognize it. It does not grow in my valley."

"This is a lotus flower. This species doesn't grow in Central America, or South America either. This particular specimen is common in Asia, specifically Egypt. It was often depicted in Egyptian hieroglyphics dating back to the time of the pharaohs."

"What does it signify?"

"Death."

Monja placed a slim hand in front of her mouth involuntarily.

"It is a warning?"

"I'm not certain," admitted Doc. "To the ancient Egyptians, this flower signified death and resurrection, because its petals opened during the day and closed at night. I do not understand how any people who live around here would know of this type of lotus flower."

"It is a mystery then?"

Doc Savage nodded. "Possibly a profound one."

Doc tore away more foliage, having discovered a crevice. Remembering the crack into which old King Chaac had inserted a special key, he wondered if the turquoise dagger might not fit.

Withdrawing the weapon from his belt, he experimented with inserting the turquoise blade into the crevice. It slipped in readily enough. He tried turning it this way and that, pushing it in and out, seeking to trigger some simple mechanism. But nothing resulted. He was afraid to force the blade in either direction, lest it crack or shatter. Turquoise might be suitable as a stabbing tool, but it would not stand up to great pressure.

Doc withdrew the blade and contemplated it.

"I do not understand how to use this blade. It baffles me."

Frowning, Princess Monja looked at the complicated thing in Doc's metallic hand.

"I have never seen my father employ this blade for any purpose. Perhaps the handle contains instructions, such as writing."

Doc turned it about in his hands. The hilt seemed to be in the form of the glyph of a god with a strange upturned nose, virtually a proboscis. Some archaeologists called it the Serpent-Nosed God. The true name and significance of this deity was in dispute.

The bronze man turned to the princess of Maya and asked, "Can you make anything of this?"

Monja took the blade from Doc, turned it about in her hands, and looked perplexed in a pretty way.

"This is the god-monster known as Cabrakan. He is the demon of earthquakes, and earth mysteries. He does not have a nose like a normal man, but instead a snaky snout like a *tzimink*—what you would call a tapir. This Cabrakan uses it to explore crevices and caverns in the earth, where dark things dwell. His long nose is for him like a great boneless finger questing into the cracks in the underworld."

Doc retrieved the turquoise blade, examined it anew and

suddenly his trilling was back, its melodic notes mixing surprise with understanding.

With a strange expression on his face, he turned, then inserted not the blade, but the ornate hilt into the crevice. It fit perfectly. The trick was to turn it. The only way to hold it was now by the blade, which was exceedingly sharp.

An ordinary man might have found it difficult. Doc Savage was no ordinary man. He pressed the palms of both hands against either flat of the blade, thus avoiding the edges. Slowly, he turned with all of the muscular strength of his upper body.

A metallic sound of mechanism came to his ears and the face of the rock, along with the glassy black lotus flower glyph, opened inward.

They stood there watching, Monja's demure expression becoming full of awe mixed with a twinge of apprehension.

Doc Savage's face settled into its customary impassive lines. His flake-gold eyes were very active now. The door continued opening, and out from the other side came a strange smell, an animal musk, heavy and bestial. Doc Savage could not immediately place it, but the odor caused Princess Monja to recoil in open-mouthed alarm.

When the door had yawned about a third of the way, something living whipped into view, snaking out from the other side.

It was long, brownish and sinuous. At first, Doc thought it was another boa. But the tip of the thing did not include a head. Unless it was headless.

Seeing this tentacle of a thing questing about, Princess Monja let out a shriek. "It is the god of the long nose! It lives! We have found its dwelling place."

Then the ugly thing wrapped its headless length around the bronze man's uplifted arm and seized it in a muscular grip that was unpleasant to the touch.

Chapter XV

THE SECRET OF CALANTIS

BOOT HEELS DIGGING in, Doc Savage set himself against the groping thing.

The ropey tentacle was hot to the touch. It gave a tug against which the bronze giant's prodigious strength was distressingly feeble.

Monja screamed again. Her golden hands seized one of Doc's arms, as if to aid him in resisting the powerful thing. But there was no resisting. It was impossible.

With a sinuous jerk, the serpentine coil hauled the bronze man through the doorway. Refusing to release her intended, the princess came with him, blue skirts shaking, stumbling with every step.

Employing both hands, Doc took firm hold of the appendage. His palms came into contact with coarse hairs that speckled its tentacular surface. The skin of the thing felt rough, corrugated, vaguely unearthly.

The bronze man had felt such surfaces before. Comprehension began dawning.

So when he saw the monster's face, Doc was prepared. Nevertheless, his trilling piped out rather wonderingly.

The thing drew him closer, staring at him with small dark eyes set in a broad, brutish face. On either side of the bronze giant, two down-sweeping tusks like elongated yellowish horns hemmed him in, keeping Doc from lunging to either side.

Pulled along with him, Monja let out another shriek. "This is no god! What is it? What manner of beast could it be?"

"Mastodon," said Doc steadily.

Monja was speechless. The word meant nothing to her.

Then they both saw the warrior astride the great rolling beast, his bare legs clamping its broad wrinkled back, glaring down at them with an expression that might have been hewn from stone.

He looked like one of the golden-skinned Mayans populating the Valley of the Vanished, and his attire was similar—essentially a cotton broadcloth and leather shoulder guard and gorget. However, this man came equipped with fragments of armor hammered from some ductile metal Doc Savage did not immediately recognize. It had a gleam of gold, but it was reddish. Red gold.

The fellow wore an elaborate wooden helmet decorated with scarlet feathers. His eyes were uncovered. He looked down upon Doc Savage and Princess Monja with an unreadable expression.

Another tentacle whipped out unexpectedly and captured Monja's golden wrist. She recoiled, but to no avail. They were separated.

"Are you mad? I am a princess!"

"Do not resist, Monja," stated Doc Savage in a calm voice. "They do not seem to mean us any harm."

The second warrior balanced atop a similar beast said something in a guttural tone. The hairy trunk of this pachyderm had hold of Monja.

Doc Savage and Monja recognized his speech as Mayan, but of the ancient, flowery variety. This was the Kulca dialect forbidden to all but the loftiest nobles, which the bronze man had been taught long ago. The warrior was inviting them to come along. His tone was that of an order, but it was not unfriendly.

The two beasts commenced backing up, drawing them along, but released them after the entry portal was closed by spear-toting guards. The long-tusked elephantine brutes turned about and lumbered off. One of the warriors glanced back to make sure Doc and Monja were following.

The princess was still clinging to the Man of Bronze as they advanced along a white causeway that seemed to be composed of finely-crushed seashells and white pebbles. *Piam-piam* birds were busy in the warm air, their noisy calls sounding like their name being repeated endlessly.

"I have never imagined such ugly beasts," Monja undertoned, watching the brown bulks lumber along.

"They are a species of elephant that has been extinct for many generations," replied Doc.

Princess Monja did not know what an elephant was, so Doc attempted explanations.

"In the modern world, elephants still roam Asia and Africa. But in prehistoric days, there were several species native to North and South America. The bones of this species of mastodon have been unearthed from Chile to Mexico. They resemble the African elephant, although not exactly. Their ivory tusks are not curved upward, but instead sweep down into a shallow spiral. They are larger and heavier than the modern-day African pachyderm."

Princess Monja nodded mutely, but Doc was not certain she completely comprehended his recitation. His eyes were on the armor sheathing the limbs of the two mastodon-riding warriors. The metal was unusual, but he began to suspect what it might be in actuality. The golden flakes in his eyes glittered speculatively at the thought.

They were taken into a small city. Small by modern standards, but it was larger than the enclave of the Valley of the Vanished. Consisting of single-story structures of hewn stone resembling alabaster, the place was dominated by a pyramid that mirrored the golden pyramid in that it was sheer and not stepped.

Unlike the other, this one came to a point at the top. The entire effect was that of a smaller version of an Egyptian pyramid. But it was not constructed of massive quartz blocks. Perhaps under the skin of the structure, such blocks resided. The four sides were faced like stucco, but the surface was not stucco, or anything like it. Rather, metal sheets had been hammered into place. Sheets of the reddish metal that held the gleam of rich gold and made looking at it too long hard on the eyes. The structure was larger than the one dominating the Valley of the Vanished, being broader at the base and perhaps fifty feet higher at the apex.

Wonder got into Doc Savage's metallic expression. When the Spanish arrived in the New World, they found that the inhabitants of Central and South America had fashioned certain religious objects out of an alloy of gold and copper, which the Conquistadors dubbed tumbaga. This structure was not tumbaga, however. Nor was it natural electrum, or the mixture of copper, gold and silver the Hellenistic Greeks called Hepatizon.

But the bronze man had no time to consider any of this. Above his head, the sky was all but blotted out by the interlacing greenery of the jungle canopy. But no lofty trees supported that thick canopy. Instead, there was a clever wooden lattice upon which was piled ferns, aerial creepers, and other sheltering vegetation.

Studying this arrangement, Monja remarked, "They have covered the valley to conceal the temple from passing aircraft."

Doc nodded. It was a remarkable achievement in cantilever-style engineering. Somehow, they periodically managed to replace the greenery so that it did not shrivel up, rot and fall down.

A pleasant chlorophyll-colored atmosphere was thus created.

They were escorted to a flagged plaza where Doc Savage recognized the elderly figure of Chi-Ahpuch, the high priest.

Doc and Princess Monja were waved toward what appeared to be an outdoor throne, made out of hardwood and studded with turquoise, emeralds and other precious and semi-precious stones. It was not the traditional Mayan platform throne, with which the bronze giant was very familiar, but a chair with a high back that was carved in serpentine coils studded with long spiky feathers.

Chi-Ahpuch sat waiting for them. He looked not much older than he had been when Doc Savage had last encountered him. He was not an old man, but his hair was a pile of cottony whiteness. The rest of him was thin and the hue of old dusty gold. His name, Doc recalled, translated as "Mouth of Death," but there was nothing unpleasant about his appearance, other than a certain austerity of demeanor.

When they stood before him, Monja bowed timidly and murmured, "I greet you in supplication, Lord Chi-Ahpuch."

The man nodded in acceptance of her worshipful words.

Assisting Monja to her feet, Doc Savage spoke up. "We meet again."

Chi-Ahpuch appraised Doc Savage with cool regard. "You are the first man of your race to pass through the sacred-flower gate. Speak."

The bronze man got directly to the point. "I have asked Princess Monja for her hand in marriage, and she has consented. Her father, the just King Chaac, has no objections. We have come before you to determine whether you bless or forbid our union."

The face of Chi-Ahpuch grew troubled.

"This is a thing not foreseen by my ancestors," he said slowly. "I must ponder this petition."

He was silent for a few minutes.

Monja stood trembling, her ornate skirts shaking in sympathy with her slim body.

Chi-Ahpuch's thin face abruptly brightened.

"I will put on a feast. During it, we will discuss this matter. I will tell you the story of my people so that you understand us, and the responsibilities we bear living apart from the world as we do."

"Thank you," said Doc. "I am very interested in hearing about your history, for King Chaac has made it clear that his knowledge of the subject is not complete."

They were separated and taken to simple quarters. Doc showed interest in the architecture and saw that it had similarities to the traditional Mayan, but differences also. These puzzled him. There was an absence of the complicated carvings which typically overwhelmed the exteriors of the Mayan structures he had encountered. These were simpler, more refined and, by virtue of their simplicity, pleasing to the aesthetic sense in a way the overbearing complexity of the typical Mayan decorative carvings and bas-reliefs could never be.

Normally, the bronze man would be immersed in study, but he was preoccupied with the high priest's deliberations. He had not expected that winning Monja's hand would be so complicated, or involve anything beyond King Chaac's paternal blessing. This interlude of uncertainty was bringing out in him an unfamiliar nervousness, and he found himself pacing.

Events had been accelerating at an amazing pace. Doc could scarcely have imagined, a mere week ago, that he would find himself in such changed circumstances, both outwardly and inwardly. He wondered if this were all meant to be in some strange, fateful way he could not firmly grasp. Such thoughts were not normal with him. He felt as if he were in the grip of forces he could not resist.

With an effort, Doc halted and placed his focus on his surroundings, away from his inner turmoil.

A guard was placed outside of his chamber and the bronze man studied him through the open door. The armor the fellow wore was of strange coloration. Definitely not copper. Not exactly gold. And probably not an alloy of the two.

The smell of cooking drifted in. Doc passed the time by trying to separate the smells with his sensitive nostrils. He recognized tapir meat, armadillo and some jungle birds, including wild turkey. Fresh corn sweetened the odors of roasting meat.

Apparently, talk of a feast was no exaggeration. They were going to eat well, if exotically.

THE SUN was still up, but sinking ponderously when another Mayan man came and spoke to Doc's guard, whereupon the bronze giant was escorted out to the central plaza. Princess Monja was already present. She sat at the feet of Chi-Ahpuch. Evidently, they had been conversing.

In the reddish light of dusk, the Mayan princess took on a beauty that all but snatched Doc Savage's breath away. He had experienced something similar when he had first met Monja, but never let on. Now the feeling was strong in him. It felt a little unreal, as if he were striding through a dream in which everything was heightened and the hues saturated like a Technicolor film.

Seeing the bronze man approach, Monja smiled. The smile was relaxed, and unworried. One slim hand toyed with her long black hair, which had been rearranged cleverly, no doubt by one of the women of this valley vale.

"I have been speaking about you, Clark," she said. "Your strength in conquering the constrictor serpent rivals those of our great god-warriors in ancient times. I have likened your prowess to that of great Hurucan."

"Thank you," said Doc, acknowledging the name of a Mayan storm god similar to the Norse god of thunder, Thor.

Chi-Ahpuch spoke then.

"I know many things about Doc Savage, except what is in his heart. Princess Monja has told me what is in her heart. Now I will hear what is in yours."

The bronze man was so unaccustomed to revealing his inner feelings that he hesitated. Monja caught his eye and signaled for him to speak up.

He began in a formal fashion. "I have always been fond of this woman. But the circumstances of our lives kept us apart. Those circumstances are changing now. We are both growing long in years, and the time to move to the next stage of our lives has come. We recognize this. In the past, we may have denied it. But we can deny it no longer."

Doc Savage stopped speaking then. He was uncomfortable. He understood that he was not professing the fullness of his feelings, but the inner reserve that had been with him since childhood was a rigid shell not easily broken.

Chi-Ahpuch nodded. "Well spoken," he intoned, sounding satisfied.

He signaled with one lifted arm and food was brought forth on platters of ceramic and calabash bowls. There were no chairs except the throne. Only woven mats. So Doc and Monja took positions at his feet while the others—and there were not many—gathered about and found spots on the stonework of the plaza.

They commenced eating. They did so in the manner of so many tribes of native Americans. In respectful silence at first, not speaking until the meal was well along.

Eventually, Chi-Ahpuch set down the bones of the bird whose flesh he had stripped from the bone with his teeth and remarked, "Marriage is about many things. Love is chief among them. The children are more important. Children make us immortal, even though we are not."

Monja smiled simply. "To bear children would be my second greatest joy in life." She took Doc's strong arm and squeezed it with both sets of fingers. "To be this man's wife would be my highest joy."

Doc would have blushed, but he was not one for blushing, either. He had the horrible sensation of his common-sense self lying prone where it had been knocked, while another part of his mind took control. It was amazing. He failed to understand how he could feel so....heady.

Doc essayed a careful smile. His golden eyes caressed her. He had difficulty keeping his attention off her lovely features.

The white-haired high-man resumed eating. His face was thoughtful. He always wore a distracted look.

"The story of my people is not known to you. If you are to marry into our race, you must learn it."

"I have studied the Mayan people and culture," said Doc simply. "I know the names and attributes of all your gods. Over the years I have come to know the people of the adjacent valley."

"That is the Valley of the Vanished. This is the Valley of Eternity. From this valley, all the tribes once radiated like spokes from a wheel—the Mayan, the Aztec, the Toltec, even the Olmec. I must tell you how we came to be."

Chi-Ahpuch's dark eyes took on a faraway light, his expression turning dreamy and remote, as if falling into a spell of second sight.

"Long, long, very long ago, our ancestors came from a distant land. They sailed across the great eastern sea. They fled the ending of their world. These people were the survivors of an empire whose memories we carry with pride. They arrived in large ships of a kind succeeding generations have forgotten how to build, and tamed the beasts of these wild jungles of plenty. Over generations, they upbuilt their villages into great cities. Their temples still dot the land. All lie in ruin now. Only the structures of this valley and the next valley are maintained."

Doc Savage was not surprised by any of this. It had always been assumed that the Mayan people had come from some other place. Polynesians had colonized the Pacific in their primitive outrigger canoes. Other peoples had migrated. The origins of the human race, especially before recorded history, were not clearly understood. Science was still trying to unravel the mysterious knot of mankind's march across the globe.

"What was the name of this land?" asked the bronze man.

"Calantis."

IT TOOK a moment for the name to register. Up until this point, the trend of the bronze man's thoughts went to theories that some of the peoples of South and Central America had migrated from ancient Egypt. Like the Mayans, the Egyptians had a high culture for its time, and erected stupendous pyramids. Doc had expected to hear something that furthered that unproven theory.

Instead, shock snatched away a shade of his bronze hue.

"Did you say *Calantis?*"

Chi-Ahpuch nodded solemnly. "It was a land very different than this one. An island. Across the eastern ocean it lay. A calamity brought it to ruin. The legends speak of earthquakes, cities crushed by the hands of the gods, with many drowned, both the wicked and the worthy alike."

"Atlantis!" Doc whispered.

"What?" asked Monja, a trifle fearfully.

Doc related, "Atlantis was the name of a small continent, or perhaps a very large island, somewhere in the Atlantic, beyond the so-called Pillars of Hercules. The name meant 'Island of Atlas.' Atlas was a Titan of Greek myth. From his legend comes the name of the Atlantic Ocean. It was said a very long time ago that Atlantis sank amid a cataclysm that virtually destroyed it. Modern science has long believed the place merely a myth, a product of ancient imaginations. But ancient Troy was also thought to be mythical until its ruins were discovered in the last century."

Doc Savage's mind flashed back to previous adventures. A decade or more ago, he had explored a portion of a sunken metropolis, which had been dubbed by its discoverers, *Taz*. The underwater city lay near Nassau, in the Bahamas, and its architecture was a blend of Mayan and Egyptian features.

There was ample evidence to suggest that Taz was a surviving ruin of Atlantis, and that its extinct people were scientifically advanced. Some time later, the bronze man discovered descendants of the sunken civilization living in sophisticated underwater domes deep in the South Atlantic. These survivors of a lost land spoke a brand of the Egyptian language as it was during the time of the pharaohs, specifically the Eighteenth Dynasty. The marvelous oxygen pills Doc carried were devised by the present-day scientists of that watery wonderland.*

There were other such experiences. Southeast of this spot, in Colombia, he had stumbled across something amazing. A titanic stone structure resembling a sleeping Egyptian pharaoh. It was no giant's sarcophagus, but a honeycombed labyrinth housing another outpost of a lost people, who had migrated from Egypt back before the days of Tut-Ankh-Amen of the Eighteenth Dynasty era. They called their strange colony Klantic, after the banished Pharaoh Klantic, who founded it.**

Klantic. Calantis. Atlantis. All the same.

Another enigmatic ruin—a temple—was found overlooking a lagoon in the West Indies.*** Early in the war, Doc and his men had discovered an ancient stone lighthouse set in the Caribbean, on a spot called Satan Cay. Beneath it lay a treasure chamber. This held many fantastic artifacts, as well as a great store of red gold. He had not seen much of this strange stuff. But it resembled historical accounts of a lost metal, orichalcum. A substance that was said to be common in the time of Atlantis, but no longer extant in the present day.****

Scientific excitement seized Doc Savage. Many of the strands of his previous explorations were coming together. He glanced over at Princess Monja's golden profile and realized that other strands were coming together as well. A warm feeling came over him, followed by a satisfied smile that naturally lit his metallic features.

Noticing this softening of his expression, Chi-Ahpuch asked, "What is in your mind, Doc Savage?"

"I have heard of Calantis. The outside world calls it Atlantis. It is such an ancient place that few believe it ever existed. But

---

* *Mystery Under the Sea* & *The Red Terrors*

** *The Mental Wizard*

*** *Phantom Lagoon*

**** *The Secret of Satan's Spine*

what I see about me proves that it did. I am glad that this ancient civilization continues to thrive in the modern day."

Now was Chi-Ahpuch's turn to smile. "Then you understand the importance of keeping the Valley of Eternity sheltered from the outer world?"

"I do."

"You have kept the secret of the Valley of the Vanished all these years. You have taken the gold which was rightfully yours by Chaac's agreement with your father. Now it is gone. Even so, you have asked the hand of this high-born maid in marriage. This proves that your interest in our people is not merely due to its wealth."

"It was never about that," stated Doc Savage. "My father was the first white man to discover the Valley of the Vanished. He recognized its value and respected its privacy. Up until the day of his death, he told no one. Not even his only son."

"Those are good words to hear," intoned Chi-Ahpuch.

He resumed his eating. There was silence for a long time. The silence was observed by the entire group, which numbered fewer than fifty inhabitants.

Doc looked about him. He studied the people of the Valley of Eternity. They possessed the same golden complexion marking King Chaac's subjects. Their clothing was somewhat different, and there were other items of note. He remembered that Chaac had told him long ago that this Clan of the Very Highest sent its own to rule the Valley of the Vanished. These were the people he intended to marry into. The unsuspected nobility of lost Atlantis, who were somehow connected with the ancient Egyptian civilization, if the architecture of the twin pyramids meant anything. It gave him a strange feeling to think that this unbroken lineage had been so important in his life.

Chi-Ahpuch spoke up. "This valley has its own store of gold, separate from that overseen by Chaac."

Doc said nothing. He wanted to see where the old man was going.

"Gold has little value here, except as ornaments. It is called flower gold for that reason. We do not have money. We work for the common good. Gold and money are not necessary to a people who toil in unison and in concert for the greater benefit of all."

The bronze man held his tongue.

Chi-Ahpuch resumed speaking. "We know that you do good work with the gold that was given to you. Perhaps we can insure that good work continuing."

"How so?"

"Perhaps the flower gold that we hold that is of little value to us could be given to you. As a dowry from the family of Chaac."

"Dowry?" Doc Savage had not considered such a thing. He fell quiet.

"It is a custom here. There was not as much flower gold as in the other Valley. Yet there are great quantities of it in our great temple. We would reserve only a fraction for our own purposes. What do you say to that, Doc Savage?"

The bronze man did not answer right away. He could see the look in the high-man's eyes and face. He would be judged upon his answer. His worthiness was being measured again, as if anew. He glanced toward Princess Monja, who looked back. The glance they exchanged told the bronze man she had picked up on the same thing.

"Tell me of this rare metal your soldiers wear," Doc invited.

"This is our true treasure. Flower gold can be had for the digging. But it is too heavy and soft for practical matters. This metal, which we call 'blood gold,' is lighter and harder. Our sole supply was carried in the great sailing ships of Calantis to this wild land. It cannot be found here. There were no mines bearing it in these jungles, or any lands we have discovered. Our ancestors sought it far to the north and south in vain."

Doc thought of the Incas of Peru, and their great civilization. When Europeans first explored what is now the United States, they discovered traces of abandoned cities in places like Illinois, Ohio, Missouri and elsewhere. These consisted of settlements arranged around huge mounds shaped like many of the pyramidal structures of the Maya, Toltec and Aztec peoples. Fascinating to contemplate that the descendants of Atlantis had expanded so far across the Americas.

"Accounts of Atlantis refer to a rare metal called orichalcum," said Doc Savage. "It is not found anywhere in the modern world. At least, its source has yet to be discovered."

Chi-Ahpuch nodded sagely. "We have long believed that the only surviving blood gold lies in the Valley of Eternity. There was none in the Valley of the Vanished." He pointed toward the towering metal-plated pyramid looming over the enclave, its reddish gold skin reflecting the diffuse sunlight. "That structure is our treasure house. The blood gold it contains is the exclusive property of the Clan of the Very Highest."

"That is not completely the truth," said Doc Savage earnestly. "There is at least one cache of orichalcum in the outside world."

The snowy-haired ruler's mouth gave a reflexive twist.

"How do you know this?" he asked sharply.

"I know this," replied Doc Savage earnestly, "because I have seen this store with my own eyes. Beneath the waters north and east of here lies a flooded chamber where artifacts of lost Calantis, as you call it, can be found. The red gold is still there."

Interest made the man's thin voice excited. "You saw this with your own eyes?"

"Yes. The red gold could not be retrieved because the chamber housed a strange crystal idol that generated extreme cold, apparently to protect it from looters. The flooded waters are frozen. To retrieve the red gold would be a massive undertaking."

Chi-Ahpuch's face fell. "Then it cannot be salvaged."

"Not easily," admitted Doc. "But it is not impossible to do so. I have long considered ways in which it might be done. I would be prepared to undertake this work on your behalf."

"You would?"

"I would," said Doc simply. "If you are offering me your yellow gold as a dowry, I must reciprocate. I offer you in return all the red gold I can safely bring out of the flooded chamber."

Chi-Ahpuch's lined face lit up. It was practically incandescent. His smile, although recondite, showed full force.

Unexpectedly, he shot to his feet, clapped his hands overhead and announced loudly, "I hereby give permission for Doc Savage to marry Monja, Princess of Maya, daughter of sacred Calantis."

The assembly broke out in what might have been applause, but most of it was vocal. Hooting and catcalling and smiles all around. A few of the men slapped their bare thighs enthusiastically.

Still seated, Doc Savage and Princess Monja turned to one another and embraced warmly.

"My dreams have come true, Clark Savage," she said through tears.

"Both of ours have," replied Doc. And he was surprised at the emotion in his voice. He had been trying to control it. It would not be tamed. A new chapter in the book of his life was about to open and emotions flooded him in a way that was beyond all of his expectations.

Chapter XVI

THE MOAN BIRD

THE COUPLE RETURNED to the Valley of the Vanished late that evening.

After being escorted through the hidden portal marked by an Egyptian lotus whose significance was now clear, Doc Savage and Princess Monja stopped to watch the ponderous entrance door to the Valley of Eternity close by steady pressure from the ponderous heads of the supposedly-extinct mastodons. Once they cleared it, the pair picked their way through the pristine glade that separated the two surviving sanctuaries of sunken Atlantis, the one of high nobles and the other of common folk mixed with the royal family.

They walked along in silence, Monja pausing often to pick wildflowers. She placed one—a white orchid rarely found outside this enclave of lost Maya—in her hair. She hummed wordlessly. The humming was pleasant, and smacked of suppressed joy.

For his part, Doc Savage kept a wary golden eye cocked for predators. He did not imagine many such lurked about, but the boa constrictor of the night before had been an unpleasant surprise.

Moonglow followed the dusk with silver dimness. A breeze blew in from the southwest, steady and cool. The lunar light etched Doc's muscular face with steely highlights, making dark shadows under his eyes, lips and jawline. More than usual, the big bronze man resembled something brought to life by a sorcerer's wand, and not a flesh-and-blood human being.

Moonlight was soft on the exquisite contours of Monja's face. The flowery perfume of her was a heady presence. The tone of her voice, the provocation of her manner, caught his senses and sent them flying in a wild way. She turned her dark eyes sideways at him.

The curve of Monja's lips, rich and warm, was limned by the slanting silver beams. He could, by lifting a hand, touch those inviting lips. The knowledge made warmth leap within him. She was like a lovely jewel, a gem that had been polished deeply by nature, breeding, and ceremony.

There was a tense pounding inside him, apprehension mixed with elation. His shoulders began to tighten up. His emotions seemed to be without armor, where Monja was concerned.

Doc moved to her and drew her close, his metallic hands on her pliable arms, close to her elbows, his fingers not encircling her arms entirely, but spread out with the firm fingertips against her flesh. She did not move. He could feel her heart pounding. His own, too. Her mouth was touched with full color, limpidly inviting him. Suddenly, it changed. Whipping across her soft face came fright, fear of something unseen. As though she was caught in something she had not expected.

A short sharp hooting coming from the west caused the bronze giant's head to rotate. Golden eyes sought the creature, found it, and the yellow eyes of the bird fixed upon the pair. It sat amid the branches of a spiny cciba tree, bathed in spectral moonlight.

Monja exclaimed, "Oh! A *muan*—a moan bird."

That was a Mayan phrase signifying a forest owl. In this case, a screech owl.

Suddenly, the princess shivered. It was not cold.

"What's wrong?" asked Doc.

"I was thinking of the H'men. He is called Chilam Muan, the Wise."

Doc remembered the individual. He was an older fellow, the chief shaman, or H'men, of the Valley of the Vanished. Like many primitive sorcerers, he also worked as a physician, demon-banisher and fortuneteller. Astrology was as strong a belief among the Mayans, he recalled, as it had been with Old World peoples going back to the Babylonians.

Doc Savage had seen Chilam Muan perform his wizardry, and found it intriguing. During his childhood he had been entrusted to some questionable "tutors," including a Hindu Yogi and an African witch doctor. These experiences had left the bronze man with a mixture of respect and curiosity about their ways, which Doc had never fully understood.

Although the man was mysterious in his way, Doc never thought of Chilam Muan as sinister.

"Why do you shiver, Monja?" he asked her.

"Now that we have permission from my father and the high priest of the Clan of the Very Highest, Chilam Muan must cast our fortune, and sanctify our union before the gods."

A troubled flicker came into Doc Savage's flake-gold eyes.

"Why is this necessary?"

"Chilam Muan is the high priest of my people. Next to my father, he is the greatest authority in our clan. Of course, he must peer into the future and see that you are worthy to succeed my father."

"Succeed?"

"Yes. My father is getting tall in years. He cannot rule forever. He has no male heir, nor any grandchildren. You, as an ordained son of Kukulcan, must take his place."

DOC SAVAGE stopped in his tracks, and pulled Monja to a halt.

"Are you saying that by marrying you I am obliged to become ruler of the Valley of the Vanished?" he demanded tightly.

"Of course. How could it be otherwise?"

Doc Savage's golden eyes took on a strange frosty light.

"My intention is to take you with me to New York City after we are wed," he stated firmly.

Monja frowned. Her dark eyebrows knitted together, creating a notch. Long lashes made thin, delicate cobwebs over her eyes.

"I could never leave the valley," she returned firmly. "For I am the last member of my family to carry the blood of my royal ancestors in my veins. My forebears of ancient lost Calantis. Now that I know my true heritage, it is more important than ever that I bear children."

Shock at her direct words caused Doc Savage's firm lips to part. Just what would have issued forth was never clear. That same shock froze his vocal cords. A pair of odd musical notes did emerge, but they died aborning, as if too weak to propogate.

Seeing the stark look on his metallic features, the princess continued. "Once we are wed, you must remain in the Valley of the Vanished as its honored co-ruler. You will not be a king, because you are not of our blood. I will be Queen Monja. You will be my consort. That is the Mayan way." Her tone was firm, unyielding.

There came a kind of roaring in Doc Savage's ears. It sounded distant. Through this inner turmoil, Monja's words penetrated. Doc could hear the pounding of his own heart, and the pulse of blood rushing to his brain. He had never had such an experience before. This must be some kind of physiological reaction to sudden shock, he realized.

"But I have no intention of remaining in the Valley of the Vanished indefinitely," he told her firmly. "My work in the outside world is too important to abandon."

Monja's face and voice became stern. "Of course, I know all of your work, but it is dangerous work. Too dangerous for the consort of a Mayan queen. Too dangerous for the father of the next king of the Valley of the Vanished, for I intend to produce a son, if not many sons."

Her tone of voice, so soft and warm before, was now insistent, noticeably flinty.

Doc Savage felt as if the earth under his feet had stopped turning. Every word he heard distinctly, but his brain refused to accept them.

He struggled to formulate some sort of response. But words failed him. Hot emotion was a flame that consumed both brain and body as if he were a rigid bundle of sticks that had been set afire.

Seeing his confusion, Princess Monja touched one bronze cheek with tender fingers. Inadvertently, a long nail remindful of a cat's claw scratched him slightly.

Doc suddenly remembered Pat's admonition that women could be she-tigers. Here was proof of the truth of that insight. Monja suddenly reminded him of a mother jaguar protecting her cubs, who were yet unborn.

"Your father has commanded you to settle down," she continued softly. "Do you think he meant for you to take terrible risks after you did so? Do you think he would want your wife and offspring to be in peril from enemies?"

"My father said nothing like that in his letter," countered Doc. "I have always assumed he expected me to carry on his humanitarian work until the day I either died or was unable to continue."

Monja's tone hardened. "That would be foolish, and dangerous. You are still strong and brave, but time is not your friend. It is truly the enemy of all of us. Each sunrise bequeaths us another day of life, but every sunset steals that day forever. Our days are finite. We must make all we can of those hours that are left to us—*both* of us. For your life is no longer your own… it belongs to the Valley of the Vanished."

Doc's confusion was unaffected by these words.

Finally, he blurted out, "The chief reason I never married was due to the danger my work created."

Monja smiled. "With your own words, you have rendered my argument sound. If we are to marry, you cannot continue to be Doc Savage."

"My father expressly requested that I train my son to follow in our footsteps," protested Doc.

Monja shook her head vehemently.

"You cannot train your firstborn to do any such thing! Perhaps your second son will follow in the footsteps of your father and yourself. We will discuss that at the proper time. But you have done enough good in the world. Now it is time to live a life of normalcy and family relations."

Doc said nothing. His mouth was dry.

Monja smiled thinly. "Your silence tells me that you see the wisdom of my words."

Doc Savage did not contradict his bride-to-be. Instead, he took her by the hand and led her through a riotous garden where the roosting owl followed them with wide eyes, his tufted head swiveling uncannily.

Then the bronze man said something peculiar.

"We will see what Chilam Muan has to say about this."

Monja looked up at him questioningly. Perfect lips opened, and on the tip of her tongue hung a question. It did not escape her mouth.

In the near distance there came another moan. It became the throaty thunder of an approaching aircraft. The sound magnified with each passing second.

Abruptly, twin beams of light were reeling about the sky, and the sound of airplane motors grew increasingly loud.

"What is that?" Monja asked anxiously.

"My men have arrived," said Doc. "They are landing."

Squeezing her hand firmly, he picked up his pace and they rushed toward the Valley of the Vanished.

Chapter XVII

THE DILEMMA'S HORNS

THE LITTLE MAYAN city—it was more of a stone village really—had been sound asleep.

The rising thunder of the arriving aircraft brought the inhabitants scurrying out into the night. A trickle of sleepy humanity seeped in the direction of the narrow lake, growing into a colorful, trudging river.

Perhaps due to the complicated nature of Mayan attire, Pat Savage was the first to arrive at the water's edge, fully dressed. She had her six-gun in hand in the event another boa constrictor lurked hungrily amid the ferns and cattails.

The amphibian plane hit the water, bounced briefly, and the pilot chopped power while throwing it about before he could careen onto the beach.

From the reckless landing, Pat easily deduced the identity of the pilot.

"Monk Mayfair, or I am a wee pixie," she murmured.

The plane soon beached itself. Visible through the cockpit windscreen, Pat spied hairy Monk shutting down the engines.

The cabin door opened and Doc's men began climbing out.

Ham Brooks was the first. He placed his Borsalino hat correctly on his head and gave his black cane a jaunty twirl, smiling appreciatively in Pat's direction.

"Where is Doc?" he asked.

"Let's wait 'til the others disembark, then I'll give it to you all at once."

Ham frowned. "Is it that bad?"

"That depends on whether or not you are wading ashore or standing on solid ground when you swoon at the news."

Renny unfolded his awkward bulk from the cabin doorway and demanded, "We're not exactly the fainting types, Pat, and you know it."

"Nevertheless, I would suggest that you boys find yourselves a nice soft patch of grass before you lend an ear."

The others came clambering out, Monk last. His grin when he saw Pat Savage was almost as wide as the amphibian plane's wingspan.

"Made it!" he squeaked. "Wasn't sure we would."

"Are you boys prepared to sit down hard?"

Monk puckered up his homely catcher's mitt of a visage. "What gives, Pat?"

"Doc and Princess Monja have really hit it off."

Assorted expressions crawled across the faces of the five men. They ranged from the expectant to the uncomfortable.

"Is it serious?" asked Johnny Littlejohn, blinking studiously.

Pat nodded forthrightly. "Dead serious. Doc asked the princess to marry him. Or maybe it was the other way around. Anyway, she said yes. Her father has consented. Now they're off in the forbidden valley getting the blessings of some high muckety-muck who dwells there."

It was comical the way that their five faces reacted.

Monk's cow-catcher jaw just dropped. Renny resembled a human steam shovel whose yawning bucket was about to gulp something tremendous. A midge wandered into his mouth and he had to pluck it off his tongue with fingers too big for the delicate task.

Long Tom reached up to rub his chin, but it wasn't where he expected it to be. He hadn't noticed that his mouth had fallen open and inadvertently touched his gleaming gold incisors.

Ham dropped his cane. He did not seem to notice, either. If

his right arm had also dropped off, it might have escaped his attention as well. He preserved a stony silence.

For his part, Johnny instantly coined a new pet phrase.

"Well, I'll be ultraflabbergasted!"

They stood around, looking dazed. Finally, Long Tom asked, "What do we do about this development?"

Pat smiled. "Pick up your crestfallen faces, boys. I trust you all brought formal clothes. Unless I miss my guess, the wedding isn't far off."

Monk frowned fiercely. "Doc wouldn't rush into matrimony like that."

"I would not," countered Pat, "be surprised if the nuptials don't commence tomorrow morning. And you can thank me for making it all work out. While you boys were dawdling along in the sky, I was busy playing matchmaker."

The eyes of Doc Savage's men grew hard and flinty.

Pat threw up her palms. "Don't glower at me like that. You all know what Clark Savage, Senior's letter said. It's not as if Doc had much choice in the matter. What's done is done. We're all going to have to learn to live with it."

Johnny rubbed his slightly lantern jaw. "I, for one, would like to hear this from Doc Savage's own lips before I completely believe it." The archaeologist's choice of simple, unadorned words told more about his state of mind than any flustery outburst he might make.

The Mayans started arriving at this point. King Chaac showed up with his colorful retinue, which included various nobles in their feathery finery.

The monarch of old Maya greeted them joyously. "I see that you have finally arrived. Have you yet heard the wonderful news?"

"I just filled them in," said Pat. "We'll have to give them some time to let it sink in. None of us ever thought we'd see this day."

King Chaac intoned, "Your leader should be returning with my daughter soon. We must await the verdict that they bring."

The group turned around and made a stately procession back to the village. By this time everyone had turned out of their houses and huts and were milling about.

They did not have very long to wait. Guards had been posted at the entrance to the inter-valley, which was actually a natural causeway between the inhabited zones. They blew conch-shell trumpets to signal the arrival of Doc Savage and Princess Monja.

Hearing the number of blasts, King Chaac's weathered features lit up joyously. He proclaimed, "Doc Savage and my daughter bring excellent news!"

Under his breath, Long Tom Roberts muttered to the others, "That's a matter of opinion, if you ask me."

Pat gave his thin shoulder a remonstrating squeeze. "Now don't be a spoilsport, Long Tom. You want Doc to be happy, don't you?"

Ham Brooks firmed his aristocratic chin. "We must congratulate him, of course. Congratulate them both. This is an amazing turn of events."

"Here come the happy couple now," said Pat, turning smartly.

WHEN Doc Savage and Princess Monja stepped into the pale blue light of the luminescent firefly lanterns, the bronze-haired girl's anticipatory smile all but collapsed.

Doc Savage's countenance was deadpan, as if graven in stone. Beside him Princess Monja was smiling. But the smile had a touch of concern at its edges. Neither one's eyes looked quite right.

"Oh," murmured Pat. "Maybe the news isn't as rosy as advance notices would have it."

Seeing her father, Princess Monja broke free of Doc Savage's hand clasp, and rushed up to him. Parent and daughter shared a warm embrace. The princess cried out, "Father, Lord Chi-Ahpuch has blessed our union."

"Congratulations, my daughter," said the king proudly. "And congratulations to you, Doc Savage. All that remains is to consult with Chilam Muan."

Doc shook hands with the king. Shaking hands was not a Mayan custom. The gesture was entirely unknown to the ancients. But old Chaac had learned the formality from Doc's father long ago.

There was nothing in Doc Savage's face to give away his inner thoughts. Given that it was normally impassive, almost like a metallic mask, only Pat Savage detected the faint indications that something was amiss. It was mostly in the animation of his remarkable eyes. The illusion of golden flakes perpetually in motion possessed an urgent, churning quality.

"Thank you," Doc told Chaac. "I would like to break the news to my men at this time."

Chaac inclined his feathered head. "Of course. Quarters have been prepared for all of you."

"I would also like to inspect the plane that gave them trouble."

The aged sovereign nodded.

Doc Savage went to his men and said crisply, "We will need to confer over this matter."

Ham's patrician face looked perplexed, "We understood from Pat that it has been settled. You and Princess Monja are to marry. Perhaps as early as tomorrow."

"I will explain the circumstances once we have privacy."

The bronze giant led his men down to the white sands of the little moon-burnished lake. To their surprise, he climbed on board the aircraft, turned, and waved them in.

The aircraft presented an awkward arrangement for a conference, but they selected seats and Doc, sitting in the pilot's bucket beside Pat, turned to face his men scattered about the cabin and said, "I have asked Princess Monja to be my wife, and she has agreed."

"Let me be the first to congratulate you, Doc," said Ham sincerely.

"Thank you," said Doc. "But matters are more complicated than they first appeared."

"How so?" wondered Johnny, fingering his monocle magnifier.

"I was completely sincere when I agreed to marry Monja. My feelings are genuine. As are hers for me."

Pat suddenly flared, "That sounds like a man getting cold feet. Already! Don't you dare stand up that poor woman. It would break her heart."

Confusion came over the faces of Doc Savage's aides. They had not recovered from the initial shock of the news. Now they were struggling to comprehend exactly what their bronze chief was driving at.

"I know," said Doc. "It would crush me, too. I'm afraid that in my rush to explore this possibility, I misunderstood the full nature of the commitment."

"Spoken like a true welsher," sneered Pat, folding her arms. "You'll back out of this over my dead body. It's for your own good, you know."

"Please hear me out," said Doc. The tone of his voice was brittle.

Doc struggled with his next words, swallowed painfully, then backed into another subject altogether. He told them of his brief sojourn in the Valley of Eternity, and the incredible revelation that the Clan of the Very Highest were descendants from the nobility of the lost island of Atlantis. Further, that they had offered the remaining store of yellow gold in return for any surviving Atlantean red gold that could be salvaged from the Caribbean.

"I'll be superamalgamated!" exploded Johnny exultantly. "This confirms the theory that I have long held that the examples of Egypto-Mayan architecture found on various Caribbean cays represent what is left of a vanished civilization of a high order.

"No doubt the Atlantean survivors scattered to other parts of the globe in ancient times. This would explain the inexplicable rise of the Egyptian culture, and the pyramid builders of the Americas, the Mayan and Toltec empires. Why, even the

Aztecs claimed to have migrated to the Valley of Mexico from a paradise they called Aztlan. To this very day, no one knows where it lay." He sounded positively giddy.

The others were unmoved. They had other concerns.

Pat blazed, "Don't you dare change the subject on us!"

Doc continued. "It was while walking back from the Valley of Eternity that I learned from Princess Monja the full extent of my obligations."

"Oh, don't tell me she wants to have a dozen children," Pat said quickly.

"Nothing like that," returned Doc. He was having trouble with his words again. "I imagine that I got so caught up in everything that I failed to foresee all the ramifications of marrying a princess."

"Ramifications is a strange word for impending matrimony," Pat sniffed. "But I suppose that I will allow it."

"During the walk back, we had a discussion. What you said about women sometimes being tigers contains more truth than I gave you credit for, Pat."

"Hah! Did she scratch you with her unsheathed claws?"

"Worse than that. She revealed to me something I failed to anticipate. Namely, that by marrying her, I will be obliged to remain in Hidalgo for the rest of my days as consort to her, the future Queen of the Valley of the Vanished."

"Holy–" Big-fisted Renny could not complete his pet ejaculation. He choked on the bovine syllable.

"Furthermore," Doc continued, "my firstborn son would also have to remain in this valley, eventually to ascend to the Mayan throne. There will be no one to carry on my father's important work, although Monja considered that a second-born son might be permitted to do so."

Doc let that sink in. He groped for further words.

"My father's directive to marry does not, in my opinion, release me from my obligation to continue doing my life's work until such a time that my own son can replace me. I am in a quandary. I do not know what to do. I have made a promise to marry Princess Monja. But that promise contradicts my solemn obligations to my father's memory. He did not envision such a conundrum."

"Conundrum," growled Monk Mayfair, "is no word for this mess. I would call it a howling calamity."

Renny grumbled, "Calamity? This is more like a catastrophe. You can't stop being Doc Savage. The world needs you. Now, more than ever."

Pat Savage had kept her tongue under control during this exchange, but now she spoke up. Her voice had lost its saucy cadences and was twisted with raw emotion.

"Oh, Doc! I'm so sorry. This is all my fault."

"No, Pat," the bronze man said firmly. "I walked into this situation with my eyes open, but I failed to think it through. I should have foreseen this. Monja made a comment yesterday that I now see in retrospect plainly indicated what she expected of me. I became so caught up in the rush of events that it simply did not register on my brain."

"Cupid got you good, huh?" Monk commiserated.

Doc nodded wordlessly.

The cabin fell silent. They all shifted about as the full weight of the problem settled in on their minds. The amphibian aircraft swung about on its anchor chain, creaking and groaning at stress points.

Doc Savage broke the interval of quiet finally. Again, he struggled to form the words.

"For the good of all, I must find a way to extricate myself from this rash commitment to marry."

"Good grief!" moaned Ham. "You realize that you risk alienating the good will of King Chaac and all of the Mayan people?"

"I understand that," said Doc. "But it cannot be helped. The two directives from my father are impossible to honor simultaneously. I cannot follow one without breaking the other."

Monk smacked one hairy fist into the opposite palm.

"You gotta figure a way out of this mess."

"Right," rumbled Renny. "But we can't exactly rev up the motors and flee into the night, can we?"

"That would be the coward's way out," agreed Doc. "But let me confess to you fellows that, for the first time in my life, I am tempted to take the easy way out."

"Have you any ideas?" asked Ham.

Doc shook his head. "I only learned of these details in the last hour. My brain has been in a whirl. I am having difficulty thinking clearly."

"Well, that could be true love talking," remarked Pat. "But on the other hand, it might be pure panic. Not that I blame you, cousin."

"There is one further formality," said Doc. "Before Princess Monja and I can become wed, the local seer must cast our fortune to assure King Chaac and his people that I will become a suitable royal spouse."

"Maybe we can bribe him to see otherwise," suggested Long Tom.

"Unlikely," said Doc. "And to be discovered doing such an underhanded thing would poison the mind of the Mayans against us."

"Then there's no good way out?" grunted Renny.

"Not unless Chilam Muan can truly perceive the future. For if he can, he might honestly blackball me. If I am not perceived as a suitable consort for Princess Monja, it is quite possible he would turn a thumb down on our union."

Ham mused, "That is not much of a hook to hang your future on, is it?"

"My future," admitted Doc Savage, "right now dangles on the thinnest of threads."

Pat Savage had been considering the problem, and now she spoke up.

"What's gotten into you, Doc? You sound like a defeated man."

Doc nodded. "I feel like one."

"The Doc Savage I know has a trick up every sleeve and in the hollow soles of his shoes. Heck, I've seen you pull a live rabbit out of your hat when you weren't even wearing a hat! There must be some face-saving way you can untie this Gordian version of a marital knot."

"I have yet to think of one," admitted Doc sheepishly.

"Well, you have all night in which to do so. Let me suggest that instead of sleeping, you stir your mighty brain cells until they hatch something clever."

"That is what I'll have to do," said Doc.

"And while you're at it," added Pat, "maybe I'll come up with something clever, too. I have a hunch it will take the both of us to get you back to New York with your scalp intact and your future marital prospects unsullied."

Doc Savage let out a long sigh of concern. He spoke the words his men never thought they would hear from his firm lips.

"I have a distinct feeling I will be happy that I brought you along on this trip, Pat. As a woman, and my cousin, you may be my best hope."

Renny finally ridded himself of his unspoken cud. "—Cow!" he boomed out. "Is the world upside down? Sounds that way to me!"

Johnny chimed in, saying, "An incontrovertible empirical verisimilitude."

Pat stared at the rail-thin archaeologist.

"You must be losing your way with words, Professor Littejohn. I completely comprehended that string of jocose jawbreakers."

Johnny blinked. He looked profoundly disappointed.

"Now you did it!" roared Renny. "The old fossil is speechless for once."

Chapter XVIII

CROSS CURRENTS

DOC SAVAGE DID not sleep that night. Not one wink. The bronze giant did not even try.

Instead, he slipped down to the moonlit lake where the two amphibian aircraft were moored amid the waving cattails and pale water lilies.

Climbing aboard the ship in which he had arrived, Doc dug out his apparatus for doing his daily exercises. For two hours he did these diligently, and they helped him fight off fatigue, as well as stimulating his stupefied brain.

At the end of the strenuous regimen, Doc was thinking clearly again. His flake-gold eyes had regained their customary steady animation.

He went to a rack in the back of the aircraft where spare equipment was secured. One of Monk Mayfair's portable chemical laboratories was stored there. He opened it up and removed a small bottle of cloudy liquid. There was also an atomizer, small enough to fit into the palm of one's hand.

Doc Savage filled the atomizer reservoir and pocketed it. Then he left the aircraft.

Instead of returning to his quarters, the metallic giant took a midnight constitutional around the Mayan village, moving with ghostly ease, not even disturbing the grasshoppers sleeping amid the ground cover of ferns and exotic foliage.

Dense leaf sage plants with tubular flowers of intense royal blue quivered in the soft night air. The plant's botanical name,

Salvia cacaliifolia, came to mind without prompting. So great was the bronze man's fund of knowledge that he could categorize and classify every plant in sight, if not the world.

He thought ruefully that the experts who had drilled such exotic knowledge into him should have devoted a measure of preparation for life to the understanding of the fair sex and its unfathomable ways. Too late for that now, Doc thought ruefully....

A howler monkey let out a trailing call, and he froze for a moment. Doc listened, detected no stirrings among the sleeping occupants of the village, who were no doubt accustomed to the occasional interruption of slumber by the howlers' weird cry.

He moved about seemingly at random, but in fact Doc had a destination in mind.

He soon came to a hut, set off from the main habitations. The hut was rather crude, and was thatched with coconut palm fronds. There was no door, only a woven mat covering. With extreme caution and uncanny stealth, he slipped up to the mat and eased it aside.

From a pocket, he took one of the thin-walled glass gas bombs that he usually carried with him, removing the fragile object from its protective case. Holding his breath, he tossed it through the open entry. It broke with a mushy crystalline shattering.

There was a stirring within, accompanied by a soft questioning grunt, but it soon subsided.

When Doc Savage was certain that the volatile anesthetic gas had dissipated, he resumed breathing and crept into the rude hut of tree bark plastered over supporting sticks.

The bronze man was inside for only a fraction of a minute. When he emerged, his flake-gold eyes glinted with a slightly crafty gleam.

Drifting back to his own sleeping quarters, Doc spied a slim form creeping about. He slipped up to it, and one bronze hand seized the figure's forearm.

A feminine gasp sounded.

"What are you doing out at this time of night, Pat?" he asked quietly.

Pat Savage quickly regained her composure. "Well, it's a good thing you spoke up. I almost gave you a Ju-Jitsu throw that would have landed you in the next valley."

"Doubtful. I taught you everything you know about Ju-Jitsu."

"And I might ask the same question of you," challenged Pat.

"I couldn't sleep," Doc said honestly.

"Same here."

The two cousins regarded one another warily. Suspicion came into Pat Savage's golden eyes.

"You wouldn't be up to some deviltry, would you?" she asked.

Doc said, "I was about to pose the same question to you."

"Perhaps," suggested Pat, "we should preserve silence on this awkward occasion and meekly go our separate ways."

Doc eyed her carefully. "You have all but admitted to being up to something, you know."

"My feminine intuition says that makes two of us," returned Pat lightly. "What do you say we both get some shuteye and see how we might surprise one another in the morning?"

Doc sighed. "I am too wrung out by worry to question you further. But I hope you have not been consulting with Princess Monja behind my back."

"Never fear," said Pat. "She has no idea what either one of us is up to—whatever that might or might not be."

"Good night, Pat."

"What's good about it?" murmured the golden-eyed girl.

They went their separate ways, disturbing no one in their passing.

SOON enough, dawn came, cracking the night open, and inciting an amazing chorus of jungle birds into tweeting, squawking and calling musically. The hum of insects loudened steadily, becoming a drone that was so pervasive it seemed part of the humidity of the morning.

Doc Savage and Princess Monja were kept separated while they went about their morning ministrations. All parties ate in privacy. An unusual quiet lay over the tranquil valley.

Doc and his aides had breakfast in a communal building dedicated to the god of maize. The food was tasty, if unusual. Roasted armadillo and a maize porridge constituted breakfast.

Midway between sunrise and high noon, King Chaac summoned everyone to the main plaza. A servant blew a conch shell for this purpose.

After the villagers were assembled, an unarmed guard came and escorted Doc Savage and his men, along with Pat Savage.

Doc surveyed the crowd. He noticed one person was absent.

There was no sign of Hun Balaam, the defeated suitor of Princess Monja.

A flicker of concern touched the bronze man's composed countenance, but he thrust the thought aside. No doubt the rejected man was still sulking. He had not been conspicuous since his ignominious defeat.

Princess Monja was made to kneel on one side of a great colorful blanket woven of cotton fibers. Doc was directed to sit opposite her. King Chaac sat on a portable platform throne nearby. He looked very pleased with the gathering. His pride in his people, in his daughter, and in the future that lay before them all, was unashamedly expressed in his placid features.

Chilam Muan padded up, looking like a caricature of a human owl. This was more of a suggestion than anything else. The H'men did not wear a giant owl costume of any kind. But his shaman's garb was carefully crafted to excite the imagination.

In contrast to the brilliant finery of the high-born Mayans, the old wizard wore dreary feathers. His cloak was a bedraggled blanket of owl tufts and other grayish-brownish plumage, many faded and unkempt. One obsidian eye was closed, permanently stitched shut, and the other stared wide-eyed. This, and the dry clicking profusion of olive-hued owl beaks and talons decorating the shaman's robes suggested that his harvest for talismans had gone awry more than once.

Anyone encountering him by moonlight would have thought Chilam Muan half-owl and half-man. He walked in a stooped manner as he approached the blanket and then he stood before it.

Chilam Muan lit two jade bowls. Bluish incense wafted forth. A bead of milky gum in each bowl produced the incense. It had a spicy scent. This was copal, a local tree resin. The Mayans called it *pom*.

Once the air was filled with the aromatic scent of copal, Chilam Muan began murmuring what might have been incantations. Doc did not completely follow them. They did not seem to be exactly words. More like cabalistic utterances.

During this procedure, he removed a stingray spine from under his cloak and used it to pierce one scarred earlobe. A stream of blood resulted. Removing the spine, he shook it, sprinkling blood droplets upon the white cotton. It made a wild spattering, like a star field of wet rubies.

Then he spoke clearly. "I will cast the stones that will foretell the future of this couple. By the images that appear within these stones will we know if this marriage is accepted by the gods."

Doc knew what came next. Chilam Muan carried a number of clear stones in a pouch of tapir hide. The owlish seer jammed a fist into that pouch now and pulled out a tight-clenched fist. Waving the fist about, he prepared to cast stones in the center of the cotton blanket.

By some means Doc Savage did not understand, Chilam Muan would divine from the way the stones scattered across the blood-spattered blanket certain portents of the future.

The sorcerer dropped the clear pebbles and they bounced and settled. Princess Monja watched them with a face that was self-consciously bland. It was not her place to expect a positive or negative outcome. What Chilam Muan would perceive through his divination was held to be sacred, and therefore not to be anticipated beforehand—or denied after the fact.

Whatever Chilam Muan perceived would determine the future of Doc Savage and Princess Monja.

The stones ceased bouncing, and Chilam Muan dropped to his bony knees, bringing his head down over the clear stones, which were infused with bright sunlight. His surviving eye must have been weak, because he had to bring his face down very far in order to look into their depths.

Doc Savage imagined that soothsayers who gazed into crystal balls did much the same thing.

A sharp hissing came from Chilam Muan's withered lips.

He looked deep into the stones, staring eye going from one to the other and back again as he sought to discern the future.

The H'men seemed to struggle with his oracular divination.

Finally, he jerked his head back, looked to old Chaac and then to Princess Monja. "I can see nothing! The future is cloudy! It is not clear, nor is it dark. It is neither of those things. It is obscured, as if the gods are undecided."

Golden fingers leapt to Monja's parted lips, and she stifled a cry of disappointment. Her eyes went to Doc Savage's face. They were imploring. The bronze man kept his composure. It was unreadable, that expression.

King Chaac came off his throne. "Look again. The stones never lie. Nor do they equivocate. The future must be seen, for good or for ill."

Chilam Muan thrust his head down and again attempted to peer into the clear stones, but it was evident that the stones were not clear. Princess Monja could see that from where she knelt. Doc Savage could see this also. There was no clarity to the stones. They were gray and cloudy.

Far in the rear of the assembled Mayan people, Doc's five aides were stifling relieved grins and surreptitiously shaking congratulatory hands. These suspicious activities went unnoticed by all.

Somewhere in the crowd came a stirring, followed by a moving commotion.

Someone was pushing his way through, toward the center of the crowded plaza.

Heads turned. Mayans got out of the way. Those who did not were pushed rudely aside. The person approaching would not be denied.

At last, the determined one broke into the open. A strange wail came over the crowd.

For the man was no less than the stocky Mayan warrior, Hun Balaam. He was garbed for war. His face was painted red and black, his fingertips dyed the scarlet of a macaw's wing. Loose jaguar-claws clicked at his wrists and ankles, held in place by silver wire. Around his waist was wound the broad girdle whose ends made aprons fore and aft, which is called an *maxtli*. His was fashioned from the pelt of a tiger-striped ocelot. A yoke of hammered and shaped copper covered his bare shoulders.

In one hand he carried a Mayan sword. In the other, a hand-crafted shield fashioned from a large turtle shell. He swept both arms up into the air and proclaimed, "I, Hun Balaam, do once again challenge Doc Savage for the hand of Princess Monja! The stones have deemed him unworthy. The gods do not lie. They are withholding judgment until he and I settle this matter once and for all."

Both Doc Savage and Princess Monja shot to their feet.

Not far behind them, Pat Savage murmured under her breath, "Hallelujah! The prodigal rival returns...."

"Hun!" scolded the princess. "This matter has already been settled by combat. Go back to your hut. You do not belong here."

Hun Balaam turned to the princess and in a voice thick with trembling emotion, said, "Since we were children I have loved you. I have worshipped you from the depths of my soul. Patiently, I have waited for you to recognize my worthiness. You have not. Yet the gods who dwell both above and below us have given me another chance. I claim the opportunity to show my worthiness to all."

His chest heaving, he pointed his sword in the direction of the metallic giant.

"*Ma,*" said Doc, using the Mayan word for no. "I do not wish to fight you, Hun Balaam. For I bear no animosity toward you."

King Chaac lifted his voice. "Silence, all!" A moment passed. A wave of emotions paraded across his aged features. Into his wise old eyes came a stab of pain. It was evident to all that the sovereign ruler of this hidden kingdom of the Maya was struggling with a difficult decision.

Then, in a tone that wavered between grief and pride for his subjects, he proclaimed, "If the gods are withholding judgment, that could only mean that the matter must be settled otherwise. I give Hun Balaam leave to battle for my daughter's hand. The winner of the trial will prevail in this matter. And, if the gods are just, the victor will one day sit beside my daughter—or upon my throne."

Now Monja shot an angry yet beseeching glance in the direction of her father. One hand seized the rare white orchid she still wore entwined in her long ebony hair.

"I love Doc Savage. No other. Have I no say in this matter?"

"The gods decree otherwise," spoke Chaac, reclaiming his throne. His face was resolute. At a signal, an obsidian-toothed sword and turtle-shell shield was brought to Doc Savage, who took them.

The bronze giant stood holding the weapons, not quite sure what to do with them.

The sword was a cross between a paddle and a tennis racket. The paddle portion was rectangular and carved with images, one of which Doc recognized as Yum Cimil, the god of the Mayan underworld. The edges of this flat length of mahogany were studded with black fangs of obsidian inset into the three open sides. These vicious teeth could cleave through flesh, and break bone when struck with sufficient force.

This is what the Mayans employed as a sword in ancient days. Some cultures called them a *macana*, but the Mayans used the word *kosmacack*. They were nothing to fool with.

The bronze man was not pleased with the choice of weapons. It would be difficult to defeat an opponent without doing considerable, not to mention permanent, damage.

Two servants brought up a heavy copper gorget and set it atop Doc's shoulders. It had been constructed to conform to the typical Mayan male physique, and was therefore exceedingly tight. In addition to protecting the wearer's shoulders, an ornate bar ran horizontally behind the neck, its jutting ends designed to catch the opponent's blade and thwart attempts to sever the exposed portion of the vulnerable neck.

Seeing that she would not prevail with her father, Princess Monja turned her hot gaze to Doc Savage. Her chin lifted, soft face firming up resolutely. She plucked the white orchid from her head, holding it up for all to see.

"In that case, my future husband must once more win my hand. And I have no doubt that Clark Savage will do so."

Pat Savage drifted up and whispered, "Now's your chance, Sir Clark."

"To accomplish what?"

"To prove your unworthiness, you towering oaf."

"How?"

"Oh-thray the ight-fay."

"Eh?"

"Let the better man, by which I mean the most suitable suitor, prevail. Avvy-say?"

"Oh," said Doc, understanding at last.

Bronze jaw squaring, he started forward.

Chapter XIX

THE BETTER MAN

THE DUEL PROVED to be short, brutal, but decisive.
Doc Savage and his Mayan challenger were escorted back to the stone ball court, and the villagers gathered around to watch.

Once they squared off, Hun Balaam gave a wild yell and charged.

Doc detected the subtle muscle movements that presaged the lunge. His lifted turtle-shell shield intercepted the blow, yet he was forcibly driven back half a pace.

The bronze giant was proficient in many weapons. He could wield a rapier or sabre with equal skill, and even knew how to manage a broadsword. But his experience with the *kosmacack* was naturally limited. Doc had observed Mayan men handle the vicious weapon during previous visits to the Valley of the Vanished. But he had never engaged in combat.

This gave Hun Balaam a distinct edge, despite the bronze giant's obvious advantage in sheer strength and reach.

Doc feinted, and slashed off a bit of decoration from Hun Balaam's costume. A jade jaguar-eye ornament clattered to the flagstones.

Seeing the speed and skill of his opponent, Hun Balaam became enraged. Venting another wild yell, he brought the toothy weapon slicing upward, then down in a crazed attempt to rcmovc Doc Savage's left arm at the elbow.

The weapon could do that. Doc had no doubt of it.

This time the bronze man intercepted the primitive blade with his own. The two weapons tangled up, got caught on one another's projecting teeth. While they struggled to disengage, Hun Balaam attempted to slam the side of Doc's head with his turtle-shell shield.

Driven by the ferocity of his hard muscles, the Mayan warrior succeeded. The hard carapace, rebounding off Doc's left temple, drew blood.

Doc returned the favor and smashed him back.

This time it was Hun Balaam who was forced backward. Their weapons disengaged, somewhat the worse for wear. Each one resembled a broken saw with missing teeth.

The watching Mayans were strangely silent. Almost to a single one, they worshipped Doc Savage as a great benefactor—an important person in the outer world who kept the valley from being discovered and pillaged by outsiders.

But Hun Balaam had been one of their own from infancy, being born into the village and growing up to be a sturdy specimen of Mayan manhood. He was of their blood. He shared their beliefs. Hence, they did not take sides. They only watched, their faces stiff and stolid.

Stepping up to one another, the two men resumed their slashing, battering combat.

Hun Balaam was good. He was no doubt an expert by Mayan standards. Having attempted a ferocious frontal assault, he now relied on quickness and skill. The fierceness of his emotion-reddened face turned to stone. He was no longer wrought up. A determined spirit possessed him now.

His descending blade scraped the copper yoke protecting the bronze giant's shoulders and neck, failing to dent it.

Hun Balaam's slashing lunge suddenly changed direction and Doc Savage's right sleeve was all but ripped away. The bronze man glanced down as he shifted to one side. No blood. This time. But that was sheer luck and not skill.

Doc's turtle shell caught the next sweeping blow, and the one after that. Obsidian thorns broke and flew off Hun's disintegrating sword.

Then the broken blade performed a dazzling dance in the Mayan's gripping fist. With a ripping sound, half of Doc's shirt was torn away. This time there was a gash that leaked gore.

A barking laugh came from Hun Balaam's confident lips.

"You are strong, eagle-eyes. But you are clumsy with a *kosmacack*."

"I do not wish to harm you, Hun Balaam."

"Do you yield?"

"No," returned the bronze man. And his own blade swept up and around, knocking the shield out of his foe's hands. It banged away, skidding noisily across the courtyard flagstones.

Now the warrior's rage returned.

LIFTING the weapon above his head with both hands, he charged like an enraged bull, with a clear intention of bisecting the bronze man's head.

Doc squatted down suddenly, bringing his own shield above his head protectively.

The terrible fanged sword came whistling down, splitting the shield, and becoming lodged in it.

The force of the blow was powerful. And Doc's defensive position weak. Yet he had set his leg muscles to absorb the impact. The bronze giant should have withstood it.

To the astonishment of all, the bronze man collapsed upon the flagstones. He was not out. He appeared dazed. In falling, he had thrown out his arms, and his shield went flying. With it went Hun Balaam's *kosmacack*. It was out of the fight.

Finding himself without a weapon, Hun Balaam bent down and tore Doc Savage's blade from his metallic fingers. He stepped back, gripping the weapon in his right hand, and his eyes were brimming with hot tears.

At the edge of the crowd, Monk Mayfair yelled, "Doc! Get up, brain him!"

"Sock him silly," added Renny.

To everyone's surprise, Pat Savage called, "This would be a swell time to urrender-say!"

Long Tom grated, "Whose side are you on, anyway?"

Pat threw up her hands in helpless confusion. But her golden eyes were brimming with apprehension.

Beside him, Ham Brooks clutched his sword cane, abruptly removed the blade-concealing barrel. He was about to toss the weapon to his bronze chief when Hun Balaam turned to face Princess Monja and King Chaac.

"I cannot slay this man," he cried out in an anguished voice. "But I refuse to lose the woman I have loved almost all of my days. What am I to do?"

The look that came over King Chaac's face was one of pride. He raised his hand and said, "Lay down your weapon, my warrior. You have won this battle. And if my daughter gives her assent, you have earned also her hand in marriage."

All eyes turned to Princess Monja. She was quaking with conflicting feelings. Her dark eyes went from the powerful figure of Hun Balaam, to the prostrate form of Doc Savage. She made fists before her heaving breast. They shook with powerful emotion. It was almost as if she were willing the bronze giant to climb to his feet and retake the advantage.

Instead, Doc Savage painfully gathered himself, lifted his head, and said words no one had ever thought they would hear.

"I yield to your superior skill, Hun Balaam. You are evidently the better man."

A throaty roar welled up from the crowd. Monk and the others groaned, yet looked visibly relieved.

Under the cheering of the Maya people, Pat Savage uncrossed the first two fingers of both hands and whispered a single word. "Hallelujah!"

For her part, Princess Monja appeared stunned. Disbelief made her eyes retreat into their sockets. She wavered on her feet. Successive waves of emotion crossed her rounded features, darkening and paling the gold of her complexion in alternation.

She stared down at Doc Savage, evidently helpless. Her gaze went to Hun Balaam, who looked at her with beseeching eyes. Then she glanced toward her father standing beside her.

Old King Chaac laid a firm hand on one trembling shoulder and whispered, "Go to the man you love. The one who truly loves you in return."

Princess Monja shook off her emotions and gathered up her vibrant skirts. She rushed into the courtyard, looked down upon Doc Savage and dropped something, whispering, "I am very sorry. And deeply disappointed."

Then she threw herself unreservedly into Hun Balaam's waiting arms, who gathered her up, lifting his emotion-twisted face skyward in thanks to the ancient gods who had answered his prayers. Tears of joy streamed from his squinting eyes.

The cheer that went up from the Mayan throng shook the myriad trees of the Valley of the Vanished. Coconut palms, chechem and gumbo-limbo trees, as well as others seemed in sympathy with their excitement. But a warm breeze might also explain their animation.

Only then did Doc Savage examine his wounds, and discover the white orchid that lay at his feet. He stood up slowly, ridges of sinew standing out on the backs of his bronze hands.

Doc strode up to the couple. "I wish you both the very best in life."

The bronze man put out a hard hand that felt like warm iron when Hun Balaam took it. Their handshake was brief, and awkward.

Doc Savage turned and walked away toward his quarters, his expression as fixed and metallic as the hammered copper sheathing his broad shoulders.

Chapter XX

THE BEST MAN

DOC SAVAGE WAS already binding his wounds when his men caught up with him in his private quarters.

Concern was written upon all of their faces; relief, as well.

Ham voiced their feelings. "Matters worked out for the best, don't you think?"

"They usually do," said the bronze man in a subdued voice. He was wrapping a bandage around his left bicep. The wound was not as deep as the flow of crimson would have suggested.

"I can't believe he beat you, Doc," muttered Monk.

The bronze giant pointed to the copper gorget lying on the stone floor. "I was somewhat handicapped by that protective device. It did not properly fit, preventing me from swinging or lifting my arms freely."

Renny regarded the discarded yoke, grunting, "Kinda looked to me like you weren't half trying."

"Perish the thought," Pat cracked.

"Furthermore," continued Doc, "Hun Balaam has practiced with the Mayan sword his entire life. I have scarcely ever wielded the weapon. It was simply a matter of superior skill and long practice."

"And good judgment," said Pat archly.

Doc Savage looked to his cousin. "You put Hun up to that challenge, didn't you, Pat?"

The tawny girl shrugged negligently. "I knew a smidgen of Mayan, and he understood just enough English for me to put it over," she admitted. "Hun was reluctant at first, because he didn't think he could beat you. But I egged him on. He took the worm like the hungry fish that he was."

The others looked to Pat Savage in bewilderment.

Renny rumbled, "You could've gotten Doc killed, you know."

"Not a chance! I knew what I was doing."

"For a change," said Long Tom sourly.

"Show some respect for my cleverness," retorted Pat. "I got Hun to throw down the gauntlet, and convinced Doc to throw the fight. I'd say that was a fair morning's scheming."

Johnny looked aghast. "Doc threw the fight?"

"I knew it!" boomed Renny.

"You'd be surprised at what deviltry Doc is capable of," said Pat. "Why, I wouldn't be surprised if he tinkered with the motor of that plane you flew down in, just to keep you boys from interfering with his romantic quest. Not that I am accusing anybody of anything, mind you."

Finishing his bandaging, Doc Savage stood up and said simply, "I did what I felt was right and best for all concerned. I have few regrets."

"But not *no* regrets," suggested Ham waspishly.

Doc nodded, eyes strangely somber. "I would rather not have initiated all this drama. But even there, perhaps it was the catalyst that enabled Monja and Hun Balaam to come together after all these years."

Ham suggested, "You will probably have to speak with the princess at some point. Without revealing the truth, of course."

"I am not looking forward to it," allowed Doc. "But in the meantime, I would like you all to do me a favor."

"What's that?" grunted Monk.

"Go about the valley, and gather six clear stones similar to the ones Chilam Muan used to cast his fortunes. Do not be obvious about it."

"Why?" wondered Ham.

"I will need to slip them into Chilam Muan's pouch before he attempts to cast the fortune of Monja and Hun Balaam. The ones presently in his pouch are clouded by a corrosive chemical."

Doc pulled the now-empty atomizer out of his pocket, and Pat Savage exploded, "Oh-ho, the truth will out! That's what you were doing sneaking around like a Comanche last night. You sabotaged that crank's magic stones."

"It was the only thing I could think to do. I hoped it would buy me time. I did not expect Hun's challenge. But it enabled me to bring matters to a successful conclusion without complicated subterfuge."

Pat Savage's grin was that of a satisfied cat sleeping next to an empty bottle of cream. She showered it over Doc's stupefied aides.

"I told you Cousin Clark was capable of just about anything."

Turning to Doc Savage, she crowed, "And after this little operation, don't you dare ever doubt that we make a great team!"

The bronze man's smile was slightly ironic.

"I do not know how I would have extricated myself from the situation without your clever meddling. Thank you, Pat."

"Meddling! That was sheer genius. I hereby petition you to formally induct me into your little band of unmerry men the minute we get back to New York City."

"We are not going back to New York City. We are heading to the Caribbean, where we will attempt to salvage the red gold of Atlantis. I promised Chi-Ahpuch that I would exchange it for the yellow gold still stored in the Clan of the Very Highest's treasure house."

Without further ado, Doc's men scattered and gathered up enough stones. Geologist Johnny Littlejohn selected the best of the lot and presented them to Doc.

BY AFTERNOON, King Chaac had called his subjects to the plaza and announced the formal engagement of his daughter with Hun Balaam.

The latter puffed out his chest and looked as though he had conquered the known world. Princess Monja smiled gamely. But in her eyes there were lingering doubts. Her fortunes had reversed themselves twice now in as many days.

Her liquid gaze went to Doc Savage often, then shifted away. Her expression was difficult to read. Disappointment was there. Other emotions, too.

Chilam Muan was preparing to cast his stones. He had set down his pouch in order to light the copal incense beads and pierce his other earlobe with his stingray spine. That made what Pat Savage had to do that much easier.

She had been entrusted with the clear stones and, while virtually all eyes were on the bride and groom to be, Monk and Ham got into a noisy and attention-stealing argument that subsided only after the sneaky deed was done. They shouted at one another in the Mayan tongue, the better to distract the crowd, who hung on every word.

While the attention of everyone was captured, Pat crept up, and swiftly exchanged the stones. Her furtive deception was not detected by anyone.

Returning to Doc Savage, she had in hand the cloudy stones and said, "You might want to bury this incriminating evidence somewhere."

Doc imparted, "Keep them as a souvenir."

"I'll put them in an honored place in my private museum dedicated to your misadventures," Pat said dryly. "Of which this may be the most notorious."

Ham interjected, "I have spoken to King Chaac. I told him about our wedding customs in the United States. Here, they do not have any such thing as a Best Man standing with the groom."

Pat scolded Doc with her golden eyes. "Don't tell me you offered to be Best Man!" she hissed.

Doc nodded. "It is up to Hun Balaam and Monja whether this will be permitted."

"I think you are fishing for trouble," warned Pat. "Perhaps it would have been better had we decamped in the middle of the night."

"I must see this affair through to its conclusion," stated Doc.

"You fail to grasp the ramifications, as you call them," returned Pat archly. "To Princess Monja, it would be like rubbing salt into a fresh wound."

Before the bronze man could respond, a cheer went up from the crowd. Doc listened. He translated the Mayan tongue for Pat, whose grasp was shaky at best.

"Chilam Muan has cast his stones. They foretell a bright future for Princess Monja and Hun Balaam. The matter is settled. The wedding is set for tomorrow!"

"These Mayans move fast, don't they?" squeaked Monk.

"This wedding can not happen soon enough for me," said Doc fervently.

Pat eyed her cousin skeptically.

"Don't think just because you wriggled off one hook, you've swum to safety. Your father's letter still stands."

"I know that, Pat. But my father stipulated no deadline. There will be ample time to conduct a careful search for an appropriate wife. I will not rush headlong into anything like this again."

"Finally learned your lesson about tigresses, did you?"

"And she-jaguars," said Doc without hesitation. "Thanks to you."

THAT night, Doc Savage made a point of seeking out Princess Monja.

She was walking alone by the narrow lake where the two amphibian planes waited to convey the bronze man and his associates home. The waning moon shed a clear light.

At first, the princess pretended not to notice the bronze giant, but Doc soon made that impossible. He cast a shadow that could not be ignored.

They spoke for a considerable period of time in low, hushed tones and the things that they said to each other would never be repeated to another human being.

THE NEXT morning the wedding of Princess Monja and Hun Balaam went off without a hitch. King Chaac had personally ventured into the Valley of Eternity to explain to Chi-Ahpuch the remarkable change of circumstances, slipping away in the dead of night and returning at dawn with the high-man's blessing.

The ceremony was simple, and strictly according to the Mayan tradition. With one exception. Pat Savage stood beside Princess Monja as Maid of Honor, while Doc Savage took the part of Best Man to Hun Balaam.

Looking like a cross between a dilapidated scarecrow and a molting owl, Chilam Muan officiated at the ceremony, which took place before an elaborate altar on which a burning taper was set at each corner, representing the four brotherly Bacabs, as well as the four cardinal points.

Flowers and feathers were everywhere, their colors incredible. Princess Monja wore a fresh white orchid in her hair, a gift from Doc Savage. But only they knew that.

Watching the ceremony conclude, Monk turned to Ham and remarked, "Can you beat it? Doc Savage as Best Man?"

"Hun Balaam," said Ham firmly, "may be the better man as far as Princess Monja is concerned, but Doc Savage is always the best man. He proved that beyond any doubt."

"Amen," said Johnny Littlejohn. "I mean, verily."

Chapter XXI

ON SATAN CAY

A FULL DAY later, the two amphibian planes were moored at a desolate cay in the Caribbean where the Antilles Current flows warmly before joining the Florida Current past the outer Bahamas to feed into the mighty Gulf Stream.

Only a few years back, this lonely spot had been thoroughly scoured by a hair-raisingly powerful hurricane. Yet it still stood, along with the jagged foundation of a primitive lighthouse that had been erected in the days before recorded history, only to be carried off by high winds in the present Twentieth Century.*

For this volcanic island had been an outpost of Atlantis during the antediluvian period, when the vanished continent—or whatever it was—stood above water.

The place was unbelievably black and devoid of vegetation. Formed from hardened lava rock, it had been thrust up from the aquamarine waters by a seaquake, early in the war. Beneath the debris-choked cellar hole lay a treasure chamber. The only way into it was by precarious steps winding down and along the wall of a man-made well that had no outer rail.

The chamber had flooded during the tempest, but the warm tropical water had congealed due to the action of a grotesque one-eyed crystalline idol which possessed the uncanny and unexplained power to radiate almost impossible cold. The frightening thing was larger than the statue of the sixteenth President seated inside the Lincoln Memorial in Washington.

---

* *The Secret of Satan's Spine*

554

Everything reposing in the chamber, including the red gold of lost Atlantis, had been permanently sealed in this immense plug of ice.

Chipping away at it had proven impossible. They had cleared the surface debris years ago, but the icy submarine waters had proven impenetrable. They had abandoned all salvage attempts once the war had broken out, for it was a task that required months of effort. Every time they made painstaking progress, additional water would pour in and freeze solid.

But this time they were attacking it with chemicals. Many years ago, Monk Mayfair had formulated a chemical solution capable of melting icebergs. They had used it during a submarine voyage to the North Pole early in their adventurous career. The stuff worked well enough, but it wasn't powerful enough to penetrate the thick ice in the underwater chamber.*

Doc had reformulated it, and the new version was making miraculous headway.

Monk was saying, "I still don't see how we're going to solve the problem of fresh water pouring in and freezing up all over again."

"I have a plan," said Doc.

The apish chemist scratched his head. "It must be a doozy. Because I can't figure it out."

"We will dynamite the idol. By shattering it and hauling up the individual fragments, each of which can be expected to radiate a weaker version of the freezing force, we should be able to retrieve the orichalcum."

Monk turned to Renny, who was standing nearby.

"That sounds like your department, big fists," he said.

"Stay clear when I drive down the plunger of the detonator, if you want to keep your head perched on your neck," warned Renny.

"Remind me to stuff cotton in my ears," squeaked Monk.

---

* *The Polar Treasure*

"Remind yourself," thumped Renny. "I'm no baby sitter."

IT WAS while they were hauling the one-eyed idol's horned head topside one morning that a boat drifted up, a stream of bubbles trailing behind it. A hearty female voice called out, "Ahoy the cay!"

Monk and Ham came up and spied a woman at the wheel. She was dressed like a conch—an inhabitant of the Bahamas. Her hair was windblown and her face glowed with healthy living.

Doc Savage was below when the boat arrived. He was attired in a rubberized diving suit and transparent lucite helmet that protected him from the cold radiations of the decapitated idol, and so failed to hear what transpired above.

The craft was a motor-sailer of Burma teakwood. It measured about forty-two feet long on the waterline. It was not under sail, and its motor impelled the shoal-craft carefully between the treacherous coral blackheads surrounding the forbidding cay, shying from the sudsy spots marking each submerged fang. Satan's Spine was the name given to the hidden reef.

The pair stared in the direction of the sailboat, shaded eyes fixed on the woman. She seemed to be the only soul aboard.

Monk squinted his tiny eyes. He was observing her shape and the expression on his homely features was approving.

She was a vision in dungaree pants with the legs cut off, and an ivory blouse with deep rust accessories. Brown as a nut, she was perhaps five feet-ten, and so well-made that it was startling. Her eyes rivaled the blue of the Caribbean Sea. Auburn was the hue of her boyishly short hair, although a better descriptive might be sorrel. The waves, moving at her back and chipped with sunlight, were all rippling gold. She looked lovely, exquisite, and carefree against that dancing background.

Ham wrinkled his sharp nose. "I say," he remarked, "that young woman looks familiar."

The familiarity was swiftly returned. "Aren't you two Monk and Ham?" the woman called over in a surprisingly deep voice.

"That's us," Monk yelled back. "Who are you?"

"Your memory is shorter than you are," the woman hurled back. "It hasn't been that long!"

Monk recognized the voice before he did the form. That was unusual in and of itself.

"Holy Hannah!" he howled. "Is that you?"

"Not much holy about me," laughed the woman, "but you got the name right." She reversed the motor, then cut it. The craft lost headway and slid into a glide like a white duck, easing through baby blue shoal water tinted with jonquil.

Digging out a kedge anchor, she tossed it overboard to create a happy splash. It caught immediately on the submerged coral outcroppings of the shallow seabed.

Hearing all the commotion, Pat Savage climbed out of the ruin to survey the situation.

"Visitors?"

"That," grinned Monk, "is our old friend Hannah."

"Willia Hannah, to be precise," corrected Ham.

Pat shaded her tawny eyes with two well-tanned hands. "Should I know her?"

Monk said, "That's the babe we tangled with over on Happy Bones Island back during the war. Hannah is the daughter of a long line of pirates." *

"She's quite the swashbuckler," said Ham, admiration flavoring his cultured voice.

"Is she now?" mused Pat, a golden glint coming into her eyes.

Calling over to the ship, she said, "Why don't you step off and stay a spell? Doc Savage is here. He told me all about you."

Hannah blinked. "Doc Savage did?"

"Absolutely," fibbed Pat through a dazzling smile. "You made

---

* *Mystery on Happy Bones*

quite an impression on him. Why don't you two get reac-
quainted? I'm sure Doc will be thrilled to see you again."

Monk studied Willia Hannah's expression. He knew something about women, and he knew that the way her expression
had changed at mention of Doc Savage meant something.

Monk and Ham eyed the bronze-haired girl skeptically.

"Don't you ever learn?" growled Monk.

Pat's mischievous smile crinkled the corners of her laughing
eyes. "I merely intend to cross two live wires together. Whether
sparks result will depend on how much juice said wires contain."

Then she rushed over to take hold of the line the beautiful
descendent of pirates threw her way.

Turning to Ham Brooks, Monk grunted, "Match you for the
duty."

"Of rescuing Doc Savage from this latest female danger?"

Digging out a half-dollar coin, the homely chemist smacked
his lips at the fetching form of Willia Hannah as she climbed
down the accommodation ladder. "She'll do for my money. She
sure will. Yeah, man!"

"I seem to recall that you distracted her that last time," the
dapper lawyer drawled as he adjusted his tie. "Pocket your money.
I believe my turn has come. Now step aside, you hairy monstros-
ity."

About the Author
LESTER DENT

ALTHOUGH HE WAS born and died in La Plata, Missouri, Lester Dent was and considered himself first and foremost a Westerner. He spent most of his formative years in Oklahoma and Wyoming.

"My dad was a chronic pioneer," Lester explained. "Soon after I was born, he dashed off to Oklahoma where he bought a farm. He sold this, though a year before they hit oil on it, and went to Wyoming. He deserted Wyoming, leaving all the other ranchers there to get rich and came back to La Plata."

During his first Oklahoma period, the future creator of Doc Savage lived in numerous localities in and around Broken Arrow, starting at age four. After a cyclone demolished their home circa 1907, the family abandoned ranching to return to Missouri briefly before resettling in Wyoming. That was the year Oklahoma achieved statehood.

Lester actually traveled with his extended family by covered wagon across the Big Powder River on their way to Wyoming, bringing in a trail-herd of cattle. Indians and horse thieves had to be discouraged by rifle fire.

The Dent family lived for a brief time in Alliance and Potter, Nebraska before settling near Gillette, Wyoming. This was back in 1908–09. The infamous Johnson County cattle wars were still fresh in memory. When the area became too settled for Bernard Dent, he moved, eking out a hardscrabble existence on a ramshackle ranch near Pumpkin Buttes, the 4-J spread. Young Lester called the Powder River Basin and the Belle Fourche badlands his "stomping ground," and lived within riding distance of Devils Tower. He was fascinated by the dinosaur bones and petrified shellfish that could be found at its base—a residue of the antediluvian era when the area was covered by an inland sea.

During his youth, Lester apprenticed as a horse wrangler, cowboy and sheepherder. None of it appealed to him.

"Punch cows?" he once joked. "Of course, I punched cows. All up and down the Wyoming slopes I punched cows. Every time they punched me, I punched them back."

When Lester became a teenager, the family once again returned to La Plata, Missouri, so he could attend high school. By 1925, now a married man, Dent took up residence in Tulsa, Oklahoma, where he first broke into print in 1929. Until he relocated to La Plata, circa 1939, Lester considered himself to be an Oklahoman by virtue of the fact that he had lived there longer than in any other state up until his arrival in New York City in 1931. His thick Okie accent was such that Missourians found his pronunciation sometimes difficult to understand.

Dent told many stories of living in the West as the son of pioneer parents. He got his first rifle at the age of eight, with which he shot squirrels.

"Did a lot of growing up in that Wyoming badlands country myself—learning about sheepherding and cowpunching, and on my back in a sheep wagon reading adventure yarns, quite a few of them in Street and Smith magazines that were coming out a long time before *Air-Trails*."

But Lester Dent did not enjoy his Wyoming years. He remembered it as a barren, lonely land, where playmates his own age were rare to nonexistent. When he began writing pulp

Western stories, he naturally used the state as a locale, but once he moved on to Doc Savage, he avoided Wyoming.

"Shucks!" he explained. "I was raised on a ranch! Now wouldn't I be crazy to go writing about something I knew all about? I never been north of southern Alaska, but I write wonderful stories about the North Pole. You're crazy if you think you're going to get me to write about Pumpkin Buttes, Wyoming. I've already seen Pumpkin Buttes...."

The 1941 Doc Savage adventure titled *The Green Eagle* was a rare exception. Late in life, Lester started cracking the slick magazine market. Westerns were booming in movies and in the new medium of television. Ironically, Dent sold to the prestigious *Collier's* and *The Saturday Evening Post* by returning to Westerns.

In the last year of his life, Lester Dent had the opportunity to script a pilot for a proposed Doc Savage TV show. Only a few handwritten fragments survive of this effort. The unfinished story opens in the Bighorn Mountains of Wyoming....

About the Author
WILL MURRAY

WILL MURRAY GREW up during the era when Westerns dominated television. This was an amazing time in which approximately one third of primetime network programming consisted of cowboys and lawmen. Of all the myriad shows he watched as a young boy, Murray's favorite Western was *The Rifleman*, starring Chuck Connors. The same Chuck Connors who a few years later would be selected to play Doc Savage in a series of pictures that unfortunately never went to camera. But in Murray's mind, Connors embodied the Man of Bronze as no other actor ever could.

All of this electronic horseplay branded him deeply. Although he never wrote much in the way of frontier fiction, Murray has turned his hand to the Western short story from time to time. One tale appeared in *Spicy Western Stories* and the other in *Weird Trails*. Both were horror yarns. A third Will Murray Western starred an ancestor of Lee Falk's Phantom. One of his proudest achievements was the well-received history of the pulp Western magazine, *Wordslingers: An Epitaph for the Western*, published by Altus Press in 2013.

With his 21st Doc Savage novel, written in posthumous collaboration with authentic Westerner Lester Dent, Will Murray has finally written a Western novel. That it's a science-fiction Western is beside the point. *Mr. Calamity* belongs to the Doc Savage tradition inaugurated with the 1933 novel, *The Red Skull,* which was set in Arizona. This was a setting Lester Dent periodically revisited. Only the states changed.

Murray has never been anywhere near Wyoming, and frankly confesses that without Lester Dent's unpublished manuscripts, this adventure would not possess a credible Western flavor.

With this volume, Murray has tripled the number of Doc Savage novels he's written since the original seven penned for Bantam Books over 25 years ago. He never thought he would turn out so many adventures starring the Man of Bronze and his iron crew, so it is with enormous pride and satisfaction that Murray offers Doc Savage fans this latest work ascribed to the imaginary Kenneth Robeson. Growing up to become your favorite author is a miracle that happens to almost no one. But it happened to Will Murray.

About the Artist
JOE DeVITO

JOE DeVITO WAS born on March 16, 1957, in New York City. He graduated with honors from Parsons School of Design in 1981 and studied at the Art Students League in New York City.

Over the years, DeVito has painted many of the most recognizable Pop Culture and Pulp icons, including King Kong, Tarzan, Doc Savage, Superman, Batman, Wonder Woman, Spider-Man, *MAD* magazine's Alfred E. Neuman and various characters in World of Warcraft, with a decided emphasis dinosaurs, action-adventure, SF and Fantasy. He has illustrated hundreds of book and magazine covers, painted several notable posters and numerous trading cards for the major comic book and gaming houses, and created concept and character design for the film and television industries.

In 3-D, DeVito sculpted the official 100th Anniversary statue of *Tarzan of the Apes* for the Edgar Rice Burroughs Estate, *The Cooper Kong* for the Merian C. Cooper Estate, Superman, Wonder Woman and Batman for Chronicle Books' Masterpiece Editions, and several other notable characters.

An avid writer, Joe is also the co-author (with Brad Strickland) of two novels, which he illustrated as well. The first, based on Joe's original *Skull Island* prequel/sequel, was *KONG: King of*

Skull Island (DH Press), published in 2004. The second book, *Merian C. Cooper's KING KONG,* was published by St. Martin's Griffin in 2005. He has also contributed essays and articles to such collected works as *Kong Unbound: The Cultural Impact, Pop Mythos, and Scientific Plausibility of a Cinematic Legend* and "Do Android Artists Paint in Oils When They Dream?" in *Pixel or Paint: The Digital Divide in Illustration Art.*

The year 2018 will see the further exploration of DeVito's Kong prequel/sequel saga in the coming book, *King Kong of Skull Island,* which is due out in December of 2017. The property is also in full development as a TV series. DeVito continues painting covers for the Wild Adventures saga (written by Will Murray), featuring Doc Savage, Tarzan, The Shadow, Pat Savage and King Kong—including *King Kong vs. Tarzan,* the first-ever authorized meeting of these iconic characters. DeVito is also gradually developing the imagery for his newest creation, a faction world of truly epic proportions tentatively titled *The Primordials.*

Joe is the founder of DeVito ArtWorks, LLC, an artist-driven transmedia studio dedicated to the creation and development of multi-faceted properties including Skull Island, War Eagles and the Primordials. DeVito ArtWorks is exclusively represented by Festa Entertainment and Dimensional Branding Group.

Regarding *Mr. Calamity,* Joe writes:

We had a great deal of fun kicking this cover concept around. It was quite unusual in many ways. From the get-go it was decided that Doc needed to be seen floating in the air. I believe it's the first time I ever painted Doc that way. It might even be the first time Doc was *ever* seen floating in the air—not to mention upside down!

Interesting problems arise/things happen perception-wise when such an approach is taken. One of the first dilemmas I had to plan around was if I were to pose Doc upside down, visually his boots could have more prominence than his face.

This dynamic was exacerbated by the best shot we had from Jim Bama's archive of photographic negatives being a perspective pose. In it Doc's head became very small as it receded from the viewer, down into the image. To make matters even worse, I knew the book title would also prominently draw attention to the area of the boots at the top of the picture as well.

What to do in order to arrange a dramatic, eye-catching Doc cover? Normally, the least desired thing would be to draw visual attention to Doc's feet, away from his iconic ripped shirt, torso and head. I decided that the solution was not to fight the compositional prominence of the aforementioned problem elements head on. Instead, I would capitalize on them by turning their visual weight in my favor. This was done by designing the other floating elements in the painting—Pat Savage and a startled horse—to assist the eye in falling away from the more prominent elements at the top. This causes the quickly diminishing imagery to work in service of the drama, which in this case is not primarily Doc's tautly muscled torso and widow's peaked head, but a strong sense of vertigo. The impression this creates, especially while floating juxtaposed high above such an enormous and instantly recognizable landmark as Devils Tower, is palpable and hopefully will resonate in the mind of Docdom as intended: As both one of the more unusual, and unusually composed, Savage covers.

www.jdevito.com
www.kongskullisland.com
FB: Kong of Skull Island
FB: DeVito ArtWorks

About the Patron

NICK "COLORADO" CAIN

"SEEK DANGER AND Adventure Each New Day!" is the motto Nicholas Cain has tried to live by since volunteering for Vietnam in 1972—a mere four years after discovering his first Doc Savage novel. He recalls:

From about 1960—when I was just the tender age of six—until about 1966, we'd hike out several miles into the blue prairies within sight of Pike's Peak every weekend, pretend we were my childhood hero, Roy Chapman Andrews, exploring the Gobi Desert for dinosaur eggs. Then, with the surplus army backpacks my father had gotten us loaded down with geodes and feldspar and arrowheads—even bottles filled with giant tiger salamanders—we'd drag our exhausted bodies after a long, sun-baked, Indian Summer's afternoon back to my house on Pueblo's South Side, "Sunset Park" neighborhood, fill our bellies with water from the garden hose until they were about to burst, and create new displays for the museum we'd named after famed paleontologist Edward Drinker Cope. My dream at that time was to someday visit the American Museum of Natural History and study at Columbia University—the most famous producer of paleo-scientists back then. Every time my friends and I explored the badlands of southern Colorado, searching for a T-Rex or Triceratops skull, but finding only invertebrate fossils and a few rare Jurassic Period sharks'

teeth, I was never disappointed. For despite aching calf muscles and sunburned shoulders, my vivid imagination told me there might—just might be a long, lost living Brontosaurus or Dimetrodon lurking around the next bend in the deep shale and sandstone canyons we spent hours exploring, armed only with pick axes, (for splitting slabs of grey shale), and plastic-handled "Indian Brave" knives (souvenirs of the Mesa Verde gift shop).

Then *Star Trek* came along in 1966 and everything changed. We all became "Original Trekkers," building and launching model rockets by day, rushing home to watch Captain Kirk and Mr. Spock explore "space, the final frontier…" by night.

And then it happened: on a muggy June afternoon in 1968, while browsing the book section of a local five-and-dime, the smoldering crimson-red cover of Doc Savage #14: *The Fantastic Island* jumped out at me. The two giant Komodo-like dragons the Man of Bronze was battling were not quite bonafide dinosaurs, but they would do! I was hooked, of course, devoured the crisp paperback in a couple evenings, and went on in search of additional installments in the adventure series. (Imagine my excitement when I came across the blue-toned *Land of Terror*, with our arch-enemy of evil confronting a Tyrannosaurus-rex while a sail-backed Dimetrodon looked on!)

Like any red-blooded, American teenager in the 1960s, I could not get enough of Doc Savage. To have to wait a month for each new Bantam paperback installment was sheer torture! My fossil museum and rocket collection fell by the wayside; my rock-hound friends were replaced by fans of Doc Savage who spent hot, summer days mowing their neighbors' lawns or delivering newspapers at pre-dawn so they could spend their evenings lining up Doc novels on second-hand bookcases newly-purchased with their hard-earned dimes and quarters.

Nineteen-sixty-eight and 1969 were turbulent years for our country in general and my extended family in particular: Vietnam reared its ugly head. I'd already taken an intense interest in law enforcement as a serious career target (after witnessing a very dramatic police chase on Easter Sunday, 1969), and after facing reality: there was no money for college, especially high-brow Columbia University).

As I progressed through high school and my interests shifted from long-dead fossils to frisky young cowgirls, I nonetheless remained faithful to building my Doc Savage library, exploring used book stores for my missing covers—even choosing dozens at a time from those tiny Bantam Book order forms at the rear of each copy. An all-seeing, strikingly-painted poster of "Doc Savage—Arch-Enemy of Evil" hung on my basement bedroom wall—right above a five-feet-long, "scale" blueprint of the star-ship—powered by a "perpetual motion" E.M.I.D. (Electro-Magnetic Ionic Device)—I'd designed.

In December 1972, I arrived in the City of Sorrows, the "Paris of the East," Saigon. Fresh from the MP Academy in Georgia, I stared out at the teeming metropolis of three million in awe. It was my first "big city" experience. We patrolled the concrete jungles in open-topped gun-jeeps with twirling red lights and "Military Police" emblazoned along the front, olive-drab wind-shield frame. We worked twelve hour shifts, six days a week, and as the battalion newbie, I was stuck on graveyard shift—which I loved. Saigon was under martial law and ringed by a constant circle of drifting security flares from dusk until dawn. Each night, the Viet Cong launched a solitary rocket into the heart of the city, and we raced toward the roar of explosions while terrified civilians fled in the opposite direction. From time to time, rooftop snipers would zero-in on the glowing white "MP" letters on our jet-black helmets. I rarely felt fear—ever–protected by my St. Michael's medal and the bronze "Doc Savage" lapel pin glued to the thick collar of my flak jacket.

I usually drove a buck sergeant around town on roving, city-wide patrol (he, coincidentally, hailed from my own hometown and lived down the block back in what every GI "in-country" referred to as "The World"). I visited the PX every week when the new shipment of books and newspapers arrived from state-side, and actually located two Doc Savage episodes—*The Metal Master* and *The Seven Agate Devils*—in this manner. (After devouring them during my off-duty hours, I would wrap each one in first-aid pouch plastic to protect them from the tropical humidity, and managed to get them back to my Rocky Mountain "fortress of solitude" after three years in Southeast Asia.)

Once, while on routine patrol, I came across a poster-sized, locally hand-painted (in bright glowing neon oils on black felt) portrait of Doc Savage in his classic *Man of Bronze* pose and snatched it up for less than 100 *piasters* (about five dollars; it remains on the wall of my private library to this day, framed in teakwood and under glass). Once, I sauntered into the Orderly Room at four in the morning in search of the "candy jar" that held each MP's daily mandatory dose of yellow anti-malaria pills and found the CQ, Desk Sergeant and Duty Lieutenant leaning back in swivel chairs, their jungle boots propped up on a bullet-riddled TV set that hadn't worked in years, all three absorbed in separate Doc Savage novels. I didn't have any of them yet, and offered half my private's pay, but none of my brother MPs would surrender their tattered paperback.

After the farce of a cease-fire in 1973, I eventually ended up in Thailand, a newly-promoted sergeant at the tender age of 19. Once known as the kingdom of Siam, this tropical paradise supposedly boasted "the most beautiful women in the world." I rounded off my tour-of-duty with six months in Korea—"Land of the Morning Calm"—where I left the Army's Military Police Corps in 1975 with an Honorable Discharge and a couple dozen more Doc Savage paperbacks in my olive-drab duffel bag.

Back in Colorado, I quickly hired on as a peace officer in north Metro-Denver, but after six years of chasing bad guys on black ice and breaking up endless bar fights, constantly drunk on adrenaline, racing Code-3 from one crisis to another, I was so burned out on "playing" cops and robbers that I no longer enjoyed the simple things in life that brought me pleasure—like my Doc Savage collection, which fell by the wayside. Before I knew it, all 181 books in the series had been published, and when "Savage Fever" finally struck again, I had to make a concerted effort to search them out; it took me nearly a decade (and probably a hundred visits to dusty, dilapidated used book stores in and around Los Angeles after I relocated to California in 1983).

After I saw *The Deer Hunter* movie, I was motivated to type up some short stories about my own Vietnam experience. Military magazines published them and I compiled most into a manuscript nearly every New York publisher passed on.

One day a phone call set my life off in a different direction: Michael Seidman, Men's Adventure editor at Zebra Books in New York City, called. They were not publishing non-fiction, but as an ex-MP himself, he had enjoyed my "rowdy autobiography." It had reminded him of books penned by "old Asian hands" or foreign correspondents who'd gone native in Indochina. "If you turn it into fiction, juice it up a bit, increase the sex and violence, I'll give you a four-book contract. What do you say, Sarge?"

Well, of course, I was ecstatic. The "Saigon Commandos" series ran to 12 books over the next three years, and was followed by a four-book spin-off which came to be known as "War Dogs." As a personal homage to Doc Savage, (and appreciation to my "writing mentor," Lester Dent, AKA Kenneth Robeson), I would sprinkle short references to the Man of Bronze throughout every manuscript I submitted: MPs were sitting around on break reading *Quest of Qui* and *The Monsters,* or came across the latest "Doc" at the PX paperback rack.

Though a "published author" now, I longed for the action of the street. Apprenticing under retired LAPD copper Larry "Shootin' Newton" Winn, I became a private investigator in the so-called "City of Angels," specializing in insurance fraud referrals to the State of California, which hired me a decade later as a special investigator. All this time, I continued to collect everything Doc related: fanzines, bronze busts, audiotapes—and the beautiful, glossy softcover reprints of both the original pulps and Bantam covers by Sanctum Books/Nostalgia Ventures. (My favorite parts of each double-issue were the segments by Will Murray giving a little "history" behind the original books.)

When Mr. Murray began publishing the new and original "Wild Adventures of Doc Savage" in hardcover, it was the latest of many Bronze dreams-come-true! By then I'd become a deputy commissioner in the Cal-D.R.E. Enforcement Division.

I retired from state service three years ago and relocated to "red rock country" in Northern Arizona. If I thought "retirement" would be filled with endless leisure hours devoted to re-reading favorite selections from my Doc Savage collection, I couldn't have been more mistaken. The "Lure of the Five-Pointed Silver Star" called and I answered, joining the Arizona Rangers, whose proud history dates back to 1901. We have over three hundred Rangers in 18 companies spread across the "Grand Canyon" state, and I have been honored with the assignment of preserving some of this fine organization's legacy as "historian" of the Verde Valley Company in Sedona—a both mesmerizing and eerie town which *USA Today* once declared "the most beautiful city in America."

I was recently appointed "training sergeant" as well, which keeps me happily in the "law enforcement loop" as I advance into my "golden years." (Never thought I'd make it to 30 when I was a "seventies copper" so long ago! Now I like to joke that it only took me 44 years to make Master Sergeant.)

When Murray and the renowned artist Joe DeVito granted my request to be a "patron" in connection with a future install-ment of the "Wild Adventures of Doc Savage," it was another dream come true! It was as if, in a way, I've come full circle: my earliest memories of "seeking adventure and danger" as a mere teenager on the streets of Pueblo, Colorado have their roots in Doc's *The Fantastic Island* and *Cold Death* and *The Czar of Fear* and *Hex*. Now I am actually participating—albeit in a very small way—in the creation and production of my favorite fic-tional character's continuing missions to seek justice, fight evil and solve mysteries around the world!

I chose to be involved with the *Mr. Calamity* project because Will's synopsis of the plot in Wyoming and Joe's description of Devils Tower making a prominent appearance on the cover seemed to segue right into my current lifestyle that includes wearing cowboy boots and a Stetson while packin' a "Big Iron" on my gunbelt!

Yet I misspoke a couple paragraphs ago when I called Doc Savage a "fictional character." We, his true, diehard fans, know that Lester Dent based his legendary character on a Man of Bronze who truly existed a hundred years ago, who really kept an ever-watchful eye on New York City from the 86th floor of the Empire State Building, who discovered a secret elixir in the jungles of Central America that gave him—if not immortality—at least extended years beyond a "normal life span" on this planet.

I have it on good authority and have been told by those "in the know" that Clark Savage, Jr., sits even now in a huge iron chair—much like the one for which he posed in nearly a hundred years ago for the classic *King Maker* cover—inspecting the galleys of one of Will Murray's manuscripts for accuracy as he contemplates releasing his files about the "lost years" surrounding Monk, Ham, Johnny, Long Tom, Renny and Pat between 1950 and these first two decades of the new millennium. He is not so much a recluse as he is a national treasure, forced into retirement by the powers-that-be when he literally stumbled upon one of the greatest scientific discoveries mankind will, unfortunately, never be told about.

I wait with baited breath for Will to someday pen that adventure... and to one day, myself, in person, shake the giant, bronzed hand of the Arch-Enemy of Evil.

Before it is too late.

Master Sgt. Nick "Colorado" Cain
Historian: Arizona Rangers
P.O. Box 20825
Sedona, Arizona 86341

Coming in 2018

THE SPIDER®

RETURNS IN EXCITING NEW EXPLOITS!

THE DOOM LEGION!

The crossover to end all crossovers,
starring The Spider, Operator 5, and
the legendary Flying Spy, G-8!

THE WILD ADVENTURES OF THE SPIDER

By WILL MURRAY

Follow us on Facebook: The Wild Adventures
of The Spider, Master of Men

THE SPIDER ®

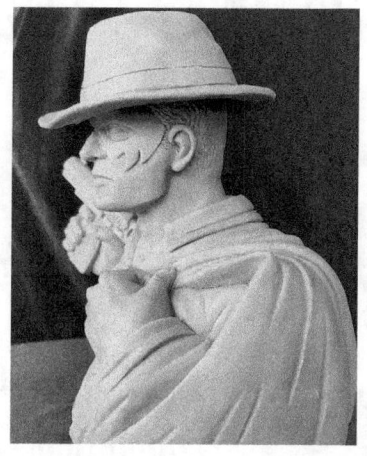 

Now you can own an authorized cold-cast bronze bust of the dreaded Master of Men as he appears in the Wild Adventures of The Spider.

Sculpted by Lawrence Elig.

Contact: ljelig03@aol.com

Note: image shown is a prototype. The finished sculpture will have a metallic surface. Price not yet set.

TM & Copyright © 2018 Argosy Communications, Inc.
All Rights Reserved. Produced Under License.

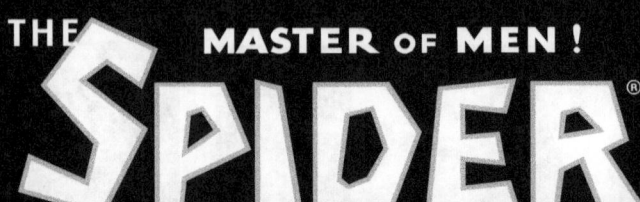

THE **MASTER** OF **MEN** !

SPIDER®

The original adventures
of the Master of Men:
coming this Spring
in affordable, mass
market editions.

Brought to you by
Altus Press, the leader
in Pulp Fiction.

TM & Copyright © 2018 Argosy Communications, Inc.
All Rights Reserved. Produced Under License.

The original adventures of the greatest
pulp heroes ever created are now
being released as audiobooks!

Now available:

 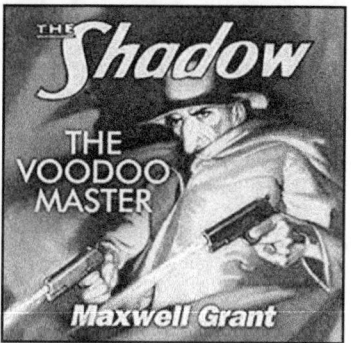

Audible Studios

Available as MP3s or as downloads
from audible.com. Order now!

THE LEGENDARY
ADVENTURES
CONTINUE!

www.edgarriceburroughs.com

Part of DeVito ArtWorks' unfolding King Kong Universe!

Limited to 500 copies!

For full details go to:

www.kongskullisland.com

www.ingramcontent.com/pod-product-compliance
Lightning Source LLC
Chambersburg PA
CBHW070344030726
47504CB00001B/62

* 9 7 8 1 6 1 8 2 7 3 1 8 5 *